VENUS BURNING: REALMS

DEDICATION

This book is dedicated to Shawna McCarthy, who was the founder and editor of 'Realms of Fantasy' Magazine, and also Tanith Lee's much-loved close friend and literary agent.

PUBLISHER'S ACKNOWLEDGEMENTS

Immanion Press would like to thank Jeremy Brett and his staff, at the Cushing Memorial Library & Archives, Texas A&M University, for providing scanned archive copies of the stories in this book, which made its compilation so much easier. Thanks also to Allison Rich, who administers Tanith Lee's online bibliography 'Daughters of the Night', for her assistance in sourcing the stories and proof-reading the finished book.

VENUS BURNING: REALMS

THE COLLECTED SHORT STORIES FROM 'REALMS OF FANTASY'

Tanith Lee

Preface by Shawna McCarthy
(Founder and Editor of 'Realms of Fantasy')

Introduction by Jeremy Brett
(Curator of the Science Fiction & Fantasy Research Collection at Cushing Memorial Library & Archives, Texas A&M University)

IMMANION PRESS
Stafford England

Cover Art by John Kaiine
Interior Illustrations and Cover Design by Danielle Lainton
Interior layout by Storm Constantine

Set in Garamond

ISBN 978-1-907737-88-6

IP0139

Author Site:
Daughter of the Night: An Annotated Tanith Lee Bibliography:
http://www.daughterofthenight.com/

Facebook Page for Tanith Lee's readers: Paradys Forum - Daughter of the Night - Tanith Lee

An Immanion Press Edition
http://www.immanion–press.com
info@immanion–press.com

Contents

PREFACE

Shawna McCarthy

(Editor of 'Realms of Fantasy')

Many many years ago, long before I created Realms of Fantasy, in a time before the internet and cell phones and Facebook, I was the editor of Isaac Asimov's Science Fiction Magazine. I'd been a long-time reader of science fiction and fantasy and I was utterly thrilled to have the job I had. One of the greatest perks for me was meeting in person the writers whose work I'd loved for years. Of course it was amazing to meet Isaac Asimov, and Ted Sturgeon, and Harlan Ellison but the writer I most wanted to meet was Tanith Lee. Like most young women of my age then, I'd devoured *Silver Metal Lover*, *Don't Bite the Sun* and *Drinking Sapphire Wine*. I thought that anyone who could write characters and stories like that must be a magical creature—someone who left a trail of glitter and fairy dust behind as she passed.

I've found, as a rule, that it's often best not to meet your idols, as you're almost always going to be disappointed. Meeting Tanith was the exception to this rule. She wafted into my office one day with, quite literally, glitter drifting off her hair and clothing. She was funny, charming, warm, kind and had a wonderful way of dispensing what they now call "shade." I had heard tales from other editors that she could be difficult to work with as she resisted most attempts at editing, but I quickly found that that this was because she knew exactly what she wanted to say and how she wanted to say it, period and comma placement included. I published a number of her stories at IA and we became friendly.

Over the years our relationship grew and deepened. I became her literary agent some time in the late '90s/early 2000s, (at just about the same time that *Realms of Fantasy* was created) and I did my best to try to straighten out the tangled web of her novel rights. We didn't get to see one another often but when we did, it was magical. (I'll never forget the time my family and I met up with John and Tanith in London (although with the amount of food and alcohol consumed, I'm amazed I can remember it!) Tanith bewitched my children, as she did everyone she met, and John (who is about 7 feet tall in his Frankenstein boots) carried my younger daughter around on his shoulders most of the day, to her terror and delight.)

When I started *Realms of Fantasy*, of course one of the writers I wanted to publish was Tanith. I asked her to send me some work for my newborn magazine, and she did. The first story I published from her was "The Story Told by Smoke: From the Journals of St. Strange," which appeared in our third issue. All told, we published 15 of her brilliant works, ending (sort of) with "Our Lady in Scarlet" in the August 2009 issue. I say "sort of" because we'd bought one last story from her, "The Pretty Knife," along with an illustration by her talented and lovely husband John Kaiine. Sadly the magazine folded before we had a chance to run it. All of those wonderful, mystical, gorgeous, glorious stories are in this volume, and I'm so glad that Storm Constantine and Immanion Press are sharing them with new (and old) readers.

Shawna McCarthy
April 2018

BEAUTY, DARKNESS AND SENSUALITY:
THE MAGIC OF TANITH LEE'S WRITING

Jeremy Brett

(Curator of the Science Fiction & Fantasy Research Collection at Cushing Memorial Library & Archives, Texas A&M University)

I never got to meet Tanith Lee. I met Tanith Lee for the first time in 1987, at the age of 12. Both of these statements are true.

I was a voracious reader when I was young, and fantasy was one of the genres I consumed the most. I read and re-read my copies of C.S. Lewis' *The Chronicles of Narnia* until I had much of them memorised. I eagerly devoured all fourteen of L. Frank Baum's Oz books (and was crushed when I was unable to find – in those days before eBay and Amazon – all the sequels written by Ruth Plumly Thompson and John R. Neill). I loved Lewis Carroll's *Alice* books, and J.M. Barrie's *Peter Pan*, and all the endless variations of fairy tales and mythologies that I could get my hands on. Like many children, I longed to travel to fantastical, magical worlds of adventures, of strange creatures, of grand heroes and terrifying monsters. Like many adults, I still do.

So imagine me in 1987. I was putting my small allowance to good use as a new member of the Science Fiction Book Club, and was having the time of my life looking through the catalog of titles and the new worlds now available to me. I remember that one title stood out among the rest: *Tales From the Flat Earth: The Lords of Darkness*. Normal, spherical Earth-residing me was immediately caught by this notion: A flat Earth? Flat? How would that even *work*? What would such an Earth look like? And what kind of people would be living on it? I didn't recognize the name of the author, although I remember even then thinking that her first name – Tanith – sounded like the name of a sorceress or a queen from the fairy tales

I loved to read. I sent away for the book, as well as several others, the titles of which are now long lost to my memory.

Several impatient weeks later, *Tales from the Flat Earth* arrived. I remember that the cover was pink, and it depicted three utterly unusual figures standing in a hazy landscape. Of course, once I began reading I would come to know these figures as Chuz, Lord of Madness; Uhlume, Lord Death; and, in the center, the dark and beautiful Azhrarn, Night's Master and Prince of Demons. But at the time I only knew that these strange (What were they? People? Monsters? Demons?) were unlike anything I had seen before, although they seemed reminiscent of various mythological figures I read about. And then I read the book (which was actually a collection of the first three books in the series).

There was much of it that a 12 -year old wouldn't have understood completely, and I was no exception. I'm sure that much of the sexual content went right over my head, for one. (On the other hand, being used to fantasy situations like the boy Tip who is transformed into Princess Ozma with no comment by Baum, I'm sure that I accepted Simmu's gender fluidity with no questions.) And as a young boy I no doubt lacked a real understanding of much of the deep emotion Tanith describes in the Flat Earth series: Azhrarn's doomed passion for the human Sivesh, the ruthless ambition of Zorayas, the unabiding and casual cruelty of the magician Zhirem. But even at my age, I saw that Tanith Lee had created something at once not unlike and at the same time far more beautiful, far more complex, than the various fantasy worlds with which I was already familiar. I fell instantly in love with this, the first *adult* fantasy I had ever read, and part of me has been in love with its author ever since. Part of me still looks for Tanith in every work of fantasy I have read since. She will always be my dark queen of literature.

Tanith's work is lush and rich with beauty, darkness, and sensuality. And she was, above all else, the consummate storyteller. Mike Ashley called her "a true Scheherazade", and it is the perfect appellation for her. She told endless tales of worlds that were ours and of those that were not, but each and every one feels very much like a half-remembered dream, or a race memory. That is, something that feels *real* to us, as if we had experienced it ourselves or something very much like it somewhere in our past. This feeling that Tanith's work inspires is a natural consequence, I think, of her innate ability to write in styles reminiscent of arcane and ancient legends, of fairy tale and old myth. More than almost anyone else whom I have ever read, Tanith sounds like someone whose work was meant to be read aloud as tales, perhaps huddled around a fire in the dark forest or in the quiet and still air within an ancient temple.

Realms of Fantasy, with its dedication to quality fantasy literature and art, was a perfect venue for Tanith. The magazine (which ran from 1994 to 2011, being passed like an Olympic torch from publisher to publisher in a valiant effort to keep it going) was a slick and beautifully produced serial, with fiction overseen from *Realms'* birth to death by editor Shawna McCarthy. It published stories by such figures as Neil Gaiman, Jane Yolen, Robert Silverberg, Sherwood Smith, Kij Johnson, K.D. Wentworth, Naomi Kritzer, Harlan Ellison, and Charles De Lint. Terri Windling wrote a column on the folkroots of fantasy. Gahan Wilson produced book reviews. Resa Nelson reviewed films. The magazine had strikingly colourful and dramatic covers from artists like Boris Vallejo, Luis Royo, Michael Whelan, and Kinuko Craft. And of course, the magazine frequently featured work from Tanith.

Tanith published 15 stories in *Realms of Fantasy* between 1995 and 2009, and among these are some of her very best work. Her first appearance was in the magazine's third issue (February 1995), with the tale "The Story Told by Smoke: From the Journals of St. Strange". It is one of her numerous stories-within-a-story, and a tale of the consequences of forbidden love (a frequent theme of Tanith's). Tanith's final *Realms* story was another addition to her Flat Earth universe, "Our Lady of Scarlet", in August 2009. Between these bookends, the pages of *Realms* saw some exquisite prose from Tanith. A few of these stand out to me as particularly representative of her body of work. "Doll Skulls" (February 1996) is a tale from Tanith's Paradys universe, of a downtrodden woman and her daughter whose lives are transformed through the acquisition of two mysterious dolls. The story is very much Tanith in its conflation of the waking world and the world we experience in dreams. As the story states, "There is always this problem, just as the real world is so often determinedly confused with the Real, so it is difficult to differentiate between others that are fantasy, or maybe madness." It's a conundrum that recurs in Tanith's work, and the slippery, dreamlike quality of her stories give them a particular and unearthly beauty.

Several of Tanith's most successful *Realms* pieces turn fantasy clichés on their heads, or bring a sense of deep emotional complexity to them. "The Children of His Old Age" (October 2000) transforms the classic dragon vs. dragonslayer story into a tale of cautious understanding between ancient rivals. "The Woman in Scarlet" (April 2000) is a story (in a genre noted for heroic sword-wielding warriors who slice their way through acres of enemies) of a passionate love affair between a man and the mystical sword he bears. (Here Tanith displays her gift for chronicling different sorts of loves and obsessions.) "Moonblind" (April 2003) tells the tale of a young hunter of werewolves, who experiences a moment of compassion and tenderness and welcomes transformation into the thing he hunts. And others, in the fableistic tradition, have wonderfully jarring twist endings in which the protagonists learn the true costs of their desires or the true ends of the roads they walk: "Israbel" (April 2004), "Ein Foret Noire" (December 2005), and "I Bring You Forever" (June 1998), for example.

As I noted above, I never actually met Tanith in person. She and I did exchange several emails in 2013-2014 in my capacity as Curator of the Science Fiction & Fantasy Research Collection at Cushing Memorial Library & Archives, Texas A&M University. Thanks to the good offices of Tanith's expert bibliographer Allison Rich, our library holds a large and growing part of Tanith's published work, used by Allison to compile her *Daughter of the Night* bibliography. Libraries like Cushing have made it part of their primary mission to preserve and provide access to the documentary history of the development of science fiction and fantasy. Tanith understood the importance of that mission, and was conscious of her own contributions to that development. Our email conversations resulted in the donation by her to Cushing of the handwritten manuscript for her 1976 novel *Don't Bite The Sun*. The manuscript (written when Tanith was 21) contains the text for the novel, as well as several illustrations Tanith made. In an effort to provide context, Tanith helpfully added notes to the first page of the manuscript before she sent it to me, allowing her 2014 self to speak to 2014 me about her 1968 self. And when it arrived here, 2014 me held the manuscript while 1987 me thrilled, and remembered his first love affair with adult fantasy.

Different voices speaking across time and distance. The power of longing and memory. How very Tanith.

-Jeremy Brett
February 2018

THE STORY TOLD BY SMOKE

From the Journals of Saint Strange

That night, in the yellow hotel high above the port, silence became my enemy, as it sometimes does. I had become used to the rush of the sea, timbers complaining, the vocal life of ships. Now the noises began in my head, the long, thin drone, the feeble futile flickering notes above. I got up and dressed in the salt-stained trousers and shirt of my voyages. Outside the room, the murky gaslight quavered, and at regular intervals the lamps had failed, giving over the long corridors, with their mottled walls and spaces of matting, to the dark.

Below, in the large communal rooms, no one was abroad. But dim sounds reached me from the port, and the droning and whining in my ear drew off. Then, sweet as crystals, I heard the song of nightingales, not one but many.

Two wide doors stood open on a courtyard. Out beyond the vagaries of the false light, a blue night sky had brought forth all its stars. The single tree that centred the court was heavy in foliage, and here the nightingales sat singing. At the base of the tree was the shape of a man like a statue, and in front of him was a glass hubble-bubble that faintly gleamed and gave off a gurgling sigh. I hesitated, and his hand came up, beckoning me. He said in French, 'Good evening. You are welcome.'

Then I approached and sat down, facing him in the dark, across his little mat. He handed me without preface or delay the mouth-piece of the smoking, bubbling hookah. It was of ancient amber, bleached in the starlight. I sucked the scented fumes into my body, and light as a cloud, a cool stillness rose up in me – opium had been mixed with the tobacco.

We smoked for some minutes without speaking. Then the old man – he looked as old as the amber – made that graceful gesture I have seen in several lands, a sort of gliding over the air before the body of a stranger, which asks some information.

I told him my name, where I had come from, and where I

intended to proceed.

His head was swathed in a white turban clean as an English blancmange, and over this rested a veil, patterned and fringed at its edges. His hands were ringed in blackened silver and green gold.

He listened courteously, and then, giving me once more the mouthpiece of the hubble-bubble, he said, 'And will you hear a story?'

'I'd do that gladly.'

He smiled. He said, 'In your childhood they told you no tales.'

'That's true.'

'And now you hunger after them.'

'Also true.'

He took the mouthpiece again and filled his old silver lungs with the smoke. So the story started, its phrases made visible. And since we continued to pass the mouthpiece between us while he spoke, his words soon seemed to issue also from my lips.

As the pot-seller came to the road, which ran across the desert, misfortune befell him. The road was broad and powdered with dust. It extended from the distant city, an artery without blood; traffic seldom moved along it – some carts, a bicycle perhaps, every third day. Now as the skinny man, with his pack of pots, ventured out upon it, he heard a curious, ominous noise.

He hesitated, looked about him. The desert was empty but for its sands and rocky slopes, bristled by a few of those thin and twisted shrubs that never hope for water. The sky was yellow, flushed blue only at its edges, and hollow and filmed at once, also empty.

The noise was on the road. It rushed toward the man. At the road's shore stood his daughter, carrying other pots, and he waved at her to be still.

From the haze, then, there emerged, throbbing and shining and smoking, a monster. It was a car, a beautiful black car with a square cabin of glass windows, and golden lamps that blinded in the sunlight.

Transfixed and half-disbelieving, though he had seen such things now and then, the pot-seller waited there, in the road's middle. And to the hooting of the oncoming and impatient car he responded only with a muttered prayer.

Too late, he jumped aside. Intolerant, the car caught his

drooping load of pots with its bumper, rounded as a hip in Paradise, and thundered on.

The pots scattered, shattered. He was left there, after the car had gone back into the haze, staring at these brown shells all over the roadway, with his daughter vainly going among them, trying to pick up anything whole.

'Leave it, Rebaidah. Leave it, I say. God's heavy on us.'

The girl glanced at him. He was a man, the superior one, and her father. She must always obey. She left the rubble, and they crossed over the road and went down a path in the desert, toward the village they had been told of.

Rebaidah was very beautiful, but she did not know this. Plump as ripened fruit, with narrow waist and wrists and ankles. Her black hair curled and hung, under its rag, to her thighs. She did not cover her face, which some eastern queen had somehow conveyed to her, through generations of ignobility. Her eyes were purple-black with a sapphire glaze.

After an hour on the path, they came upon the village. Its name was Murum, and it was an oasis of the desert, full of deep wells. Along the streets of windowless stone houses, huge trees lifted their pillars, wreathed in foliage that gave only a glint of green.

Into the shade of these giants they walked, the pot-seller and his daughter. He said to her sharply, 'Don't look up. Such trees are full of evil spirits.'

But Rebaidah was glad of the coolness on her skin.

Soon enough, they came into the village market, where there were no trees at all, and going humbly to the place where itinerants were allowed to crouch, the pot-seller laid out the pitiful remnants of his wares. The girl assisted him, then stood by and fanned him with a plaited fan.

As was usual, only servant women came to inspect the goods in the market, and even their faces were covered over with thick dark veils, showing just the eyes. But close by there was a shop with a red awning, and under this the barefaced men of the village of Murum sat drinking coffee and smoking cigarettes. One of these men began to stare at Rebaidah. Now this, of course, had happened before. She was poor and worthless and did not hide her countenance. However, something in the man's persistent scrutiny unnerved her. She sensed some new element, not solely passing lust mingled with contempt. Here there was a hunger.

17

And presently, the man got up, leaving his companions, and strolled over to the pot-seller's station.

'You've done well, to sell so many so quickly.'

'No, alas, bless God. My pots were broken, by a motorcar.'

The man smiled, finding this funny. 'We shall all have motorcars quite soon.' He smoked his cigarette, then threw it down half-consumed. He was rich, and in the village, they called him "Handsome", although his looks were not exceptional.

'I'll buy the last of your pots. My servants are clumsy and break a great number.'

The pot-seller made a fawning gesture.

The rich man, Handsome, looked full at Rebaidah, and she lowered her eyes, because naturally he was superior.

'And what else will you sell?'

The pot-seller was surprised. 'What, do you want the girl?'

'I'll take her and give you – oh, the price of a fat goat in milk.'

'But she's my daughter,' said the pot-seller, thinking no doubt of how she cooked his food at night, rubbed his feet, fetched water, and fanned him.

'As you wish,' said Handsome. He turned slowly, and the pot-seller said, 'Two goats.'

Handsome laughed out loud. 'Is she worth so much?'

'She's all I have, and she's a virgin.'

The bargain was concluded on the spot, a pair of the other men coming to witness it, and a boy servant sent to fetch the money. The notary drew up a contract that neither the pot-seller nor Handsome, and certainly not Rebaidah, who anyway was not shown it, could read. Each man made his mark.

As the hot sun set upon Murum, the pot-seller sat alone in the dust, and a woman led Rebaidah away to the house of her new master.

Her life had always been hard. Now it was as soft as cream. Her world had been large and arid, now it was condensed, blue with shade, and punctuated by liquid.

The house had several rooms, which gave on a courtyard, and here there was a tank of water. Steps led up onto the roof, where stood a pavilion patterned with vermilion. Orange trees grew in pots and vines clung round and flowers bloomed. Here Rebaidah might sit all day and eat sweets, hidden from the roofs of other houses. Her tasks commenced at evening, when Handsome came home from his day of business and coffee in the market. Then she would wash his hands and feet, serve him the meal the servants brought, and finally go to bed with him in an upper room. Of her duties she liked this the least, but it did not trouble her unduly. Once the first pain was over, she found it quite easy to please Handsome, whose nose would run in his paroxysms of joy. Only, from time to time, he liked to sleep with his head on her belly, and then she lay for hours awake, pinned down and unable to move, in the close black night of the room.

Handsome was delighted by her, called her his gazelle, but soon became quite used to her, seldom bothering her more than once or twice a night. He adorned her with silver bracelets and gold earrings. She wore light silky garments, and though she must go veiled in the house, once up on the roof she might remove this safeguard. Otherwise she must never leave the premises.

Her entire existence, from her earliest memory, had been one of wandering about, sleeping more often than not on the ground, sometimes chased by dogs, frequently without food. She was accustomed to her father's grumbling, and the grumbling of Handsome was new yet familiar. On the wall of one of the rooms, he kept a curved sword with a crimson tassel at the hilt. It meant no special thing to her. It was a man's.

She had asked nothing of her previous life and expected nothing. Surely, she had been lucky, and comfort must be better.

Yet, even so, she found that strangely her eyes would stray to the outer door. That she would gaze at those servants who passed in and out. At night, pinned by the hairy boulder on her stomach, she would strain to catch some outer noise of the village, the mew of a cat or the whisper of the large tree which grew beside the house.

It was this tree, more than the vines of the arbour, that made Handsome's roof so secluded that Rebaidah might unveil there. From the start the tree had been a thing of marvel to the girl, for it seemed the tallest tree in the world, going up and up beyond the house, its leaves so massed that they were black, and only the midday sun would sew among them a handful of green sequins.

Yet Handsome spoke ill of the tree. 'A haunt of demons, so my father would have said. We'll cut them all down before too long, cut down all the trees in Murum, and the streets will be wider and more modern.'

Rebaidah did not debate with Handsome, would not have thought to. She said only that the trees gave shade to the streets, meaning that this was why she had noticed them.

But Handsome, thinking she had put up a tiny, frail opposition, cuffed her gently. 'No shade will be necessary. Soon we men will travel by motorcar. In the morning, I'll drive to the marketplace to meet my associates, and they too will drive there. In the evening, we'll return, and at the sound of the cars, our women will come through the rooms to meet us. That's a fine smell, the blue smoke of the gasoline. The air will be perfumed by it. And I'll build up the wall. You won't miss your tree.'

Rebaidah sat on the roof and thought of this. She began to look up into the tree, which her father would have told her not to do. She had heard old stories. Of creatures like enamelled snakes that lived among boughs, luring the foolish to commit wrong acts, tempting with gifts of fruit. Such ideas seemed nonsensical to Rebaidah. Life was very simple. You had only to do always as you were told.

Sometimes in the afternoons, as she lay on her cushioned couch beside the pavilion, Rebaidah heard faint laughter sprinkling over the sky. She knew that other women, the possessions of the richer men of Murum, were also up on their roofs, among the pots of flowers. She did not think that any of these would visit her, stepping over from one roof to another, for she was an alien and not even a wife. However, one day, near sunset, when the sky was the colour of apricots, Rebaidah opened her eyes from her doze, and a figure was moving out from the limbs and leaves of the tree. She wore, the newcomer, a dark silky dress like Rebaidah's own, and like Rebaidah was bright with ornaments, with little golden discs even tied into her hair, like stars in the night. She too was unveiled, and Rebaidah, who had never seen her own beauty, caught her breath at the beauty of this other.

The visitor did not speak but she laughed. Her laughter was like water in a fountain, or a breeze through the tree. She came forward in swift brief glidings, stopping always after a few steps and tilting her gorgeous head, as if to see what Rebaidah would do. And Rebaidah, rather shy, did not speak either, but only held out her box of pink sweets.

Finally, the visitor reached Rebaidah. She put a slim hand into the box and drew out a sweet. Raising it to her lips, she licked the sweet with a tongue even pinker.

'Sit down, if you will,' said Rebaidah.

And the girl sat down by her side.

A lovely smell came from her. Not of perfumes, or even of cleanness. It was a natural aroma, like that of a scented flower. Rebaidah breathed it in, and they ate the sweets, not speaking.

Then the girl lifted her hand to Rebaidah's unveiled face. It was a contact as mild as a leaf. Oddly, it made Rebaidah laugh also.

Then the girl leaned and kissed her, full on the mouth, in a delicious kiss, like kissing a sun-warmed nectarine.

Rebaidah had no recollection that she had ever been kissed by a woman, and only one man had ever pressed his lips on her, and that was Handsome in his snotty transports of joy.

She was at first startled and, at her reaction, her companion drew back, as if in fright. It was Rebaidah who must reach out and take the girl's hand, to show that she had not minded.

When she did this, the girl with golden stars in her hair leaned forward and kissed Rebaidah over the heart.

There could be no wrong in this. Only one man might touch a woman in such a way, but women, who were inferior and without soul, did not matter. Even so, Rebaidah was amazed. A lightning had gone through her. She did not know whether to jump up and run off, or to sit still and discover what would happen next.

At that moment she heard the well-known steps in the street below of Handsome, returning in company with two or three of his peers. At the door of his house they were parting with loud sounds, as unlike the feathery laughter of the visiting girl as could be imagined. And already the girl had sprung to her feet and was gliding away. She vanished in among the branches of the black tree, no doubt stepping off from there onto the adjacent roof, which was her own. It had not occurred to Rebaidah that some considerable distance separated the house of Handsome from his neighbour's. In her obedience and docility, Rebaidah had never much looked at or thought upon anything.

In any event, a real star had burst out in the sky, which was now losing its amber and turning blue, and the door had let in her lord, so she hurried down.

Obviously, Rebaidah did not tell of her encounter with the beautiful visitor. What Rebaidah did away from him was of no importance to Handsome. The servants ignored her.

Thereafter, though, Rebaidah would sit on her roof, with boxes of green and rose sweets and thirst-quenching drinks set by, and she would wait. Nor was she disappointed.

After the first occasion, the wonderful acquaintance would come to her every afternoon, always about the same time, in the hour before the sun set. Now she did not hesitate, but walked directly to the couch, seated herself, ate the sweets and sipped the juices. After this, she would begin to caress Rebaidah in the same appetising way, tasting her and giving back to her mouth the essence of lemon and peach.

Soon enough they would stretch out, face to face, on the cushions, under the cool shadow of the protecting tree.

'Oh, I love you,' said Rebaidah, her head on the other's breast. 'Tell me your name.'

Her lover laughed. Rebaidah did not mind this. For now, she knew that the laugh itself was the name.

Handsome frowned as he ate his spicy mutton, cleansing his fingers at intervals in the water bowl on which petals floated. 'That tree,' he said, to no one in particular, for only Rebaidah and a woman servant were there, 'that tree angers me.' Then he ate some more of the saffron rice, drank his sugared coffee, and said, 'My father would have cut it down. Old men talk of evil spirits. We must respect old men, God says so. Well, the moment has come.'

That night he mounted Rebaidah three times, so that she was sore and ached, and now this deed of his made her nauseated, and she was astonished that she should mind it, for he was her master and she must serve him the very best she could. But Handsome did not notice her retching; he thought these were spasms of enjoyment.

When he slept he did not put his head on her belly, but one leg had swung across her, fastening her down.

She lay and listened for the murmur of the tree, but no wind had risen from the desert. Not a sound was to be heard.

It seemed to Rebaidah that an illness settled on her, and she might die. She did not know that she was heart-sick or that there was anything she might do. For what could she do, after all? A laugh was not a name, a woman did not matter, a tree could not defend itself.

In the morning Handsome rose early, washed himself and prayed, and ate a meal of bread. Then he went out and called men, labourers who were ready for any work. They came at noon and circled round the great dark tree, where it towered up like a column from the dusty street. It was as ancient as the oasis, perhaps, but it was bad luck. It might fall upon the house. Vermin climbed the limbs. Demons *loved* it. God did not care so much for a tree as for His prime creation, a man.

Rebaidah had been told to avoid the roof that day. So she sat, veiled, in a room of the house, which seemed hot as a furnace. Sometimes she retched into a bowl, like the bowl in which her lord had rinsed his hands. The older servant women muttered. They thought she was pregnant.

Oh, the thunder of axes. Unlike God, had Rebaidah ever truly cared for anything? Now she did not know what went on in her. She vomited and sank back in a sort of faint. Dimly, from a great distance, she heard the cracking, tearing and dreadful falling of the tree, down into the gap of the street, and the smashing of its branches and the rustling sigh of all its broken leaves.

When Rebaidah went up onto the roof after this event, she was screened by the green lattices of the vines. She noticed that the other houses were too far away for anyone to have stepped across. Although she still heard the laughter of women, it was at a distance and, unlike that of her visitor, it was graceless and stupid.

The debris and corpse of the great tree had been removed. It would be burnt in ovens, so that men could be cooked for and fed. Stools would be made from it that wives might kneel beside and lave their husbands' feet.

Rebaidah knew that her beloved would not return to her and yet...

And yet...

Again and again now she would go down into the lower house. She would stand and stare at the outer door. It was always locked, opened only by the male servant just before her master's return.

All her life, she had wandered the earth so wide and so cruel. But now she was confined within a cage.

Did she hear the sweet wild laughter out there on the sunset street? The girl from the tree could not have vanished. Women had no souls, and so, how could they die?

Five nights later, when Handsome, lingering in the market with his friends, was late, Rebaidah went to the preparatorily unlocked door and slipped through it. One servant saw her go and gaped in disbelief.

But Rebaidah was not herself. She had begun painfully to grow. She had rebelled. She was full of hurt and panic and the desire to run into the desert.

Despite all this, or because of it, she lost herself in the village of Murum. Fearful, fretting, she slunk about the streets where the other trees stood so tall. She was veiled; she had remembered enough to do that, and most took her for a servant. Often, she concealed herself, and generally behind the trees.

Darkness came, the shadows clustered. In the stone houses the oil lamps were lit, unseen. The village was black, and overhead now the stars shone hard as the points of swords – as hard as the point of the curved sword Handsome kept upon his wall. Rebaidah started to think of this sword, and suddenly she became aware that the crimson tassel that dripped from it was like a gout of blood.

Then she turned to fly away along the streets, but Murum held her in. She was soon lost again.

Meanwhile, he had come home and found Rebaidah gone, and the female servant had come grovelling and confessed the appalling thing she had seen, how Handsome's possession had sneaked out of the door, out onto the public and forbidden street.

His rage was terrible. He roared like a lion, so neighbours arrived, asking what was amiss. Handsome told them freely. Their faces turned to stone, like that of the houses, badly-made and windowless.

At last, Handsome strode into the room where the sword hung on the red cord. He lifted it off and held it a second, stricken and non-plussed, in his reasonable hands. Life was so simple. How had this madness come about? But he knew, they all would, what he must do. He left his house alone, the sword balanced firmly in his right hand. He stalked the thoroughfares, and people shrank from him. As the facts of the affair came drifting down in his wake, men cursed their need of womankind, and women fell on their faces and grieved.

She was not so far away. She had come about in a circle. She stood there pathetically, in a dry little space beside a well, and here a lamp rested on the ground to give light to those who sought water.

Handsome sought only her and, very clearly, he beheld her, curved like an instrument of pleasure, her face veiled like the moon in cloud.

'Bitch,' said Handsome.

Rebaidah only gazed at him in despair. She had gone as far as she could. The logic of existence returned to her. There was no escape.

So she stood meekly, her head slightly raised, not in pride, but to assist him.

And he, with a terrific swing of his arm and the flash of the sword like a wave, struck the head off her body. For a few moments she continued to stand upright, headless, and by the time she had toppled down, her head had rolled into the lamp and put it out.

She was thrown into a hole, unmarked. Her head was another item altogether. For Handsome, there was only praise. He had done the correct thing, setting an example to other less steadfast men, and teaching a lesson to disobedient women, who must be virtuous.

Rebaidah's head was set up on the wall of Handsome's house, on a spike. It gazed sadly and stoically down into the street, and men looked at it sternly, and the servant women averted their eyes, lest the wickedness of Rebaidah infect them too. There was no veil, of course. She had lost her right to modesty.

Sometimes crows flew over to inspect the head, but they did not peck at it. The sun dried it, and gradually, rather than rotting, it became old and withered. The eyes turned white, and the hair was like black straw.

Every evening, Handsome gazed up at the head. He thanked God for delivering him from the toils of Woman. But sometimes in the night he would dream that Rebaidah came to entice him, and as she rubbed her naked form against him, his seed would jet out into the bed. This caused him great humiliation, and he filled the mattress with stones to worry him in slumber and keep the sin of waste away. The trees of Murum began to prey upon his mind also. He urged the other men of the village to have all the trees cut down. He was influential and rich. Eventually he got his way. And hour by hour, for seven days, the streets rang to the thud of the axes.

As they sat under the red awning and debated the unwisdom of the earth, the men murmured that now all the shade was gone from Murum. Handsome reminded them that the village was prosperous, and soon they would each be very wealthy. Every man would have his cool motorcar and need not fear the heat of the sun.

That night, in the first lilac of evening, as Handsome returned to his house, he looked up at Rebaidah's head fixed on his wall.

A horrible shock passed through Handsome, as if he had been suddenly plunged from crown to toe in icy water. For there on the spike above the wall was fixed, not the head of the slut, but his own head, with its black moustache and small sharp eyes.

Handsome dropped to his knees and entreated God for mercy, but as he did so, he noticed that the head, his own, disappeared entirely, and instead he saw up on the wall a piece of the neighbouring house.

Presently Handsome got the boy to fetch a ladder and go up the wall to see. The mystery was soon explained – or deepened. For Rebaidah's mummy had gone from the spike, and in its place a mirror had been attached, slanted somewhat toward the street. It was an ordinary mirror that any rich man might have in his house. For sure, Handsome believed that it did in fact belong to him. And for this reason, he flogged his servants, male and female both, and the dark was noisy with outcry. But from none of them could he get the avowal that they had set out to trick him. Nor could he anywhere locate the missing head of Rebaidah. At length he learned that her markerless grave had also been despoiled and lay empty as a gourd.

'She has had some lover,' shouted Handsome.

Then there were quarrels. Men swore, and doors slammed.

A silence came down on the village of Murum, unlike the midnight silences which had been before.

And out of the silence, as figments blown by the fierce warm night wind of the desert, came the cars.

In the morning, Handsome thought he had been dreaming, for he had heard them all night long, driving with a low harsh purring that reverberated inside the base of his skull, up and down the streets of Murum.

Out on the thoroughfare he found their tracks, like the pad marks of animals. There were very many, and every street was the same.

The other villagers stole forth timidly. The women whispered at the wells, the whisper trees had once made. The men met in the marketplace.

'What can it mean?'

'Who has so many motorcars?'

'I saw them, twenty or more. They rolled by, one after the other. Beautiful machines – but I didn't like them. I stepped back inside.'

'It went on all night. Who slept?'

Handsome said, 'Why are you afraid of cars? It's a symbol of the prosperity to come.'

That evening at home, when he had eaten his meal – which was tasteless and had been so since Rebaidah had ceased to wait on him – he walked into the room where the sword hung on the wall. From a cabinet he took out a bottle of arrack and, begging God's pardon, drank a small amount, which quickly rushed to his head.

Then he strode up to the roof, to the garden with the pavilion, and here he sat under the wide black sky, into whose hair the stars had been tied. He smoked, and he waited.

How intent, the silence of the village, and it seemed to Handsome he must strain to hear anything, but there was nothing, not the mew of a cat, or the rustle of a leaf. And then the low and trembling purr of engines blew from the desert.

It was an awful sound, so thick and live, like the rumble of a panther. It poured into Murum and engulfed it, and from a hundred roofs, the startled faces stared down, and below the black cars passed, at no great speed, one after another.

They were very beautiful, the cars. The vehicles of the very, very rich. The dim roof lamps of Murum shone on their sides like water, but the cars had lights of their own. Gold and silver headlamps blazed and flashed, and in the square black cabins of glass, bold yellow glimpses; a smooth hand with diamonds, a silk-stockinged shameless foot in a ruby shoe.

How black the cars were, and in their flanks, a glimmer of green. They were like reptiles which purred. They rubbed their naked scales against the night.

Round and round Murum they drove, up and down and back and through. They came from nowhere and they went to nowhere. Murum was theirs.

A score of men, of whom Handsome was not one, ventured out

into the streets. They stood transfixed, and the cars drove by them.

The men saw into the high black cabins, lit and sparkling only with glimpses – a cigarette holder of crystal, a bare pearl shoulder – between and above the bumpers and fenders like coal, and the spokes of wheels picked out with honey flame. But the lamps splashed out their sight, and the purring roar made them giddy.

You could not stand in their way; plainly they would run over you.

The men who had gone out hurried in again.

The cars drove on and on, round and about, up and down and through.

When the dawn came, in a thin line like blood, they ebbed away, drove off into the wasteland in a cloud of vapour.

The village smelled sweet as jam with gasoline. There was an oily film on everything. On the rooftops, the gardens of the opulent died quietly. The water of the wells tasted of metal and ozone.

The men met in the market under the awning. The coffee congealed in the cups and the cigarettes burned away like cinders.

They were hollow-eyed. There was nothing to fear. Why should they fear this? No harm had been offered. But Murum lay spread out like a man pinned to the desert for a whipping. It waited, brittle and taut. The noise of the cars still hung in the ear and the fumes of the cars were between men and the sky, between them and God.

'What's caused this?'

'It is a curse.'

'But why?'

Handsome said, 'It's that bitch. She brought some evil. Oh, I would have called it superstition. But not now.'

'Demons,' said an old man.

They sat hunched over, bowed by terrible fate, which had struck them undeservingly.

But as the day flowed out they dispersed hastily to their homes and shut and locked them.

Only Handsome came that night down to the entrance of his house and positioned himself there, with the sword in his hands. As he did this, his servants ran off by a back way to other buildings, where they took refuge.

The cars arrived as the black bloom of night's flower filled all the sky, and one by one they drove by Handsome's house, until the last one appeared, and this one stopped before his door.

It was a car made of jet and sprinkled by jade. A figure had the wheel, which seemed of polished gold. He looked like a man, in the black and white evening dress of the city, his hair a black mirror, his face in shadow. But behind him in the glorious light, on the black velvet seat like a shell, were two women. Both were beautiful and dressed also for the city, in dark satins shot with lizard blue and serpent green, beaded as if with rains. Their black hair was piled up with combs. Emeralds coiled their arms, which were uncovered. And their silken ankles were bare and their feet in slippers made of water.

They laughed and played together, like two pretty and innocent, sensual children, but to Handsome it was the game of harlots, and one of them was Rebaidah. He saw her there, safe in the armour of the motorcar, which did not need a tree to shade it, even from the bone-hard moon. He saw her wealth and her happiness, her unveiled face and hair, her naked limbs, her jewels. And he saw too how her neck was joined to her shoulders by a ring of delicate twigs and leaves twisted with opals.

He wished to tell her that she had offended God and was condemned. But Handsome had no voice. He wished to use the sword but had used it up. He moved into his house, and soon he heard the car drive on, and its motor was lost in the motors of all the other cars, which were now once more driving round and round Murum, round and round, and round and round, forever.

Yet as they passed, from their golden windows these creatures threw out on the earth handfuls of seed. Or was this only a fancy, for who else had seen them?

The village of Murum lies dead now, out in the desert beyond the city road. The stone houses crumble and have lost all semblance of human habitations. Crows perch on the walls. The wells are wet yet unwholesome.

Even so, they quench the thirst of the gigantic trees which grow there, trees black as coals and jets, with only a hint, at midday, of green. Cars cannot go down the streets, through which enormous roots have pushed their way. Those that venture there hear laughter but meet no one. Those that laugh there fall silent.

Only picture those pale hands with their long, unearthly nails, casting out those handfuls of glittering seed, like gemstones. Only picture how Rebaidah's lover scrabbled her out of the hole in the sand, and brought down her poor dried head from the spike, and kissed it back to loveliness, and put her together like a perfect doll, with a binding of pleasure and vegetation.

But do not picture the people of Murum, how they ran away like beaten dogs, weeping and calling on God at the injustice. Do not picture Handsome, with his chest of valuables strapped to his back, pushing along the road. Or the village left behind them to the cars and the trees and the laughter, like the demons of childhood we would like to love.

When the old man had finished his tale, he sat looking at me, still puffing slightly on the amber mouthpiece of the hookah, whose spirit had lasted all this time, which was probably not possible.

'I thank you,' I said, 'for the story. I like it very much. Can I repay you?'

He grinned, quite uncouthly, showing all his blackened teeth. The light was coming, and his air of mystique and holiness was fading. His turban no longer looked white. 'There is my bowl.'

I put some money into this and, satisfied, he nodded and bowed his head. I was dismissed.

I stood up. At that moment, all the nightingales, which had sung on and on in the court, took flight at once. They flew up into the sky, which had now a heart of aquamarine, and turning, darting, fled away. The tree was dead, I saw, and had had no foliage. Only the birds had covered it, like leaves.

But already the day was full of other sounds, coarse and unimportant. I could sleep if I wished and dream of Rebaidah in her earthly Paradise.

'Go in peace,' muttered the old man, from his dirty head-cloth.

I thanked him again and went out, trusting as I did so, that to go or be or live in peace would never be my lot.

DOLL SKULLS

It was the last evening of the old year, but also of the century. As the winter dusk fell like grey powder, a million lights appeared across the city, the rich glow of oil lamps and the fainter bluish glim of gas, the cold bold electric windows, and the electric pods that marched along the higher streets, the rouged neons of the cafés, the soft blush of candles. With such a massing of lit eyes, Paradis meant to watch nightlong, to make sure the ship of the city should sail through that terrifying gate, into her future.

On the boulevards there was, too, some frenetic hilarity already, crowds that surged and laughed and blew whistles, and a scatter of motorcars that rattled by with their own great lamps alight, charged with shouting revellers. From the large mansions about the Obelisk, an occasional premature firework escaped. Children ran through the avenues, half unaware of the momentum of the time, yet primed to it, calling and shrieking. The cathedral on its hill was bright as a jewel box, its glorious windows like cut fruits on fire, signalling God for protection, perhaps.

Fear and festival were in the air.

The mother, as she trudged homeward, however, paid small attention to all this.

Ten years before she had been a young girl herself and would have laughed and been whirled about in a fashionable frock, willing to drink wine, and to perch in the back of a polished car. But since then she had been in love, and been in abandonment, and next in pregnancy, and so in childbirth. As the moon changes, so did she. Her slender shining nights were gone. Now she was thin and worn, and in her hair something had clawed out the colour in long strands. She was drab, weary; at twenty-seven years old.

As she walked up the long hill toward the clockmakers, she thought of her child. This child it was who had taken away her life, stopped her, the young girl, and gradually yet quickly altered her into this withered, partly-stooping crone. Despite that, the mother – which was all she had become, there was no other name for her save drudge – loved the child very deeply, loved the child with all her soul. And the child, a girl of nine years, loved her mother in return, with so much love that the whole city could not really hold it, and so it had escaped like the fireworks, up into the sky.

It was a fact that, when together, the mother and the child blossomed a little, were increased and better. But all else in their lives was difficult and unyielding. And, through that too, they were often apart for long hours, during which, lacking each other, they were also exposed to strangers who mistreated each of them in crass or subtle ways.

The mother slaved underpaid in a shop, for instance, where her fellow workers were cruel and stupid, mocking not only their intolerant customers, their base employers, but also each other and all the world. They took delight in playing quite dangerous practical jokes, such as filling dusters with pepper, or making the winter roadway outside extra slippery with spilled liquid. They sneered at the elderly and courteous woman who came there to buy laces for her stays, overcharged her, and kept the money, saying she could afford it. They laughed openly at the flushed girl sent to purchase intimate underclothing. (Abashed, the mother had tried to be especially helpful to both of these victims.) Everything the assistants did, all told, was revolting, and the mother shunned them as best she could. Even so they stuck pins upside down into her tray of ribbons, put salt into her water glass, and called her to her face, the Imbecile.

The child, conversely, had been sent by law to school, and here her thinness and pallor, her lack of energy and her dim sight, had won her the reputation, too, of being a simpleton. Both larger and smaller children tormented her, called her foul names, and sometimes beat her – although not often, for the mere threat of violence elicited from her such utter terror, indeed to the point of vomiting, that it was enough for them. Her teachers regarded her with disgust, for she was not seen to be intelligent, and since she could not always make out what they wrote on their blackboards, or through fright assimilate what they said, they either ignored her, or rapped her with a ruler on her thin white knuckles and put her to stand in corners.

In such a nightmare, mother and child existed. For either of them there seemed no end, no rescue. At home, nevertheless, they did not speak of the agonies of that outside world, called by fools, real. They shut it from them with the strength of the embattled warriors they were.

Their home was a tenement, which leaned. The stairs were partially rotten, the roof leaked, and sometimes a rat would arrive in their apartment. But the mother said they should not fear the rats, which were living things as they were. So she gave a little food to them, and each of the rats, three or four of them, became as docile and soft as a kitten, one tusker especially, who would sit, pale as snow, on the mother's knee, and allow her to feed him crumbs of bread and cheese, or suck milk from her fingers.

Actually, the child, so afraid, and with such cause, of human beings, had no fear of any other creature. She found beetles as fascinating as birds, and did not shy away from huge carriage horses on the street, only looking up at them in admiration. At school, one day, when the bullies hid a large spider in the child's hat, she coaxed it out on her palm and carried it to a window, where she let it go carefully into some ivy. This earned her their respect for a week. (Of course, had she been afraid of spiders, the shock might have sent her into hysterics.)

The mother earned little enough, and she and the child, the rats and beetles, ate very meagrely. Tonight, the mother had wished things to be different. It had come to her that she and her daughter were to see the turning over of one century into another, and that this was a remarkable occasion. The child, to whom the mother frequently told beautiful stories of a magic world that, fortunately, made the 'real world' truly appear a thing of sawdust and lies, became filled by her mother's excitement. And so they planned a small feast. To this end the mother had saved, and this evening, released early from her hell, she had gone about the shop and market eagerly. There was now in her basket fresh bread and a portion of butter, some cheese, and cold meats, an onion, herbs and apples, milk and chocolate. This was satisfactory, but still all was not quite well. She had wanted to buy the child a gift. In vain, the mother had looked into the glass walls, like prisms of ice, the windows of the better shops. She had seen velvet dresses and sequined fans, and toys without number, brilliant and entrancing. And all of them as far beyond her means as the Milky Way.

At last she turned to go back, knowing she must not be too late, or the child would be frightened, aware too of the storybook cliché:

she had become the poor slattern who cannot afford, for her bastard child, a starry present. And now a benign witch should step down from thin air, and offer her this present, because it was the hour for it, the moment, this sinister and sorceress night between two vast rifts of time. And the mother laughed a bitter tiny laugh. Her dreams were full of loveliness, and this she had imparted, unsullied, to her child, her poor, skinny, ugly little child that she loved so much. But though she might pass the wonder on, in her heart it had died. She had been forced to believe at last in reality.

Halfway up the hill, the mother paused. The sky was all dark now, and she saw the old clock tower in this darkness, lit too with a misty light in its crown. Nearby, at the gates of a little park, by the glimmer of lanterns, a few persons were selling things.

The mother went closer, unsure, not wanting to linger. There were pictures in cheap frames, not well-painted, and this made her quite sad, for either the artists had not troubled, or else they had no talent for this work, and had not yet found out their proper talent. Also there was various bric-a-brac, and some rickety chairs despoiled from some lost home. At the end of the line waited an old man, shabby and bent over, with long grey hair. Before him on the ground stood a box, and out of it, as the mother drew close, he produced two bright small objects. These he held out to her, and as he did so, his face lifted from the shadow. She had been about to flinch aside, but the look of him stayed her inadvertently. How handsome he was; he must in his youth have been a prince among men. Her heart actually fluttered because ten years before, she had been something of a gem herself.

'Dolls for you, madame. Two lovely ladies. For your children.'

The mother looked down, and there they were, the dolls. Plainly they were sisters, and she saw at once one was a few years older than the other. Their sweet faces were pale, and shaped as the faces of two cats, and their great smoky eyes had been rimmed by gilt. From two gilt hats furled long milky plumes. Their dainty china hands were an iota larger than their perfect little feet encased in charcoal shoes with gilded heels. Around their throats were sombre ruffs edged with glitter. The elder had dark curls and a dress of rose satin. The younger was blond and clad in aquamarine silk. Beneath the skirts were glimpsed some creamy layers of lace.

'Yes, madame. Now, how can you refuse? Think how your children will delight in them.'

'Just my daughter, monsieur,' said the mother, surprising herself. She did not often now confide in anyone.

'Ah, just your daughter,' repeated the old man. One of his eyes had a drooping lid, a sort of wink. It seemed to say: *I knew all along, but we must pretend, mustn't we?*

'She would love them,' said the mother.

'Then surely she should have them. The world teaches that denial is good, but this is one of the great lies. Fulfilment is good, providing no one is harmed. And the truly happy do no harm.'

The mother's eyes burnt as if they had filled with tears, but they had not. She said, tentatively, 'How much is it you're asking?'

The old man spoke a price. It was quite cheap.

The mother thought she could go without stockings for another month. What did stockings matter?

'Then I could afford one of them.'

'Ah now, madame. Could you be so heartless as to part them? They're sisters, as you can see.'

'I can only afford one doll,' said the mother, firming herself, as she forever had to.

The old man said, 'Well, tomorrow is another century, or perhaps we shall be swallowed by a star, as some have predicted. So, I'll give you both my dolls for the price of one. My box is empty. These are the last. Tomorrow I go far away. Two for one.'

'Are you certain?' said the mother.

The old man looked at her again. His winking eye said, *Come now, you know I don't say what I don't mean. Don't you remember, three hundred years ago, when you and I, both of us young and fair, danced on a floor like ice, with champagne in our blood and wings on our feet?*

The mother blushed faintly. She fumbled for her purse, and found the money and handed it to him. He bowed to her as a count would do to a princess. Then he put the two dolls gently down into her basket, laying them between the bread and chocolate, between the staff of life and the sweet unneeded comfort that life makes so necessary.

As he did this, she beheld an odd ring on his hand. It was set with a miniature skull, carved presumably from bone. Sallow and ominous. She did not care for it and wondered if this meant some bad thing, and she should beware. Her embarrassment altered into slight fearfulness, and she thanked him and quickly turned away.

She was almost apprehensive as she went on, that he would now call loudly after her, demanding more money, perhaps with a harsh and sneering laugh. He did not. And as she turned upward into the leaning canted rows of ancient houses, slums now, mostly all darkened after the carnival of lights below, she saw the stars visible overhead. She pulled her skimpy scarf from her neck to cover the dolls, lest some thief notice their finery. She had the urge, as she did so, to explain to them what she did. But she had learned not to talk to inanimate objects.

When she reached home, she found the child anxiously waiting in the larger of their two rooms, but the anxiety was, this time, more of impatience than unease, because the child too had been busy.

She had washed and dressed herself in her best frock, and undone her long rat's tails of hair, and combed them. Then she had laid the table with the embroidered cloth kept for birthdays and put out the cutlery and the plates and cups. Obviously, too, the child had been setting aside some of her slight allowance of money, which was meant to gain her a glass of milk and a piece of bread during the school day, or a fruit-cake on her days of holiday. In the middle of the table, stuck to an azure saucer, was a tall vanilla candle marked with the hours from eight until midnight. And by it, some primroses gleamed in a bottle.

All the shabby furniture had been dusted and the cushions plumped up, and a painted shawl spread on the best chair. Their two pictures, one of which showed knights riding beneath a balcony of graceful women, and the other one, a lion asleep, had been decorated by paper bows. Best of all, perhaps, in the narrow window hung a string of paper birds, superbly cut out and coloured by the child herself, in secret, with sequins winking on their wings.

'Oh,' said the mother.

'Do you like it? Do you?' asked the child. Her mother was the only one in the world to whom she ever dared to offer anything of herself.

'Oh yes – oh yes. It's so pretty – it's so exactly right. And the candle! And the wonderful birds. But you didn't have your milk...'

'Yes,' said the child, 'every other day.'

They regarded each other solemnly. Man has never lived by bread alone, and these two both knew it very well. The mother conceded the child's common sense, and better yet, her uncrushed imagination, her ability to ascend.

Then the child darted to her and they embraced. It had been a terrible blow to them both that, due to the dangerous nature of the house stairs, the child was no longer able to fly down them and meet her mother at the lower door.

'I have a surprise for you,' said the mother presently, 'but I want to take it into the bedroom and wrap it up for you. You must have it at midnight. And after dinner you should have an hour's sleep, so you're awake when the century crosses over.'

'Oh no,' said the child. 'I won't need to sleep before. There's no school in the morning. You promised not.'

'So I did. No, no horrid school. No horrible shop. We'll stay up until one in the morning, and then we'll sleep until ten.'

They gave a mutual cry of happiness and victory. For a moment the foulness of Reality fell down and was trampled underfoot by two pairs of slender feet, both in ill-fitting shoes.

As the mother wrapped the two dolls carefully in silvery paper, in the cramped, damp-darkened bedroom, she heard the child bustling about, washing the salad of herbs in a basin, cutting up the onion and apple and heating the oil in the pan.

The dolls were so beautiful, and so pleasant to touch, to eye and fingers, like *lakoum* to the mouth; honeyed, soothing, voluptuous, nearly drugged. The child would love them utterly, for she loved beautiful things. The mother acknowledged, with vague shame, that her child thought she too, the mother, very beautiful. But the mother knew that she was not, and knew that the child was not, except to her mother.

However, when the apple and onion were fried, and put with meat and cheese, and the bread and butter set out, and the hour candle duly lit, and the cranky gas lowered, they sat there in a sort of glow, eyes luminous and cheeks warm, laughing and telling silly stories that made them shake with mirth. And when the hot chocolate was prepared for dessert, and the mother added a dash of brandy, they became quite drunk and began to talk to each other of kings and enchantresses, as if they knew them well, which in a way they did. (Only once or twice, did the mother think of the curious skull ring the old man had worn. She had been taught fairly remorselessly that nothing good could ultimately come of anything, even of joy. With great skill she still tried to push this lesson from her. The old man did not matter at all. Only the present of the two beautiful dolls.)

They found it really quite easy to keep awake, although both had had to rise about six that morning. It was after all a night that arrived only once in a hundred years. They sang, and danced even, pecking round on the worn carpet to three hummed waltz tunes. When a wind blew up over the city, as if responding to the speed with which now – it was after eleven – Paradis rushed toward the future, the paper birds flew about on their strings. And the mother realised that perhaps her child could have been clever, if she had been given some chance. And it seemed to her that possibly she could save to have the child's eyes looked at, and glasses prescribed, and, even if this should mean more cruelty and invective for the child to endure, it might also permit her to learn more. And the mother would not remember just then that the teachers in the poor school were ignorant and useless, at best stupid and at worst monsters, and glasses might not help at all, since there was not much of worth to be seen with them.

By five minutes to midnight, when they had made a second chocolate with a second wisp of brandy, the mother was childishly dreaming that there was a way to be found through the labyrinth of terrors. It was the food and the chocolate, the brandy and the flying birds. But she did not remind herself of that.

Tonight, they were a queen and a princess. They could feast and stay up late, and tomorrow sleep on, regardless of the dictates of the world.

'Mama – it's true. The bells are ringing!'

They went to the window hand in hand, and looked out into the clustered dark, which was one moment dense and impenetrable, and next – alive, alight, blazing like a sudden morning. From somewhere a thousand extra lights were born, actually from the very meanest windows, where in a sudden unreasoning festival of amazement, the despairing doomed and damned had all at once thrown off the darkness and reached out to the promise of hope. And in the sky, a thousand other lights were breaking, pink stars and gilded, hail of tinsel, fireworks like flakes of the moon. The clocks struck and the bells clamoured, and up from the city rose all the pent screams of arrival and astonished greeting, as if every citizen was only in that instant born.

The threshold had been passed. The sky had not fallen, and the earth still bore everything up. The moment had come – and was gone.

'Isn't it wonderful?' said the child.

'Yes,' said the mother. 'Yes.'

And they opened the window to hear the noises better, the car horns and the whistles and trumpets, the dogs barking in front, the smashing of glasses for good luck.

'And now,' said the mother. She put the silvery package into the palms of her child.

The child parted the paper carefully.

The mother stood as if high up or far away, watching her child. She saw a shadow spread over the face of the child. The child stood speechless. She was too old for dolls. The mother had misjudged. How could she have been so foolish as to buy them? They were shoddy, this was the reason for their inexpensiveness. An awful mistake.

The child said, stiffly, 'They're more lovely than anything.' She looked up at her mother. The child's face had changed with the passing of the century. What was it? 'Their names,' said the child, 'are Miralda and Dianelle.'

'Do you like them?'

'Yes,' said the child.

Abruptly the mother saw what had happened. It was not disappointment. One of the great shocks of existence had occurred. The child was in love.

The mother went to her, and gently, almost timorously, touched her hair. The mother did not touch the dolls anymore. They had become attached to the child, as if by strings of metal, and gone with the child away, into a cube of crystal.

One of the reasons for festivals is the belief that through them, something may change for the better, that by toasting a new year, it may bring different and kinder fortune, that a corner has been turned, a door gone through. Most humans hold to this dream stubbornly, and when it is finally, utterly lost, they grow old.

The mother credited herself with having grown up. Yet, the festival had galvanised her, and when a couple of days later she found herself back in her awful place of work, with everything grey and abysmal about her still, some inner child in her that was herself, raged and wept. This is the price that hope extracts. Hope is one of the best gifts, but also one of the harshest masters.

Because she had returned a day late, on pretence of illness, her colleagues had a story that the Imbecile had been sick with drink. She had been seen, they jeered, soliciting sailors on the antique quay of the Angel, only the basest of whom would go with her because she was so unappealing.

The mother bore this because she had to. But as the days and weeks went by, and nothing improved, chalk was rubbed into her threadbare coat, and coins stolen from her purse, she found herself struggling with her own pain. This was much harder, for by now something had truly been changed, and for the worse.

There had always existed solace for the mother in her child. At this stage, without the child, the mother would probably have sunk much lower, even under the river, maybe. And the child too had needed the mother. Now however, the child was otherwise absorbed.

At first, the mother was captivated, on coming in, to find the child there playing with the two dolls, Miralda and Dianelle. This play involved the table, and the piling up of some books, or the placing of the fern from under the window, a lamp, cards, perhaps two thimbles of water, the painted shawl. The child greeted her mother affectionately, and did everything she was asked, even cleared the table instantly. But when they sat to their supper of bread and coffee or thin soup, the dolls sat with them.

By the lamp's low light, their smoky eyes gleamed, their curls, dark and blond, glistened and their finery shone.

The child did not speak very much, unless questioned about the dolls.

Then they had all three been walking in the park, by the great fountains, and here Miralda, the elder of the dolls, had spoken to a handsome duke, who much admired her, but Dianelle had been more interested in sporting with her little dog. Or they had been to a theatre, where half the audience rose to glimpse them, and seen there a wonderful performance in five acts and, in the intervals they had eaten sugar almonds and marzipan, and drunk transparent wine. Sometimes they had stayed home, however, in their mansion, where marble statues held torches, and there was a domed conservatory up three hundred steps, from which it was possible to observe, through a telescope, the planets of other galaxies.

The mother listened, in delight herself, to the child's inventions. In the past, it had been she, the mother, who had told the stories. And for a while the twenty-seven-year-old woman, bent and elderly, and worn out as a glove, had been lifted from herself and floated there, her eyes fixed without focus on flighty Dianelle and wise Miralda, partaking of their freedoms, decorum, education, and opulence. Through a sort of shimmering haze, she saw them, like candlelight. She almost fancied that their heads would graciously turn upon their white necks in the sombre ruffs, or that, when the children lifted them to show them dance, they did so.

But in the end, the child grew more reticent. She would say now only that all was well, that tonight Miralda and Dianelle were to take her to another country. This, when pressed, she would explain to be a very cold one, with mountains diademed by ice, or a very hot one, where enormous beasts prowled, and parrots laughed in the cinnamon trees. Or there would be cities with minarets. Or a sea, where temples came down into the waves.

'In your dreams,' said the mother, at last.

'If you like,' said the child.

And this cool little phrase turned the mother aside, as if now she had spoken in the wrong language, the language of a stranger.

Sometimes the mother would wake too, in the big bed, and see, as if miles away, the child quietly sleeping. Previously, the child had been inclined to snore in her sleep from winter congestion, but now she was so still that, once or twice, with a pang of fear, the mother bent over her to see that she breathed. And on the pillow sat the dolls, Miralda, Dianelle, like two little fairies or angels set to act sentinel. How hard their eyes in the packed darkness, hard as tears that had become granite. The mother remembered that, unlike other dolls, they did not smile, and she recalled they had no colour in their cheeks. Somewhere away within her own skull, the child was dancing, boating, riding in bright carriages, or on the backs of dove-skin horses. Miralda was introducing her to painters, poets, and musicians. Dianelle was guiding her through picnics of frosted sweet-meats and champagne. How old was the child in these dreams? Perhaps the timeless age of a doll, between maiden and baby.

'And what did you eat?' the mother asked of the great dinner, where every goblet and plate had been of sheerest glass.

The child told her of dishes from the Arabian Nights.

'And what dress did you wear?'

'Oh, it was silk. And I had pearls in my hair, and feathers.'

The mother knew that in her dreams, and in her playing when

awake with Miralda and Dianelle, the child was not without beauty – or, now, accomplishments, for one evening she had entered the apartment to find the child singing in a hoarse, thin voice some song, she said – when asked – she had composed to her imaginary guitar.

This waking and sleeping dream-world, then, initially appealing to the mother, began to unnerve her as it closed her outside.

There is always this problem, just as the real world is so often determinedly confused with the Real, so it is difficult to differentiate between others that are fantasy, or maybe madness.

Christ Himself seemed to have found this an obstacle with some of his listeners.

The mother began to brood upon what went on now with her child and the two dolls, bought so easily, on the Night of Passage.

Surely the child's complete immersion in their invented life could not be healthy, might indeed be a danger – but then what was there to offer in return?

She became lonely, too, the mother. Her child was considerate to her, the way a loving daughter would be, as she went into the distance, with new inspiring others.

There was no one to seek out for advice. For ten years or more, the mother had had adult conversation only with horrors, and what humanity sometimes calls beasts, forgetting beasts do not merit such connections.

Sometimes she tried to tempt the child to different things. A book of pictures bought at some cost, an outing. But the books were received with gratitude and carried off to furnish more fuel for the adventures of Miralda and Dianelle. The outing could not compete with them. And the mother noted, as well, a politeness in the child, a patience – not to hurt the kind parent who meant so well and could provide so very little. Only now and then, some element would attract the child. And she would say, 'Oh, Miralda's swans are like that one!' Or, 'Dianelle came down in a ball gown just the colour of the sky.'

One night, as the mother walked home, about two months after the start of the new century, like many other nights, she found she had begun to cry. And she leaned on a wall, out of sight, lost as a girl of nine whose mother has left her.

The months went by. Spring fluttered down into Paradis, the new moon of seasons. The mother did her accounts carefully, for now the time was coming when the expense of the winter stove would be balanced by the summer turning of milk, and the sometimes-undrinkable quality of the common tap water.

At the shop, the assistants found a new game, remarking that something had begun to smell. It was of course untrue, unless they scented the stench of their own souls. The mother bore with it, as ever. But she sensed now, abruptly, a day was drawing near when they would manage to oust her, and what then would she do? Perhaps she might find work in the poisonous laundries, but these would probably kill her in a year; she was no longer physically strong.

That evening she returned to the tenement, with some fruit and chocolate that was bought in a fit of recklessness, feeling her death, the death of everything, although the spring night was fresh and starred by buds.

When she opened the apartment door, fear leapt at her throat.

There at the table sat the child, still as stone, and down her face the tears were streaming, pouring, like rain.

'What is it?' cried the mother. And she ran forward, and grasped the child, as if to get between her and whatever novel dreadful force was now at work.

'No, Mama, I'm safe. I am. No, nothing happened to me.' The child held the mother as protectively as the mother held the child.

This the mother became aware of, and reassured somewhat, loosened her grip. 'What, then?'

The child indicated the table. The mother now saw it – she had seen nothing in the room but the child until that moment.

There, on the softest cushion, lay the elder doll, Miralda. She was stretched on her back with her arms at her sides. Her curls and the plumes of her hat framed her pale exquisite face. Beside her had been positioned the other doll, Dianelle, sitting stoically upright. The hard, clear eyes of both of them reflected the lamp, but in a glassy, sightless way, like the eyes of a dead fish.

'Miralda died,' said the child softly.

'But…' said the mother. She checked herself at once. 'How terrible.'

'She was very old,' said the child, still weeping, but without any expression, and the mother noticed oddly that her nose did not run

– she wept herself like a weeping doll. 'Older than she seemed. Much, much.'

'Yes,' said the mother humbly. 'And poor Dianelle must be so sad.'

'Dianelle is dying too. She told me, when I found Miralda. Only a few hours.'

'But can't she be saved?' said the mother, unaccountably, perhaps anxious now. 'They're great ladies, Miralda, Dianelle. Some important physician…'

'There's no cure. They're so old. They've done such a lot,' said the child.

The mother shuddered. She wondered, caught herself wondering, if Dianelle would require a priest. And, horribly, unavoidably, if she herself would want one, at her own deathbed.

As if the child knew what she thought, or some of it, she said, 'There's no need for any fuss. They're not frightened. Dianelle told me, only the body dies. And she wants to be with Miralda. She always has been.'

Suddenly, the mother glimpsed – absurd, fearsome – what it was that alarmed her. The child, contained in this world of dream and fantasy, had become one with the two dolls. If they died – what did she expect for herself? Before she could resist the impulse, the mother touched the forehead of her child, to test for fever.

'No, no, Mama,' the child said again, very gently. 'I'm quite well.'

The mother got up. She stood there and did not know what to do. At length, she made the chocolate, and put the cup beside her daughter's hand. The child's tears had ceased.

'Drink what you can.'

The child nodded, tasted the cup, and set it down.

The mother withdrew to the bedroom, and here she took out some stockings that needed to be darned. As she did this, she began to pray. She reckoned herself peculiar, foolish, an imbecile for sure, for, although she did not now believe in God, or thought Him wicked, she would always pray to Him in her direst moments. It seemed to her there had never been any answer, except perhaps further punishment. And yet, to speak to Him eased her. Of course, there was no one else to whom she could turn.

After about two hours, she stole out, and saw that the child was sitting as before, with the cold chocolate congealing beside her.

Both dolls now lay on the cushion. Mysteriously, aptly, the lamp was burning low. It was a room of shadows and mourning.

'Oh...' said the mother.

'It's over now,' said the child, almost the words of the Cross.

The mother clasped her hands together.

'But we must bury them,' said the child.

The mother cast about her mind wildly. She must not upset the child further. But what was to be done? And in the centre of her confusion a voice rose in her, which said, *What nonsense. Throw the things out with the rubbish. Or better still, sell them in the market.* This voice, which had the exact tones of her colleagues' in the hell-shop, she recognised immediately and pushed from her with enormous invisible violence. And it seemed to her she saw the voice falling miles down, back into some pit.

'There's a paper box,' said the mother. 'Do you remember? I brought it from the shop to keep gloves in. It is only paper, but if they're wrapped in the painted shawl – will that do?' Her own voice was full of apology and pleading.

The child said, 'Oh, yes.'

'And tomorrow we can go to some place where there's – some open space. And I can put the box into the earth.'

The child looked up now. She smiled at her mother. 'We can keep the box,' she said. 'It will be all right. You see, really the funeral will have carriages made of glass and dark horses with plumes, and hundreds of people will walk behind. And there will be a mass, with two thousand candles.'

'Yes,' said the mother.

But then she fetched the box, and put into it the painted shawl, that was the only thing which remained of the coloured, lighted days, ten years before. The child lifted the dolls into this cocoon, and quickly covered their faces. Then the lid was put down.

They lowered the box into the deepest drawer of their chest, where it need not be disturbed.

And then they stood there, in the gloom of the bedroom as mourners do, at a loss, once the coffin has gone down into its hole.

Later, when they had eaten their bread and cheese, and were in bed, the mother lay awake. She was not afraid, but full of an ominous sadness, a sickening uncertainty. Beside her the child slept, silently as now she always did.

Finally, the dawn remade the sky, and the noises of the day

commenced in the street below. The child woke, and said softly, 'Mama, may I have a book – a book with words to read?'

'Yes, my love. But you know how trying it is for your poor eyes – we'll go to see a doctor soon.'

'My eyes are much better, Mama. I can even see the things on the blackboard at school.'

The mother did not believe this, but she did not say so. She promised the book. She had partly noticed the child's knuckles were not so often split open and bruised by rulers, but she had put this down to a random upsurge of mislaid humanity in the teachers.

While they drank their coffee, she watched the child surreptitiously. The child seemed calm, no longer distressed or tearful.

She has forgotten it, the mother thought, hopefully. And she has grown out of the dolls. That's good. It must be good.

The end came very simply.

By then it was summer, hot and steamy in the lower city as if Paradis lay in the heart of a primordial swamp, as once it had.

Entering the shop, at the usual early hour, the mother met one of the assistants skipping toward her, while the others waited, leering and sneering.

'Monsieur wants to see you.'

It has come. Oh God, what shall I do?

But in the wooden bravery of despair, the mother went without delay to a dingy room, where the overseer of hell awaited her, his congested face swollen further with displeasure.

'You are to go and see someone. You're to go now. I don't like it. I won't be told what's what in this way.'

The mother poised before him, astonished.

He thrust at her a letter, and she read it, but it made no sense.

'Go on, go on,' cried Monsieur, flapping her off.

Outside, the colleagues clustered. 'Got shot of you, has he, Imbecile? Oh, what a shame!'

The mother did not speak. She sat down on a chair, while they capered around her.

'Want some brandy, do you? You'll be lucky. You can have some of my snot if you like!' And at this witticism they were so convulsed they barely saw her pass out of the door, which perhaps peeved them later, for they were never to see her do it again, or pass in, for that matter.

At a small office on another street, the mother was treated more humanly, if with equal patronage. These, too, supposed her slow or retarded. At least the facts were persuaded into her.

Then she walked away, up through the city, wandering, not knowing where she was, and as this went on she seemed to catch sight momentarily of bizarre things, a bird that flew about with wings of softest fire, an arching rainbow, pink and honey, that described the towers of the cathedral, a boat on the river with dragonfly sails, a car driven by a bear.

Finally, she went into a café and ordered aniseed liqueur that she had not tasted in ten years. And this she drank, startled at herself. And when she burst into laughter, the waiters thought her tipsy, but only smiled, because she was a good-looking woman, worth a glance or two, and why should such an interesting woman not drink a liqueur at nine in the morning?

After the liqueur, the mother knew where she must go and there she went, to the tumbling swarthy house that held her daughter's school. The children had just been let out for some recreation, which entailed sitting in a shadeless yard with three stone walls to look at and, over one of those, the unswept street. A single child, however, was seated on a bench, and another girl was holding up over this child's head a dilapidated sunshade. Like a little queen she sat there, the favoured one, and others sat at her feet, two cutting up an apple and a pear for her, and another begging for something – this was quite evident from her gestures. Then all the girls begged too. Suddenly the seated child began to sing. She had a sweet high voice, a voice like that of a well-tuned instrument. The song she sang the mother did not know, and yet it entranced her, as if it had come from some place where she had been in dreams, some marvellous country forgotten through amnesia, and now glimpsed once again with a pang of memory, nostalgia, and wild excitement.

The other children were also affected by this singing. They drew in close, craning, their eyes fixed on the child who had the bench. Even the rough boys, who played on, tussling, ceased to make any noise. Had they been older, they would have listened frankly.

When the song was over, there was a space of silence, and then the mother, half-embarrassed, raised her own voice and called to her child.

The girl on the bench got up instantly and came running over to her.

But as she came, the mother saw it all, all that she had not seen. How the child's hair was full and shining, her skin like porcelain, the soft flush at her cheeks, the deep shade of her eyes. And in those few seconds, like an hour of careful thought, the mother beheld not only how her child was changed, but saw through her, as if through clearest water, to what she would become. She saw her lifted up upon some spire of celebrity, and dancing in the sky, with pale emeralds on her fingers, and Paradis at her feet; the world at her feet.

'I've something to tell you. It's wonderful.'

'Yes,' said the child. She was not surprised, only ready. She expected the best news.

'An elderly lady used to come into the shop. She was so courteous, old-fashioned. The others were so rude to her. Poor creature, she died. But oh – she's left me some money. A lot of money.'

'Oh, yes,' said the child, happy, not surprised.

'She didn't know me, you see. She said – that I was kind to her.'

As they looked at each other, the woman and her daughter, they were not privy to what else the elderly lady had bequeathed. The pretty little bow-tied presents soon to be delivered to all the remaining assistants in the shop. Which each contained the turds of dogs and other, even more prolific, animals.

They did not know, or need to know, the woman and her daughter. They were already quite busy talking of the small house they would inhabit, with milk-washed walls and polished floors, with mirrors having pictures of butterflies in their corners, and the knights and ladies, and the lion, in areas of honour above a piano, overlooking the walled garden with tea-roses. Nor had they forgotten the three or four rats, the white one particularly, and planned how they might be induced to move with them from the tenement.

As the mother and her child went away from that school, the pupils grouped by the wall, looking out like convicts, watching two freed prisoners escape. They had only the apple left to them, the convicts, and the pear. Which they ate, and so had no more.

Love can take many forms, even that of a perfect and beautiful man, abused and whipped, bleeding and asphyxiating on a cross. Love is bewildering.

In the night, the young woman woke and got out of bed, leaving her daughter sleeping. She went by stealth to the chest and from it she took the coffin, the paper box, and carried it, closing the bedroom door behind her, into the outer room.

Here she lit the gas, and taking one breath, drew off the box's lid, and delicately pulled away the folds of her shawl.

Not much was left of Miralda and Dianelle. Some threads of their glamorous dresses, aquamarine, rosy, some sprinkles of gilt, their dainty shoes. And there was some sawdust, such as might be used to fill the interior parts of dolls. Other than this, there were only two tiny skulls, about the size of acorns, well-shaped, complete in every way, even to the minuscule teeth, which were charmingly clean and wholesome, like seed-pearls, though otherwise the bone had darkened.

Death Loves Me

Sitting in the tavern after the race, it was just because he had not seen her, that he began to shiver. The three rich men with him, buying him Thracian wine, since he had won for them, never noticed, or put it down to nerves, the kind a thoroughbred horse might exhibit. When he was shot of them, and went out in the dusk, the summer air was heavy and ripe over the port. Down below, the ships lay at anchor, and the stink of turning fish rose from the market. But there was incense too from the temple of Kore, and the smell of oranges and pomegranates from her groves. The day was flying, and lamps coming alight like jewels. As a child, he had liked this time; it had seemed magic to him the way men could make light return, though darkness drew her cloak across the world. On the plaster of the inn wall some educated drunk had scribbled, *Xetis it is who loves me*. Evidently, he did not know the reputation of Xetis.

Lukon walked back up the hill to the stadium, and looked in on his horses, which, well-groomed and fed, stood burnished as coals in the torchlight, tossing up their long heads for his caress.

'You did well, my dears, did I tell you? You, Bull, so strong, and you, Bird, fleet as an arrow. And my clever Eros. Yes, my love. My son, my brother.' Lukon embraced them all. They were his family. He had no other, probably wanted none. 'I'm sorry I left you to the boy. But he's seen to you very well, and he needs to learn – but, no excuses. It wasn't what I should have done. No, Bull, you shake your head. No. But I wasn't myself. You know I can't say. You know I don't tell you that one thing. But there it is.'

Lukon had come from the chariot, the sweat streaming on him, and the garland of victory on his head, and puked behind the bath house, as if it had been his first race.

It was because she had not been there, in the crowd. Although he had scanned it closely, skinned it with his eyes. Nowhere. The first race in seven races he had not seen her. And he had been sure, although this had only come to him when the race was done, that this time she would be in the very front of all the benches, right up against the barrier of the track. Yes, he had been certain of that.

He stood staring now at the temple of Kore. Should he go in? She was not here in her aspect of shadow, but shown as a young girl, with the poppies painted red in her hands. But he did not like priests. Not since he had been poor years ago and seen what they really were.

Instead he turned away, up toward the houses by the tent-makers. Tilat was there, who would welcome him. She would send the slave running for cakes and flowers and wine. She would lie back and draw him down against her pale smooth body. He had won the race embraced the horses, got drunk. What else was there, now, but Tilat?

'Shall I sing you the song about the dove?'

'If you like.' His voice – ungracious, unkind. He amended, 'Any song is good, if you sing it.'

'You don't think so.'

'Yes, of course I do, Tilat.'

She turned her face a little away, her dark hair shining under its chaplet of flowers, the loose robe slipping from her burnished shoulder. She had been, as always, pumiced and soft and fragrant. She had rejoiced at him and made the evening into a festival, but once he had possessed her, he had known she was, after all, not the same. Her little cries might not have been real. At supper she was sulky. He should have brought her a present, she preferred it to money. He said, 'I don't deserve your sweetness, Tilat. I'm sorry.'

'When I love you so much,' she said.

'I know. You're my darling.'

'And you won. I heard them cheering, the way they do only for you.'

'Or for Shaizek,' he said.

She made a sharp little gesture. 'Shaizek – what is he? An Egyptian. A foreigner.'

It might have amused Lukon, for Red Shaizek had raced in many places and was highly thought of, besides which Tilat, with her Semitic eyes and the moon-coins in her ears, was no less a foreigner herself.

'You didn't come to watch me, then.'

'A respectable woman can't go there, except veiled. And you know, one can see *nothing* through a veil.'

This too he might have laughed at. Was she trying to entertain? Or would she take affront? She was quite wealthy from his patronage and from that of others before him. Even so, she was hardly *respectable*. And he had seen her first, unveiled, or barely, sitting in the women's stands where no "respectable" woman was ever allowed, with a crowd of five other girls such as she, her friends.

That had been at a time, last year, when he had only seen *that other one* rarely. He could count them on one hand the times he had seen *her*. Until this last month.

Tilat's wine was sour in his mouth. He did not wish to be here. He must go, insult Tilat by leaving her before the sand had even run from her day-clock, marking midnight.

'I think you're tired of me,' she said.

'Not at all. Some trouble, Tilat. It's made me unsociable, and I regret that.'

Tilat raised her face, and taking up the little harp, began to strum the sad melody of the dove song. The notes fell like beads into the lamp-lit pool of the room, and oddly detained him.

'She mourns, poor dove, for her lost lover. Caroo, caroo. She mourns for him. Her broken heart, I pity her, for once I flew as flew this dove. Caroo, caroo.'

Lukon drew an apricot from the silver dish and turned it in his fingers. His hand was muscular, calloused, and brown, scarred white across the knuckles. All of him was this way. A man of brown marble with pieces chipped and ripped out of it. Why did she like him, and the other girls who liked him too, and not only Lukon, but any successful charioteer? Did they not say, in the lower streets, *Lying with Death?* – Death took the form of a king to a woman, Hades, also a charioteer. But for a man: Persephone, Queen of the Underworld, Kore the Maiden.

The song had stopped.

Lukon said 'Tilat – can I tell you a secret?'

Her little face flashed up. Her eyes flashed too, with sudden tears. 'You love elsewhere. You're done with me, and came to say so.'

'No – no, Tilat. Pretty girl.' He dropped the apricot and went to her, and held her, gentling her, as once, one horrible time when he was only sixteen, he had held and stroked the golden neck of a broken horse, quieting it, before the merciful smith smashed in its skull. And as he thought of that, the tears, to which only his horses now could move him, coursed down his face.

Weeping, they lay on the mosaic floor, and presently made love again, with a clutching violence. Her scream was real enough now, and he was drowned in her. Spent, he rested against her breast, and soon they rose, and he told her, as he had never told another in all of the past five years *it* had been his to tell.

Just after lamp-lighting, Urtemis stood on the house roof, gazing down toward the port, and seeing something quite other. Below in the house was the familiar evening movement, and the faint smell of cooking, and of flowers.

When I was young, Urtemis thought, *I should have wept if he were not coming home to supper.*

That, of course, was long ago. She, who had been wed to her husband at fourteen, was now ten years older. She had, through those years, grown accustomed to the ways of a man, learning that, although he might honour her and be well-pleased with her, still he might also wish often to be elsewhere, and sometimes in the company of other women. She had been warned long before her wedding of the customs of the two sexes, that she must be circumspect and chaste, and he at liberty.

She had always loved him. From the moment they had let her peep around the screen, and see him ride into the courtyard, and dismount so gracefully, for in those days he was an athlete, and stand under the tree of green figs. He was very tall, with fair, gilded skin, black and curling hair, and eyes as blue, she believed, as the ocean.

It was a lucky marriage. His wealth and status – everyone had been delighted. And even he, drawing up her veil for the first time in the lamplight, had said to her things she did not ever forget.

When she did not quicken with child, Urtemis had sought a wise woman at her own mother's instigation. And then had come a strange regime, potions that stank and after which she chewed mint leaves, for fear he would smell them on her and be sickened. Curious amulets under the pillow, under the bed frame. Nothing worked. She was barren, she had disappointed.

Then the wise woman – another one by this time – had said, 'There is always this: you won't lose your looks as a mother may.'

Urtemis saw now before her what she had just seen in her

apartment below, her own face swimming in the bronze Egyptian mirror, between its upright ibises of gold. The bronze was kind and did not show the dry thin cuts at either side of her mouth, and at the corners of her eyes. The mirror still showed Urtemis the wholeness of her beauty, and the wheat-gold of her hair coiled upon her head.

She need have no fears. She was lovely, and besides the legal wife of Karestes, who once had exclaimed, kissing her fourteen-year-old breasts, *'These are the doves of Aphrodite herself.'*

Urtemis turned from the unseen view of the town, the fading violet of the sky. She went down again into the house of her husband, across the floors of marble that glimmered at this hour like still water.

She looked into the supper room, where perhaps he would come, or not, to dine alone, and if so she might wait on him, and sit by him, and eat sweetmeats from his hand, and place the garland on his darkly-curling hair that had now a little grey in it, and lastly lead him, she faint with desire, to their chamber.

It was not that she had ever experienced physical ecstasy in his arms. She did not know how to take such a gift – of which she had heard only the coarsest whispers. The holy joy she knew was emotional, a paroxysm of surrender verging on the spiritually divine. It was this she longed for, this she pined for, when he removed his body and gave it instead to other women.

Feet ran lightly along the watery floors.

'Lady…'

'He will not be home tonight,' she said.

The slave lowered her head, and her face, its eyes cast down, was like a stony mask.

'It is a woman of the docks.'

'No. No, he hasn't any reason to go there. It's the new one, the Rhodian hetaira…'

'Lady, why should I lie to you?'

Urtemis looked into the lizard gaze of this wise woman, who was yet another wise woman. Along with her bag of unguents, herbs, and charms, she might bring news for a price, and had done so.

One day, I shall be as old as she is. Who will help me then?

'He has – gone with many women. Never a woman of the

streets. Karestes is a great man...'

'Great men like sometimes to descend. She's called Phebo. She lives now in a little house behind the market. She has a knack of pretence.'

'What do you mean?"

'She makes believe to be certain things she isn't. Very young, perhaps little more than a child. Or some sort of animal.'

Urtemis shuddered. 'I don't want to hear.'

'You *asked* to hear,' said the woman sullenly, fingering the cloth Urtemis had given her with coins in it.

Urtemis got up. She walked about, not far, for this side room was small. The lamps cast a rich, hot light and beyond the windows the sky was black.

'He's so often with her – I've never known him so often to go with any of them. A week, a month. Then he tires.' She thought proudly, it had been a year before he tired of *her*. But then, he had been bound to her and must make the best of it.

The wise woman crouched under the lampstand, one blot of dark night that had got in. 'Phebo has a particular trick I've heard of. Very strange. Perverse, against the gods, perhaps sacrilegious.'

'Tell me!'

'You said you didn't want...'

Urtemis raised her hands to her face. Both her wrists were clasped by gold and suddenly the bracelets were her shackles, but to what? 'Don't,' she said, 'speak aloud. *Whisper* it.'

The woman whispered, and Urtemis turned to her with her eyes widening – surely, she had not heard aright? 'But – she does *this?*'

'She does.'

'Why would he – Karestes...?'

'Sometimes,' said the wise woman, 'as a man ages... and he has no son to remind him of youth and the immortality of his name.'

Lukon spoke softly.

'Remember, soon I race again. But it wasn't here I first saw her. No, I was in another town. I was sixteen. I'd been racing for a year and won quite frequently. You know how they make a fuss of you. I was full of myself, Tilat.'

She poured more wine into his cup. The lamps burned low and caused her earrings to shine like little cool flames.

That perhaps was what had made him truly notice *her*, the first.

Or an absence of that. For unlike the other women on the terraces of stands, she did not glitter and gleam in the afternoon sun. The town was a ramshackle one, but it had some decent buildings, and a stadium. They had been happy enough to enlist him, and his team, the copper-coloured horses and the chariot with its stars of gold.

When the chariots came out, it had been then, in the very first minute. He was young, and once he had got up on the track, he would feel the power come into him, the racer's hubris – dangerous perhaps, but until then a wonder, and fortunate. So he turned about, seeing how the crowd received him, and what women were there, behind their often flimsy veils. There were several pretty ones, all grouped together in the women's stand. But then, his eye still travelling, he saw another woman, standing where she ought not to be, among the men. She was so different from them, the curves of her body, like the amphora. And her black clothing, swathing her, and covering almost all of her face. She was not so far off that day, toward the middle, and he thought she was some loose woman, smuggled in for an indecorous joke, in this lax, ignorant, unimportant town. He could just make out the marking of her eyes and brows on the pale bar of her upper face. Her lack of ornament. That was all.

Then, he lost interest.

The race started. Most of them were clods, but there were a couple of men from the sophisticated west, and they were not so bad. The first lap came and went with a pair of spills for the local flowers, and the second lap, and then he was pulling into the third, with the best of the charioteers, the one who claimed to have come from Corinth, though perhaps he had not, over to the left, driving Lukon in and in, to squeeze him up against the stadium's central hub, and so cut him out.

Lukon knew the trick, and let it seem he would be stubborn, try to ram a path through, and so get jostled. Once the horses lost their step that way, it could be hard to get them back together again, and in this five-lap race, there was no time to be wasted. He meant, in fact, to let the Corinthian through. The man's pace was still uneven, the horses not well-matched, and the Corinth chariot rather on the heavy side. Lukon thought it would be easy enough to fall back and catch up again, trying next the other trick of driving straight across the mouths of the Corinthian team, which in turn would jostle *them* and put them out of stride.

As Lukon flicked up his whip in the air, as if to urge his copper horses on, he called low to them the words that would hold them steady, and he pulled down on the corded reins. They knew this double signal, and which part of it to obey, and although they flinched at the note of the whip, ignored it, and began to drop back. The Corinthian seemed to guess before he could see it, what Lukon was at, and a leer of anger chased up his face. But in that moment a cloud went over the sun.

It was an expression of the chariots, that about the cloud. A swoop of sudden darkness, when the laurel had seemed to be just before you, and all at once Sunny Apollo turned his face away, and shadow fell. But to Lukon the shadow was actual. It spilled across his way, unseen – yet definite as octopus ink in water. The horses felt it too; they swerved at nothing – and at this second the chariot and team of one of the local fools came head-long against Lukon's flank.

He learned later from a review of the straight, that night torch-lit by a grumbling slave, what must have happened. Scraps from a previous wreck had rolled about on the ground. One of these, some cog or piece of metal, unnoticed, had caught the right-hand wheel. The chariot had slewed a very little, but, concentrating on the other matter of misleading the Corinthian, Lukon had not been aware of it. His car had accordingly tipped some inches from his control, and so the tumbling idiot behind, too stupid to go wide, ran into him, and caught him a thick, disabling blow.

At once Lukon's vehicle was slung sideways. And as the team, running slower but too fast, dragged everything out of joint, the yoke-pole cracked.

Lukon saw it all, the way the drunk beholds the earth rush suddenly up at him. He could do nothing, and next moment he was out, and down in the stadium sand. A tempest of hoofs and wheels burst by, and that was some other, marvellous fool, who had saved Lukon's life by clumsily riding clear. But the chariot was buffeted a second time, caved in, and all the gold stars fell off like omens.

The horses lived and were whole but, as could sometimes happen, were useless after. They had not been in the game long enough to forget one horrible fright. He sold them to a farm in the hills for stud at quite a reasonable price.

It was two days following that when he recalled the woman in black veils who had stood above him, where she should not be. He went back – why? why ask, why? – and inquired of the stewards, who told him harshly, (one had had a bet on him and so lost money), that all women kept to the women's place, and were not allowed in any other. Did he suppose this some town of barbarians?

Later again, a month or more elsewhere, he had commented upon seeing a woman once among the terraces where she should not be, clothed in black. The old groom he spoke to made the sign against something maleficent.

'What is it?'

'Nothing, master, nothing.'

'Tell me.'

The old man pointed. Across the street from the stables was a little shrine dedicated to Kore Persephone. The small, crudely-carved and painted statue showed her as she sometimes appeared during the Mysteries. The Priestess of the Lands Below, the consort of Hades, Queen Death. She held her significant pomegranate in her hand. She was curved, and swathed, and only her eyes showed, looking right at him across the street, the shade of black onyx.

'But – did you see her again?' asked Tilat, now, in the breathless, wondering voice women had, so Lukon thought, when they were afraid, and yet admiring.

'I said I did. Yes, I saw her seven months after, and miles away from both those spots. That time, someone had played with my wheel. It came off and rolled. Somehow, I reached the barrier, and lived. She had been farther off, that time, right to the back – it was sheer chance I saw her. Maybe. But a year on from that day, I saw her much closer. She *was* in among the women's benches then. About four or five rows up. I could see the lights in her eyes, and some of her long hair had dripped under the edge of her veil – yellow hair, like the hair you see on the statues of Kore the Maiden. She made – the strangest movement. Rather like the way a woman will move her dress, in private, to bare her breast for her child. And I knew if I saw her breast... But she didn't do it. And she wasn't quite at the front, not quite...'

'One of my horses, it can happen, I'd heard of it – his heart rose and choked him. He dropped dead. The others fell, and I was thrown out, right across their bodies, so I saw them dying and then – do you see my hand? Look, this finger. Yes, Tilat, another chariot took most of it away. But another instant, it would have been my legs, both of them. I rolled so fast my skin tore open all down my back. You know the scar.'

Tilat covered her face with her hands. He heard her weeping.

'I understand, when she's finally there, against the barrier... Or if she shows me her femaleness – *then*. To see her hair almost killed me. She's death.'

'Did you – today...?'

'No. Today, she wasn't there. Not at all. And every time, for the past seven times, I've seen her. Now on the upper farthest benches. Then with the boys, and none of *them* seeing her, though she was right in among them. And another day, in among the men. And next, with the women too, but eight benches up. I *counted.* And every time, Tilat, some mishap. A little one, or a bit worse. Bull cast a shoe the last occasion. We ran with it anyway – and *won.* He is a hero, Bull. But *she* – she's Death. Mine.'

In the hour that followed midnight, after the slave had turned the vessel of sand in Tilat's day-clock, the porter let in a man at the gate through which, a few minutes ago, Lukon the charioteer had gone away.

Very dark, the newcomer emerged from the night only slowly, and as he entered Tilat's sleeping room, the lamps could make him merely into the most sombre bronze, all but his red hair, which in his own land years before, had caused women to sign themselves against evil, and boys to throw stones. That was all behind him, now. As Tilat ran to him, he offered her the cheek to kiss that fascinated her the most, the cheek with the white scar like a sickle moon, and then the left side of his hard, bronze breast.

Then he handed to her, without a word, a jewellery garland for her hair, gold leaves and grapes of amethyst. She liked best to be given a gift, not money.

Then he kissed her until her limbs gave way and she hung in his arms. She could not even speak his name after that – Shaizek, red-haired as Set, the demon god of Egypt, the Betrayer and Enemy.

But when he had lain down with her, and all the house had heard her voice, springing like a water or a blood of sound from her convulsing body, then she too told her secret, which was not really hers, to the one she loved the best.

A brace of days had passed, and Urtemis's husband, Karestes, was going hunting with some of his friends, a gentleman's pastime.

She stood watching him as he selected his spears, and then he turned and looked at her, smiling.

'What a woeful face, Urtemis. What is it?'

'I shall – miss your presence in the house.'

'Nonsense. Come, cheer up. You'll make me think you've had some premonition of distress.'

Urtemis lifted the corners of her unkissed mouth. She constructed a smile, raising the stones of it against the sinking counterweight of her heart. He did not like to see long faces. Had he not always told her so? The sadder he made her by his neglect, the more he would wish to neglect her.

After he had ridden off, with his slave and his dogs, Urtemis went to her chamber. Iris was sitting at the loom in the corner, busy, her earrings winking, her hands flying

'It must be done, I've decided. I can't rest.'

Iris glanced up. Her hands fell to her lap and her wide eyes grew anxious. Even her earrings ceased to twinkle. She had been Urtemis's personal attendant since childhood and was five years younger than her mistress. She loved – or believed she loved – Urtemis who had always been gentle and besides, a slave, the fate of the girl named for the rainbow, was inexorably bound to the woman who owned her. If Urtemis's feet came on flinty ground, so did the tender feet of Iris. 'Lady, it's not right for you to go there.'

'Of course. Of course, it isn't. But I must see her. I must talk to her. I must *know*.'

'She – may refuse,' stammered Iris.

Urtemis lost for an instant her appearance of despair and wilting. She stood straight and her eyes burned. 'She won't dare.'

The next hour was spent on their method of disguise. Urtemis, unpractised, must be guided by Iris on the mode of the lower streets, and must select from the washed garments Iris had gained for them. All jewellery was removed, replaced, where thought needful, by coarser stuff.

They crept out when the noon meal was to be served, by a side entrance, if seen taken, so Urtemis trusted, for women who had visited the kitchen. Although, naturally, the few who spied them knew precisely what went on, as slaves had to know everything in good houses, and so grasped their lady went to call on the low whore of her tasteless husband, a thing that shamed the house further, shamed all of them, by proxy. For as they said, poison carelessly dropped from the table, makes sick the roaches on the floor.

The rooms of the harlot Phebo lay behind the market, reached through a large and raucous courtyard, where types of trade went on not usual in the upper streets: knives glinted, dice were thrown, betting on the arrival of ships, and on the races that evening, mongrels and naked children ran about, and two scarlet parrots screeched ceaselessly. A narrow passage led from the yard directly to a slab of wall. Here a door was opened by an elderly, thin, dwarfish woman only the height of a child herself. But in one nostril there was a stud of gold.

'What do you want? You've no business with her.'

'If I pay what she asks,' said Urtemis through her veil.

The old dwarf cackled. You could see in her youth she had been very beautiful. She was the tutor of Phebo, who had learned such a lot. 'I'm supposed to argue, lady, and say, "How can a poor woman like you afford the pleasures of Lesbos with my girl?" But it's plain enough, despite your rags, what you are.'

Urtemis said, 'I want only to talk to her.'

'I'll go and ask,' said the woman. She went through the dark and grimy space and behind a curtain.

Urtemis and Iris soon heard, dismayed, two female voices projected in cruel and feral laughter.

Then the dwarf came out and beckoned Urtemis through, only staying Iris. 'You must wait with me. My, and if you were a free woman, my girl, I could make your fortune, with a little teaching.'

Iris scowled, but behind her hyacinthine eyes, something stirred, for a moment.

Urtemis, oblivious, went by the curtain, and so into a roughly-plastered chamber that had a painting of flowers and oranges and mating animals on the walls. Beyond a washstand with its bowl, and a bed of cushions, there was little else. Phebo stood idly by a tiny barred window that displayed the crook of the building, and a slice of the sky.

Phebo was not, after all, so young. In her twenties probably, and across her paint time showed a touch. Nor was she especially comely, her breasts sagged in her loose dress. Had she borne a child? Perhaps she had. Her hair glowed as yellow as a paste of saffron and urine could get it.

She was common, surely cheap. And yet, her demeanour was haughty, not perhaps in the way of arrogance, this temporary ascendancy over a higher-class woman. It seemed more habitual. But then, in her own walk of life, Phebo had been, and was, a success.

'What do you want? I don't generally assist women.'

'My husband is – your customer.'

'Oh? Is he so? Have I somehow impaired him?'

'Yes,' said Urtemis with a low hoarse passion, 'since he prefers you.'

'Don't fret,' said Phebo lightly. 'They all return to their wives. Men of his age – I assume he isn't young – tend to boys, or those desires I can gratify. This is the last flush of their stronger lusts. Then they go home and want their lawful women.'

'What do you do for him?' asked Urtemis, her face in the veil scorched with blood.

'Who is he?'

'Karestes.'

Phebo smiled. 'Ah yes. He's a handsome one. I can understand your grievance.'

Urtemis stood swallowing back her fury and pain like hemlock, until she grew frozen and numb.

The harlot let her do this, then she said, 'It's a particular thing he likes. I have others who like it, this thing. I have a reputation for it, and so he heard of me and sought me out. He wouldn't ask it of *you.*'

'*What?*' croaked Urtemis. 'Tell me…'

'But surely,' said Phebo, 'someone has *already* told you? Some helper you have.'

'I didn't believe her…'

'Believe her,' said Phebo. 'Or, do you want to see? My friend outside keeps all the clothes ready in the chest. If you care to pay, I'll give you a performance. Would you like that?'

Urtemis dropped her veil. She stood like a white and trembling pillar. 'Don't show me, show me how to do it myself. Dress me as you dress yourself, to please him.'

Phebo uttered an oath and, slipping up, excused herself to the higher-class woman. Then she composed her face and said, solemnly, 'The Brightest god tells us to look into ourselves and know what we are. For a man, what he fears must be faced and overcome. This is the root of it this thing he – and others – like. To treat with his fear, and then to *possess* it. To – I won't use the word. You know what I'm saying to you.'

Urtemis bowed her head. Karestes, with the skein of grey in his hair, Karestes boldly hunting boar, Karestes the athlete who was now a little stiff in one leg. His father had died at the age of forty, and now Karestes was thirty-seven.

'I'll pay double your usual fee,' said Urtemis.

'I have a better plan,' said Phebo, and suddenly Urtemis saw how guarded her dark eyes had become, stupid, cunning, and cold. *What will she want?*

'What will you want?' said Urtemis.

'It's simple. Someone is coming in the afternoon, a new client. He desires the very thing Karestes does. You want to see, don't you, if you're any good at it, if you can delight your man as I have? Oh, don't look so upset, lady, *this* one today doesn't want much else. He's shy. His slave called to say what he will have. A caress or two, I'll show you how. Nothing properly to besmirch your honour. And then you can be sure of yourself.'

Urtemis stared. This was the woman's revenge. Doubtless she would give nothing unless she could exact it. Rage, humiliation, pure caution fought with desperation in Urtemis's heart and brain. And, as almost always, desperation triumphed over all.

When the new customer approached Phebo's house, he did so alone. He was huddled in a musty cloak, a fold of it pulled up over his head and much of his upper face. Nevertheless, he moved strongly, his legs were muscular and his shoulders wide, even though it seemed he tried to bow them *over*. His jaw too was that of a young man, dark of skin, and one time, when four urchins had bothered him near the fish market, he had sent two spinning with a negligent slap. There was a knife in his belt, just visible.

When he reached the doorway, which was where he had been told it would be, he saw three women standing about there. One was plainly a prostitute, and he took her for Phebo, though she was dressed in yellow. The second of the women was old and malformed, and the third young, but *very* alarmed, wriggling, and muzzled up to the eyes in a shoddy but decent veil. An apprentice, possibly.

'Oh, are *you* he...?' said the woman he had supposed was Phebo.

You look a fine virile master. I'm sorry now it isn't to be me. Do you really only want what your man asked for?'

'Perhaps not,' said the arrival. 'But my business isn't with you, apparently. Is she inside?' He had the accent of a foreigner, and the yellow whore shrugged as if to say, if he were not a man of her own lovely race, she was less regretful at not serving him. She indicated the door, and so he went in, and next through a curtain that had been pulled open. He sensed as he did so the youngest nervous one make some gesture toward him, but the others stopped her. He was not concerned at that.

Now, anyway, he saw before him the woman who must truly be Phebo, for she was garbed as he had been assured Phebo would garb herself, for the proper price. What surprised him was that she did not, despite her garb, look at all as if she were in the trade she evidently was. No, she looked like a chaste woman of some noble house, and her skin, where he saw it, on her arms and forehead, was like cream. A pang of desire surged through him after all, but he put that off. He might try her after, when the other thing he wanted most was seen to. For his scheme, anyway, this unanticipated fineness in her was all to the good.

'Your sisters were outside. I'd send them off, but they seem to have departed. I want to share a secret with you.'

The woman stood up. Her veil fluttered down. He saw she was quite beautiful, remarkably so, and her hair, that coiled free over one breast, was the colour of summer corn. Despite this, she was frightened, unmistakably. Far worse than the girl had been outside.

He turned back and armed shut the curtain that divided off the rooms. The alley beyond the door was indeed empty

'Very well, you know who I am. I was too modest thinking you wouldn't.' He too pushed off his covering, to reveal the architectural body and russet hair of Red Shaizek the charioteer.

This exquisite Phebo shook her head dumbly.

Shaizek laughed. 'Don't dissemble. I won't hurt you. It's another I've got in mind for that. The bastard has beaten me all of five times, but last time was the last time.'

Phebo spoke. Her accent was educated but, still confused by the plethora of dialect, and other vocal flutes in foreign places, Shaizek did not really notice. 'I think you require something I can't give. You see – there has been a mistake, a trick. My fault. You must pardon me…'

'Shut up.' He ordered this quite amiably. 'You'll do as you're told. You may have a quaint face, but I can still beat it to a pulp. That would be a problem, I think. So, you'll do what I say. I'll pay you lavishly. Much more than the slave promised. And you won't even have to indulge in your usual work... unless you want to.'

Phebo stood before him, and he saw her quivering like a graceful slender tree.

He folded his arms. 'It's well done,' he said. 'I'll give you that. It must be, if your clients like it as much as I've heard. But *he* won't like it, by my own Sutekh, no. Lift your veil again, up over your mouth, nose. Like that. Yes.'

Urtemis stood before Shaizek, not knowing him at all, for she had never seen a chariot race in her life. All she did know was that she had made out the two women running away along the alley laughing, taking Iris with them, unwilling or eager – and leaving Urtemis helpless here, with this dangerous brute, a man. And what he seemed to want, although she did not yet know what it was to be, she somehow sensed was worse than any sexual act he might have demanded. But she could not tell him the truth of her situation for the sake of Karestes's honour. In any case, Urtemis had realised that trained from her birth to the utter obedience of female to male, she could no more resist this terrible masculine will than fight him physically. She must do all, and everything. Probably the gods, wishing to destroy her, had made her mad. How else had she come to this? With a stab of sheer pain, that might have been anger, in another, she gave herself *over*.

Shaizek, however, was happy. For just as he had formerly heard, Phebo clad herself for her more perverse clients in the exact likeness of the Death-Persephone of the Mysteries, swathed in black, white-faced, her eyes ringed round, her yellow hair falling free, and if he had not known these gods were nothing to the true gods of his homeland, seeing her as he found her, with this aura of fineness, of fear and fate and shadow, and, worse, of awful purity, he too might have been, one second, afraid.

'Drink,' said the dwarf woman to Iris in the hot little neighbouring cell. 'It's sweet, isn't it? Yes, what you'd like. And you could have this every hour. And jewels. You should see the trinkets my Phebo has. When I was a little past my best, I trained her up. And now she's a little blown, like the pretty roses, she'll train you, she and I. So, you're a slave. There are ways around that. And do you think anyway, your mistress will ever allow them to pursue you, after what you know she's been up to this afternoon?'

Beneath the writing on the tavern wall – *Xetis it is who loves me* – the expected wit had scrawled: *Best seek a physician then.*

You did not go drinking before the race. Lukon had never done so, knew not to do so. Yet he had come in here and asked for a scoop of water, like a beggar off the street. They gave it him gladly, clapped him on the back. They thought he was showing himself to his patrons, who cheered him loudly. But he was saying farewell.

He had not known what to do about the horses, but in the end, he had accepted their destiny was tied with his, as the reins would be tied about him today. He made an offering at the temple of Poseidon, who had a special fondness for the swift horses of sea ports.

Once Lukon paused. *I must not think after this fashion.* But it was on him like a fever, slight, pervasive, unmistakable. Ever since he had told the girl, which he had thought would make it less. Ever since, growing heavier and more sure with every hour. It would be now. This evening. Under the low golden sun that shot his arrows sidelong down the straight, the Bright god who spoke of self-knowledge, and every night, without fear, descended into the dark.

Death. It would be death.

In the stall, he went to them, his gleaming black horses: Bull, named for his strength, and Bird for his speed, and Eros – called for love.

He always talked to them, before a race, telling them what they must do. This evening he told them nothing, only praised them. He hoped they would survive what was to come, and on their bridles hung the new amulets, the tiny silver Poseidons. They never deserve it, princely beings broken like firewood. He was sorry for the chariot, too, poor thing.

He had been conscious, about the stable court, of other racers, speaking to him, if they must, briefly. No insults, no wishes for ill or good. And one of the foreign ones, the boy from Caria, who would not even allow Lukon's shadow to pass over his own.

The Egyptian was there also, flaunting his well-groomed bays, riding his chariot round and round, with the mask of his peculiar demon-animal on its front. The Egyptian greeted Lukon, 'Smile for me, Lukon!' It was the most luckless thing you could say, and someone spat, for the smile of the stadium was pain, and ultimately the grin of the naked skull.

'Red Shaizek, outland scum,' said the man from Lydia. But he did not say it to Lukon.

When it was time, they rode up, flat-faced and straight as effigies, every man, and the sun came over on them from the edge of the stadium roof, shining up the horses, and the metal, and all their eyes.

Lukon had not prayed. To whom could you pray, when this was already with you? Now, he turned his head, and looked carefully and directly, face by face, along the benches of the terraces. As if he searched for a dear friend or sworn foe.

And – he did not see her there. He did not see her, Queen Death.

For she was not among the benches of the men, or the seats of the boys, or the seats for favoured servants and freedmen.

Even so, as they rode forward, to the starting point, he looked on and on, face by face. His heart was beating as though he could die of it, but he would not, not of that.

And then. He found her.

She was there.

Among the women's seats in the most decorous place. Yet, as he had known, she had come to the very front, the most unabashed spot, the most advantageous and yet uncertain spot, right against the low barrier, where the wreath of laurel, done in green and crimson and gold, curved only a few feet above the sanded straight. No other woman had been bold enough for that. If any saw her, they must think her one of the primest, choicest, and least wise. But no one, of course, could see her. Only Lukon.

Something made him glance across the lines of his fellow racers. Their eyes were to the front. Now the quick offering was being made, smoke, a glimpse of flame. He should look at that. But there was no use in offerings now.

He turned and stared again at her. She had never appeared so near to him – or so *real*. It seemed she had put on flesh of alabaster and hair of corn-gold. Just for him. Her eyes, above the partly-raised black veil, were blacker than any veil in the world, but as he gazed, she lowered them. Death would not meet his eyes. Or no, it was not that, she meant him to see something else. Under the wing of the veil, she had opened her dress, the way a woman does in private, to suckle her child. He saw the creamy globe for one split second, just the perfection of it, the eye of the nipple that had been enamelled, or *was,* like her eyes, *jet black.* Then she was covered, and through the sparkling, thickening air, the signal came.

They burst forward, all the chariots, Lukon's chariot with the rest.

They were galloping before he had time to know how it had come about, and he thought that he should have taken note of what he did; it was the last time he would ever do it.

Swept up, he beheld the turn, the golden, sun-fired dust, the Carian boy out ahead, and two others curving in behind, and then himself, caught between the Lydian and Red Shaizek.

Lukon heard Shaizek singing some chant to his animal gods.

But they had squealed around the turn – another episode gone forever. They dashed up the opposing straight, and the sun ran over them, over and down, and threw its flame before them now, but between lay the moving hedge of their own shadows, like a black pit into which each must fall, but it would be only Lukon who must fall.

He raised his head and glared into the sky. He would never see it again. In the land of the shades, there was no sky. His eyes seemed to shatter with tears, and so, blind, he took the second turn, and the Lydian had thumped his flank, and the horses seemed a moment all scrambled together, but then free, and he did not, could not, care anymore, for *she* was ahead of him again, there on his left hand.

And it would be now.

He felt all control go from him, and then the chariot went from him, but he was carried with it.

The horses, bellowing, thrashing and out of rhythm, rushing as if downhill, clear of everything, and the world cast away, but the barrier, the terrible pigsty barrier, with its badly-decorated laurel wreaths, looming up as if it were a mountain, that thing which was only a few feet high and half a foot thick…

Lukon screamed. The horses were screaming. He felt nothing, only a sort of whiteness splintered with shards of orange and red.

The chariot buckled. He sprang as if winged, lurched out and down, and the reins snapped off from him, burning him nearly in half. He crashed forward into the abyss of endless Night.

On the edge of the path that leads to the shadows, Urtemis lay, looking up at the fading sky. Hades, King Death, who had ridden to her out of the sun, his black chariot fuming and coal-black horses breathing fire, sweeping her up, crushing her down, now covered her body with his.

She felt only her utter shame. That she had done what she had been told to, baring herself – even that – and everything was lost, as it had been from the moment she gave herself to her madness, and she must die now, because her honour was riven from her, and so she had forfeited eternally the love of Karestes, her husband.

Thus, she did not watch how, as Shaizek was winning the race, men were lifting the charioteer from Urtemis's dead body. Her spine had been broken by the impact of the chariot and team, as they clove the barrier, and her head had one little cut at the temple, which nevertheless had veiled her face in blood. No one knew who she was.

Nearby, the horses, standing mysteriously and miraculously unharmed among the smashed benches, were shivering as if it were their first race. Yet Bull, the valiant and loyal one, hearing Lukon's voice go on screaming, turned his head, and tried to understand, before grooms led them all away.

You may see him yet about the port, Lukon the One-Legged. He lives on the charity of the town, and they are kindly to him. He tells a story, if you would hear, of how he met and killed Death in the stadium. But naturally it was only some accident and some whore who died – despite that different tale, which anyway, was hushed up.

Lukon's horses were sold to a young charioteer from Caria, who races them now in the East. That is, if they are not already too old for it, and have become instead the fathers of other racers.

Urtemis's tomb you will not find, search as you wish. But there was a girl called Tilat, who hanged herself when Red Shaizek left her, and she had bought a tomb, so you may go and look at that.

For Shaizek the Egyptian, he wins, he always wins, and they say he always will win. But one day too, he will also die, as all men do.

> *Death loves me.*
> *For however much I keep myself from death,*
> *However often I misremember death,*
> *Death will stay for me,*
> *Always faithful.*
> *Until at last*
> *I will leave everything,*
> *Honour, riches, love, fame, all –*
> *Only to be one with death.*

Anonymous Greek from a wall at Thrace. Probably 3rd Century BC.

Old Flame

From the Journals of St. Strange

The moth came from somewhere and flew into the lamp. Meeting the hot glass, it seemed dismayed. The ship's Mate rose and held out his hand to the moth. 'Now, Pretty. Don't scorch yourself.' And the moth dropped into his hand, its fans folded, and waited as, careful not to brush those fragile wings, he took it to some dark place of the ship. When he came back we had refilled the glasses, his too.

'The sea's as calm as honey in a dark jar,' he said. 'And the stars are spilled sugar. A sweet night.'

'He's drunk,' said the Captain to me. He hugged the Mate.

'And a poet,' I said.

The Mate smiled. 'Shall I tell you a story, then?'

Plainly he did this often, for their faces opened, easy as the oiled hinges to windows. We sat expectantly, I no less than the others.

In the brown later summer weather, the town of San Dove baked on its hill, as it had for five centuries. The walls were of medieval design and studded by towers. All around, the vineyards and the field hung heavy with the noise of cicadas. It was not the time, as spring is, to fall in love. Yet it happened.

Angesia was coming from Mass, with her Spanish duenna. The duenna was suitably a thin crone, in black, with a black spider web veil; Angesia a goddess, with hair the colour of golden coins beneath a veil of old white lace.

When Raolo de Cerini saw them, perhaps he thought he had seen them before. It was Sunday, and he was on his way to take some wine with a friend at a reputable tavern, which stood in the shade of an olive tree. But then, it must have seemed that, even if the wine had its origin in the personal vineyard of God, something new had occurred. Journeys and friendships were set adrift. It was the first day of the world.

Raolo crossed the square and reached Angesia and her duenna

just where the basilica cast the last of its burnt purple shadow. Angesia stopped at once, lit by the rays of the sun.

'Signorina, pardon me. I mistook you for another...' and he bowed to the duenna, '...the little cousin of my father's uncle.' Then, to Angesia, very softly, 'No, actually for an angel from the church.'

'Don't whisper to her, young man,' said the duenna, who, despite her accent, was no fool, nor deaf – he had hoped her to be both.

'Again, your pardon. Let me remember my good manners. My name is Raolo de Cerini.'

The duenna made an accented noise. Angesia crossed herself, and her peach-like blush paled entirely away.

Raolo said, guessing only too well, 'What's the matter, ladies?'

'She,' said the duenna, moving between Raolo and his angel, 'is Angesia, the daughter of Alessandro Versuvio.'

Raolo lifted his face to heaven. He addressed God, not caring for a moment who heard. 'Sir, you're unkind. I would have gone to evening Mass. You know that I often do. Why punish me this way simply over a cup of wine at *The Olive Tree*?'

For he now knew that he had fallen in love on sight with the daughter of his father's closest enemy. Indeed, there had been a blood feud between the two families for twenty-seven years.

There are other stories of this sort. Two houses at war with each other, two young lovers, one of each name. Especially there is the famous story.

However, things did not fall out quite in that way, although the feud casts itself a shadow over everything, longer by far, and darker than the noon shadow of the basilica tower.

Raolo went home and pleaded eloquently. Angesia wept and refused food and prayed every hour to the Madonna. After two weeks of this, perhaps worn out by the energies of youth, Alessandro Versuvio sent a servant to his enemy, Thomaso de Cerini. There was presently a meeting by night in an obscure library, with a priest and a scholar to keep the peace. Then another meeting, less formal, in a wine shop which was, to *The Olive Tree*, a full moon to a star.

Rumour went around the town. Could it be that despite the spilled blood between them, the angry ghosts of nine men, the houses of the wax taper and the volcano were to make friends? San Dove hoped so, for it would mean a party. Both families were wealthy, and each had two or three marriageable sons and daughters.

In the end the news was out. Angesia Versuvio was betrothed to Raolo de Cerini. There was to be a wedding and a feast with tables set in the square, and pieces of money distributed, and side-shows, dancing dogs, and cannons fired from the old battlements.

Raolo met his beloved once more on a high terrace where her hand was put into his. She was pale as a lily, then red as a poppy. This he told her and that he would love her forever. She believed him, naturally. That night the house of Versuvio was full of orchestral music and dancing.

Some might have noted a woman standing aside. She was very beautiful, and yet the beauty had been overlaid, as if by a curious smoky powder. Grief, they said; those who noticed, and knew. She was tall and slender, her black hair caught back in a style that would not have looked amiss in the paintings of the early 1500s, when the town was less than two centuries old. A circlet of antique sallow pearls coiled about her throat. She was not more than thirty, not too old yet for marriage herself. But there was no chance of that. The smoky powdering aside, Livia de Cerini had given herself to love only once. The night after that night, they had found him dead by the town wall. The dagger was gone from his ribs, but someone had written a malediction in his blood. It was the Versuvios who had killed Livia's husband. And though the feud might now be healed, her heart had not healed, nor ever would.

What did she think, then, watching the golden lovers dance by, under all the burning candles of the volcanic house? No one could tell. She smiled at them. She bowed courteously to her soon-to-be relations. She spoke politely of small matters. She accepted a dance even with Alessandro Versuvio. He remarked after, 'I thought she'd dance well; she's a graceful woman. But she was stiff as an iron spike.' Even so, to be, while dancing, an iron spike, is not to be unlikeable, or bestial, or unholy.

And yet ...

Livia had climbed the stairs to her room in the house of De Cerini.

It was now after two o'clock, and at last all the human noises had died down. A mouse stirred somewhere, and the wooden partitions creaked as the cool of earliest morning briefly relieved them of a lingering day's heat. Soon enough it would be dawn again. The light of truth, that brooked no duplicity.

The room of Livia had a yellowish tinge; the old plaster, certain hangings. And her bed, with its canopy of yellow wood. It was a room left over from long ago, 1500 perhaps. And still, it was even older. In one corner stood a priceless statue of tawny marble that had been dug up at Rome. It was of the goddess Diana. Livia's husband had given it to her upon their marriage, when Livia was just sixteen. In the opposite corner stood a Virgin. But one might be excused for thinking this, too, pagan, and besides, an image of Hekate. It was so dark. But how had the darkness been achieved? Some oddity of shadow. Some weathering of the stone of which the icon was made. The blue veil was inky, and the white gown, painted with golden stars, gauzy-looking, almost stained. And the lowered face, usually in such a statue so serene and gentle, appeared clandestine – sly. Some trick of the candle that burned before it? An unfortunate trick.

Livia did not kneel to pray. She put a dish of wine before the Virgin, and a withering blood-red rose from the dance.

'You were a woman,' said Livia de Cerini to the Virgin Maria. 'You know a woman's heart. A sword went through you, so it says.'

Then she crossed the room and put her hand on the shoulder of the Diana, whose face was simply pure and cruel.

'Let us go hunting,' said Livia de Cerini. 'Bring down a little deer in the wood. Bring down the great black boar and lop his tusks.'

Then she turned away and went and lay on her bed. Her eyes, which often were unsleeping, stared up into the yellow canopy.

When the candle at last went out, the room was black. The window faced across a passage onto another wall. She had chosen it for this reason. Livia did not want to look out between her grill and see children playing or the garden trees.

Once the dawn began to filter down, she got up again. She changed her clothes, put on her cloak, and stole out from the room and down through the house. Generally, a woman of her class would not go out into the streets of town without a servant, but now she did it. She would say later she had gone to early Mass.

Instead, she took a byway, and walked briskly, ignoring the women who were already stealing out to fetch milk or water. Grey cats, coming home from killing things in the alleys of San Dove, saw Livia with their yellow eyes, and knew her as one of their own.

Eventually she went through a narrow, overhung street, behind an orchard, and out through a little ruined gate into the fields beyond. Soon she came to a grove of trees. The sky was only just properly light, and the grove very overcast. In the middle of it was a lump of stone. Once it had been an altar, no one knew to which ancient god. But now and then, even in this day and age, the altar had been visited. Blood had marked it less than a year old, and there were some recent feathers scattered. Livia brushed these aside.

She put her hands, one palm down, the other a fist, on the altar. She looked up into the sky between the trees, rather as Raolo had looked up after the face of God.

'I have no name for you. I remember my grandmother told me... Our house was glorious once and had its roots in the Old World. We were named for wax. For a candle. But my grandmother told me, the candle is different when it's lit.'

A breeze stirred the boughs above. Cow-bells sounded unreal, across fields where lines of poppies dripped blood-red in the corn.

'I call the fire,' said Livia de Cerini. 'I call the fire to the wax taper. The old fire, old as destruction. She told me. It's ours. Give it to me.' She raised her open hand, her fist now, as well as her face. The light pared her skin of many of her thirty years. She might have been sixteen again. But her eyes were black as wells from pain and rage, hatred, and a terrible strength.

'Send down the fire to me. The fire old as our house, for the destruction of our enemies. They all forget. I won't.'

And then she leaned and spat on the altar and opened her hand over it. Something like a red poppy splashed there. She had been working all this while at her palm with a brooch pin. There is a picture of Medea the Sorceress at Pompeii that looks just this way.

Nothing stirred in the grove. Legions had marched past the place long, long ago. And nearby, during the plague, heaps and mounds of corpses had been burned.

The birds did not sing. And when Livia walked back through the gate and was going under the orchard trees, a dead russet finch fell from among the apples at her feet.

She retired to her room that day. When someone or other sent asking, she replied that they must forgive her. It was an accustomed ailment.

Thomaso never heard of it. He was a busy man, and everything had been settled. He had forgotten the noise fourteen years since of Livia screaming and weeping over her husband's body.

But Livia lay on her back on her bed, sometimes taking a little sip of water. She lay thinking of the archaic fire, that the name of de Cerini, with its ideas of tapers and candles, truly represented.

And on her table by the mirror stood one pale ochre candle, with its grey virgin wick poking out. There was a small red streak of blood near its base, which, as the day went by, turned brown, like a fault in the wax.

That night there was a great storm. These were not common at the summer's end. But it was almost quite dry, with just a dash of rain. The thunder boomed and cracked, and the houses seemed to shake, and off some of the medieval wall-towers pieces burst at the vibration. There was lightning too. A stone pine was struck just below the town and blazed so violently, the fire brigade was called out with six mules pulling the engine and the pipes attached to the fountain in the basilica square.

Raolo, the young lover, stood at his window. His eyes also blazing, hoping Angesia was not afraid, or wishing she was and he there to comfort her.

Thomaso de Cerini and his secretary ignored the noises and the flashing of the bolts, working late in a room over the gate of the house.

But Livia had closed her shutters. She stood at the centre of her chamber and waited for the old fire of heaven to come in to her, bypassing roof and walls.

She had no fear, even if she had gone up in flames herself. Indeed, she had water ready, for though she cared nothing for her life, she needed to do one more thing before she perished. However, the levin-strike did not come. Neither the room nor she were seared. Near four in the morning, not long before the dawn, the storm beat away on huge black wings.

Then Livia went and stared down at the virgin candle, standing there by the mirror in the middle of the room, between the cold virgin Diana and the ominous Virgin Maria. Livia stared and stared. The chamber was in a twilight darkness, for there were no lights, and yet some sort of sheen or gleam had come in there that might have been an uncanny glow emanating from the woman herself.

There was a faint, rich, gilded cast also now to her like that of all the paintings she resembled, the plotting, child-slaying Medea on the broken wall that the true Vesuvius had destroyed, and the doomed duchesses and queens of the 1500s, who had poisoned or sent hired assassins by night, and who died by their own cold hands.

As she stared at the candle then, quite ordinarily, as if she had touched it with a taper, it came alight.

'Ah,' said Livia. This sound was a deep sigh. Had she been holding her breath since yesterday morning? 'Ah.'

The flame seemed of the usual sort, yellowish, yet very clear. A very clean flame. With at its base, about the wick, a tempting friendly rosiness of colour.

How kindly it looked, the sort of light to give a child in the dark.

Like the lit lamp, perhaps, Medea carried, her other hand having the sword to hack into bits her younger brother and later, once he had betrayed her, her own sons by Jason.

'Yes,' said Livia now.

And then she breathed fiercely on the candle, to blow it out.

The flame bent, flickered. It straightened up. Its light was stronger. Livia blew on it more harshly. The lame flattened – and arose. Livia took up the candle-snuffer and held its cup down over the flame for the count of seventy-one heartbeats.

And when she drew off the snuffer, the flame burned out like a golden flower, and the rosy core was for a moment like a drop of blood, before it melted down again – into a rose.

'That's good,' said Livia.

She drew a chair near to the candle. She sat, smiling. Not so many had seen her really smile, and never like this.

'Take what you want from me,' said Livia. 'Leave me just enough to carry you where you are going. And there you'll feast flame. A marriage breakfast.'

She was received with great courtesy at the house of Versuvio. Small cakes were offered, and coffee, and a glass of a famous wine. Angesia, her mother, and the duenna, met Livia de Cerini in a parlour made over to the women of the house.

'It was most thoughtful of you to call. We shall be friends now, I hope?' said Angesia's vague and gracious mother.

Livia bowed. She was very pale and seemed tired beyond any tiredness her carriage drive across the town could have occasioned. But then, she was no longer young. She had had, they said, her sorrows.

On the ebony table she placed a narrow, upright box.

'Indulge me,' said Livia. She glanced at the girl, Raolo's beloved, through whom the feud had been ended. 'A foolish tradition of long ago. I can recall my grandmother told me of it. I wanted to do the same.'

'A present?' asked the duenna.

'Nothing so glamorous. I'm sorry if I disappoint. It is a burning candle. The flame is sanctified. For Angesia. A symbol of what she has achieved between our families.'

Then the box was undone, and there the candle stood, beaming its soft topaz welcome.

'But... still alight?'

'Oh yes,' said Livia. 'Sanctified, as I told you. An old custom.'

'But how did the flame not go out?' asked the duenna, twitching her pinched nose.

'I was very careful. Besides, a specialty of the wax. It burns slowly. It should be thirty days before the flame consumes the taper. Just the time till her marriage day.'

Angesia sparkled. 'I'll put it in my window.'

'No,' said Livia, 'by your bed. So that it can protect you.'

'A holy flame?' said the mother. 'I see, it has been sanctified by the church. How thoughtful. Will you take some more wine?'

'You're too hospitable, Signora. But I have my little tasks in the house. I must go back.'

In the returning carriage, Livia, her body aching, her head filled by a black stone, smiled. Dozing, she dreamed of Angesia's funeral, the flowers thrown on her coffin. All roses die. Even angels fall.

Three days later, Raolo met his lover in the garden of the Versuvio house. The duenna sat in an arbour some way off, stitching.

'What is it, my love? Don't you care for me today?'

'Oh, Raolo. How can you say it? But I'm weary today. I've had such strange dreams.'

'Of me? Or of whom? I'll kill him.'

Angesia laughed, but she was not herself. There was no colour in her cheeks that always bloomed for him. Even her hair had lost some of its lustre. Some woman's trouble? Or perhaps nervousness. A bride might be uneasy, even if very much in love.

He took her hand.

Angesia said, 'Always I dream something flutters down. For

three nights I dreamed it.'

'Something? What?'

'Oh, golden and shining, with a sweet face.'

'Yourself, then. I'll allow it. You may dream of yourself. Why, even I do that.'

'No, no, Raolo. It isn't that way. It settles on my chest. At first, it's so light. And it fans me with its bright wings. And then... then it becomes so heavy. I try to push it away. I beg it to go. It only smiles at me, and all the while it's heavier and heavier. And then ... I forget. But when I wake up my head hurts.'

Raolo held Angesia in his arms. He kissed her. 'A natural fear. You're such a gentle girl.'

But the duenna, when five days later Angesia told her worry, replied, 'You must visit the priest. Some demon is jealous of you.'

'There aren't such things as demons,' declared Angesia, but she seemed unsure. Even her mouth was pale. Her hair was lank and once or twice she complained of dizziness.

Neither had the duenna felt so very well, but at her age she did not often expect to. She subscribed to the belief that to be old was to be enfeebled and so thought herself, though others had seldom observed it.

Alessandro, however, was suffering with his gout, shouting with pain as the doctor attended to his foot. His wife was liverish. A younger daughter lay in bed with a fever, but she was prone to such things. The servants were irritable. Even the horses stamped and shied in the stable, and the dogs howled at night until threatened.

Birds which had nested in the garden trees flew off. But who marked the birds?

When Angesia visited the priest, he gave her a benign sermon on the virtues of fear in a young wife. He told her she was blessed in her reticence and should put herself in the hand of the Almighty.

The following morning, Angesia, having got up, fell back again in a faint. But she told the duenna that the priest had explained everything to her. There was nothing to be alarmed at. Once with her husband, she would lose her difficulty and become, she hoped, a perfect wife.

Meanwhile, the sick child vomited into a bowl, Alessandro found he had a rotten tooth that must be drawn, and the two oldest servants of the house were discovered dead in one afternoon. But the old die and sometimes the young also.

During this time, too, the sanctified candle burned mildly on the night table by Angesia's bed. Through the day it was barely visible, so soft and circumspect the flame they forgot it. And at night, as the house lay tossing and murmuring, and Angesia became a stone in her strangled stupor, the flame blazed like a good heart in a faulty world.

They said in the streets of San Dove there was something amiss with the house of Versuvio. God prevail and save them all, or the wedding would not be celebrated, the tables not be laid, the money not be given out, and not a single dog would dance.

Livia de Cerini had recovered from her brief illness. She was very sorry to hear of the sickness in the Versuvio house. But autumn was a time of chills and maladies. These things would pass. She would pray.

On the seventeenth day, Angesia was to try on her wedding dress, but Raolo found her lying on a couch in the garden. The duenna had hung about Angesia's neck, along with the golden cross, an amulet that smelled of rosemary.

'You must see a doctor,' said Raolo, his heart blundering in his breast.

'Oh, I'm well. Only tired. It's so hot. The trees have fruited twice. Not ours, of course. There's some pest in the orchard. Not a single apple.'

Raolo stared at her face. It had grown thin and waxen. All at once, he glimpsed how she would look when very, very old, her beauty gone and all her strength. And he knew with a piercing clarity that he, also then old and frail, would love her still as utterly as he did now.

'Angesia,' he cried, and caught her to him. But she had fallen into a deadly slumber. She, who had hung upon his every word, was oblivious to him.

Her lids were blue. Her wrists showed every vein.

And upstairs, the sick child was being despaired.

Raolo looked about him and scales fell from his eyes. He saw how the autumn leaves had turned black on the trees, not falling but decaying where they clung. He saw the sculpted evergreens infected with a yellowish pall. Near the little fountain, a frog crouched on a stone. It was quite dead, and when he touched it with

80

a stick, dropped forward in the water.

Raolo had left Angesia on her pillows. He went to the duenna, who started at his approach.

'How are you?' he asked.

'I feel my age,' she replied. 'Not well.'

'There's too much sickness in this house. How's the little girl, little Aelia?'

'Alas.' The duenna had a look of cobwebs where before she had had a glint of steel.

'Someone,' said Raolo 'has put an evil eye on you all.'

'What nonsense. It was only in my youth they believed in such things.' But the duenna's eyes had sharpened, coming out of a mist like hard black flints. 'Who'd do it?'

'God knows. We ended the feud. Are there other enemies?'

'Not one. Signore Alessandro Versuvio is honourable. There were no other quarrels.'

'What, then?' Raolo looked about again.

In the aging morning's sultry light, the old house of Versuvio leaned. Every crack and fault was apparent. The sun sent down here a yellowish glaze. And oddly, in an upper window, there was a faint yellowish gleam which answered it... Was it a face that looked out? A smiling face of some strange type, foreign, but not in the sense of race... but of time?

'What window is that? Is it Angesia's room?'

'So it is. Where the doves nested in the vine. Though they flew away seven days ago. And see, the vine is dying. It was a hundred years old. Here's a lesson to us all.'

No there was no face. Only the mysterious light.

Raolo said angrily, 'What is shining in the room?'

'Shining? Nothing. Unless... could it be... the holy candle? I thought yesterday its light had grown brighter, but that would be as it burns down. It's to last thirty days. A clever contrivance.'

In the town, the bell of the basilica began to ring on a dull, sunken note. 'That is the dirge,' said the duenna. She crossed herself, and a look of sadness not fright woke in her eyes. 'The tolling bell. We are always reminded.'

'And so I have been. I won't lose her! Tell me, old lady, about this candle – from where does it come?'

'Why, from your own house. Your kinswoman brought it, as a gift.'

'Who?'

'Livia de Cerini. A good woman. It was to guard Angesia. It had been sanctified.'

'By whom?'

'She didn't say, young man. By the church, surely?'

Raolo turned about. He heard the bell, he saw the strange glimmer in the window, the dying trees, the shape of the girl who was everything to him lying like an empty doll.

Livia... Raolo could remember that, as a child, he had always been afraid of her. But they said to him she was a poor tragic woman whose husband had been stabbed to death the night after her marriage night. Raolo had trained himself to think this of her too. She was not sullen but sorrowing, not a witch but a widow.

'Take me up to Angesia's room,' said Raolo.

The duenna roused. 'Not proper!'

'She's there, and you're with me. Do what I say. Or do I go to Alessandro?'

Grumbling yet galvanised, the old duenna led Raolo up through the house and, reaching Angesia's door, pushed it wide, then stood there in the doorway, like a centurion guarding the route from both sides.

What an adorable room it would have been to him. The slender maiden's bed with its floral curtains. The wallpaper of flowers that had been laid over the ancient plaster. Her little prayer place with a tiny dainty Virgin of white Carrera marble. Her Bible with a red ribbon lying on a table, some flowers in a vase, her rosary, a pair of embroidered gloves – his present – which every night were put beneath her pillow, and now lay there on it, waiting.

By the bed on the table was an innocent novel, a pitcher and glass, and one candle in a sconce. But the candle burned by day.

'That,' he said. 'Is that the one?'

'Yes,' said the duenna.

Raolo strode across the room, came to the candle, and looked into it. Ah, but it smelled, like the room, of Angesia. Honeysuckle and salt, vanilla, and clean sand. The perfumes of a girl.

The light was docile, slight. How had it been evident from the window?

No, there was nothing here.

Raolo had turned, and as he did, he saw his shadow cast huge on the opposite wall by the dim, dulcet light. His shadow was brutish, uncouth, horrible. He knew from that. He turned back and hissed, 'Magic!' And then he blew with all the might of his strong lungs, to quench the candle flame.

The flame would not go out. Seven or eight or nine times he tried, till black stars stood in his eyes. And when he could not put it out, he seized the sconce and the wax splashed red-hot on his hand.

'No – don't try to move it!' said the duenna, distressed in her turn.

But Raolo did try, and the sconce would not move. The candle would not move, either, when he tried. And at last, trying this too, the table would not. It seemed each had been cemented to each. Or each was iron.

'She mustn't sleep here,' he said, breathless and nearly faint from his exertions, with red stars now on his sight from the flame, so he could not see anything as it should be, and all the room seemed now grotesque.

But the duenna said, 'It's in all the house. That Smell – I smell it even in the garden. I hadn't thought. May God forgive me.'

'Then she must leave the house.'

'Young man,' said the duenna, 'think what you say. You will have to give a reason. This witch Livia has practiced against us. It will start up the feud again like a hungry wolf.'

Raolo thought. He left the candle, walked out of the room, moved the duenna and shut the door. He was young. Never in his life had he met such a terrible and stupid dilemma, caught between the horns of pure evil and immovable etiquette.

'Where do you sleep, old lady?'

'That room... there.'

'Take her in with you. Say you're ill, old, say you're so sad to be losing her. Just a night or two. She has a heart like a cherry, so sweet. She won't refuse.'

'Even there...'

'But better than in that room!'

Raolo went to the basilica. There he asked to speak to an important man, a priest and scholar, educated, and a friend of his father's.

It took some while to explain, and Raolo was impatient. Besides, there seemed to be two entirely separate conversations going on. Raolo would talk of the feud, and of Livia and her resentment, and that she might be unwhole of heart, and the priest would begin to question Raolo, tactfully and sympathetically, as to whether he, Raolo, had inflamed thoughts of his bride.

At length, Raolo told the story of the illness at the Versuvio house and of going to the room of Angesia who lay below so sick, and of seeing the candle which could be neither moved nor blown out.

Then the priest began to lecture Raolo quite sternly on the effulgent and apparently immovable properties of lust.

'Sir... please... I don't refer to that, I'm content to wait – after all, it will only be some thirteen days now till our consummation...'

'Nevertheless, she is a young and innocent girl, little more than a child. Your urges must be controlled. Remember, the main purpose of the act is the procreation of children for God's glory. If there is pleasure in the doing, that is God's beneficence. And for a woman there seldom is pleasure. All she may hope for is gentleness, respect, and dutifully to please her husband.'

Raolo cursed, which was a mistake. The priest then lectured him upon oaths and their imprudence.

Raolo burst out: 'Father, it's an exorcism that's needed here! Her life's in awful danger.'

'My dear, misguided son, it is all too plain. You only want to wrest her from her house. You must be guided by me or your marriage will be a disaster.'

After a portion of another hour of this, Raolo bit hard on his tongue. He bowed his head, consented to pray with the priest, did so, accepted a penance, and left him with thanks, saying that now he saw his own error. Raolo at least was no fool.

But having escaped the priest's chamber, bereft of hope, what now? He could not go to the de Cerini or to Versuvio, for they were older men, both swept up in their own concerns. Having mended the feud, as they believed, to assist their children, they expected no further requests. And everything the duenna had said, besides, was crystal clear.

Raolo passed down into the body of the basilica. It was by now well into the afternoon. The light hung in long amber curtains between the pillars that were of a colour like sour cream. On the altar was a white cloth with gold and above were paintings, quite good ones, of angels and of the Virgin, beautiful in blue, with a lovely mouth. This mouth indeed spoke for all the world to God, when He, so busy at His affairs, must be reminded.

Raolo kneeled alone on the stone floor. Somewhere he heard the chanting of priests less wise, less powerful, perhaps less stupid than the man to whom he had spoken. But Raolo gave up his faith in men for a moment. It was for a woman he prayed, and to a woman, a Woman beyond all women.

'I salute you, Maria, perfect rose.'

His whispered words lifted into the cool air. An old adage came to him: *It takes a stone to crack a stone.* And a woman, maybe, to stay a woman.

'Help me... help me...'

He prayed for Angesia. Again, he told it all. The candle, witchy Livia, the wall of etiquette; the trap in which he found himself.

When he was done, tears were on his face. He stood up and brushed them away. Then going out, the fermented heat of the ebbing day struck him. Mounting his horse, he rode quickly up the winding streets of San Dove, passed the beckoning inn of *The Olive Tree*, and made his way from the gate and down the dusty road among the fields. He did not quite know what he did. In this manner we are sometimes guided.

Night spread her canopy over the town. It was deep blue gemmed by stars. Below, lights were answeringly lit, and then mostly extinguished. In such places you get up at dawn, or an hour or so after, and seek your latest bed, except for festivity, at ten.

In the house of Versuvio, the poor child Aelia survived. She was drowsy and had slipped into a sort of sleep.

Angesia, who had gone to the bedside to pray for her sister, fainted on the stair and woke up in the room of the duenna.

'Stay here with me, little girl. Your poor old lady needs you.'

So Angesia stayed. But about one o'clock she woke, and seeing the duenna slept, Angesia crept away to her own room.

On former nights, Angesia had lain here thinking of her lover. Although she had been kept ignorant of most of the private delights of marriage, her body had some notions of its own. The educated priest had been stupid not merely in his theories of evil.

Now, though, she was far too exhausted, and, had she known, too weak, to think of anything of or for Raolo beyond a loving blessing, like that of some aunt who venerated him. She lay down on her bed and in the dark the candle, which never lost its light,

Tanith Lee

seemed to blossom into a golden tree.

And so Angesia prayed to the candle. Can anything have been more natural, or more appalling?

'Keep me safe. I'm so foolish to be afraid. Watch over me, dear light.'

And then she closed her eyes.

Her dreams now had ceased to be unpleasant, nor did she remember them. She seemed to be floating through the midnight sky, and all the stars spangled around her. The candle was no longer a candle, but a softly golden companion whose enormous wings bore her up. Now they passed over the sinking moon and the smiling divine face of Angesia's guardian was bent over hers. 'May I kiss you?'

'Oh, dear friend, what else?'

And so the beautiful calm face leaned near, the tender face, like that of a mother, and with its silken texture brushed Angesia's brow, her eyes, her lips.

And such a delicious sleep came in then, into the sleep of life, that – had she been anything save dreaming – Angesia would have known that it could only be the honey of death.

The candle flame was nothing but a vampire. God knows how often it had aided the more evil members of the ancient house of de Cerini before. Now it sucked the vitality from every stone and every beam of the building, and out of every breast it drained, drop by drop, the vibrancy of the heart. It seems that never before during the feud had anyone thought to call this fire. No doubt it took a special talent and a particular pain, an old pain, aged like itself.

And from Angesia the flame seduced not only her life, but all her spirit.

Was ever anything so filthy? Perhaps.

In Livia's room, the occupant slept peacefully, making not a sound. A shimmer lay over all things, a gilding not quite visible, by which however, one might see the oddly sly and malevolent Virgin, and before her the dish of wine. And there the pagan Diana whose arrows brought death. Under her feet stretched a mouse, slain not by an arrow but a rodent-catching mechanism of the house. The creature was very fresh, an offering garnered when the servants had gone to bed.

And the face of Livia, so unlike the face in Angesia's deathly dream: a face of wax, composed, in the way one sees faces of the dead, who have forgotten all and know everything.

The inn that Raolo came to after a long ride in the gathering dark was itself very old. In the courtyard, a lamp hung from the bough of a twisted, ancient fig tree, and here white moths were circling. Every so often one would reach the lamp flame and burn up with a green flash.

The young man saw this omen with a heavy heart. But he dismounted, securely tied the horse, and walked into the dimly-lit inn. He was thirsty and weary, at a loss. The processes of thought had stopped in him and lain down to sleep, or they were also quite worn out.

Sitting at a rough table, he let the woman who waited bring him wine, and some bread. No one else seemed to be in the house, save for a white cat that lay, paws tucked in, on a bench, watching him like a sphinx.

Presently a clock struck near the stair. It was 11 p.m. The hour itself seemed desolate, a final aspect of his depression. He drained his cup and poured another.

Then he noticed someone else had come silently into the room. The cat saw too, got up, and went at once to the arrival. It was a priest who bent down and smoothed the cat over with a lean hand. He seemed, the priest, to be of some wandering mendicant order. His coarse, dark robe was belted by a rope. But when he pushed back his hood, a face appeared that matched the hand, lean and pale, without any tan from the weather. Where had he been wandering, to get no sun? His head too, though shaven for the tonsure, had elsewhere long dark hair. When his wine was served him, he drank it in a slow graceful way. Raolo was reminded, despite his trouble, of some old painting of an apostle perhaps, taking rest on his endless journey.

Then with no warning, the priest spoke to Raolo. 'Will you join me, my son. There are only the two of us, and this cat. And see, the cat is already here.'

Raolo did not have it in him to protest and so he took his drink to the priest's table and sat down. The cat now lay under the priest's right hand purring, her eyes shut to midnight slits.

'Do you go a great distance, father?' Raolo asked, from courtesy.

The priest replied, 'I go with you, my son, to San Dove.'

Startled, Raolo said, 'With me...? What do you mean?'

But the priest said, 'Eat your bread for the strength it will give you. In an hour we shall be on the road. It is a long ride.'

'If you – if you wish to ride with me, father, then of course. But... do you have business in the town?'

'Your business: that is the business I have.'

'How can you know it?' blurted the young man.

'You told it in the church. You asked for help there. One refused you, but news travels. At the house of the Versuvio, I will do what I can.'

Raolo frowned. It seemed to him some other had overheard him, either his pleas to the important religious who would not listen or believe, or his prayer. Somehow some message had been sent ahead of him.

'But do you know it all? Something vile and supernatural – an exorcism...'

'I know it all. I am here. In an hour, we will ride together for the town.'

When they entered San Dove, it was dawn – the canopy drawn back and the sky a creamy blue. Cocks crowed, and birds sang, and soon the basilica bell began to sound.

But when they reached the house of Alessandro Versuvio and his kin, there was no sign of activity. No bird of any sort trilled in the garden. No morning noises came of broom or bucket, and not one shutter opened.

Raolo banged on the gates loudly with his heart pressing at his throat like a knot of thunder. Finally, an old servant opened up, wrapped in a blanket, shivering and watery-eyed.

They met, Raolo and the priest, with Alessandro in his library. He was dressed for he had not been to bed. His face was swollen still where the tooth had been pulled, and his eyes were heavily blotted with shadow.

'This is an early visit. You catch us unprepared.'

The priest answered. 'The house of de Cerini wishes you and yours nothing but good; witness the young man here with me. But there is one woman who has wished you nothing but ill. You sense some evil on you? Her curse is destroying you. May I continue?'

Alessandro sank down in his carved chair and gripped the arms. He said, 'My wife is ailing. They're all sick. My horses fret, my dog lies on his side. My daughters...' And then, with a lash of rage, 'Who has worked against us? Raolo, tell me who.'

Despite the warnings, Raolo saw he would have to speak. He did so.

Then the priest raised his hand for silence. Rage, shame, terror, each lay down, as the cat had done at the inn.

The priest gave all the story quickly and in such a way that the de Cerini were vindicated. Then he took the hand of Raolo and gave it to Alessandro Versuvio.

Raolo said, 'My own father will judge that woman.'

'Swear that, and there is still no feud.'

It was sworn on the name of God.

'Now,' said the priest, 'we will go up to the chamber of your daughter Angesia. The old lady, her chaperone, shall come in. A cure works best by night, when the flame is at its strongest. Till then, we will watch.'

So they climbed the stairs and the frightened, pasty servants stared at them. The duenna was summoned and arrived coughing, brittle as one of the black leaves in the garden. Yet at the sight of the priest, she curtseyed.

Angesia lay in her bed. She could not wake, though the duenna and Raolo coaxed her. Raolo tried to lift her in his arms to take her out of the room. But somehow he could not. He, young and very strong as he was, could not raise her up. She was heavy and stuck as if cemented to the bed, as the candle in its sconce to the table, and the table to the floor.

The candle burned kindly all this while. None attempted to put it out. They did not look at it at all, not even the priest. He told them only to open the window and let in the sunlight. He said Raolo must sit to one side of the girl and hold her hand.

'Press her fingers sometimes and tell her things you have done when happy. Speak of your wedding.'

At this Raolo shed tears. Would the wedding ever be? But then he did as bid, talking now and then to her white fallen face that had crumpled down like a flower after heavy rain. To her lank hair spread deadly on the pillow, he spoke. Her beautiful body under the coverlet might only have been a bolster. They could just see her breath. That was all.

The duenna sat in a corner telling her rosary, praying softly, sometimes in her native Spanish. Alessandro paced the room, sat, then paced the room.

It was the priest who kept quite still, his head hooded and bowed. But from him there radiated a quietness that began to fill up the space. It became easier and easier to forget the unquenchable candle squatting there, drinking up the life of the house, sucking out the soul of Angesia.

Was night the time for exorcism? If he said so, then so it must be.

Sometimes servants rapped at the door. Some food was brought. Otherwise they were sent away. Occasionally one or the other of the people, aside from Angesia and the priest, had to absent themselves briefly. Save for these comings and goings, they did not stir.

The room became like a sundial, for it had the sun most of the day. Now the rays passed over the floor, gilding this furnishing, next that one, tinting this face with colour, now drawing all colour away.

Time passed with a curious motionless quickness.

Far beyond the house and garden of Versuvio worked the muted noises of the town, its carts and horses, bells and shouts. But *they* were held fast in a tomb of silence.

In the afternoon's ending, the sun touched at last Angesia's face, and for a second the father and the lover saw reflected there a blush of life. Gold in her hair, a kiss on her cheeks. But then the sun moved on and shadow came back, and they saw the true foreshadows of death.

By then the bizarre nature of that room, keeping together candlelight and sun, male and female, sleep and waking, life and unlife, had hypnotised them. Raolo's eyes were reddened but dry. The duenna had left off her prayers, though she watched under her crinkled lids like a snake.

The sky beyond the window turned to amber, then to pearl, and then to lapis lazuli.

The priest rose, and as he did so a huge ripple seemed to break about him and spread, ring upon ring, through the chamber.

'Close the shutters now. The sun is down, and night is beginning.'

And as they closed the shutters, Alessandro and Raolo together, a deeper darkness formed and then a wilder light. The candle flamed now. It was pure gold, and at its core a petal of ruby. It was a second sun that had a heart of blood. And it was still as if made of coloured vitreous.

'Stand away from the bed,' said the priest.

But in that golden candlelight, he seemed now only thin and insignificant and human. What could he do? Surely nothing. Some ritual, some prayer. He would try and fail. They would be lost.

The era would have become again that of Diana the huntress, Medea the sorceress, and of Hekate the witch-goddess before whom were cut the throats of black dogs. While she, their own Angesia, must float down that River of the Dead, which had belonged, not to a modern Christian century, but to that age of Night which had preceded it. A night embodied not in blackness, but in the burning flame of the candle.

'Oh God!' cried Raolo.

'He is here,' said the priest, 'as in all places.' And he opened the breast of his robe and took out of it a tiny, tiny thing, and they could not, for a moment, decipher what it was.

Years after, when Raolo and Angesia had two or three gold children playing at their feet, only certain things were spoken or credited to that night. It was the night Livia de Cerini had died. They said she had been walking downstairs, lost her footing, and fell. They found her rigid as a rock at the bottom. Her eyes were wide, her lips stretched in a rictus, and her tongue sticking right out of her mouth. Her neck was also broken, doubtless from the fall, and her pearl choker had snapped. There were the beads of it, like whitish drops of blood, scattered everywhere. They said that far more pearls had been found, in the end, than could have been in the ornament.

But it was that night too that Aelia Versuvio's fever broke and she began to mend. The night when all the house of Versuvio turned for the better. An ailing horse stood up and wanted bran. A dog started to bark vigorously for his master. Apples appeared late in the orchard under the moon, and a wonderful crop they were. Doves flew back the next day, after the night, to nest in a vine that had been thought dead but came alive again in enormous luxuriance.

Alessandro, too, said later that this was the night, or dawn, that a new sound tooth commenced to come in where he had had to have one pulled out. And for his daughter Angesia who had been close to death... suffice it to say, she lived.

Those seeing the prosperity and health of the houses of the de Cerini and the Versuvios in after years tended to dismiss any tale of ill luck. Who could ever believe that exquisite Angesia had ever been near to death, with her golden hair, her apricot bloom, her luminous children, and her handsome husband.

But then, very few had been in Angesia's room that night – that particular and peculiar night.

After a little while, in the weird glow the candle gave, so vivid, so aureate, and yet so sickly, Raolo made out that what the priest held up was a tiny cage.

The bars of it were small as wires and set close. What was there? Never a bird. Perhaps a cricket?

Then the priest undid the cage, and something actually flew out.

As they watched it flit about the chamber of the dying girl, at first they could not understand what it was. But then, by the very action it performed, they knew. It was an act as old as the lights of mankind, as old maybe as the first lamp, the first candle.

Out of the cage had come a moth, the colour of paper, dainty and flimsy as a little ghost.

This, then, darting about the room, going to the wall, a picture there, to the Bible, to the vase of fading flowers, and about the head of Alessandro Versuvio, who stared at it, about the duenna, who raised one hand and the moth skimmed over it. Such a faint translucent, insubstantial thing. And drawn always one way.

No one made a sound.

Outside, cicadas would have given their percussive music, but the garden of Versuvio was dumb. In the house not a note, not really a breath.

The moth now reached the candle. As moths will always do. Nearer and nearer, drawn by that inevitable fascination which is death. Upon the filaments of its slender antennae, the eyes of the moth winked silver. But the candle gleamed more brightly.

'Come to me,' the candle said, the evil sorcerous candle, but as all candles do, 'come to me to be warm.'

And all at once, as a million, million times at any moment of any night, the moth dashed straight into the flame.

There was a splash of tigerish green. It lit the room. By its glare they saw, the three who watched, and perhaps the priest, the moth transfixed there in the heart of the ancient fire. And as they looked, they beheld how the flame was burned up by the moth. Drawn in, crushed, devoured, and turned to ashes. The flame burned in the moth. Went out. Was gone.

The room was black, and in the black the little being flew back into its travelling cage, and the door was gently closed.

Do not protest. Say no word. Moths are consumed in flames. But in the hand of God, all things are one thing, and a flame may be consumed in the fire of a moth.

He looked at me, the captain's mate. Our cups were empty and had grown stale. 'She heard him, then, the Virgin.' I said.

He shrugged. 'Something heard. Better to call power always by a lovely name.'

Beyond the cabin, daybreak was spreading on the sea. The seagulls cried with mimic voices, the braying of asses, clucking of chickens: a sure sign of land.

We drank one cup more for the departing night.

On the deck, we saw the ocean was barely moving. The poet Mate stood looking after the dark.

'A fine story. Thank you. May I use it?'

'It's yours. Everything belongs to each of us. Only, we seldom see.'

THE LADY-OF-SHALOTT HOUSE

A river like black glass ran by the place. Above, bone pale, stood the old house with its dark, sloped roofs. It had one of those towers, too, where a pair of windows face each other, so the light of the sky through one, shines out through the other, and this other window, looking down to the road, seemed even by day to have a lamp in it. All around went the hills, also pale and bleached by the sun. Trees grew on some with sombre leaves. And by the river grew strange huge marigolds – if they were – the colour of orange curd.

Carey Pearce, who had not yet become a well-known painter, paused on the road, staring across the river, up at the house, and the hills behind. He began memorising the scene for a canvas, especially the marigolds, which looked primal and nearly carnivorous.

It was late afternoon, and he was on his way to the home of distant cousins he had never met. The train ran only to the station he had left an hour before, and here the horse he had been promised was out on other business. Carrying his bag, therefore, he had started to walk. He found this a haphazard country all told, but one he liked. He did not think he would reach the house of his cousins until evening.

Down in the valley to the south, he could see the black trail of the railway, and along it another toy train was just now puffing, its smoke-stack sending up a plume into the westering sun-ambered sky.

When Carey glanced back at the pale house, he saw a woman was seated on the veranda. And she had hair, he afterwards said, definitely the exact shade of the marigolds by the river.

He thought she had not been there before, but now she was. She looked at the road, or maybe at the train below. In any case, he raised his hat.

Her dress was dark, caught with a silver brooch at the throat. She was of that slim small type, and her face seemed an unusual one under the pile of remarkable hair.

Carey moved off the road, went over the river by a narrow bridge, brushed through the marigolds, and came up to a white-painted picket fence. Here he stood and gazed up, and the woman looked back at him.

'Can you tell me; am I on the right road for the Hannifer house?'

He realised then she had not been looking at him, or not truly, for now her eyes seemed to change. It was, he thought, as if a cloudy liquid grew suddenly clear.

'Oh, yes,' she said. She had a sweet voice. He decided she might be able to sing well.

'I hope it's near. I've walked from the station, and it's a hot day.'

All this was blatant deception. He knew perfectly well he was on the right road, and knew too he had another hour's walk at least before him. He was fit, his bag was light enough, and he was used to walking; he had climbed fells in England, and small Alps in France, from dawn to dusk, in search of images to paint.

What he wanted was that the woman with marigold hair would invite him to step up and sit with her. She was beautiful, and in an almost classical way. Just as he knew when he had found the view he wanted, so he knew he had found in her a portrait. No doubt there was a husband, even children, and probably servants, in the pale house. He must charm them all and be asked back.

She did not speak at first, then she said, 'It's a long way, I fear.' She sounded remote, like a well-schooled infant that does not know the precise meaning of the lesson it has learned.

'Very long?' inquired Carey, putting a querulous note into his tone. 'Oh, I was on that train for thirteen hours, cooked alive. They said I'd find a horse to ride at the station, but no such luck.'

In the garden that climbed to the house, bushes of fiery flowers had run wild. A parrot tree stooped almost to the ground with unpicked fruit.

She said, 'You must be tired.'

But nothing else.

Then he looked more attentively at the house. The sun was on it, burning on the windows, just as the bright north sky burned through the window of the tower. But he seemed to see curtains drawn, or absent. The veranda was in want of repair. There was an old rocker in which she sat, and one other chair, a notable one with carved back and arms. A cane table had been set between, and he noticed now all at once it had a decanter on it and a crystal jug, and two tall glasses and two glasses for wine. But in the decanter and the jug and the glasses was nothing, nothing at all but a thick smoke of dust shining in the low sun.

Carey Pearce said, 'I wonder if I might come up and sit with you for a few minutes. Forgive my boldness. Perhaps your husband –'

She said, 'My brother has gone away. But come up if you want. I have nothing to offer you –' this struck him oddly, she did not say it in a churlish way – 'but the river is very pure, if you wish to drink.'

Carey took her at her word. He went down the bank, knelt, and cupped up in his hand a couple of mouthfuls of the black, bright, transparent water. It was clean and pleasant. But he had wanted to show her he was accepting her hospitality, such as it was.

Something must have happened here, some family matter. The brother gone away, the servants vanished.

He opened a little white gate in the picket fence and went through. He went up the garden path under the parrot tree, and so the steps to the veranda. As he stood over her, she lifted her pale quiet face to his. His heart stopped a moment. She had that kind of loveliness which makes its subject seem known, as if we half recall something very beautiful from another time and place, for here is its reminder.

'I'm sorry to trouble you,' he said.

'It's no trouble.'

'My name is Carey Pearce,' he said. 'My cousins are the Hannifers, but we've never met. May I sit down?'

She looked at the other chair, and then back at him, and all at once she laughed. It was a soft melodious laugh, not exactly mocking – more playful. 'Please do, Mr Pearce.'

He sat. And there was another odd thing. The chair, though such a good one, felt extremely uncomfortable. He thought at first he was more travel-worn than he had believed; and serve him right for pretending to be so. Then he concluded that it was simply a badly-made chair, all show and no substance.

But he opened his bag and took out a bottle of fruit cordial.

'May I offer you some of this?'

'Oh no. Nothing, thank you.'

'Then, do you object if I drink it alone?'

She said then, without the least sign or nuance of rudeness, 'Don't use the glasses, Mr Pearce.'

He supposed she was sensible of their dirtiness, so he nodded, and drank the cordial from the bottle.

Then she folded her hands in her lap and rested her wonderful head back on her chair, and she began gently to rock. She said not a word, yet it was not from shyness, he thought, nor coldness. It was as if she knew him well, and might be silent with him without offence.

He was used to silence himself, and unlike most people often alone, he rather liked it.

So he sat in the uncomfortable chair as comfortably as he could, which was not very, and looked down the hills to the valley and the snake coils of the train track, looked at the exotic sombre-leafed trees and the flames of the flowers. He listened to the hush of that wide, scorched land, broken only now and then by a daytime cricket, and once at the whistle of an unseen bird.

The sun slanted more and more to the west, and a line of clouds, a herd of them, tumbled slowly before it.

At intervals, he turned and studied the woman very carefully. She did not seem to mind this, if she was aware of it at all. Throughout his life Carey had had the knack of making a mental sketch, for he had begun early to want sometimes to create pictures of things and spots where sketching on paper was either inadvisable or frankly impossible. But he drew the lines of the woman's face over and over in his mind, cautiously etched in the translucent first shadows, and the dilute clear amber of the light – and the wash of hair that would be so easy to paint with some splash of colour direct from a tube, which meant he must be more subtle and try to capture it another way.

She was about twenty-five, he thought, not quite young, but not turned either, as women often did in this climate, to that dryness and toughness of skin the critic termed *leathering*. Her eyes were grey-azure, opaque yet glimmering as moonstones. If he could reproduce that, and the angle of her brows, the lilt of her throat with the small winking brooch at its nadir, he would have something very fine.

The sun was now into the clouds, herding them down beyond the valley. A certain alteration of blueness was at the core of the sky. The day was working toward sunset.

He said, rather low, not to break her reverie harshly, 'It's late. I'd better be getting on. Thank you for your oasis.'

She did not look at him now. Her eyes were back on the road.

She said, 'Go safely.'

'You're kind. I will. And you.'

'Oh, I am safe enough,' she said.

But when he was out of the awful chair and standing, a compunction seized him as if he had only just become aware of things.

'Are you quite alone here? Is everything all right with you? Shall I...?'

'Everything's well,' she said.

That was all.

But when he gazed down at her, she was smiling. He thought she seemed happy and at ease. And so he only offered another farewell and left her, walking down through the garden, and closing the gate with elaborate care.

Once over the river and on the road, he turned again to signal goodbye, but the sun had reached just that point to dazzle away the images of the veranda. Indeed, the whole building appeared curiously to float like a bubble, suspended in the air. He could not make her out at all, and perhaps anyway she had now gone inside.

Carey reached the Hannifer house in the last of the dusk. He was struck at once by its bustle and life. Kerosene lamps hung along the veranda, every window was lit behind its lace rosy yellow, and men and horses came and went through the pastures behind.

Soon enough all the cousins swelled out in a swarm. His hand was wrung, a large beaming woman embraced him. He was led into a parlour with a rose lamp in its window, and presently into supper under a chandelier, with two rough and massive dogs lying for contrast by the hearth.

They were as hungry for his stories of the world as any people he had ever come across. He had to tell them anecdotes of a ship in Africa, and of a French village, *and* even about the great city he had just left, which most of them had never seen. Between whiles they poured him wine and loaded his plate of pleasing brown and white china with potatoes, vegetables, pie and relishes. Afterwards there was a lemon dessert, and cigarettes and brandy were brought, and he sat alone with the men in an up-country English sort of way, hearing the women's bright laughter in another room.

All this time there had been no opening to speak of anything close to home. Even the omission of the station horse they had swept quickly away with an, 'Of all the lousy shows!' But as he and the men now lounged, with the veranda doors wide, and the crickets sounding in their silver night chorus, counterpart to the croak of frogs in the swamp beyond the river, Carey turned to his new cousin, Joseph.

'Before I reached your house, there was another. Just off the road. About three, four miles back. A white house, with a tower.'

Joseph Hannifer nodded idly enough. 'Yes, that's the Collins place. Run down now.'

'I thought I might paint it,' said Carey. It was as if something whispered to him, the crickets perhaps, that he must beware what he said. 'Who lives there?'

'No one at present. It was Tappy Collins' place, but he moved away years ago.'

'Tappy Collins? Now the man at the station mentioned him, I think,' lied Carey nimbly, sipping his brandy. A great moth, large as a dollar bill, had come from the night and hovered over the veranda rail above the lamps. The flicker of its wings was like one more warning. 'The man said Collins had a sister – or do I have it wrong?'

'Old Ned's a rare old gossip. Right enough, Tappy had a sister.'

Carey waited, and as he did, considered the tense of the word *had*.

'Had he? I thought –'

'Oh, it's a sad story. A bad story.'

Old Uncle Someone – Carey did not yet grasp all the names – had fallen asleep. Two male cousins mildly joked about this. Two others had gone out to see to something in the outbuildings and stables, the dogs padding after them.

From the women's parlour winged up more laughter, and the notes of a tinny but game piano.

'Can I know the tale?' asked Carey.

'We're not proud of it,' said Joseph. 'But there. You'll make a painting of it, maybe.' And Carey was alerted to the first hint of acrimony in Joseph Hannifer, his cousin.

Then Joseph told him the story, and the other men were, mostly silent, but for the mild-snoring uncle. Now and then, one added something. They shook their heads. The room was warm, and smoky from the pipes, and outside stood the black walls of the night, into which the giant moth flew away.

Tappy Collins had had the house from his father. The mother

was long dead, though it was she had given the property its queer and fanciful name. It was the title of some poet's poem – Carey forbore to speak the other name of Tennyson – a crazy notion that was talked about.

Lady-of-Shalott the house was called, after this ballad about a damsel who drowned herself. And Carey forbore to correct them, since the Lady of Shalott had not drowned but only lain down in a magic boat and died of love.

'Well Tappy kept his sister – Maudra, the mother had called her – to look after the house, and it was a downright waste of her. She was a pretty thing, but day-dreamy – perhaps too much that way for some. But she could have made a marriage, no doubt of that. Tappy, though, he shut her up at home, and she never saw another soul but him and the maids. They said he promised her, "When I get wed then you can do as you like". But perhaps he never said that.'

'The man at the station – Ned – told me she had strange-coloured hair.'

'Orange,' said Joseph, and one of the other cousins added, 'Yes, Orange as marmalade. But apart from that, she had good looks.'

Joseph continued. He said that a day came when a man rode out to the house on business with Tappy Collins, and he took one look at Maudra and wanted her, body and soul. And it was the same with her.

'Trouble was,' said Joseph, 'the fellow was married already, hard and fast, and no getting out of it.'

Carey listened, until the cigarette burned his fingers and *the men* laughed slyly at him. But his hands were as hard from paint as theirs from manual work, and he did not mind.

He was seeing Maudra and her dreaming eyes, seeing her in love. The man they did not much describe – he had a shock of thick blond hair, enough to turn any silly woman's head. Enough money as well to dress elegantly and smell of cologne. Edmund Dyle was his name.

'Well, he had his way with her. Tappy was off in the city, and they used his house to their own advantage.'

'I heard,' said another cousin, 'they lay down in every room.'

Joseph said, 'You've got a course tongue, Matt. But so they did, probably.'

'What happened then?' said Carey softly.

'Once he'd had his fill, Dyle ran back to his wife,' said Joseph. His was, thought Carey, a cruel voice, judgmental and now slightly shrill.

Carey no longer liked Joseph. He said nothing.

Joseph said, 'He's stayed with the wife, too, though off and on he has another fling with some girl or other, with her head on backwards and not got the sense she was born with.'

The cousin who had also spoken said, 'But Maudra died.'

Carey breathed out a long sigh. 'Did she?'

'Died of a broken heart,' said the other cousin.

'Poor little thing. She was twenty-five years old.'

'She took a fever,' said Joseph. 'Brain fever. That was how she died. There was a story she drowned herself like the girl in the ballad. But she didn't.'

Yet, Carey Pearce thought, Maudra had died rather in the way of the Lady of Shalott after all, if she had died of love, breaking her imprisonment. He said, after a moment, lighting a cigarette, attending the advice of the cautioning crickets, 'Ned told me there was some idea the house was haunted. Now I see why.'

'Tappy went off soon enough,' said Joseph. 'But Tappy was a fool.'

The Hannifer uncle had woken. He spoke without emphasis. 'Two or three persons have seen Maudra Collins sitting on her veranda, since her death, in the old rocker. She looks out to the road.' He seemed to watch Carey acutely; maybe it was only the light on his spectacles. 'If you wave, she may wave back to you. She's a polite little creature still.'

Carey said, 'How long ago did she die? Was it recent?'

'Fifteen years,' said the uncle. 'Sixteen, next March.'

Later, Carey climbed the stairs and found a milk-white bedroom, washed himself, and got into bed. He blew out the lamp; there was no gas here, let alone electricity.

In the night peculiar sounds came from the hills beyond the house of the Hannifers. Carey knew, from all the alien nights he had slept and lain through, in russet little rooms up under thatch, in barns and empty sties, in the wide chambers of hollow, dark hotels, where golden beetles ran about the floors, that the noises of unknown night are always uncanny. He was not alarmed. Nor did the ghost of Maudra dismay him. He had been privileged to get so much more than a wave, to come so close. And he was glad she had not seemed afraid or sad, or shown any vestige of her pitiful, lonely unloved death. She was peaceful now, hopeful almost. Yes, he was glad.

The next day Joseph Hannifer wanted to ride with his Cousin Carey to the town, ten miles east. The women cousins protested that Carey was too tired, but Carey was not tired, and he was intrigued by Joseph, even not liking Joseph, because Joseph had mostly told him the story of Maudra Collins.

They started early enough, and the sun was white, and the sky that unique brazen sheet that is not blue at all, and the parched hills rolled round them, with their tufts of trees, and the occasional groves of farms, and the woods, and the swampland with its spears of razorous grass and muggy lilies. The horses were strong and courteous. But Cousin Joseph still kept expecting Carey Pearce to make some mistake. When a rabbit bolted across the road, for example, Joseph looked at Carey, all crinkled up in the face, to see the horse shy and throw him. But Carey and the horse were quite calm. Joseph seemed to have made up his mind that a man who painted pictures would be able to do nothing else. Soon Joseph began to talk about illnesses of the region, brainstorms and ailments of the bowel from poisoned water, and about renegades and thieves. All this, it seemed, to see if Carey would get nervous. But Carey only listened and asked reasonable questions.

They were about four miles from the town when Joseph said, almost violently, 'Why, see that fellow walking down there, on the road?'

'Yes, I do.'

'See his hair?'

Carey looked more fully, and saw the man was flaxen fair, which was not very uncommon here.

Joseph said, 'From the style of him, he goes on like that wretch I told you of, Edmund Dyle, Maudra's fancy. Only I'd expect him to be riding.'

The sun was going over from the zenith, and it shone from behind them all down the road, and made it, but for their shadows, white and polished as glass. The man appeared half there and half not in this devouring light. He came on at a steady pace, striding west as they rode east, to meet them.

'Edmund Dyle,' said Joseph. 'It could be. Maybe that rich wife of his got sick of his escapades and threw him out at last.'

They rode on, and the man who might be Edmund Dyle drew closer. *Carey* was interested. He wanted to *gaze* into the face of Maudra's betrayer, wanted to scan it for future use on canvas. Judas has always been of artistic value, in whatever form.

Even so, Carey felt a little ashamed. Because he thought he understood already that something of Maudra was drawing Edmund Dyle, if so the man was, drawing him to her despite himself. For him she watched the road. For him the best chair waited, unwelcoming of any other – and for him it would be comfortable. And the decanter and the crystal jug would sparkle full of wine and lemonade.

The countryside was empty here, excepting the stands of umbrous trees. Soon enough they came up with the walking man, and when they were some thirty feet from him, Joseph swore. 'It's him. I tell you,' he added, as if Carey had argued, 'it's Dyle.'

Joseph reigned in. And so Carey copied him.

'Hey, Dyle! Is it you?'

The walker came on, then stopped. He was near. He looked up at Joseph's face, and as if finding the paucity of it, his eyes continued until they found Carey.

'Sir,' said the man on the road, 'I've lost my way. I used to know these parts, and yet... I'm searching for the Collins house.'

Joseph vented another curse. But along Carey Pearce's spine there moved upwards a pale, quiet, electric tremor, as when grass turns before the wind and whitens.

'Follow the road,' said Carey. 'Just follow the road and you'll come to it. But it's a long way.'

'Yes, a long way,' said Edmund Dyle. 'But I've come a long way already.'

Carey meant to say something else, but the words stuck in his mouth. Then, as the man walked by him in his elegant dusty coat, he found to his surprise he said, 'God bless you. God bless you both.'

Joseph sat his horse, snorted, and kicked its shanks. They rode on again.

'He's gone daft,' said Joseph. 'It was him, all right, but addled. His tie was all undone. His gloves were stained. And that's no coat to go trekking in.'

Carey glanced back. He watched Edmund Dyle walk west along

the road, the white sun blazing above and before him. But when Joseph half turned and said angrily, 'What's up now?' Carey only answered, 'Nothing.'

'Is he still there, the idiot?'

'No.' to deflect Joseph, Carey lied. 'I think he's gone off the road into the trees.'

'Good riddance,' said Joseph. His face bulged now with malevolence and scorn, and for a while, though never looking back as Carey Pearce had done, Joseph Hannifer railed against the Dyles, all of them.

But when they came to the town and went into a bar there, he had to alter his tune.

So Joseph got drunk, until he had to hurry into the yard, and Carey held his shoulders as he threw up, and then supported Joseph when he sank down.

'We never met that bastard,' said Joseph, through his fits of shaking. 'Never. Not us. For Christ's sake,' said Joseph, as though they had committed a crime on the road, 'don't tell a soul we met him.'

For Edmund Dyle had, the previous evening, shot himself point blank through the heart and dropped dead in his wife's fine house. He left a letter, which was now common property, that is, what it said, for he told her he had only ever loved one, and that one not her, but Maudra Collins who had died because of him.

Fifteen years and more the worm of regret had gnawed through Edmund Dyle, and in the end, to stop the pain, he had fired into himself the worst pain of all, which ends all others.

At sundown, Joseph begged Carey that he would not speak of any of this to the family in the Hannifer house, and Carey agreed to be silent.

But in the end, Carey Pearce was not silent at all, for he painted those two pictures, which anyone may see, where they hang in the gallery, or in reproduction. And the pictures speak loudly enough.

The first is the landscape with figure, which he called *The Lady-of-Shalott House*, a rich study of terrain, but mostly of a girl with extraordinary hair, seated in a rocking chair on a veranda, above the wild garden, and the black river with marigolds.

The second picture is more simple, and stranger. *This* is called only *Going Home*.

It shows a sun-blasted track, which carves between pale hills, and on the track a man, walking away, his back turned to the onlooker.

It is either the worm of regret, or the bullet of a pistol, which has cut right through him, showing what Carey Pearce saw so clearly on the road: how the sun shines straight as a spear through Edmund Dyle's body, at the area of the heart, forming one blinding ray of otherwise inexplicable light.

I BRING YOU FOREVER

Did the sages say, in Jeshlah, each human thing is but a little place of life surrounded by the desert?

Just so, the palace towered on its rock like the back of a lion, and all about, the town, pinned to the earth by towering trees and stems of water. But beyond – beyond the great lakes of dust, whose close, hot breath is the desert wind. Gardens falling like green steps. A fountain that sprinkles, by night, the water drops of the stars. But beyond, beyond the hot white Moon that has the face of the skull of a gazelle. There are bones under the dust. And bones in heaven, too.

When she was a year old, the king saw his daughter for the first time. He had been at war, triumphed, and come home. Three beautiful wives had already given him several strong sons. But his favourite wife, the fourth, had borne during his absence a female child. The woman approached, her soft hair falling to her waist and filled with tiny golden bells that made a placating noise. Her lambent eyes were downcast. (A nurse held the child sidelong, as if to hide it.)

'Forgive me,' said the fourth wife.

'I shall only,' said the king, catching her to him, 'not forgive you for thinking me such a savage. Forgive you for what? For bearing me another such as you, to charm the hearts of men like music?'

Presently he took the girl child, who smiled and waved little fists, trying to snatch his jewelled earring. 'See, she wants this.' The king removed the costly earring, broke off the sharp hook by which it had held to his ear, and gave it to his daughter. 'She must have everything she wants,' he said, warm with victory, homecoming, lust, and simple happiness. 'Always.'

They had not named the child, for fear he would not want it to have even a name.

So the king named her Zulmeh, which in that tongue meant Diamond – the gem she had reached for.

The diamond child grew up. A clear child, like cool water slenderly poured. And her hair was like dark copper, and her eyes a smoky green, like jade.

As she grew, so grew the town of the desert king. Long channels were made to conduct the water of the oasis, enamel roofs arose, and towers and lions of white stone.

By the day she was, Zulmeh, ten years of age, the king was called Great King. And by the year she was thirteen, he was dead. A tomb was built for him that the desert people said was a wonder of the earth and travelled far to see. Pillars and stairs raised it up to Heaven, showing it to the sky and the gods above, as if to ask them: *What have you done?*

But the Princess Zulmeh was only thirteen. What was death to her? It was true she wept beautifully as she followed the king's bier among the flowers of his weeping women. But it was only that the sad songs made her cry. She had scarcely known him. He had always been away at war, and in the end, war had claimed him utterly, with the spear that pierced his vitals.

Her mother had died too, somewhere in those years. But her mother had not meant very much either. Her mother belonged to the Great King.

Only one thing Zulmeh knew for sure. That whatever she asked for she was given. How strange, perhaps, she never thought to ask, as another child would, for her father or her mother. She must have learned very early, perhaps even that morning in the arms of the king, that she would be given bright and shining things, valuable things, mystical and longed for. Hard, too. Hard as diamond. But nothing easy. Nothing that was hers – by right?

It would seem then she was a demanding child. Not so. She learned also, and quickly, to choose with care what she would have.

At seven years, asking for a particular beast, which she had been told of, she saw a caravan dispatched for a foreign land, to fetch it. One year later they returned, those who had survived the dreadful trek, and they brought her, stiff and stuffed, the animal she had wanted, since it too had perished on the journey. One more lesson. Hard lesson. Diamond lesson.

When she was fifteen, Zulmeh's brothers fell to fighting among themselves for the crown of Great King. Their armies clashed out in the desert, and from a place high on the city walls, one might see a flash of swords and arrows, over and over, and the dust rising like a purple column to uphold the indifferent sky.

The victor presently returned. His name was Hazd.

He swept the city like a broom, and settled on the golden lion throne, and called them all to admire him there. He asked who the girl was, the royal girl with dark red hair. They told him. Hazd said he would marry this girl, to uphold his claim to his father's throne. They were only half brother and sister, he and the Diamond, and Hazd was a bastard.

Strangely, again, for one taught she might have anything she asked for, Zulmeh must have known not to ask to be spared her half-brother. But then, he was ebony-skinned, with corded hair that fell to his knees, lion-strong, a warrior and a poet. And she had never known him as a brother, as she had never known, let us be exact, father or mother.

They were wed, and he led her to a pavilion high on the palace roofs, and from there he showed her the enormous desert of dust in the settling dust of evening.

'What do you see, Zulmeh?'

'The Great Sands,' she answered.

'No, you see my kingdom. Soon that absence of life will be covered by the life of my city.'

But then they sat drinking sweet wine, and he played a melody for her on a lap-harp of ivory. He sang a song he had made for her. It compared her to the Moon, now lifting over the desert. But Hazd did not say the Moon was a skull. No, it was a young girl, whose eyes were green, if only one might see them. Of all his fine songs, this was, at that time, the most beautiful.

Zulmeh listened. Perhaps she thought, if she had not already, 'I want and must have this man...'

At midnight, coloured birds were uncaged above the roofs of the palace, where, behind the highest lighted windows, the city knew that Hazd and his bride were mated and made one.

Their love was glorious. He told of it in his songs, carved into the stone pylons of the city, beside his lion songs of war. But Zulmeh left no record of this love. For some reason, she did not conceive his child. He would have assured her not to mind it. He had plenty of women who could do that in her stead.

Was there ever a night or morning then, standing in the high place, when Zulmeh invoked magic from the stars or those strange otherworlds, the planets, or the gods, or the Sun or the Moon, saying: *I want and must have the child of Hazd – I – I...*

No. There never was. She had learned her lesson, had she not? No father nor mother. No child. And, at last, no lover-husband either.

Zulmeh was seventeen years, when one brother returned across the desert, a true son of their father. His name was Hroor. He slew Hazd in single combat, before the gates of Jeshlah. Did she see? Yes. But she was high up on the walls. Such little figures – so far off. Did she ask the gods for his life? Perhaps she thought of the exquisite living animal brought dead and mummified and laid before her. Perhaps she asked a moment too late – even as Hazd fell, dying – but by then her request would have been only a denial, *Oh, let it be not so!* A prayer must always be framed, the sages tell us, in the positive mode. Never *do not*, but only *Let it be so*.

If she thought she would be given to Hroor, the victor, with the other wives, she was correct. But Hroor was not a man for women and did not trouble any of them. Also, not being a man for women, he was kind to them. Seeing Zulmeh stand alone, white as ivory in her red hair, dry-eyed green among the wailing queens of Hazd, Hroor asked who she was.

Then, 'Ah,' said Hroor. 'The Diamond. I remember well my father's decree. Take heed, all of you. Give her always what she wants.'

She never wept when others were by, not for grief, she who always softly and publicly wept at melancholy music.

She sat alone, high up in the women's courts, in her own luxurious pavilion, which Hroor had not taken from her. She gazed away over the desert. Once or twice someone will have asked Zulmeh what she desired. She will have answered, 'Nothing.'

Hroor ruled three years.

One warm evening, with a Moon like a bow in the sky, the faction that had risen against him took their omen and shot him full of arrows.

He lay unburied in the street, flighted like some old dead bird, while the sections of Jeshlah fought together. When the fighting was done, in the hour before dawn, men came to Zulmeh's pavilion.

They kneeled down to her.

'You,' said they, 'are the last descendant left living of the blood of the Great King. Only you, our Diamond, are fit now to rule.'

She saw their smiling, crafty, blood-streaked faces. She would be Queen, but they would rule through her, for a woman was only an ornament, as the Moon only gave light.

But it was not a time to argue or declare what instead one wanted. She acquiesced meekly.

So Queen Zulmeh took the throne of Jeshlah.

And sages tell us, wisdom comes with the years, as with pain. We are scourged in the school of life that we memorise the lessons. To rule, even as a puppet and a woman, was dangerous, and so Zulmeh now encouraged, secretly, her own faction, those who revered her true royal blood, or were struck by her beauty and her sorrowful widowhood. Those too who liked power, but preferred it second-hand, the natural captains of a king.

When the fruit was ripe, Zulmeh the Diamond addressed them.

It was a night of feasting in her private apartments. Cloth-of-gold, velvets strewn, tame birds with long tails of amethyst that stalked about, perfume playing in the fountains. The gold cups were raised high to praise the Queen and the gods.

Zulmeh spoke. 'Never compare me to Heaven. They are perfect and eternal, and I have only my little span of being, which any moment may be wrenched away.'

Then they cried out that they would serve her with their very lives. What did she wish of them?

She said: 'I want safe rule in Jeshlah. I want the crown of Jeshlah and not its shadow. I must be rescued from those who, today or tomorrow, will cast me down, and all you with me, in a grave. I must have their heads.'

The colour crimson was on the room, crimson, purple, and gold. Before the lamps failed, on golden trays they brought her, her faithful men, twenty-four severed heads, dyed in their own red-purple blood.

Then Zulmeh truly was Queen in Jeshlah. And she had been given what she wanted.

Seven years passed, and the city grew like a natural thing, until it filled the horizon on four sides. Then Jeshlah was called the Great

City, and the Queen of it, Zulmeh, the Diamond, the Moon of Jeshlah. Whatever she wanted, she was given. A thousand towns and cities paid tribute to her. From the four corners of a horizon beyond the horizon of the Great City, came the merchandise of the world. Silk and sandalwood, precious jewels and priceless stones, trees of resin and cedar, baths of oil and wine. Men came there too, mighty soldiers and princes, musicians and poets, acrobats, magicians and scholars. All to the white wheel of the Moon of Jeshlah, wrapped in her copper cloud.

Feasts and shows of great extravagance were continually arranged. Here men fought to display their skill rather than to kill each other (although, quite often, kill each other they did). But also sorceries were worked of incredible kinds, to thrill and astound. And there were competitions for music and the making of songs. Jeshlah was civilised. Towers of books stacked scroll on scroll, volume on volume, the height of many tall men. Instruments that made a hundred ravishing sounds.

Zulmeh was in her thirtieth year. Among the poor, such an age was a crone's age, but among the royal kindred it was not much.

A competition there was to be, at which the best songs of all the world, as the world was known, were to be sung before her. Judges would award the prize not to the singer, but to the poet who had made the winning song.

As Zulmeh was carried to her stadium of music, she glittered flawlessly on her people. She had earned her name, they said, she blazed so bright with her riches they could hardly bear to look at her. Her face too, might have been cut from diamond, they said. So pure and radiant. (So hard?)

She sat and heard the songs. If her mind wandered now and then, no one could be sure. If she wanted anything, everyone might see it, a cup of wine, green figs or honey, the breeze of fans, and these things were given her at once.

Then a whispering began all about that did not quite centre on the Queen. If she had been thinking of other things, this noise recalled her. A man waited below, tuning a little lap-harp modestly. Presently he sang.

His voice was fair, but it was the song which held the stadium.

The song told how a poet had seen a woman and thought her at once a harp of ivory but strung with his own black hair. By herself, this harp could sound him, as if he had been will-less. Yet without the strength of her strings, these long black strands, her music must be dumb.

When the song ended, the world seemed itself made dumb.

Zulmeh inclined her head, on which an unaccountable fortune flamed and spangled. Who could miss the flash of these fires, like swords at work in the desert far away?

She was not unloved, but the love had come with her station, the accessory of her rank belonged to the Great King. Doubtless what they had devised had been meant to please her, honour her, to be, even, kind. When finally the judges rose, they sky was red. But if any other songs had been sung, Zulmeh at least had not heard them. There was no deliberation. Naturally not. The judges declaimed their verdict to the stadium, which roared back its approval. Perhaps it truly was the best of all the songs, for Hazd had made it for Zulmeh, in the first year of their marriage.

It was the custom at such a festival, after the announcement of the winner, for the victorious poet to be called by a herald, three times. Nor did they omit this custom.

Loudly the name of Hazd was called, once, and then again, and then again.

And then all that stadium packed with people cried aloud for Hazd, and the noise rocked the sky, as if it were one huge bell of ruby glass.

Yet after the tumult, a silence fell, profound and terrible. The silence of a grave.

The Queen alone spoke softly, and none heard her. It was a silly childish thing she said: 'He cannot take his prize. He is dead.'

Darkness swept over the stadium. And all the kindled lights became little hopeless wisps beneath it. Anything might snuff them out. And nothing light up the black of the sky but the careless stars. Zulmeh raised her face to these stars, and the tears glinted on her cheeks, and were, of course, taken for yet more jewels, by the crowd.

It must be said, if they had heard what she uttered, they would have taken the words for the moistureless wit of kings.

But if they had thought to please or honour or be kind, they failed. They had only taught her one more lesson. For though she had known in her mind for ten full years that Hazd was dead, only now did she know it. So long it took the message to sink home, like a slow, slow knife.

All that night she walked about the palace's high places. She touched the birds upon their gold stands, so they trilled or spoke, the leaves of exotic shrubs, so they gave off myriad scents. She looked through the magnifying lenses of her mages, and saw the stars more closely, tinted rose and sapphire and bronze.

Later she whispered, 'But even the stars go out.'

And she gazed to the edges of the city, to the desert that surrounded all things.

Her counsellors were anxious. They stood in anterooms, puzzling, planning, not yet plotting.

At first light she came back among them all.

She had no appearance of madness, rather she was implacable, as some had seen her father, the Great King. They bowed to the ground. 'Now I will tell you,' said Queen Zulmeh, the Diamond, 'what I must have. What I will have. What you must get for me.'

Never had they heard her so clear, so sure.

They waited in instinctive terror. They were wise.

'Bring to me,' said Zulmeh, 'immortality.'

Only one year passes now, perhaps more swiftly all the others. Experiments of all sorts took place in Jeshlah, acts of magic and religion, of devotion, of cruelty, elixirs, mythology, drugs, philosophy, poison. Men died, so that the Diamond might learn how to live.

Yet she did not learn. None learned, save only a few old tales which none could credit. All lessons require canny teachers.

Of her punishments for failure little is recorded. Possibly she was merciful. Only her looks of disappointment killed.

At the year's end, the city stood in its magnificence, yet about it hung a kind of smoke. And this inchoate thing towered up to the sky, like a pillar, a tomb. As if to ask the gods: What have you done?

'Oh, Great Moon!' cried the girl, casting herself down before the Queen, 'someone has come to the palace.'

Zulmeh lifted her head, she stared, her green eyes fixed as a hawk's upon far distant prey. 'Who now?'

The girl replied rapidly. 'An old man, from the desert. But he says that he has heard of your quest – and has the remedy.'

It was the hour of lamp-lighting. But the slaves stopped still and the tapers blew out in their hands.

'Bring him to me!' cried the Queen.

She rose up, thin and white and gleaming. Hard, hard, hard. Diamonds last, but they scratch scars on things, even merely by looking from their burnished eyes.

And the appalled girl rushed away, and then returned, with the man from the desert, evenly flanked by twelve guards. (Strangely, one for every full year since the death of love.)

Others had come, of course, to Jeshlah, promising they could find the way to get the Queen what she wanted. Perhaps none had said so decidedly that he possessed the goods already.

He was a tall old man, narrow as a stick, but straight and strong, sunburned, with a life carved on his face. Much scarred by years, he seemed unwary of the Diamond's scratch. But he was anomalous. So ancient a creature, to hold the secret of ageless eternity?

His clothes were ragged hides. He had no adornment but for his silver hair and the blackest black of his eyes. Such as he wandered the deserts, living in caves, feeding on sand, and drinking the dew. So poor a beggar to hold a secret that might have made him rich as any king?

'Kneel, old man,' said the nearest guard. 'On your knees before the Moon Queen of the Great City of Jeshlah.'

At this, the old man smiled. Then he knelt with surprising agility on the tiled floor.

'Are you of this land?' asked the Queen's steward.

'Am I of any land?' asked the old man.

'What is your name?' frowningly asked the Queen's steward.

'What is a name?' smilingly asked the old man.

The steward indicated that the guard might strike the old man. Who laughed. And Zulmeh spoke to prevent the blow.

Then she ordered every one of her people from the room and stayed alone there with the old man who kneeled, smiling, on the floor. One so old and so poor and so arrogant and so unafraid must hold some secret, after all.

Then a while passed. A fly might be heard crawling on the wall. At last the Queen herself instructed the old man: 'Speak.'

He rose, and his smile was gone. He looked into her eyes and said, 'I bring you forever.'

It seemed to Zulmeh then, that all the lights that had been lit, faltered and went dark. But a moment after, they burned up again, bright as before. As if time itself had blinked.

'What must you do,' said Zulmeh the Diamond, 'to make this so?'

'What indeed?'

'Tell me,' she said.

'I have told. And I have done.'

'Is it done, then? But – is this all?'

'It is everything,' said the old man.

He had stepped farther off, although she had not seen him do so. Maybe in that moment of the blinking of light and time. He seemed in shadow now, and the black of his eyes was almost violet – or red, a red-violet burning through the fabric of him, from within.

'Well,' said the Queen, 'you shall remain as my guest. There must be trials made, to see.'

But across the room, a curtain turned to a wind and blew, and he was gone in it, gone away, gone out like a lamp that did not rekindle.

The Diamond stood alone and touched her face with her smooth fingers. (And how smooth they felt.) Am I changed?

The Moon of Jeshlah ruled in her city.

'She is the Diamond,' they said. 'See how smooth and burnished-bright she is, graceful and slender, her metallic hair and expensive eyes. Not a mark on her. Always the same.' But they squinted, as if also they beheld that now each day was for her like each previous day. And each night all other nights. One eternal day and one night of forever.

Times unravels, samenesses, changes...

All the days and nights the same. Where do they go to? Changing into what?

Zulmeh left her bed early, and her women brought her a cordial of roses and mint. As she drank it, she saw them changed and changing. There a pale young girl, but now more sallow than pale. And there a voluptuous girl, whose figure drooped. And there, and there, a thread of grey in the silken hair, or hair too colourful, dyed to hide the grey.

When they laughed or sulked, Zulmeh saw the cracks time made in their enamels.

They clothed her and brought her jewels. Their hands were not so deft as they had been. Their perfume not so fresh.

Zulmeh gave an audience. Gnarled hands on yellowing papers...

chipped voices... Now Zulmeh walked in her gardens. On the green steps, places opened slyly in the arbours. The white marble of the seat, as she sat admiring it, realising that it had lost its glow. Flowers had burned themselves out. The vines were ancient and the grapes that hung to be plucked, no longer tempting. Green droplets of juice shrivelled to raisins.

Zulmeh looked aside into the palace courts. Children had become stubborn adults and moved grumbling and fussing there. Already their shoulders were bowed. Their tones coarsened.

The sun rushed to the apex. She was left behind it.

She re-enters a great pavilion...

She ate a meal in one of the great pavilions, among her nobles and captains. The grey is creeping in their hair. Rheumatic hands, old wounds that hurt them. The dogs are thin, with filmy eyes. Young dogs stand up on wild ungainly legs – steadied – and began at once to stiffen like the beautiful dead mummy brought her once across the world.

The lilies that had been wound in the garlands crumbled away. The bread has a taste of mildew.

Zulmeh gives another audience. Over the floor, feverish ambassador, the Sun hurries, moving so fast.

Old men paraded before her who had entered the palace young men. The tribute of sparkling veils spread for her delight were fraying at their edges. Only the hard jewels dimly shone.

Soon the palace and the city slept in the heat of afternoon. The Queen prowls like a panther up and down.

Over the Earth the Sun now shuffled. The Sun was old, and surely had lost some of its light. The sunset burned out like the dullest flower.

Zulmeh bathed once more and was dressed once more. Morning? Night? Old women tended her, she sees the bones behind their faces, their breasts are fallen empty bags.

The tiles in the floor had been rubbed almost clean of their pictures.

Time flew, flies, has flown. It flew, flies, had flown, over and over, circling the dish of the world. Like the blinking of the lamps, the sunrise and sunset, the flicker of the black-blue eyelids of night.

A dead bird lay on the terrace. It always lay there, lies there, or another bird. No more songs.

Zulmeh looked out to the four corners of the horizon, and her powerful city was laid like a carpet before her. But the wind and sun had pared away the colours of the city. The old trees leaned or had fallen or been cut down. An axe strikes. There, another will fall, falls, fell.

At last, one day, someday, Zulmeh has them bring her carriage, and was carried through the streets. She watched the elderly people bowing to her, painfully, and the children stand taller and gain their first true balance – and stiffening there at once to statues of pallid wax. She watched the lights die in their eyes already long ago, heard their shrill bright savage voices tamed to monotonous regret.

Dead flowers littered the carriage, thrown in alive. Thrown in, yesterday, tomorrow?

'How wonderful is the Queen-who-is-a-Moon?' she heard the fissured voices croak. 'She has not aged one hour.' Or do they only mutter against her, that she is a witch?

The guards marched by the carriage, and their breathing rasped, their footfalls rang heavy, exhaustedly.

Now the buildings of the Great City of Jeshlah are and were partly ruinous, with stones fall-fallen out. The inhabitants crouched in hovels made from bits. The dust of the desert had come in and covered everything it could, thick as yellow flour.

There was a huge gateway, a gate of triumph inlaid with blue lapis, and guarded by two lions higher than the towers around. But the lions had lost, one, his forepaws, and the other his head. And the lapis rains out of the doors. Had rained out of the doors. Here and there a blue petal of lapis lay and lies, in the dust. One petal that would not fade. Already fading.

Zulmeh left the carriage.

The ancient men in their tarnished armour stared at her with half-blind eyes. When the Queen said that she would walk a little in the desert beyond Jeshlah, they remonstrated, but feebly.

'Rest,' said Zulmeh. 'Rest a while.'

She thought that when she turned back to them they must be skeletons, fallen or propped on their shields and spears.

It seemed to her she moved like a slim white knife and cut a way through dust and age and time, and as she cut, her own cutting made her sore. And conversely the rush of everything toward death, leaving her behind, as did the Sun and the Moon and the stars, rubbed on her, grazed her. But a Diamond is polished finer by abrasion. So they say and said.

When her feet, in priceless sandals, (of which now the straps gave way), met the flame-harsh grit of the desert's back, Zulmeh paused a moment.

'This I know,' said the Queen. 'For you are made by the grinding up of all else, as now, it seems, am I.'

So she walks among the sloping dunes.

The racing hound of the Sun ran more slowly yet, aging, losing ground.

Zulmeh stared after its bled-out shape, all wrapped in a distant storm of dust. She would, then, outlive the Sun? She would outlive the world? She, and the desert.

The frayed veils of dust, the desert's tribute, furled over the city, which seemed finally like a mirage. Soon every tower would drop down. Every wall collapse. Jackals would howl among the wreck – for a moment, only for a moment. The Moon would set behind the Sun, and darkness would come, but not the dark of night. Night too will have died, with all the stars, for she has said before, the stars go out.

Zulmeh walked, and the Sun came and went, comes and goes, and night likewise, and she reached and reaches a little place of life surrounded by the desert.

Two trees rose above a pool. A deer was drinking there, and seeing the blown white brilliance of the Queen, the deer sprang away. But as it touched the Earth again, it lost its vivid momentum. Through the flesh, Zulmeh saw its Moon-skull stare at her.

The Queen of Jeshlah sat down by the pool of the oasis. She thought she must be thirsty, and so cradled some water in her hands and drank it, before the pool should dry up and shrink away.

From two trees spread a shade that seemed cold, and almost still. Zulmeh sat down there.

But, as she spread her hand in the shade, the shade seeps off, as soon, surely, the pool must do.

Zulmeh sat beneath the trees, and the shade came and went, comes, goes, the cool of it, never staying long, the heat. Somehow the pool was replenished from some fountain under the ground. She thought achingly of Jeshlah. But Jeshlah must now be dust. A place of bones.

'Time moves so fast,' said Zulmeh to the desert, 'but only adds to you, and never diminishes me.'

Winds blew, hot as the sting of a scorpion, and burnished the Diamond more.

'I wish,' said Zulmeh, 'how I wish I do not have forever. How I wish that I am dead.' (The denying prayer that does no good.)

Then she lay down in the moment of the shade under the trees, to sleep. For she seemed not to have slept at all, for many hundreds of years. And after she had slept, this once, she might never sleep again. Although, when she woke, she knew the Earth too might have vanished, will have done, dashed and rushed down into the bottomless abyss of nothing. Opening her eyes, she would find only the desert and the darkness left, and the cry of the soulless winds of immortality, the music of unforgiving forever. (No more songs.)

But, even so – even so, she slept, she sleeps.

Zulmeh dreamed. For the sages said, even the eternal gods have dreams.

A man was walking over the sand, in the dream, and Queen Zulmeh got up and followed him. He was changeable, this man. First, he was black as her lost lover, Hazd, or blacker perhaps, but his hair was not black. Then he seemed gold-haired, but also grey-haired. And then he had no hair, his head was smooth as a brown nut. And then his hair was black, and then silver. And then his hair was a wave or a wind which blew the world sideways.

However, changeable as he was, he did not dash only one way, toward the pit of silence and dissolving.

Halting, Zulmeh thought he was, after all, the forever-bringing man from the desert, who must be a mage, and so quite capable of constant change.

'I will give you all I have,' said Zulmeh, no longer running at his back but standing deadly still, 'if you will take your curse from me.'

'Did I curse you?'

'Yes. With your venomous blessing.'

'I only gave you, Diamond,' he said, 'what you wanted.'

'No one,' said the Diamond, 'ever gave me that.'

Then he laughs and turns and faces her. She cannot see at all who he is, for he is all shapes, all colours, coming and going, chaotic, elastic – terrible. Yet, his voice is like a song.

'My father,' said the Diamond, 'gave me a gem in place of my mother. The animal I loved they brought me made into wood, with cold hard fur, and eyes of vitreous. They gave me the heads of men in a pond of blood. They gave me the heavy crown of Jeshlah. Only one thing I never did ask for, and that was my marriage to my husband. And this was the only thing I ever wanted. Yet I did not know I wished for it till he was by my side.'

'Hazd is gone,' said the whirlwind upon the sand.

'Hazd is dead. I wish for death.'

'You asked for never-ending life. Wished for and wanted it.'

The Diamond said, 'Did I not tell you? It has always been my way to ask for and receive that which I do not want?'

'You are a fool,' said the thing before her. 'Go back to Jeshlah.'

'Jeshlah has fallen,' said Zulmeh, 'I have lived on, and centuries have passed. I have felt every one of them drag over me as it went. It has been centuries.'

'Fool,' said the thing, which had given her forever, 'it has only been thirty days. The number of the years of your little human life.'

Zulmeh opened wide her eyes. 'Then have you not,' said she, 'made me an immortal?'

'I gave you forever in thirty days. I did not promise you your wish, but its remedy.'

Zulmeh opens wide her eyes once more, and this time wakes. The night is spread above, black and still, the stars fixed in their places, each sparkling hard and enduring as any diamond.

They say, it is true, that Zulmeh returned to her city, over the desert. She was very strong and not old. But the rumour of her journey, and her brief, (it had been brief), sojourn in the waste, became a legend of that land.

When she came near the city, peasants at a well saw her walking toward them, and knew her as the Queen. They brought her milk in a clay cup, and she clasped their hands, those of young and old alike, laughing like a girl, so they laughed too. She petted the goats of their wild herds as if goats were quite new to her. The herders said never was there a king like this.

But for Zulmeh, what? The frantic race of time, which she had only imagined, or been spelled to see, or spelled herself to see, had ceased. What she had witnessed in her sensation of eternity, the line beside the mouth, the fallen stone, were those intimations that all men, and all women too, will notice now and then. But not as she had done.

For had she ever noted a grey hair in the black harp-ropes of Hazd? No, never. But they were there, since he had been many years older than she. Had she thought the Sun ran across Heaven?

Never, until she was given forever. (The remedy.)

Nothing is forever, unless, like the demon creature in her dream, it changes. Youth to age. Age to death. Death to birth to youth...

Re-entering the gate of her city, it stood high as Heaven, and full of its blue petals, the lions proud, their paws and peerless heads only a little worn. While on the avenue her soldiers raised their spears in salute, young men, mature men, strong and valid. And beyond, the people called for her, and the children timelessly played, and roses fell, firm and fragrant, the colour of a sunset that was not blood, nor decay, but like a young girl's blush.

And in the city, the towers and the walls they soared up. And in her private rooms, her lovely maidens welcomed her, peaches, jasmine, with teeth like pearls.

Zulmeh had seen what immortality might entail. Now she saw again what mortals see, dancing together on the floor of life, whose tiles are whole and perfect. Yet never would she forget her vision, her thirty days in a wilderness, static, and about her the whole wheel of time revolving and revolving. Poor child, she saw what men should never see. Wise child, she learned, and left it and came away, and lived. Hard lesson. Last lesson, perhaps.

In Jeshlah, Zulmeh the Diamond raised a pylon, which at midday held the Sun upon its tip. She would watch this phenomenon through a lens, a third jade eye. It always took the proper time. By night she traced the measured progress of the planets.

Also, in her thirty-first year, she married again, a prince of another land. He was not black, but the colour of honey. She bore for him, and for herself, three children, who ruled the city when Zulmeh's mortal time was done.

Long, long before that hour had struck, one night, near dawn, there was a shooting star. It flashed like a jewel across the firmament.

Zulmeh's lover-husband kissed her, and he said, 'If you wanted it, I would give you that brilliant thing – if I could. I cannot. But I will love you forever.'

The Diamond said, as the sages record, 'We love. But nothing is forever, as forever is nothing. Forever is this moment. The world in a grain of sand.'

The Woman in Scarlet

It was always one way when he met them, on the long roads, high lands, low lands, rich or not, at the little villages, in the towns too, and in the slim white cities, even there, or under the green roofs of forests, or on a seashore washed by the sea empty of most things but air and light.

'*Look*,' he noted them whisper, the men, the women, the children, the slaves. '*Do you see him? He is a Sword's Man.*'

Sometimes they would follow him a short distance. If not, they stared till he was out of sight. Occasionally, not that often, they might approach, more likely send a servant after him. Otherwise, the approach came from strangers still unseen, who had heard tell of him, or sensed his arrival, like a season. The men generally wanted straightforward help, rescue, or to train some rabble of an army, or teach their sons to fight. The women usually required him to murder somebody. Then again, men and women both, now and then wanted him for other things. To show him off, display him, to bed him or own him, if only for a night. He said 'No' more times than he said 'Yes', to all the requests. But for the beds it was always 'No'. They should remember, and they did, but hoped he might forget: He was wedded to his Sword. All his kind were. Married to her, and her possession, never theirs.

'Coor Krahn, must you be going?'

'I must.'

'Can't I tempt you to remain a handful more days? There's the horse I spoke of… why don't you come and see if you like it?'

'I walk where I go, Lord Juy. It keeps me fitter.'

'Oh that. You're fit as three men. Stay for the dinner tonight. It's my daughter's birth-feast.'

'My work's done here, Lord Juy. My thanks, but I'll be on the road by noon.'

'She's restless,' said the rich aristocrat, half contemptuous, and half jealous, frowning, admiring, uneasy, 'is she?'

'Maybe.'

'Tell me her name again.'

Coor Krahn did not like to say his Sword's name to others, but also he did like to. He stayed in two minds on this. 'Sas-peth,' Coor Krahn said, unsmiling, his black eyes burning up, so Lord Juy slightly recoiled. 'Sas-peth Satch.'

'And that other name she has – no, don't say that one. I recall that one. And why she has it. It's a good name, Coor Krahn. And you are a mighty Sword's Man. Now, because of your skills, my lands stretch to the Black River. I'm grateful. The slave will bring your fee. It's as we agreed.'

'I never doubted that,' said Coor Krahn. He bowed and turned his back upon Lord Juy. (They both understood he had referred not to a lord's honour but to a Sword's Man's power and rights.)

A few minutes later a slave came, and presented the wallet of gold, crawling on his knees.

The Sun was high over the scaled towers of Juy's mansion as Coor Krahn turned on to the road out of the valley.

The wallet was stowed in the leather pack across his back. No sane man in half a world would ever dare to try to steal it. Nor any of the ornaments a Sword's Man wore, nor any piece of his armour or arms.

At Coor Krahn's side, she hung from the belt of red leather in her scarlet silk scabbard. Although young still, he had walked so long, so many years, with that feel of her beside him, that to walk without her would have seemed like lameness. And in the same way, to sleep without her lying along his body and under his hand, like death.

'Sas-peth,' he murmured once, as he walked up from the glowing valley, 'Sas-peth Satch.' But now he smiled, to himself, or to her. He often spoke a little to her, though he never spoke very much to other men, and to women, less.

Tonight, he dreamed of her.

In the dreams he saw her in her spirit shape, which naturally was female. But also, in dreams, she put on flesh and blood. They were walking in a night garden, high on a roof above a city, perhaps Curhm-by-Ocean, or Is-lil in the north. Slender and dark, the sculptured trees rose from stone pots, and a stone lion, polished smooth as water, held the round orange Moon between his ears.

Coor Krahn could smell a perfume, like a spice, which in her woman shape the Sword had put on. Her hand rested lightly on his arm. Her face too was powdered pale, as the faces of aristocratic women always were. (Although in other dreams, when she strode or rode with him into battle, she was tawny as any peasant boy.) Her long hair looked smooth as the lion, as night water. She wore her colour, as she always did: deep red, bordered with flame red. Her eyes were black as his own.

'Why are you up here, Lady Sas-peth?' he asked her courteously. He was unfailingly formal, when first addressing her, even when, as in some dreams they did, they lay down together.

'There is the sea,' she said, pointing her narrow finger away across the houses and the temples, to a curving line of fine white fire, which described waves breaking on the city stones. This was Curhm then, yet it had a look more of Gazul, which rose by a desert.

'Do you wish to go to the sea, Sas-peth?'

'No. Away from the coast.'

'Tell me, then, where shall we go?'

Then she turned her narrow, perfect face and gazed at him. Her gaze was not like that of any woman he had ever met, high-born or lowly. Nor, for that matter, like the gaze of any man.

'At this time, I grow tired of our wandering about, Coor Krahn. Let us rest soon.'

In the dream he was startled. But she sometimes made him start. During the first dream in which she had bared her breasts and kissed him and drawn him down, he had been amazed, so amazed that it amounted to fear, until, presently, everything was lost in her.

'Then – then, lady, we'll rest a while. Where would you wish our rest to be?'

'Some small place,' she said, idly now, more womanly. She glanced away, and smiled secretively, as sometimes she did before they coupled. But she drew her hand from his arm, and the long tail of her scarlet sleeve slipped over his wrist, cool as a snake. 'The next small place, perhaps.'

'It will be some upland village…' he said, almost protesting.

She did not reprimand him.

Instead, she drifted off, crossing over the face of the Moon, moving away through the garden, until she vanished behind the trees.

He woke, disturbed slightly, and lay thinking of the memory of her, her shadow-silhouette against the face of the Moon.

But under his hand, she lay silent now, and steel hard, out of her scabbard.

'Whatever you wish, Sas-peth Satch. As always. I am your warrior, master of all but you. Your slave, Sas-peth.'

He had slept that night under the pines and sobe trees of a little wood, and in the morning, when he walked out of the wood, he could see nothing below but the track and the sloped shoulders of the hills. At once he felt relieved and wondered at himself. In the past, now and then, she had come to him asleep and told him they must do certain things, take a certain direction or avoid another. So far as he knew, no loss had ever resulted from his obedience. Why should it? A Sword could only bring her warrior good; fame, wealth and kudos, through lawful battle, which was the reason for his life.

He walked on, along the hills, she at his side.

Coor Krahn had been born in a poor town, whose name meant Pigs City. Undoubtedly pigs were kept there and provided the mainstay of the town's economy. Coor Krahn grew up in a thatched house-hut, one of three belonging to the town's overseer, and overlooking five courtyards, each full, like all the town courtyards, and the town streets, of pink and grey pigs.

When Coor was nine, some Sword's Men entered the town. The overseer had himself called them, because Pigs City was experiencing conflict with a neighbouring brigand across the river. (There had been trouble for months, and one night part of the town burned – Coor remembered well the cries and shrieks, the streaming metallic flames, and the odour of roast pork – that in later years he realised was not all attributable to unlucky pigs.)

Waiting on his father the overseer's table, with several other older sons, Coor was dazzled and astonished by the four warriors, the Sword's Men. They blazed in the greasy torchlight in their mail and ribbed plates of armour. These carapaces had been decorated with chasings and bosses of gold and silver so intricate they seemed embroidered there, while jewels blinked and gleamed like coals, or witch's eyes of glacial ice. The men were tanned to bronze, their hair long, braided or worn tied high, as the tails of the horses they had brought. One had a scar across his cheek that pulled his face that side always into a grin. It was a wonderful scar, and he was rightly proud of it, sometimes fondling it, and he had given it a name: The Moon's Tooth, which Coor never forgot, though afterward he forgot the names of all four men.

Their Swords also had names, and these names Coor forgot as well, but for perhaps another reason – they daunted him so. Slanting from the belts of their men, as the warriors sat at the overseer's dinner, each Sword leaned in her scabbard of silk over leather over steel over velvet, and force swirled from them. The Swords were four queens, four enchantresses, and this was made most plain. A cup of hot wine was set before each Sword, which drink her Sword's Man never touched, also a platter with a little of the best meat, and a flower laid on it, as if for a great lady.

Within a single day, the Sword's Men had settled the brigand across the river. His head, and those of his two lieutenants, were fixed on poles by the wooden town gate, for everyone to delight in. The heads had not even quite rotted down to the skulls when Coor ran away from Pigs City and followed the road the Sword's Men had taken, eastward, to Curhm.

He had seen the warriors paid in silver and gold coins, all the town could spare. It was not that which made him run after them. He knew they, and their kind, maintained the fabric of law and justice across the sphere of lands too great for him, then, ever to imagine. It was not that either. Coor was strong and healthy and bored almost to a stone with pigs, and of course the men, their magnificence, had impressed everyone. Nor was it that. It was the swirl of half-seen lightning, the presence, the essence of the four Swords, and of one in particular. He learned after, this was not quite unheard of. The Sword had "flirted" with him, as an empress might, leading him on just a short way, to bring him to awareness of his fate. She had been sheathed in jade silk. Not recollecting her outer name, he had yet some idea she was also called for something green, but that inner name her Sword's Man had never revealed. Any more than Coor, when once he had become a Sword's Man at the Sword-School of Curhm, would much reveal the inner name of Sas-peth Satch. For the inner name was given mostly at the first meeting, awake or in dream, after the man was wed to her. Only those you allowed to hire you, or were close to you in other ways, had a right to hear it. And then, generally, they – like Lord Juy – were too afraid to speak it aloud

The sword-school was harsh. It needed to be, to slough off quickly those who had mistaken their destiny. Some few died in their first months. Not many. Most simply failed and went home, or to other vocations. Sad, bitter even, but resigned. Only now and then one who failed killed himself. There was one of those during Coor's second year. This boy, called Fengar, threw himself from the top of the Sun Wind Temple, and died on the pavement below, an offering to the wind goddess.

Coor had known, or believed he had known, he too would rather die than fail.

But he did not fail, he did extremely well. He rose straight, like a star, as if all of him, body, mind, and spirit, had already been honing itself, unsuspected, for this work.

At first his teachers were stern with him, zealous in case he should turn out only to be a star which burned up and fell. But after five years at the School, they were stern in another way, harsher if anything, to hammer him flawless.

From a yokel of the low lands, just able to scratch his name, he became educated and fined. He learned not only the arts of the warrior, but some of the knack of a scholar, able to read and to write, and of a courtier, who can speak and behave gracefully, unless provoked. No Sword's Man ever had a wish to insult through ignorance, for any unwise enough to anger him he would be able to destroy. But these were material things.

In his seventeenth year, the mystery began to be taught him.

This was the mystery of the Sword, the core of the ethos of a Sword's Man. Until reckoned ready, the apprentice owned no sword of any type. The blades he fought with and learned by were common property. But now the night approached when the School would give to Coor his own individual weapon. Not a sword, but a Sword. An artefact which had been forged for him alone, occultly, hidden from all but its makers. In other hands, it was not yet female, only he would wake it to its feminine life, and to its power.

At phases of the Moon, junctures of the zodiac, the concealed artisans of Curhm-by-Ocean created a Sword for Coor, as they, or their forebears, had done, through a thousand years, for every Sword's Man of that School.

First came the ceremony that made Coor a warrior; before it he was starved a month of food and sleep, and drawn by draughts of midnight herbs and tart, transparent smokes, into some other state, half from his body, which in turn seemed eccentric, wilder, and curiously less finite than he had ever known it. In this strange condition, he viewed eternity, the unimportance of everything else, and its contrasting utter necessity, for trivia held the seeds of different, higher matters, to be discovered only after death.

Thirty-one endless days and limitless nights Coor lived in this mode. On the evening of the thirty-second day, as stars dewed the twilight over Curhm, they led him to his wedding.

A Sword's Man stayed celibate. That is, he was faithful only to his Sword. Although female, it was his phallus. Yet it – she – and only she – might make love to him. And her only might he ever take. She would lie at his side, in his arms, every night. And in dreams, if by his courage and his genius in combat he made her care for him, then she would give him pleasures no human woman ever could.

Coor, now named Coor Krahn, stood naked in the unlit dark of that huge granite chamber, and when they brought her to him, his steel mistress, without a scabbard, naked too, his sex rose hard, and he shook as if meeting at last his one true love.

He made his vows. In the luminous darkness, he thought he heard the Sword faintly singing at each resonance of his voice.

Then, as he gazed at her, a hooded man was there, and as always he did, with exaggerated gentleness, lifting Coor Krahn's left forearm, made a long thin cut in it with a virgin razor.

The blood ran out and dripped away and away, ruby beads, and finally they brought her his Sword, to drink his blood, and as she drank, he kissed her, her silken skin of steel, for the first time.

When he did so, his erection faded and sank down. But he was appeased; as if he had reached a climax, and that energy was spent. While from the lessening of his flesh, vast vitality seemed to burst back through him. And in that moment, he knew the Sword's inner name.

After the marriage, they took him to a couch, where he was to lie down and hold her, and sleep, and have the beginning dream.

The wine was drugged, and he slept instantly.

He found himself on a mountaintop, among the white, cold snow, under a sky glittering light, without colour. But the Sword stood before him, and she was a woman, and clothed in red, and so he knew he had been right in the name. Touching his body lightly with pearl fingers just above the heart, the Sword spoke to him in her woman's voice, while her beauty scorched him like the fiery sky.

'I am to be called Sas-peth Satch. Say my name.'

'Sas-peth... Sas-peth Satch, my lady.'

'My inner name you may also speak, since I informed you at our kiss, and you heard me.'

Then he said that name, and she nodded, and the dream was gone. After this, he slept for a hundred hours.

Waking, he remembered as they always did, and both the names. Sas-peth Satch was The Woman in Scarlet.

When it appeared, five days after she told him of it in the garden dream, the "small place" turned out to be attractive enough.

The hill itself was terraced for agriculture, and brilliant as if carved from emerald. There were fields, and yards of vines. A river, crystalline and thin in spots as a rope, threaded all through, and sallow willows hung over it, and then an orchard of ash-plums, and hyacinth trees.

The town was prosperous. Having reached the wide main street, which had been paved, he looked through to a second hill, and there was a lord's mansion on it, with dragon-tinted roofs. Had the Sword brought him here for war? It seemed unlikely. Even the people on the street, (who stared after him in the usual way), looked otherwise carefree.

Coor Krahn went to the inn. The slave by the door was well-fed and went down on his knees, smiling, to welcome a guest.

The inn master saw to the care of a Sword's Man personally. It was his pert wife, eyeing Coor Krahn in a fashion he knew quite well, who said to him, 'And why can you be here, a great Sword's Man, in *our* peaceful little pond?'

'I'm on my way somewhere,' he answered. When she tried to improve on this, he did not reply, and sat as if thinking, until she left him alone.

The day passed with sunlight and the mooing of cows in the water-meadows. As evening stole through, Coor Krahn heard the inn filling up below, and kept to his chamber. They would be discussing him sufficiently as it was.

Lanterns lit in the courtyard. Moths danced. Cool breezes blew the veils of night, and a firefly winked on and off by the well.

He was restless. He did not know why he was here. Did she mean him to stay here for sure; as she had said to *rest* here, and as the inn slut had said, in this peaceful little pond? He was young, not yet thirty. Sufficient time for restful dawdling in a decade or so.

'Why have you sent me here, Sas-peth?' he asked her softly, as she went up and down with him across the room. 'Why must I loiter? Do *you* aspire to loiter – to rest – *you*? Or were you only playing a game with me?'

He thought, if he slept, he might dream of her and then she would tell him why, or what she really wanted. Or even that she had been testing him, his loyalty to her that she had never, in any case, doubted. And that tomorrow they would go on, away from here.

But when he fell asleep it was late. The youthful Moon had sailed over, and the town was silent as a grave. And he only dreamed, incredibly, as he seldom did, that he was once more living in Pigs City. The change was, in this dream, he was a man full-grown, yet not a warrior. He was the overseer, since his father and the other sons were all dead. He was sitting in a courtyard, with pigs everywhere, seeing to a judgment of some errant wife. She looked, of course, exactly like the pert wife of the inn master, who had tried to interest him earlier.

When he woke, dawn was ahead of him, the sky beyond the window like a peach. He caressed the steel skin under his hand, his wedded wife, the Sword.

'Perhaps, lady, I need some sign from you. Pardon my asking it of you. But I'm foxed. I don't understand. Perhaps give me some sign today, why it is you truly want to remain in this *small place*. Have I mistaken it? Was it some other town you had in mind? Guide me, Sas-peth Satch. Or maybe I'll have to go on anyway, a little distance, to make sure I didn't mistake your meaning.'

When he said this, a shudder went over him. The dawn was cold, despite its flush, and he had thrown off the blanket. But it was not because of that. He felt his words had been dismissive, a threat that he would have his own way in spite of what the Sword wished. And that could never, must never be.

'Whatever you want, lady,' he said.

As he got up, his limbs seemed stiff. For a second, he caught sight of the ghost of some man's old age. But Coor Krahn was young, and in a moment was as he had been. He put himself, his character, on again, like his clothes.

But buckling on the belt of the Sword, for the first time in his life, it slipped through his fingers. He caught the scabbard before it met the ground. The Sword had not been in the scabbard, or the omen would have perturbed him more.

At noon, an elaborately-dressed servant was waiting for him downstairs.

'From my master, I bring you greetings, Sword's Man. And this modest trinket.'

Coor Krahn accepted the modest trinket – a broad silver arm-band set with several clear gems – such tokens were frequent enough. He thought, *Now I shall discover why I was brought here.* He said, 'What's the name of your master?'

'The Lord Tyo Lionay.'

Coor nodded graciously. Of course, he had never heard of him.

Lord Tyo's house was very fair, not large, but exquisite in all apparent detail. Beyond, elaborate gardens ran down the hill, and next there was Lord Tyo's game park, full of spotted antelope, blond foxes, and rare tigers whose eyes were blue.

The aristocrat met Coor Krahn in a marble yard. It had a marble cistern of water, where great gold and black carp swam, or put up bold heads to look at them – at which Tyo laughed, and fed them dainties, and stroked them, too. A nightingale sang by day, in a mulberry tree of purple fruit.

'How may I assist you, Lord Tyo?'

Tyo only smiled, and the servant refilled their cups.

'I need nothing, Sword's Man. I have no enemies. Nor any war-goals: I possess already almost everything I want.'

Coor did not frown, though he suspected now duplicity. Tyo was handsome, perhaps a year or so younger than himself. Tyo's manner was frank and charming.

'Then, my lord, you're too generous. If you require no service from me, I'm uneasy at accepting your gift.'

'Please keep the armlet. I collect such things – it's my pleasure to gift them. Your service to me you perform in allowing me to meet with you. I'd heard much of you, Coor Krahn, your valour and ability.'

'You're again too generous, Lord Tyo.'

'Then permit my excess. Dine with me – stay in this house and lie soft for once. There are many diversions here. I also collect curious creatures... and there are lovely women, if you incline to them.'

Coor Krahn did frown. He said, 'I am a Sword's Man. When you heard of me, had you never heard that?'

'And married to the blade? Naturally. But surely that isn't always so...'

Coor Krahn felt a low dull anger. (In his mind he remembered the falling empty scabbard.) Did this lordling dare insult him? 'With myself, Lord Tyo, always it is so.'

'Forgive me ignorance, then. I'm sorry to have offended you, my noble guest. But, stay and dine.'

'I'm bound elsewhere.'

As Coor said this, the Sword lay heavy at his thigh. He was very conscious of her. No, he was not bound elsewhere, for she had bound him here. But why – for this? To bear with this rich fool and his rich fool's whims?

'Must you hurry on your road? Is it an urgent mission?'

Now Coor did not answer, scorning a lie.

And his silence, Lord Tyo Lionay took, it seemed wilfully, for agreement.

He dreamed of the Sword that night, when he slept on the silken bed, at Tyo's mansion. A girl had come to bathe him, a lovely girl indeed, with skin like cream and hair like night rain. But he sent her out. After this, and the heavy food and wine, sleep and the dream came swiftly.

Sas-peth Satch lay by him on the bed in Tyo's house. She was naked as a moon, and at once put her hands upon him, watching him as his excitement mounted, playing his body like her instrument until orgasm released him with its death.

'You see that I reward you,' said Sas-peth then.

'Yes, my lady. I'm rewarded beyond all treasures.'

'Then you will cease your argument with me.'

'I'd never argue against you, Sas-peth.'

'But you have.'

'How have I?'

'You resist my will that you remain here.'

'Ah, lady,' he sighed. '*Here?*'

'Here.'

'In this house?'

She said nothing.

'If you demand it, I shall. But won't you tell me...?'

She rose, and stood, garbed suddenly again, in the facile way of dreams (and magic) in her scarlet garments. She turned her face aside from him. For a second, she seemed to him nearly evasive. 'Do you question me still?'

'Not your *right* to command me, lady, only the reason. A warrior isn't made for much of such a life. Perhaps with me – not even for a single day. To *lie soft*, and eat and drink over and again, and talk and talk – to tell stories of his acts that sound like boasting, to listen constantly to some lord's worthless chat – *he* jabbers like some farm-girl...'

Between one word and the next, she was gone. Like the firefly by the well, her glow winked out, and he lay alone in the dream, and waking, under his hand her steel was that of an icicle, so his palm seemed stuck to her and scalded by her coldness.

'How have I angered you, Sas-peth, Sas-peth Satch?'

He knew. He had resisted. She was his empress; he must obey.

Coor Krahn turned over sullenly to his left side, letting go of her as sometimes – rarely – had happened in sleep. He lay with his back to her, and in the marble court below the nightingale sang on, like a clockwork engine, itching inside his brain.

'May I see it? – pardon my clumsiness – may I see *her*? I mean, the Sword?'

It was the second day here. Coor looked at Lord Tyo, who stood there, mannerly, groomed and good-looking, ingenuous perhaps, or merely stupid.

'A warrior doesn't give over his Sword to any man but his brothers, his master, or his smith.'

'I meant, evidently, that you should hold her, but perhaps I might look. Her power's very glamorous. It attracts me.'

'Let me enlighten you, my lord. What you ask is like wanting a squint at my prick.' Coor Krahn had intended uncouthness. But Tyo only put back his head and laughed. Coor Krahn said ironly, 'She is only drawn out for me, in privacy. Unless I draw her to kill. If another man sees her, as you ask to do, she must taste his blood.'

Tyo gazed straight in his eyes. Tyo's eyes were steady and pure. 'If that's the price, I would pay it. I take it you mean a sip, not my life's blood. I've heard of this custom, I believe. Yes, why not.'

The provision of the blood – a sip, as the wretch had said – had been made of necessity. There could come certain occasions when, as Coor had mooted, a Sword must be drawn outside the need of war. For repair, or before a peer. Then the Sword's Man himself did not give her his own blood. Some fitting other was selected, by the warrior, his School or the smith, one who reckoned himself honoured to be used, and would wear the scar of her bite with colossal pride.

'Again, I've offended you, my dear,' said Tyo familiarly, and Coor wished to slap him like some silly slattern fumbling him at an inn.

'You make light of what is profound,' said Coor Krahn.

'Not I. I'm caught in the web of her fascination. Soon you'll be gone. I must take up again my restricted life. Do you really grudge me this? Oh then, I'll say no more.'

A board game was brought. They ate ash-plums, and played it, as if it mattered.

In Coor Kahn a fury was rising like a storm. It began in him on the second day at the mansion, by which time anyway he was already sick of the place and everything it held. The decorative food curdled in his belly, the nightingale hurt in his ears. The tamed beasts that strolled about the marble corridors, and lay sunning themselves in Tyo's park – where his lordship did not even hunt them – seemed to be other versions of Coor Krahn, also trapped and tamed, his teeth grown sticky from candies. Ten days and nights went like this. All alike. Music was played them, girls rippled in lascivious dances, board games were set for table-wars, intellectual verses read out. The lord and Coor rode and dined, and talked, and talked, and separated only to sleep. Tyo was affectionate and nearly deferential, so that Coor came to believe this lord found him most amusing. Not one dream came to Coor, not one dream of her, to tell him what he should do. Except, alone with her one night, he said, 'Let me go from here, my lady. Or I must go from here – without your letting me.' And in the dark spaces of sleep after this, he thought he caught a glimpse of her, faint as a candle flame, miles ahead and carried away from him. And he followed in vain.

Perhaps the eleventh night arrived, or the twelfth; twelve – the number it was sometimes believed was unlucky. He had that day ridden all over the park (as if searching for escape) and the tigers had watched with lolling tongues. In sleep he saw Sas-peth walking under the Sun with a tiger, which had red eyes, not blue. And he followed, but now not in vain, although he did not instantly catch up to her.

If it was the fool's park they were in, he was not sure. But it was a park, cultivated, the trees grown for effect, pruned to ardent shapes that obscured no possible vista.

He came on Sas-peth Satch again suddenly. She waited under a cedar, and the tiger was gone. She looked away and away, and when Coor spoke to her, she did not reply, or turn to him. And then he realised that another was there with her, someone that he, Coor Krahn, could not see, so that at first he took the vague figure only for a shadow – although Sas-peth, in dreams, cast no shadow at all.

'Here I am,' she said, 'do you see?' But not to Coor Krahn.

The shadow-figure became a little less vague. It held out its arm, and Sas-peth put her hand on this arm.

Who is this that she touches?

Then there was nothing there, and she looked back at Coor Krahn, and her face was expressionless as she said to him, 'I have not called you to me, Coor Krahn. What do you want? Must I forbid you, like a child, to follow me at such times?'

She had been communing with some spirit of her own kind, he reasoned. He felt shamed and begged her forgiveness. But she merely looked away once more, and then he woke, and the fury stirred blindly inside him, like thunder under a hill.

Still, time passed. It hurt him, each wasted hour an injury. But why was the hurt so much? It was a pleasing place, this small place. No, it was a hell for him. Sleeping or waking, here he was, with this pampered lord fool, like the lord fool's slave. And the fool wanted a look at the naked Sword, and would pay in fool's blood...

They were in the marble courtyard when the fury burst, staining the air, and the aura of Coor Krahn's soul, with a black shot by fire.

But Lord Tyo did not seem to notice. Urbanely he toyed with an ivory game piece, smiling on.

'*Then,* my lord, if you *say* no more, *I* say as you did, *why not?*'

Stunned, bewildered, Tyo blinked at him.

And Coor Krahn put his right hand over on to the hilt of his Sword.

When he touched her she was like some electric thing. Sparks flew up inside his arm, but he wrenched her from the scabbard with a noise like a rusty scream, and in the air she blazed and rang, slicing the light of day like gauze. The whole landscape seemed to gasp and petrify in awe. The Sun, wounded, trickled sparkling on her blade's edge. And Tyo stared up at her, where the Sword's Man had lifted her high into the sky.

Tyo was white, he was trembling. He said softly, 'So beautiful she is. Better than any jewel. Better than anything, even a woman dressed in lilies.'

'Yes, so she is. Better than anything.' The rage now had remade Coor Krahn. He was remote and in control of himself. It was like a battle-anger, and yet, not quite. 'She's thirsty, too. Are you ready?'

'Yes.'

'So brief a word. Only one? I thought you'd talk more. Bare your arm for her, then.'

Tyo rent his sleeve. Expensive sequins spun off like tears, or like the blood to come.

Coor Krahn slit the aristocrat's skin with great delicacy, being careful not to cut too deep, as he longed to do, careful not to shear off his foul and hated head.

Tyo made no sound. The blood welled up, and Sas-peth Satch drew herself along, by means of Coor Krahn's grip, all the flat of her shining blade, until she was scarlet from hilt to tip.

And in that moment, as once before, long ago, Coor Krahn knew her secret.

He snatched her off, and in that same movement, she dropped from his hand, his fingers nerveless. She fell away from him. She fell at the feet of Tyo Lionay.

Tyo whispered, 'What – what is it? Pick her up, man. She's not some stick – she's a Sword.'

'Pick her up? No, let her lie there.'

'What – what are you thinking of, Sword's Man? Have you gone mad?'

'Yes. It could drive me there.'

'*Take her up.*'

'You take her.'

Tyo gaped at him, his colour oddly coming back from shock, though he swayed like an uprooted tree.

'You take her, Tyo Lionay. It's you she's chosen.'

'This is madness.'

'I told you, perhaps it is. But now I see. Why she sent me here. She *smelled* you, like the fruit trees. I should have seen through her, she showed me often enough, in her own woman's way.'

'Coor Krahn...'

'Don't speak my name to me, you thing of shit. Take her and keep her. Here's the scabbard too.' It went down by her, on the marble, with a crack. 'Keep her with your other collected stuffs. Take her to bed at night. See what you dream.'

And turning, he left Lord Tyo, still somehow standing, among the scattered Sun on gold and red, and above the faithless Sword that had named herself The Woman in Scarlet, since she must always be sheathed in blood.

Only when he reached the city of Gazul did he stop for as long as a day and a couple of nights. And then he left Gazul and went on, into the desert beyond.

Events had happened before that, during three months of travelling. He had been called for by a pair of lords, to fight for them. He said 'No'. But then a peasant village had entreated him to rid them of a local tyrant, showing him the bodies of four young men whipped to death. So there Coor had paused for an afternoon. He had had to ask them for a sword. It was a rough old thing, some tarnished heirloom of the village overseer's, but it did his work well enough. He saw then, with a deep bitterness, that it was his own skill in combat, as much as any weapon, which gained results.

Afterward, they begged him to keep the sword. They said they would be vainglorious, telling others they had given the sword to a Sword's Man whose own blade was currently under repair. (They were so restricted in their knowledge, they had not faltered at his lack of his Sword and concocted this explanation from spontaneous ingenuity.)

He accepted the old sword and refused other payment. He left the slain tyrant for them to tear into ritual pieces and bury in twenty different unmarked graves. (The man had been a monster.) In as much as he could feel anything, save his bitterness and insane agony, Coor was not sorry to have helped the village.

The ugly old sword was quite good, quite reliable. At another place, after another fight, he had it new-surfaced and strengthened, and made a little heavier, to suit him. Here at the smith's, no one offered comment. Only the smith's boy asked anxiously if he should find a worthy man, so the drawn sword could taste blood. Coor Krahn did not answer. It was the smith who shut the boy's mouth with a glare. Even fancied up, it was sufficiently obvious this sword was not any sort of Sword.

Coor Krahn did not speculate on how others regarded the facts. Probably they invented halfway logical tales, as the village had. The Sword's Man's true Sword was being mended or specially garnished. Instead of impatiently awaiting her, he had journeyed on, and would then go back to collect her. Or maybe some of them realised he had lost his Sword, supposed she was broken, or taken from him, perhaps even dishonourably. But where they required his talents, and he gave them, no one expressed an opinion.

He slept under trees, under hills, in caves, at the way-side. He would not go in to sleep in any house, hovel, or palace.

There was, in the third month, a woman in a town a few miles from Gazul. She was a paid girl of the streets, but clean and pretty and young. When she spoke to him he went with her through the back alleys to her tiny dwelling. He had lain with only one, and that in dreams. This girl was limber and cunning, and scented with jasmine, but although he could rise up and enter her gate, though he could ride her well enough that she sobbed and melted like warm honey, there was no resolution for him. He could not reach it. And at last he pretended, as she herself might normally have done.

She would not presently accept payment, not, she said, because he was a warrior, but because of the pleasure he had given her. She vowed too, on a mighty god, she would tell no one he had lain down with her.

'Tell any you like,' he said. 'Tell them, Coor Krahn had you.'

And then she shrank from his face.

There were never any dreams save the dreams any man might have, save once. Then he did dream, he thought, that far off he saw her – saw *her* – Sas-peth. She was standing up in water, like the sea, the waves shattering round her in white mirrors. But she was a woman only to her hips, and from there she was only a Sword, her female centre locked in steel, impenetrable. And her face was averted from him, and anyway at a distance.

Gazul was closing the gates when he reached them. It was night, but a city night, thick-starred with lit windows and gaudy paper lanterns. He stayed that night, and the following day and night. He entered nowhere, not even an inn. He wandered the streets, the marketplace, and was stared at, and he heard the mutter: *Look! A Sword's Man.* But then he heard them saying, *But whose sword is that? Never his. That old battered black cleaver. What can that be about?*

Of course, this was a city. They were sophisticated and had no manners. Next morning, when the gates were opened, he walked away.

Look! Look! He thought he heard them cheeping. *There he goes into the wasteland. What is he at? Why? Why?*

Oh, I could tell you, he thought.

And then, when he looked back, and Gazul was only a smudge of Sun on the horizon, and the barren Earth, powdered with dust, unrolled before him like existence, he wept. The tears were hard as bits of marble to shed. They tore his eyes and lay salty on his face like blood.

He sat under a lean, crippled tree and crumbled the dry dirt in his fingers.

Coor Krahn recalled the first Sword he ever saw, the Sword in the jade scabbard, when he was nine, at Pigs City. He had learned then that such a blade was always capable of seducing another, man or boy, of leading him on. But she did not then give herself to him. She stayed faithful to her husband. Only his Sword, only Sas-peth Satch, The Woman in Scarlet, had betrayed her bonded warrior.

He thought he might as well sit there, in the dust, under the tree, until he died. He drew the black sword, which was sexless, not even male, and laid it down. Coor told the sword he was sorry and thanked it for its service.

He would bury the sword, it deserved that much. But first Coor Krahn would use it to cut his veins.

However, he had not slept for two nights and two days. He fell asleep before he could pick up the black sword again.

She came to him in the night.

The desert, in the dream, was gilded by faint fires. A round Moon of red amber was nailed in the sky above.

Sas-peth had been brought here apparently in a roofed litter, tasselled and draped with silk, by slaves, and these all waited for her some way off. She wore her scarlet, and many jewels. Her hair was elaborately dressed.

'Coor Krahn,' she said, 'say my name to me.'

He looked at her. He paused, and then said, 'Your name is *The Bitch*.'

Her face did not alter. He had never seen her angry, only stern for battle. While during love, she had been amorous, sly, coaxing. Never passionate, or tender.

'Why are you here?' he said.

'What do you believe the reason might be?'

'To show me he adorns you with silk and jewellery. Does he wear you to war, too, that little boy, Tyo?'

'There are no wars in Tyo's place.'

'Rest there, then. Rest and rust.'

'Shall I come back to you?' she asked, surprising him, jolting his heart to the core. 'What would you do?'

'How can you come back, unless I go and fetch you, Sas-peth? Do you want me to fetch you? Want, then.'

'You will do without me? How?'

He said nothing.

'And now,' she said. 'Imagine I were to say, I am here to show I am ready to be with you again.'

'I would say, Sas-peth, that I won't have you.'

'Even in your dreams? Even as a woman? Even in love?'

It was an awful thing to know, as Coor knew it, that to take to her again would be worse even than when he had been robbed of her.

Coor Krahn, in the dream, shut his eyes and commanded himself: *Wake* now.'

But when he opened his eyes, he was still in the dream with her. And now she stood naked, pale as ivory, her hair combed down and down.

'No, Sas-peth,' he said, 'it was Tyo you wished to have. Fill his dreams, not mine. Let him wear away his spirit on your edge. In all the lands, I never heard a story of one such as you. Did I shame you in combat? Did I fail you? Did I abuse the poor, insult the helpless? Was I a drunkard, a cheat, a coward – was I a weakling or an idiot? Or *unchaste*? Go out of my dream, you whore.'

She turned away. It seemed to him then, in all his dreams of her, she had so often, just like this, turned from him, hiding, masking herself in his trust or his lust. Worse than that, in his respect for her.

'What life will you have,' she said, 'without me?'

'What life indeed?'

'It was a passing desire,' she said, head turned, strands of her fine hair blowing like smoke against the Moon. 'A momentary, weightless thing, to be with that other one, to live another way. But only for a while, a little minute. And perhaps, I tested you.' (He knew she lied.)

Bluntly he said, 'What could he give you?'

'Nothing,' she said softly, the woman Sas-peth.

'And that,' said Coor Krahn, 'is all now you will get from me.'

Then she turned back, and she was beside him, lying against him on the dust, her arms wound round him and her lips on his. 'I have been everything to you,' she said. 'I am your life.'

'So you are. I see it now, Sas-peth. I'd thought I would have to die, and I was wrong in that.'

He held her fast with his left arm, and with his right hand, drew up the old black genderless sword, which had come into the dream with him, as it seemed for this purpose. Coor Krahn drove the sword into her, up through her belly into her heart.

Her head curved back, and she looked at him, his Sword. She looked at him a long while, not speaking, until her eyelids fell like two white petals.

Raising his face from hers, Coor Krahn saw a lion standing on the desert, the red Moon between its ears. Eventually it vanished, but Sas-peth Satch did not. She lay heavy as lead in his arm until he let her go and woke at last.

With sunrise, he buried the black sword, as he had promised.

In the sword-school of Curhm-by-Ocean, he was questioned all the days of three more months, terrible questions on and on, over and over. They examined his dreams too (in none of which did she appear). They drugged him and beat him and starved him and made him drunk. And in the end, when they were sure he had not lied, they made him well again, scoured out like a shell. That day he was brought a new Sword that had been made randomly for him, or for one in his predicament. It was one of only twelve hoarded at any given time, in a secret store against such a need as his own. Coor Krahn was told, and it was the elderly master who told him, so he should grasp it could not be false, that though it had not often come about, the thing which had happened with him, yet, along the years, still it was clandestinely known. He was not the only one to die this death.

The new Sword was male. It had no name, was his to name. It was a slave, not an empress, but a mighty slave, headstrong, gorgeous, and as dangerous as that other slave who might rebel: fire.

Once Coor had come to know it, and wore it at his side, and walked with it, he met it in a dream. In the flesh it was himself, but younger, and a little less, and a little more crazy. It – he – laughed, the new Sword, clowning, amusing Coor. Coor Krahn called it, therefore, Coor's Brother.

Then the master took Coor Krahn half a mile down to a small room in the rock below the School's temple, and showed him a horrible thing, which was a line of narrow vitreous boxes. These were the graves of some twenty-five or twenty-six or seven Swords, mostly broken in pieces. And the last of the metal corpses was Sas-peth Satch. But she was pierced tidily right through, not mutilated. She had kept her glamour. Even ruined, she was beautiful, peerless.

'He sent her here to us,' the master said, 'Lord Tyo Lionay. He found her lying so on his floor one morning. She'd cut him as she fell. He will always carry the scar. He knew enough to want her, and enough to know what had been done. He sent jewels with her, rubies and pearls. Removed, as you see. He begs your forgiveness.'

'He will never have that,' replied Coor Krahn, without interest. Then he said very low, 'But is she dead? Yes. She's dead. I see she is. Sas-peth, better than rubies and pearls.'

The sword shone, even without light. In memory he gazed again at the closing of her petal lids, her smooth hair poured in the dust. He murmured to himself, 'Perhaps.'

THE CHILDREN OF HIS OLD AGE

To John Kaiine-with thanks for this scenario.

Ioll

When he came to live in the valley, at first I hoped that no great strife would result from it, since he was old. Even from the height where I watched him, this much was evident. Aside from anything else, he moved crookedly, limping. Yet, I could see he was strong. His scarred, pitted, olive hide seemed impervious to wounds – but he had the tokens about him his kind have in age. Keeping out of sight, I thought, perhaps he will cause us no real trouble.

There was plenty of game in that valley, I knew this well enough, deer and pig and, on the higher ledges, wild sheep. The broad stream had fish. He could have a pleasant time there, sunning himself, taking life easy, this old one. His dwelling had belonged to others, once, but lain empty some while. He saw to it, making it good for himself in the way they do, dragging in what he wanted, and his mighty treasure hoard, the things his kind gloat over. Old enemy. I hated him, of course, feared him. But I hoped. I hoped for peace. It was not to be. There was fire in him still.

Well, this is a tale, then, of the war that goes ever on between dragons and men.

A month later, I went to visit the Wise Thinker. She resides over the hills, quite a way off. I had not travelled so far in many summers, and in the winter now, I keep at home. But it was autumn yet.

She sat outside her place, on the stone terrace under the crag, in the yellow sunlight. She is old as the hills, but beautiful still. I respectfully inclined my head, and stayed some distance from her, until she indicated I might draw near.

'Greetings, Ioll,' she said. 'What brings you?'

I told her of what had come to live in the valley.

'Indeed,' she said. She moved stiffly, but with grace. Raising her head, she looked up at the clear fall sky. 'I do not smell his smoke,' she said.

It is true; their fires do not smell anything like our own. But did she think she could scent that stench from here? I said, 'There has been not much of that. He keeps warm other ways so far. The dwelling he chose is snug. And he is past his prime, though he has the marks all over him.'

'The marks?' she said. 'Scars got from battle?'

'Yes Thinker. Scars made by warriors such as I once was.'

'But he is old,' she repeated.

'He is not the difficulty,' I said. She nodded, and I seated myself. Then I told her the rest.

Some days after he had installed himself, I had seen that he had young.

Whether they had come with him, and I had missed them, or they had arrived after, also unseen by me, I have no notion. But there they were.

I counted five. Five fierce and strong, leggy males, glossy-skinned with health, savagely playing together below his fastness, on the turf under the changing trees.

They had a look of him. They were more like he was than like each other – perhaps all born of different mothers.

I heard their raw bellowings, and caught the sharp metallic flash as they lightly wounded each other in their game.

After I had told the Wise Thinker this, we sat in silence for some while.

At last she said, 'Ioll, am I right, you have your own sons?'

'A few,' I said. 'They are with their two mothers, in the north or westward.'

'Are they strong, Ioll?'

'Thinker, they are strong – but for this they are much too young.'

I saw her reckoning out the years. She sighed. 'Yes. You are sensible, Ioll.'

I said, 'I do not believe it quite an accident he has come to the valley. This is an empty land, but he knows or senses…'

'His ancient enemies?' she asked, nearly flirtatiously. 'Does he sense *you*, then, Ioll, who have slain so many of his kind?'

'Maybe,' I said. 'I think he would like his sons to cut their teeth on one such as I.'

She rose. Smoothly black, only a little faded, she stood above me. Sometimes her advice is enigmatic, or a riddle. Sometimes outrageous, blatant, or apparently unhelpful.

'Will it be so, then, Ioll?'

'Do you say it should, Thinker?'

'God decreed the war between his kind and ours. We will fight until one of our peoples is ended. You, therefore, or your sons.'

'Am I not too old to fight?' I asked.

'Am I not,' said she, 'too old to counsel you?'

Flenz

It was my mother told me I'd be going to him, that morning, the very day I had to leave.

She called me in from the work I was doing, grinding down the bones by the bone-rock outside. She looked bitter as bad water, as she always did, but worse.

'Well, he wants you.'

'Who wants me?' I was insolent to her now. The days when she used to knock me down, strike me, claw me, were gone. If I wanted I could break her long, ugly neck.

'Your sire.'

That made me pause.

I had heard of him, of course. He was, seemingly, a mighty warrior, victorious over men and beasts. But if he had shown any interest in me, I'd never been aware of it.

'Let him,' I said, 'go wanting.'

'Don't be a fool,' she cried at once. 'Do you think you have a choice? You have no more choice than I had, when he pinned me to the earth and got you on me.'

'I won't go.'

'You'll go. You'll go and grovel and thank him, and call him your master. Is your life so splendid here, doing the tasks none of the others will?'

'Why,' I said, altering my voice, 'does he want me?'

'You're his,' she said.

'He took a while to remember.'

'Now he has. Prepare yourself. You're to leave within the hour.'

And so it was. I gave in quickly. It's no longer my way to make a great fuss over the unavoidable. If there's something I don't like, still I'll usually give in, or seem to. What I think, or mean to do later about this, isn't always so obvious.

Anyhow, it was a long, uninteresting journey, the only good part stopping once, to hunt, through the auburn woods. But finally I reached his lands.

His manner of living was one I'd seen plenty of already. He had his own style, of course. And he was greedy, a tyrant. That was clear from his dwelling, and how he managed it, and everything around. He had laid the country to waste for miles. Trees down, ground dug up, rivers polluted, burned areas crushed too often to grow a single thing anymore.

The moment I set eyes on him, I thought, *One more to hate.*

He was very big, I'm not full-grown, but still as brawny and powerful as many get by twice my age, but he towered. Old, naturally, with a limp, but that seemed to have stopped nothing, only marked him, in passing, like his combat-scars.

'Flenz,' he said, showing me he knew my name. 'Welcome, my son.'

So I lowered my head respectfully. And he clouted me, as if playful, really to show me his vitality and supremacy. He nearly knocked me over.

There were the others I met presently, the other sons. I made out to be pleased. Doubtless so did they. We wrestled and showed off, and he looked happy

That night we feasted. Meat and smoke and fires, the usual. But this time, no one sent me out to see to the bones.

Ioll

During the days of my youth, in such a situation, I would not have made much of a plan, nor consulted with another. With age, that had changed. And I valued my hiding-place on the high hill, from which I could watch my enemy and his brood, unseen.

They have some myth, I suspect, that we are always to be noticed – smelled – that we leave careless evidence of ourselves in every spot we frequent. But this is not so. Or not so of us all, especially those of us who have had to contend with *them*.

However, unseen and careful though I was, my study of them did not cheer me.

In the past, I would already have made my challenge. But now I was unsure. He alone I might deal with, but the young ones, no doubt, would attend him. So I would be, for all my remaining might and my guile, one against six. And those odds, now, did not seem ideal.

After nightfall, and seeing the flames flicker from their habitation among the stones, it did occur to me to go down and try to fire the evil nest entire. But I was not confident enough of my skill in that. Which is not to say I had grown nervous, only prudent. For if I failed, and even one of them escaped – as well they might, for I am not as robust as once I was – then everything could be to do again.

Besides, there is a story they are, being so friendly and extravagant with fire, immune to it. I know that is not always the case. I have seen several examples to the contrary. But some of them, for all I know, may be. And what if these ones were?

Eventually, then, I made a decision. It went against my heart, but there. I thought that I must enlist the help of my sons, though young and untried.

They should not be alone, after all, but with me. I would teach them, stringently, what they must do. If all of them proved able, we should then be six to six.

Flenz

We'd been with him less than a month when he told us what was up.

A couple of them looked scared enough. I admit, a coil of sparks sprang off up my spine, and every inch of me tingled with something – fear, astonishment – *wonder?*

To kill one of those monstrous creatures – those *things*...

'I thought there was nothing like that in this country,' I boldly said to him, my *father*. 'I thought these lands belonged to our kind.'

'Think again,' he said. And cuffed me, but in his most *playful* mode – I only rocked where I stood.

Next day he began to train us.

It was tough, bloody. We got smashed about and no mistake. One of them – my half-brothers – muttered, *'He's worse than an army of them.'* A couple more agreed, secretively – when *he* was near, they fawned.

But to say he was worse was rubbish. *They* and they only, were the true enemy. God decreed the struggle between them and us, a contest for everything, land, water, peace – even riches, for I too had heard of their hoards of gold and jewels – for the whole earth. They were formed in the image of the Devil. Although I hated my father, and mostly everyone I'd met so far of my own people, *they* were the kernel and essence of *all* hates. And they hated us too. Men and dragons – eternal foes – by God's will.

An evening came, and he swaggered before us, and he said, 'You've done well. You're ready. So, it's tomorrow.'

Then we knew it was only one night from us, and tomorrow we would go out to join in war. To the death.

I went up to sleep in my own cramped space, among the others. Aside from me, I didn't know who slept or who didn't, pretending. We hadn't confided much in each other. Or, they didn't in me...

I myself didn't sleep, but lay as if I did. Then I acted coming to, and stumbled off heavily, as if to make water. But that wasn't what I was at.

Outside, the Moon was full, a tawny fall Moon, heavy with the aging year.

I looked around, away. In the lit-up dark, anything might be anything. I chose my path with care.

Ioll

The one who was to take my message north and west, was gone with it, and I had come back to my watching-place. I had been away three days, two nights.

When I peered over and down, their nest was in darkness, just a heap of stone, where I might imagine nothing lived at all, saving the strange look of it.

Although I had sent for my sons, I remained uneasy. I had even told my messenger to state that, if unready, they were not to come. It was a great way for them to travel, besides. Might they even not be strong enough yet for such a journey?

And then, oddly, I thought of the old one's young, how they too were so youthful, and perhaps not ready, and that I should not relish killing them, for it was hard to hate a thing unformed.

Musing on all this, I kept my watch, and then the Moon came up from the valley, growing always whiter as it left the Earth farther and farther below.

I had lifted my head to gaze at the Moon a moment when I heard something moving on the track beneath.

My eyes are older, as all of me is, or I should have seen him before that. My ears too, those years ago, would have detected him long before.

Now he came toward me, stealthy – he thought. Cautious, he thought.

I waited, still as the rocks around.

Flenz

There hadn't been much of worth in my little existence. Nothing very kind, and never beautiful, except, if I'm honest, the world. I mean, what's natural – the woods and hills, the sky – everywhere people haven't touched.

And then, I saw him.

How to explain this. I can't. Yet I have to, since otherwise I'll seem a madman, and worse, a traitor. But maybe I am. Well.

But he was beautiful. Like the world is. Like the starry night. Just like that. Dark and glimmering and still as stone. His great head turned and his eyes, like polished diamonds, were watching me, expecting me.

Although I saw his beauty, that wasn't the first thing I thought of, of course. The first thing was – *terror*. Too afraid even for a prayer to God, too terrified even, strangely, to wet myself. I, too, turned to stone.

What I'd intended was simply to escape. From my father, from his stinking dragon-chase – from all of it. All the cruelties and petty bullyings and big, violent bullyings. I don't know even if I *did* credit the dragons we'd glibly spoken of. I'd gone along with it, had to. Then I'd run off, and I'd thought I could be away over the hills and somewhere else by morning. But now I'd met a dragon on the hill. And it was real as the Moon above.

Then – it breathed. Just the slightest vapour of smoke came from its jaws. But I thought I was dead at once.

No point in lying. My legs gave. I went down flat. I just lay there, smelling the hill grass and thinking nothing but fear.

And then, then he spoke.

I'd never been told this, that they can speak – and they can speak in our language too, the tongue of men. Although it sounds peculiar in their mouths, like something coming through a cave full of water, so for a while I didn't know he was speaking at all, so perhaps that's why no one else had ever known they speak, or informed us of it.

'Get up,' the dragon patiently said to me, for the twentieth time.

'What?' I gabbled.

'Stand. You have no claw. I am not in need of food. Shall I not harm you?'

'Claw – a sword? No, he locks the big weapons up at night. I don't even have a knife, like the others, not of my own.... Not hungry?'

'The valley has food animals,' the dragon said, reasonably.

I was finding it easier to understand him. My fear had vanished – died. His breath was wonderful – like incense. I'd always heard in the songs and tales they reeked.

'Why are you here?' he asked.

I said, 'Running away. Fighting dragons isn't my ambition.' I don't know how I was so coherent now. I'd gone mad, no doubt.

The dragon said, 'You are of mankind, but do not wish to kill a dragon or to see one killed?'

'No.'

'Why is that?'

'I've no quarrel with dragons. I mean, I don't *know* dragons... I...'

He said, 'Then I may be glad to let you live.'

Did he lie? Had I lied? Why did he trust me – why did I trust him? Where had my fear fled to?

He seemed to see into me. Right inside. Not body-mind. History. Every blow, and every blow I'd turned away. My measure. Perhaps I wasn't important.

'You are his son,' the dragon said. 'What of him?'

'They say *he's* killed dragons many times,' I answered. 'That's his fame. I was always hearing about it. He's killed plenty of his own kind, too. I mean other men.'

'And the rest of his young?'

'Young? His other sons, you mean? I don't know. I think they're scared, like me. Of him – of you.'

The dragon said, 'Long ago, men lived in your father's house. They hunted my kind, they slew us, we were driven away. It is God's law.'

'God's law,' I agreed, lamely.

He looked at me with his marvellous eyes. 'I am old,' he said, 'but when your grandsons' grandsons are old, I shall still walk in the world.'

'Yes,' I said.

'Your life is too short to rob you of it.'

The weirdness of all this had gone to my head – or it was the wine from the feast earlier. 'Are we breaking some holy rule?' I asked him. 'I mean, by not fighting?'

'Yes.'

I said, 'Perhaps God isn't a tyrant. Perhaps God is just, and we don't see it. Perhaps God prefers us *not* to fight.'

'Then God must give a sign,' said the dragon. 'For I will let *you* go by. But those others below I must hate and I must kill. And I and my beloved sons may die in the attempt.'

'Don't die,' I said. My voice was nearly pleading, startling me. 'You've said, you're meant to outlive us all.'

But then he turned from me. I was dismissed. Something happened inside me. Again, I can't explain it. But I ran away, over the hill, I ran away into the night, to the next part of my short human life. And yes, before two days had passed, I wondered if I had dreamed it. Until I heard the news from there. And then – then I truly believed in God and dragons – both.

Ioll

To begin with I debated with myself, when he had gone, why I had let him live, that boy, that man-child, young of the old one in the house in the valley. Even though I knew why, and had even told the boy why

I too have sons. I too – am old.

In youth, I had considered them pleasantly, my children. In age they are much more. And even the children of my ravening enemy in the valley – even they.... The Wise Thinker may one day, perhaps, unravel these thoughts for me, or not, depending on her mood, and if her scales have been sufficiently warmed by the Sun.

I let him go, the boy He ran away. But I had seen before he did that, he was no longer afraid of me. No, in his face was that expression, that emotion I have found otherwise only in the faces of my kind, when they bow their heads before one that they revere – and love.

How curious. It puzzles me very much. For it is yet to be war between us, to the end, of this I am certain even now.

Yet, too, I had asked for a sign of something other, and this sign came.

All night I waited there. In the morning, I looked for the usual activities and business in the old enemy's dwelling.

At first they seemed as ever. Then all changed.

There was a loud outcry. The sort of shouting and clamour that might have started if they had distinguished me upon the hill – which they had not. Then the noise died, and the whole place seemed to sink in upon itself, to a silence and a shadow.

I waited on. I watched.

Night came, and then another day. The skies moved, Sun, Moon, and stars, but in the dwelling made of stones, nothing moved at all. And then dawn again broke through the east and showed me the people who had been in the old one's place, spilling out of its openings, and pouring away like a rushing river. They carried their possessions with them, and some of his, too. I saw many of them pulled along chests or sacks, and I heard these clinking, even from the high hill, and caught now and then the glitter of gold. It came to me they robbed him of his hoard of precious things. They took his animals too, the creatures kept for food or riding.

In the end, the habitation appeared empty. Birds flew round, and then they flew away. Evening drew in, then dark. Not a single one of their tame fires burned up.

Thinking of it, what I had seen, how they had deserted that place, I knew that he alone I had not seen emerge from there – he alone, and his five remaining sons.

Then those five boys did come out of the place. I saw them clear in the Moon's light. They ran away and away, just as the other had, the one who climbed the hill. But these other five, they ran in crazy fear – as if followed by nightmares, that was how they ran, though none – nothing – pursued them. I noted plainly enough then, they were not anything to dread. They were afraid amply of men – no dragon-slayers.

But even after this, *he* did not leave his dwelling.

Thereafter the place looked void.

So it has continued.

He must be there, in the pile of it. But he makes no sound, he lights no fires.

Winter has arrived by now, and turned the bare trees white. The stream which curls through the valley is changed to something like the gleaming pale drops that I keep in my own treasure hoard, under the hill. And still, he does nothing in his place of stone, and so I know that he is dead, my enemy, and that peace has returned, for this while.

Just before the whiteness fell, two of my sons reached me. They are lean, limber, perfect. The joy I take in them is beyond all joys, and doubled because I need not risk them so early.

When winter is done, I shall conduct them to the Wise Thinker, so they may learn their secret names. For now I am content. The ordained conflict with mankind – if so it still is – seems far away as that solitary star I see shining, above my enemy's empty house.

Flenz

It was his other sons killed the old man. I heard it in the first town I reached. The market was buzzing with the gossip. Seemingly they were more frightened of meeting a dragon than of him. So they went in a gang and hacked our father to bits in his bed. So much for him. They had made the plot, but not trusted or told me, only hesitating that night until I went out, to put it into action.

God knows what kind of story will get made of all this. Men will say the dragon did it, I should think, killed him, and all of us. What do I care? I've seen a dragon, spoken with him, and lived. And it was he who taught me, when I have sons of my own, to be kind to them. It's the easiest thing in the world to make a life, or to take a life – but to let another alone to *live* – yes, that's the hard thing. It's the thing God does.

THE MAN WHO STOLE THE MOON

A Story of the Flat Earth

As so often from an idea by John Kaiine

Several tales are told concerning the Moon of the Flat Earth. Some say that this Moon, perhaps, was a hollow globe, within which lay lands and seas, having even their own cool Sun. However, there are other stories.

One evening Jaqir, the accomplished thief, rose from a bed of love and said to his mistress. 'Alas, sweetheart, we must now part forever.'

Jaqir's mistress looked at him in surprise and shook out her bright hair. 'You are mistaken. My husband, the old merchant, is miles off again, buying silk and other stuff, and besides suspects nothing. And I am well satisfied with you.'

'Dear heart,' said Jaqir, as he dressed his handsome self swiftly, 'neither of these things is the stumbling block to our romance. It is only this. I have grown tired of you.'

'Tired of me!' cried the lady, springing from the bed.

'Yes, though indeed you are toothsome in all respects, I am inconstant and easily bored. You must forgive me.'

'Forgive you!' screamed the lady, picking up a handy vase.

Jaqir ducked the vase and swung nimbly out of the high window, an action to which he was quite accustomed, from his trade. 'Although a deceiver in my work, honesty in my private life, is always my preferred method,' he added, as he dropped quickly down through the vine to the street below.

Once there he was gone in a flash, and just in time to miss the jar of piddle the lady that moment upended from the window. However, three of the king's guard, next second passing beneath, were not so fortunate.

'A curse upon all bladders!' howled they, wringing out their cloaks and hair. Then, looking up, they beheld the now no-longer mistress of Jaqir, and asked her loudly what she meant by it.

'Pardon me, splendid sirs,' said she. 'The befoulment was not intended for you, but for that devilish thief, Jaqir, who even now runs through that alley there toward a hiding place he keeps in *The House of the Thin Door*.'

At the mention of Jaqir, who was both celebrated and notorious in that city, the soldiers forgot their inconvenience, and gave instant chase. Never before had any been able to lay hands on Jaqir, who, it was said, could steal the egg from beneath a sleeping pigeon. Now, thanks to the enragement of his discarded lover, the guard knew not only of Jaqir's proximity, but his destination. Presently then they came up with him by *The House of the Thin Door*.

'Is it he?'

'So it is, for I have heard, when not in disguise, he dresses like a lord, like this one, and, like this one, his hair is black as a panther's fur.'

At this they strode up to Jaqir and surrounded him.

'Good evening, my friends,' said Jaqir. 'You are fine fellows, despite your smell.'

'That smell is not our own, but the product of a night-jar emptied on us. And the one who did this also told us where to find the thief Jaqir."

'Fate has been kind to you. I will not therefore detain you further.'

'No, it is you who shall be detained.'

'*I*?' asked Jaqir modestly.

But within the hour he discovered himself in chains in the king's dungeons.

'Ah, Jaqir,' said he to himself, 'a life of crime has taught you nothing. For have the gods not always rewarded your dishonesty – and now you are chastised for being truthful.'

Although of course the indifferent, useless gods had nothing to do with any of it.

A month or so later, the king got to hear that Jaqir, the Prince of Thieves, languished in the prison, awaiting trial.

'I will see to it,' said the king. 'Bring him before me.'

So Jaqir was brought before the king. But, despite being in jail, being also what he was, Jaqir had somehow stolen a gold piece from one jailor and gifted it to another, and so arrived in the king's sight certainly in chains, but additionally bathed, barbered, and anointed, dressed in finery, and with a cup of wine in his hand.

Seeing this, the king laughed. He was a young king and not without a sense of the humorous. In addition, he knew that Jaqir, while he had stolen from everyone he might, had never harmed a hair on their heads, while his skills of disguise and escape were much admired by any he had not annoyed.

'Now then, Prince of Thieves, may a mere king invite you to sit? Shall I strike off your chains?' added the king.

'Your majesty,' said one of the king's advisers, 'pray do not unchain him, or he will be away over the roofs. Look, he has already stolen two of my gold rings – and see, many others have lost items.'

This was a fact. All up and down the palace hall, those who had gathered to see Jaqir on trial were exclaiming over pieces of jewellery suddenly missing. And one lady had even lost her little dog, which abruptly, and with a smile, Jaqir let out of an inner compartment in his shirt, though it seemed quite sorry to leave him.

'Then I shall not unchain you,' said the king. 'Restore at once all you have filched.'

Jaqir rose, shook himself somewhat, and an abundance of gold and gems cascaded from his person.

'Regrettably, lord king, I could not resist the chance to display my skills.'

'Rather you should deny your skills. For you have been employed in my city seven years, and lived like the prince you call yourself. But the punishment for such things is death.'

Jaqir's face fell, then he shrugged. He said, 'I see you are a greater thief, sir, than I. For I only presume to rob men of their goods. You are bold enough to burgle me of my life.'

At that the court made a noise, but the king grew silent and thoughtful. Eventually he said, 'I note you will debate the matter. But I do not believe you can excuse your acts.'

'There you are wrong. If I were a beggar calling for charity on the street, you would not think me guilty of anything but ill luck or indigence. Or, if I were a seller of figs, you would not even notice me as I took the coins of men in exchange for my wares.'

'Come,' said the king. 'You neither beg nor sell. You thieve.'

'A beggar,' said Jaqir, 'takes men's money and other alms, and gives nothing in return but a blessing. Please believe me, I heap blessings on the heads of all I rob and thank them in my prayers for their charity. Had I begged it, I might, it is true, not have received so great a portion. How much nobler and blessed are they, then, that they have given over to me the more generous amount? Nor do they give up their coins for nothing. For what they buy of me, when it is *I* who steal from them, is a dramatic tale to tell. And indeed, lord king, have you never heard any boast of how they were robbed by me?'

The king frowned, for now and then he had heard this very thing, some rich noble or other reciting the story of how he had been despoiled of this or that treasure by the nimble Jaqir, the only thief able to take it. And once or twice, there were women, too, who said, 'When I woke, I found my rings were gone, but on my pillow lay a crimson rose. Oh, would he had stayed a while to steal some other prize.'

'I am not,' declared Jaqir, 'a common thief. I purloin from none who cannot afford the loss. I deduct nothing that has genuine sentimental or talismanic weight. I harm none. Besides, I am an artist in what I do. I come and go like a shadow and vanish like the dawn into the day. You will have been told that I can abstract the egg of a pigeon from beneath the sleeping bird and never wake it.'

The king frowned deeply. He said, 'Yet with all this vaunted knack, you did not, till today, leave my dungeons.'

Jaqir bowed. 'That was because, lord king, I did not wish to miss my chance of meeting you.'

'Truly? I think rather it was the bolts and bars and keys, the numerous guards, who granted you wine, but not an open door. You seem a touch pale.'

'Who can tell?' idly answered pale Jaqir.

But the king only said, 'I will go apart and think about all this.'

And so he did, but the court lingered, looking at Jaqir, and some of the ladies and young men came and spoke to him, but trying always not to get near enough to be robbed. Yet even so, now and then, he would courteously hand them back an emerald or amethyst he had removed from their persons.

Meanwhile, the king walked up and down a private chamber where, on pedestals of marble, jewel-coloured parrots sat watching him.

'He is clever,' said the king, 'handsome, well mannered, and decorative. One likes him at once, despite his nefarious career. Why cast such a man out of the state of life? We have callous villains and nonentities enough. Must every shining star be snuffed?'

Then a scarlet parrot spoke to him. 'O king, if you do not have Jaqir executed, they will say you are partial, and not worthy to be trusted with the office of judge.'

'Yes,' said the king, 'this I know.'

At this another parrot, whose feathers shone like a pale-blue sky, also spoke out. 'But if you kill him, O king, men may rather say you were jealous of him. And no king must envy any man.'

'This is also apt,' said the king, pacing about.

Then a parrot spoke, which was greener than jade. 'O king, is Jaqir not a thief? Does he not brag of it? Set him then a test of thieving and make this test as impossible as may be. And say to him, "If you can do this, then indeed your skill is that of a poet, an artist, a warrior, a prince. But if you fail you must die".'

Then the king laughed again. 'Well said. But what test?'

At that a small grey parrot flew from its pedestal, and standing on his shoulder, spoke in the king's ear with a jet-black beak.

The king said, 'O wisest of all my councillors."

In the palace hall, Jaqir sat among the grouped courtiers, being pleasant and easy with them in his chains, like a king. But then the king entered and spoke as follows:

'Now, Jaqir, you may have heard, in my private rooms four angels live, that have taken another form. With these four I have discussed your case. And here is the verdict. I shall set you now a task that, should you succeed at it, must make you a hero and a legend among men – which happy state you will live to enjoy, since also I will pardon all your previous crimes. Such shall be your fame then, that hardly need you try to take anything by stealth. A million doors shall be thrown wide for you, and men will load you with riches, so astonishing will your name have become.'

Jaqir had donned a look of flattering attention.

'The task, then. You claim yourself a paragon among thieves. You must steal that which is itself a paragon. And as you say you have never taken anything which may be really missed, on this occasion I say you will have to thieve something all mankind shall miss and mourn.'

The court stood waiting on the king's words. Jaqir stood waiting, perforce. And all about, as at such times it must, (still must), the world stood waiting, hushing the tongues of sea and wind, the whispers of forests and sands, the thunder of a thousand voiceless things.

'Jaqir, Prince of Thieves, for your life, fly up and steal the Moon from the sky. The task being what it is, I give you a year to do it.'

Nine magicians bound Jaqir. He felt the chains they put on him as he had scarcely felt the other chains of iron, thinking optimistically as he had been, that he would soon be out of them.

But the new chains emerged from a haze of iridescent smokes and a rumble of incantations, and had forms like whips and lions, thorns and bears. Meeting his flesh, they disappeared, but he felt them sink in, painless knives, and fasten on his bones and brain and mind.

'You may go where you wish and do what you will and suffer nothing. But if you should attempt, in any way, to abscond, then you will feel the talons and the fangs of that which has bound you, wrapped gnawing inside your body. And should you persist in your evasion, these restraints shall accordingly devour you from within. Run where you choose, seek what help you may, you will die in horrible agony, and soon. Only when you return to the king, your task accomplished fully, and clearly proven, will these strictures lapse — but that at once. Success, success alone, spells your freedom.'

So then Jaqir was let go, and it was true enough, honesty being the keynote to his tale so far, that he had no trouble, and could travel about as he wanted. Nor did any idea enter his mind concerning escape. Of all he was or was not, Jaqir was seldom a fool. And he had, in the matter of his arrest, surely spent sufficient foolishness to last a lifetime.

Since he was *not* a fool, Jaqir, from the moment the king had put the bargain to him, had been puzzling how he might do what was demanded.

In the past, many difficult enterprises had come Jaqir's way, and he had solved the problem of each. But it is to be remembered, on none of these had his very existence depended. Nor had it been so strange. One thing must be said, too, the world being no longer as then it was, Jaqir did not at any point contest the notion on the grounds that it was either absurd or unconscionable. Plainly sorcery existed, was everywhere about, and seldom doubted. Plainly the

Moon, every night gaudily on show, might be accessible, even to men, for there were legends of such goings on. Thus Jaqir never said to himself: *What madness have I been saddled with?* Only: *How can I effect this extraordinary deed?*

So he went up and down in the city, and later through the landscape beyond, walking mostly, to aid his concentration. Sometimes he would spend the night at an inn or in some rich house he had never professionally bothered, but which had heard of him. And occasionally men did know of him to recognise him, and some knew what had been laid upon him. And unfortunately, the nicest of them would tend to a similar, irritating act. Which was, as the Moon habitually rose in the east, to mock or rant at him, 'Aiee, Jaqir. Have you not stolen her yet?'

Because the Earth was then flat, the Moon journeyed over and around it, dipping after moonset into the restorative seas of chaos that lay beneath the basement of the world. Nor was the Moon of the Flat Earth set very big in circumference (Although the size of the Moon varied, influenced by who told – or tells – the tales).

'What *is* the Moon?' pondered Jaqir at a wayside tavern, sipping sherbet,

'Of what is the Moon *made?*' murmured Jaqir, courting sleep, for novelty, in an olive grove.

'Is it heavy or light? What makes it, or she, glow so vividly? *Is* it a she? How,' muttered Jaqir, striding at evening between fields of silver barley, 'am I to get hold of the damnable thing?'

Just then the Moon wilfully and unkindly rose again, unstolen, over the fields. Jaqir presently lay down on his back among the barley stalks, gazing up at her as she lifted herself higher and higher. Until at length she reached the apex of heaven, where she seemed for a while to stand still, like one white lily on a stem of stars.

'Oh, Moon of my despair,' said Jaqir softly, 'I fear I shall not master this riddle. I would do better to spend my last year of life – of which I find only nine months remain! – in pleasure, and forget the hopeless task.'

At that moment, Jaqir heard the stalks rustling a short way off, and sitting up, he saw through the darkness how two figures wandered between the barley. They were a young man and a girl, and from their conduct, lovers in search of a secret bed. With a rueful nod at the ironies of Fate, Jaqir got up and meant to go quietly away. But just then he heard the maiden say, 'Not here, the barley is trampled, we must lie where the stalks are thicker, or we may be heard.'

'Heard?' asked the youth. 'There is no one about.'

'Not up in the fields,' replied the girl, 'but down *below* the fields the demons may be listening in the Underearth.'

'Ho,' said the youth, (another fool), 'I do not believe in demons.'

'Hush! They exist and are powerful. They love the world by night, as they must avoid the daylight, and like moonlit nights especially, for they are enamoured of the Moon, and have made ships and horses with wings in order to reach it. And they say, besides, the nasty magician, Paztak, who lives only a mile along the road from this very place, is nightly visited by the demon Drin, who serve him in return for disgusting rewards.'

By now the lovers were a distance off, and only Jaqir's sharp ears had picked up the ends of their talk, after which there was silence, save for the sound of moonlight dripping on the barley. But Jaqir went back to the road. His face had become quite purposeful, and perhaps even the Moon, since she watched everything so intently, saw that too.

Now Paztak the magician did indeed live nearby, in his high, brazen tower, shielded by a thicket of tall and not ordinary laurels. Hearing a noise of breakage among these, Paztak undid a window and peered down at Jaqir who stood below with drawn knife.

'What are you at, unruly felon?' snapped Paztak.

'Defending myself, wise sir, as your bushes bite.'

'Then leave them alone. My name is Paztak the Unsociable. Be off, or I shall conjure worse things – to attack you.'

'Merciful mage, my life is in the balance. I seek your help and must loiter till you give it.'

The mage clapped his hands, and three yellow, slavering dogs leaped from thin air and also tried to tear Jaqir into bite-size pieces. But avoiding them, Jaqir sprang at the tower and since he was clever at such athletics, began climbing up it.

'Wretch!' howled Paztak.

And then Jaqir found a creature, part wolverine and part snake, had roped the tower and was striving to wind him as well in its coils. But Jaqir slid free, kicked shut its clashing jaws, and vaulted over its head onto Paztak's windowsill.

'Consider me desperate rather than impolite.'

'I consider you *elsewhere*,' remarked Paztak with a new and ominous calm.

Next instant Jaqir found himself in a whirlwind, which turned him over and over, and cast him down at last in the depths of a forest.

'So much for the mage.' said Jaqir wiping snake-wolverine, dog and laurel saliva from his boots. 'And so much for me. I have had, in my life, an unfair quantity of good luck, and evidently it is all used up.'

'Now, now,' said a voice from the darkness, 'let me get a proper look at you, and see if it is.'

From the shadows shouldered out a dwarf of such incredible hideousness that he might be seen to possess a kind of beauty.

Staring in awe at him, then, from his appearance, and the fabulous jewellery with which he was adorned, Jaqir knew him for a Drin.

'Now now,' repeated the Drin, whose coal-black, luxuriant hair swept the forest floor. And he struck a light by the simple means of running his talonous nails – which were painted indigo – along the trunk of a tree. Holding up his now flaming hand, the Drin inspected Jaqir, gave a leer and smacked his lips. 'Handsome fellow,' said the Drin. 'What will you offer me if I assist you?'

Jaqir knew a little of the Drin, the lowest caste of demonkind, who were metalsmiths and artisans of impossible and supernatural ability. He knew too, as the girl had said, that the Drin required, in exchange for any service to mortals, recompense frequently of a censorable nature. Nor did this Drin seem an exception to the rule.

'Estimable sir,' said Jaqir 'did you suppose I needed assistance?'

'I have no doubt of it,' said the Drin. 'Sometimes I visit the old pest Paztak and was just now idling in his garden, in chat with a most fascinating woodlouse, when I heard your entreaties, and soon beheld you hurled into this wood. Thinking you more interesting than the mage, I followed. And here I am. What would you have?'

'What would *you* have?' asked Jaqir uneasily.

'Nothing you are not equipped to give.'

'Well,' said Jaqir resignedly, 'we will leave that for the moment. Let we first see if you are as cunning as the stories say.' And Jaqir thought, pragmatically. *After all, what is a little foul and horrible dreadfulness if it will save me death?*

165

Then he told the Drin of the king's edict, and how he, Jaqir the thief, must thieve the Moon.

When he had done speaking, the Drin fell to the ground and rolled amid the fern, laughing, and honking like a goose, in the most repellent manner.

'You cannot do it.' assumed Jaqir.

The Drin arose, and shook out his collar and loin-guard of rubies.

'Know me. I am Yulba, pride of my race, revered even among our demonic high castes of Eshva and Vazdru. Yulba, that the matchless lord, Azhrarn the Beautiful, has petted seven hundred times during his walkings up and down in the Underearth.'

'You are to be envied,' said Jaqir prudently. He had heard too – as who had not? – tales about the demons, of the Prince of Demons, Azhrarn. 'But that does not mean you are able to assist me.'

'Pish,' said the Drin. 'It is a fact, no mortal thing, not even the birds of the air might lie so high as the Moon, let alone any *man* essay it. But I am Yulba. What cannot Yulba do?'

Three nights Jaqir waited in the forest for Yulba to return. On the third night Yulba appeared out of the trunk of a cedar tree, and after him he hauled a loose, glimmering, almost-silky bundle, that clanked and clacketed as it came.

'Thus,' said the Drin and threw it down.

'What is that?'

'Have you no eyes? A carpet I have created, with the help of some elegant spinners of the eight-legged sort, but reinforced with metals fashioned by myself. Everything as delicate as the wings of bees, strong as the scales of dragons. Imbued by me with spells and vapours of the Underearth, as it is,' bragged on the Drin, 'the carpet is sorcerous, and will naturally fly. Even as far as the gardens of the stars, from where, though a puny mortal, you may then inspect your quarry, the Moon.'

Jaqir, himself an arch-boaster, regarded Yulba narrowly. But then, Jaqir thought, a boaster might also boast truthfully, as he had himself. So as Yulba undid the carpet and spread it out, Jaqir walked on there. The next second Yulba also bounded aboard. At which the carpet, with no effort, rose straight up between the trees of the forest and into the sky of night.

'Now what do you say?' prompted the Drin.

All the demon race were susceptible to flattery. Jaqir spoke many winning sentences of praise, all the while being careful to keep the breadth of the carpet in between them.

Up and up the carpet flew. It was indeed very lovely, all woven of blue metals and red metals, and threaded by silk, and here and there set with countless tiny diamonds that spangled like the stars themselves.

But Jaqir was mostly absorbed by the view of the Earth he now had. Far below, itself like a carpet, unrolled the dark forest and then the silvery fields, cut by a river-like black mirror. And as they flew higher yet, Jaqir came to see the distant city of the king, like a flower garden of pale lights, and farther again, lay mountains, and the edges of another country. 'How small,' mused Jaqir, 'has been my life. It occurs to me the gods could never understand men's joy or tribulation, for from the height of their dwelling, how tiny we are to them, less than ants.'

'Ants have their own recommendations,' answered Yulba.

But the Moon was already standing high in the eastern heaven, still round in appearance, and sheerest white as only white could be.

No command needed be given the carpet. Obviously Yulba had already primed it to its destination. It now veered and soared, straight as an arrow, toward the Moon, and as it did so. Jaqir felt the tinsel roots of the lowest stars brush over his forehead.

And what was the Moon of the Flat Earth that it might be approached and flown about on a magic carpet? It was, as has been said, maybe a globe containing other lands, but also it was said to be not a globe at all, but, like the Earth itself, a flat disk, yet placed sidelong in the sky and presenting always a circular wheel of face to the world. And that this globe or disk altered its shape was due to the passage of its own internal sun now lighting a quarter or a half or a whole of it – or, to the interference of some invisible body coming between it and some other invisible light, or to the fact that the Moon was simply a skittish shape-changer, making itself now round, and now a sliver like the paring of a nail.

As they drew ever nearer, Jaqir learned one thing, which in the many stories is a constant, that heat came from the Moon. But (in Jaqir's story) it was an appealing heat, quite welcome in the chilly upper sky. Above, the stars hung, some of them quite close, and they were of all types of shape and shade, all brilliant, but some blindingly so. Of the closer ones, their sparkling roots trailed as if floating in a pond, nourished on some unknown substance. While below, the world seemed only an enormous smudge.

The Drin himself, black eyes glassy, was plainly enraptured by the Moon. Jaqir was caught between wonder and speculation.

Soon enough, the vast luminescence enveloped them, and the heat of the Moon was now like that of a summer morning. Jaqir estimated that the disk might be only the size of a large city, so in his story that is the size of the Moon.

But Jaqir, as the carpet began obediently to circle round the lunar orb, gazed at it with a proper burglar's care. Soon he could make out details of the surface, which was like nothing so much as an impeccable plate of white porcelain, yet here and there cratered, perhaps by the infrequent fall of a star. And these craters had a dim blue ghostly sheen, like that of a blue beryl.

When the carpet swooped yet nearer in, Jaqir next saw that the plate of the moon had actually a sort of landscape, for there were kinds of smooth, low, blanched hills, and here and there something which might be a carven water-course, though without any water in it. And there were also strewn boulders, and other stones, which must be prodigious in girth, but they were all like the rarest pearls.

Jaqir was seized by a desire to touch the surface of the hot, white Moon.

He voiced this.

Yulba scowled, disturbed in his rapturous trance. 'Oh, ignorant man, even my inspired carpet may go no closer, or the magnetic pull of the Moon will tug and we crash down there.'

As he spoke, they passed slowly around the globe, and began moving across the *back* of the Moon, which, until that minute, few mortals had ever seen.

This side lay in a deep violet shadow, turned from the Earth, and tilted upward somewhat at the vault of the sky. It was cooler here, and Jaqir fancied he could hear a strange sound, like harps playing softly, but nothing was to be seen. His hands itched to have something away.

'Peerless Yulba, in order to make a plan of assault, I shall need to get, for reference, some keepsake of the Moon.'

'You ask too much,' grumbled Yulba.

'Can you not do it? But you are *Yulba,*' smarmed Jaqir, 'lord among Drin, favourite of the Prince of Demons. What is there Yulba *cannot* do? And, I thought we were to be friends...'

Yulba cast a look at Jaqir, then the Drin frowned at the Moon with such appalling ugliness, Jaqir turned his head.

'I have a certain immense power over stones,' said the Drin. 'seeing my kind work with them. If I can call you a stone from the Moon, what is it worth?'

Jaqir, who was not above the art of lying either, lied imaginatively at some length, until Yulba lumbered across the carpet and seemed about to demonstrate affection. 'Not however,' declared Jaqir. 'any of this, until my task is completed. Do you expect me to be able to concentrate on such events, when my life still hangs by a thread?'

Yulba withdrew once more to the carpet's border. He began a horrible whistling, which set on edge not only Jaqir's teeth but every bone in his body. Nevertheless, in a while, a single pebble, only about the size of an apricot, came flying up and struck Yulba in the eye.

'See – I am blinded!' screeched Yulba, thrashing on the carpet, but he was not. Nor would he then give up the pebble. But soon enough, as their transport – which by now was apparently tiring – sank away from the Moon, Jaqir rolled a moment against the Drin as if losing his balance. Thereafter the moon-pebble was in Jaqir's pocket.

What a time they had been on their travels. Even as the carpet hopped, wearily and bumpily now, toward the Earth, a blossoming of rose-pink appeared in the east.

This pretty sight, of course, greatly upset Yulba, for demons feared the Sun, and with good reason; it could burn them to ashes.

'Down, down, make haste, accursed flea-bag of a carpet!' ranted he, and so they rapidly fell, and next landed with a splashy thump in a swamp, from which green monkeys and red parakeets erupted at their arrival.

'I shall return at dusk. Remember what I have risked for you!' growled Yulba.

'It is graven on my brain.'

Then the Drin vanished into the ground, taking with him the carpet. The Sun rose, and the amazing Moon, now once more far away, faded and set like a dying lamp.

By midday Jaqir had forced a path from the swamp. He sat beneath a mango tree and ate some of the ripe fruit, and stared at the moon-pebble. It shone, even in the daylight, like a milky flame. 'You are more wonderful than anything I have ever thieved. But still I do not see how I can rob the sky of that other jewel, the Moon.'

Then he considered, for one rash moment, running away. And the safeguarding bonds of the king's magicians twanged around his skeleton. Jaqir desisted and lay back to sleep.

In sleep, a troop of tormentors paraded.

The cast-off mistress who had betrayed him slapped his face with a wet fish. Yulba strutted, seeming hopeful. Next came men who cried, 'Of what worth is this stupid Jaqir, who has claimed he can steal an egg from beneath a sleeping bird?'

Affronted in his slumber, Jaqir truthfully replied that he had done that very thing. But the mockers were gone.

In the dream, then, Jaqir sat up, and looked once more at the shining pebble lying in his hand.

'Although I might steal a million eggs from beneath a million birds, what use to try for this? I am doomed and shall give in.'

Just then something fluttered from the mango tree, which was also there in the dream. It was a small grey parrot. Flying down, it settled directly upon the opalescent stone in Jaqir's palm and put out its light.

'Well, my fine bird, this is no egg for you to hatch.'

The parrot spoke: 'Think Jaqir, what you see, and what you say.'

Jaqir thought. 'Is it possible?'

And at that he woke a second time.

The Sun was high above, and over and over across it and the sky, birds flew about, distinct as black writing on the blue.

'No bird of the air can fly so high as the Moon.' said Jaqir. He added, 'but the Drin have a mythic knack with magical artefacts and clockworks.'

Later, the Sun lowered itself and went down. Yulba came bouncing from the ground, coyly clad in extra rubies, with a garland of lotuses in his hair.

'Now now,' commenced Yulba, lurching forward.

Sternly spoke Jaqir, 'I am not yet at liberty, as you are aware. However, I have a scheme. And knowing your unassailable wisdom and authority, only you, the mighty Yulba, best and first among Drin, can manage it.'

In Underearth it was an exquisite dusk. It was always dusk there, or a form of dusk. As clear as day in the upper world, it was said, yet more radiantly sombre. Sunless, naturally, for the reasons given above.

Druhim Vanashta, the peerless city of demonkind, stretched in a noose of shimmering non-solar brilliance, out of which pierced, like needles, chiselled towers of burnished steel and polished corundum, domes of faceted crystal. While about the gem-paved streets and sable parks strolled or paced or strode or lingered, the demons. Night-black of hair and eye, snow-frozen-white of complexion, the high-caste Vazdru and their mystic servants, the Eshva. All of whom were so painfully beautiful, it amounted to an insult.

Presently, along an avenue, there passed Azhrarn, Prince of Demons, riding a black horse, whose mane and tail was hyacinth blue. And if the beauty of the Eshva and Vazdru amounted to an insult, that of Azhrarn was like the stroke of death

He seemed himself idle enough, Azhrarn. He seemed too musing on something as he slowly rode, oblivious, it appeared, to those who bowed to the pavement at his approach, whose eyes had spilled, at sight of him, looks of adoration. They were all in love with Azhrarn.

A voice spoke from nowhere at all.

'Azhrarn, Lord Wickedness, you gave up the world, but the world does not give up you. Oh Azhrarn, Master of Night, what are the Drin doing by their turgid lake, hammering and hammering?'

Azhrarn had reined in the demon horse. He glanced leisurely about.

Minutes elapsed. He too spoke, and his vocality was like the rest of him. 'The Drin do hammer at things. That is how the Drin pass most of eternity.'

'Yet how,' said the voice, 'do *you* pass eternity, Lord Wickedness?'

'Who speaks to me?' softly said Azhrarn.

The voice replied. 'Perhaps merely yourself, the part of you that you discard, the part of you which yearns after the world.'

'Oh,' said Azhrarn. 'The world.'

The voice did not pronounce another syllable, but along an adjacent wall a slight mark appeared, rather like a scorch.

Azhrarn rode on. The avenue ended at a park, where willows of liquid amber let down their watery resinous hair, to a mercury pool, black peacocks with seeing eyes of turquoise and emerald in their tails, turned their heads and all their feathers to gaze at him.

From between the trees came three Eshva, who obeised themselves.

'What,' said Azhrarn, 'are the Drin making by their lake?'

The Eshva sighed voluptuously. The sighs said, (for the Eshva never used ordinary speech), 'The Drin are making metal birds.'

'Why?' said Azhrarn.

The Eshva grew downcast; they did not know. Melancholy enfolded them among the tall black grasses of the lawn, and then one of the Vazdru princes came – walking through the garden.

'Yes?' said Azhrarn.

'My Prince, there is a Drin who was to fashion for me a ring, which he has neglected,' said the Vazdru. 'He is at some labour for a human man he is partial to. They are *all* at this labour.'

Azhrarn, interested, was, for a moment, more truly revealed. The garden waxed dangerously brighter, the mercury in the pool boiled. The amber hardened and the peacocks shut every one of their four hundred and fifty eyes.

'Yes?' Azhrarn murmured again.

'The Drin, who is called Yulba, has lied to them all. He has told them you yourself, my matchless lord, require a million clockwork birds that can fly as high as the Earth's Moon. Because of *this,* they work ceaselessly. This Yulba is a nuisance. When he is found out, they will savage him, and then bury him in some cavern, walling it up with rocks, leaving him there a million years for his million birds. And so I shall not receive my ring.'

Azhrarn smiled. Cut by the smile, as if by the slice of a sword, leaves scattered from the trees. It was suddenly autumn in the garden. When autumn stopped, Azhrarn had gone away.

Chang-thrang went the Drin hammers by the lake outside Druhim Vanashta. *Whirr* and *pling* went the uncanny mechanisms of half-formed, sorcerous birds of cinnabar, bronze, and iron. Already-finished sorcerous birds hopped and flapped about the lakeshore, frightening the beetles and snakes. Mechanical birds flew over in curious formations, like demented swallows, darkening the Underearth's gleaming day-dusk, now and then letting fall droppings of a peculiar sort.

Eshva came and went, drifting on Vazdru errands. Speechless inquiries wafted to the Drin caves: Where is the necklace of rain vowed for the Princess Vasht? Where is the singing book reserved for the Prince Hazrond?

'We are busy elsewhere at Azhrarn's order,' chirped the Drin.

They were all dwarfs, all hideous, and each one lethal, ridiculous, and a genius. Yulba strode among them, criticising their work, so now and then there was also a fight for the flying omnipresent birds to unburden their bowels upon.

How had Yulba fooled the Drin? He was no more Azhrarn's favourite than any of them. All the Drin boasted as Yulba had. Perhaps it was only this: Turning his shoulder to the world of mankind, Azhrarn had forced the jilted world to pursue him underground. In ways both graphic and insidious, the rejected one permeated Underearth. *Are you tired of me?* moaned the world to Azhrarn. *Do you hate me? Do I bore you? See how inventive I am. See how I can still ensnare you fast.*

But Azhrarn did not go to the noisy lake. He did not summon Yulba. And Yulba, puffed with his own cleverness, obsessively eager to hold Jaqir to his bargain, had forgotten all accounts have a reckoning.

Chung-clunk went the hammers. *Brakk* went the thick heads of the Drin, banged together by critical, unwise Yulba.

Then at last the noise ended.

The hammering and clamouring were over.

Of the few Vazdru who had come to stare at the birds, less than a few remarked that the birds had vanished.

The Drin were noted skulking about their normal toil again, constructing wondrous jewellery and toys for the upper demons. If they waited breathlessly for Azhrarn to compliment them on their bird-work, they did so in vain. But such omissions had happened in the past, the never-ceasing past-present-future of Underearth.

Just as they might have pictured him, Azhrarn stood in a high window of Druhim Vanashta, looking at his city of needles and crystals.

Perhaps it was seven mortal days after the voice had spoken to him. Perhaps three months.

He heard a sound within his mind. It was not from his city, nor was it unreal, nor actual. Presently he sought a magical glass that would show him the neglected world.

How ferocious, the stars, how huge and cruelly glittering, like daggers. How they exalted, unrivalled now.

The young king went one by one to all the windows of his palace. Like Azhrarn miles below, (although he did not know it), the young king looked a long while at his city, But mostly he looked up into the awful sky.

Thirty-three nights had come and gone, without the rising of the Moon.

In the king's city there had been at first shouts of bewildered amazement, then prayers. Then, a silence fell, which was as loud as screaming.

If the world had lost the Sun, the world would have perished and died. But losing the Moon, it was as if the soul of this world had been put out.

Oh, those black nights, blacker than blackness, those yowling spikes of stars dancing in their vitriolic glory – which gave so little light.

What murders and rapes and worse crimes were committed under cover of such a dark? As if a similar darkness had been called up from the mental guts of mankind, like subservient to like. While, earth-over, priests offered to the gods, who never noticed.

The courtiers who had applauded, amused, the judgment of the witty young king, now shrank from him. He moved alone through the excessively lamped and benighted palace, wondering if he was now notorious through all the world for his thoughtless error. And so wondering, he entered the room where, on their marble pedestals, perched his angels.

'What have you done?' said the king.

Not a feather stirred. Not an eye winked.

'By the gods – may they forgive me – what? What did you make *me* do?'

'*You* are king.' said the scarlet parrot. 'It is your word, not ours, which is law.'

And the blue parrot said, 'We are parrots, why name us angels? We have been taught to speak, that is all. What do you expect?'

And the jade parrot said, 'I forget now what it was you asked of us.' And put its head under its wing.

Then the king turned to the grey parrot. 'What do you have to say? It was your final advice which drove me to demand the Moon be stolen – as if I thought any man might do it.'

'King,' said the grey parrot, 'it was your sport to call four parrots, angels. Your sport to offer a man an impossible task as the alternative to certain death. You have lived as if living is a silly game. But you are mortal, and a king.'

'You shame me,' said the king.

'We are, of course.' said the grey parrot, 'truly angels, disguised. To shame men is part of our duty.'

'What must I do?'

The grey parrot said. 'Go down, for Jaqir, Thief of Thieves, has returned to your gate. And he is followed by his shadow.'

'Are not all men so followed?' asked the king perplexedly.

The parrot did not speak again.

Let it be said, Jaqir, who now entered the palace, between the glaring, staring guards of the king, was himself in terrible awe at what he had achieved. Ever since succeeding at his task, he had not left off trembling inwardly. However, outwardly he was all smiles, and in his best attire.

'See, the wretch's garments are as fine as a lord's. His rings are gold. Even his shadow looks well-dressed! And this miscreant it is who has stolen the Moon and ruined the world with blackest night.'

The king stood waiting, with the court about him.

Jaqir bowed low. But that was all he did, after which *he* stood waiting, meeting the king's eyes with his own.

'Well,' said the king. 'It seems you have done what was asked of you.'

'So it does seem,' said Jaqir calmly.

'Was it then easy?'

'As easy,' said Jaqir, 'as stealing an egg.'

'But?' said the king. He paused, and a shudder ran over the hall a shuddering of men and women, and also of the flames in all the countless lamps.

'But?' pressed haughty Jaqir,

'It might be said by some, that the Moon – which is surely not an egg – has disappeared, and another that you may have removed it. After all,' said the king stonily, 'if one assumes the Moon may he

175

pilfered at all, how am I to be certain the robber is yourself? Maybe others are capable of it. Or, too, a natural disaster has simply overcome the orb, a coincidence most convenient for you.'

'Sir,' said Jaqir, 'were you not the king, I would answer you in other words that I do. But king you are. And I have proof.'

And then Jaqir took out from his embroidered shirt the moon-pebble, which even in the light of the lamps blazed with a perfect whiteness. And so like the Moon it was for radiance that many at once shed tears of nostalgia on seeing it. While at Jaqir's left shoulder, his night-black shadow seemed for an instant also to flicker with fire.

As for the king, now he trembled too. But like Jaqir, he did not show it.

'Then,' said the king, 'be pardoned of your crimes. You have surmounted the test and are directly loosed from those psychic bonds my magicians set on you, therefore entirely physically at liberty, and besides, a legendary hero. One last thing…'

'Yes?' asked Jaqir.

'Where have you put it?'

'What?' said Jaqir, rather stupidly.

'That which you stole.'

'It was not a part of our bargain, to tell you this. You have seen by the proof of this stone I have got the Moon. Behold, the sky is black.'

The king said quietly, 'You do not mean to keep it.'

'Generally, I do keep what I take.'

'I will give you great wealth, Jaqir, which I think anyway you do not need, for they say you are as rich as I. Also, I will give you a title to rival my own. You can have what you wish. Now swear you will return the Moon to the sky.'

Jaqir lowered his eyes. 'I must consider this.'

'Look,' they whispered, the court of the king, 'even his shadow listens to him.'

Jaqir, too, felt his shadow listening at his shoulder.

He turned, and found the shadow had eyes.

Then the shadow spoke, more quietly than the king, and not one in the hall did not hear it. While every flame in every lamp spun like a coin, died, revived, and continued burning upside down.

'King, you are a fool. Jaqir, you are another fool. And who and what am I?'

176

Times had changed. There are always stories, but they are not always memorised. Only the king, and Jaqir the thief, had the understanding to plummet to their knees. And they cried as one, *'Azhrarn!'*

'Walk upon the terrace with me,' said Azhrarn. 'We will admire the beauty of the leaden night.'

The king and Jaqir found that they got up, and went onto the terrace, and no one else stirred, not even hand or eye.

Around the terrace stood some guards like statues. At the terrace's centre stood a chariot that seemed constructed of black and silver lava, and drawn by similarly laval dragons.

'Here is our conveyance,' said Azhrarn, charmingly. 'Get in.'

In they got, the king and the thief. Azhrarn also sprang up, and took and shook the reins of the dragons, and these great ebony lizards hissed and shook out in turn their wings, which clapped against the black night and seemed to strike off bits from it. Then the chariot dove up into the air, shaking off the Earth entire, and green sparks streamed from the chariot-wheels.

Neither the king nor Jaqir had stamina – or idiocy – enough to question Azhrarn. They waited meekly as two children in the chariot's back, gaping now at Azhrarn's black eagle wings of cloak, that every so often buffeted them, almost breaking their ribs, or at the world falling down and down below like something dropped.

But then, high in the wild, tipsy-making upper air, Jaqir did speak, if not to Azhrarn.

'King, I tricked you. I did not steal the Moon.'

'Who then stole it?'

'No one.'

'A riddle.'

At which they saw Azhrarn had partly turned. They glimpsed his profile, and a single eye that seemed more like the night than the night itself was. And they shut their mouths.

On raced the dragons.

Below raced the world.

Then everything came to a halt. Combing the sky with claws and wheels, dragons and chariot stood static on the dark.

Azhrarn let go the jewellery reins.

All around spangled the stars. These now appeared less certain of themselves. The brighter ones had dimmed their glow, the lesser hid behind the vapours of night. Otherwise, everywhere lay blackness, only that.

In the long, musician's fingers of the Prince of Demons was a silver pipe, shaped like some sort of slender bone. Azhrarn blew upon the pipe.

There was no sound, yet something seemed to pass through the skulls of the king and of Jaqir, as if a barbed thread had been pulled through from ear to ear. The king swooned – he was only a king. Jaqir rubbed his temples and stayed upright – he was a professional of the working classes.

And so it was Jaqir who saw, in reverse, that which he had already seen happen the other way about.

He beheld a black cloud rising, (where before it had settled), and behind the cloud, suddenly something incandescent blinked and dazzled. He beheld how the cloud, breaking free of these blinks of palest fire, (where before it had obscured said fire), ceased to be one entity, and became instead one million separate flying pieces. He saw, as he had seen before when first they burst up from the ground in front of him, and rushed into the sky, that these were a million curious birds. They had feathers of cinnabar and bronze, sinews of brass; they had clockworks of iron and steel.

Between the insane, crowded battering of their wings, Jaqir watched the Moon reappear, where previously, (scanning the night, as he stood by Yulba in a meadow), he had watched the Moon *put out*, all the birds flew down against her, covering and smothering her. Unbroken by their landing on her surface, they had roosted there, drawn to and liking the warmth, as Yulba had directed them with his sorcery.

But now Azhrarn had negated Yulba's powers – which were little enough among demons. The mechanical birds swarmed round and round the chariot, aggravating the dragons somewhat. The birds had no eyes, Jaqir noticed. They gave off great heat where the Moon had toasted their metals. Jaqir looked at them as if for the first, hated them, and grew deeply embarrassed.

Yet the Moon – oh, the Moon. Uncovered and alight, how brilliantly it or she blazed now. Had she ever been so bright? Had her sojourn in darkness done her good?

End to end, she poured her flame over the Earth below. Not a mountain that did not have its spire of silver, not a river its highlight of diamond. The seas lashed and struggled with joy, leaping to catch her snows upon the crests of waves and dancing dolphin. And in the windows of mankind, the lamps were doused, and like the waves, men leaned upward to wash their faces in the Moon.

Then gradually, a murmur, a thunder, a roar, a gushing sigh rose, swirling from the depths of the Flat Earth, as if at last the world had stopped holding its breath.

'What did you promise Yulba,' asked Azhrarn of Jaqir, mild as a killing frost, 'in exchange for this slight act?'

'The traditional favour,' muttered Jaqir.

'Did he receive payment?'

'I prevaricated. Not yet, lord Prince.'

'You are spared, then. Part of his punishment shall be permanently to avoid your company. But what punishment for you, thief? And what punishment for your king?'

Jaqir did not speak. Nor did the king, though he had recovered his senses.

Both men were educated in the tales, the king more so. Both men turned ashen, and the king accordingly more ashen.

Then Azhrarn addressed the clockwork birds in one of the demon tongues, and they were immediately gone. And only the white banner of the moonlight was there across the night.

Now Azhrarn, by some called also Lord of Liars, was not perhaps above lying in his own heart. It seems so. Yet maybe tonight he looked upon the Moon, and saw in the Moon's own heart, the woman that once he had loved, the woman who had been named for the Moon. Because of her, and all that had followed, Azhrarn had turned his back upon the world – or attempted to turn it.

And even so here he was, high in the vault of the world's heaven, drenched in earthly moonshine, contemplating the chastisement of mortal creatures whose lives, to his immortal life, were like the green sparks which had flashed and withered on the chariot-wheels.

The chariot plunged. The atmosphere scalded at the speed of its descent. It touched the skin of the Earth more slightly than a cobweb. The mortal king and the mortal thief found themselves rolling away downhill, toward fields of barley and a river. The chariot, too, was gone. Although in their ears as they rolled, equal in their rolling as never before, and soon never to be again, king and thief heard Azhrarn's extraordinary voice, which said, 'Your punishment you have already. You are human. I cannot improve upon that.'

Thus, the Moon shone in the skies of night, interrupted only by an infrequent cloud. The king resumed his throne. The four angels – who were or were not parrots – or only meddlers – sat on their perches waiting to give advice, or to avoid giving it. And Jaqir, Jaqir went away to another city.

Here, under a different name, he lived on his extreme wealth, in a fine house with gardens. Until one day he was robbed of all his gold, (and even of the moon-pebble), by a talented thief. 'Is it the gods who exact their price at last, or another, who dwells farther down?'

But by then Jaqir was older, for mortal lives moved and move swiftly. He had lost his taste for his work by then. So he returned to the king's city, and to the door of the merchant's wife who had been his mistress.

'I am sorry for what I said to you,' said Jaqir.

'I am sorry for what I did to you,' said she.

The travelling merchant had recently departed on another, more prolonged journey, to make himself, reincarnation-wise, a new life after death. Meanwhile, though the legend of a moon-thief remained, men had by then forgotten Jaqir. So he married the lady and they existed not unhappily, which shows their flexible natures.

But miles below, Yulba did not fare so well.

For Azhrarn had returned to the Underearth on the night of the Moon's rescue, and said to him, 'Bad little Drin. Here are your million birds. Since you are so proud of them, be one of them.' And in this way Azhrarn demonstrated that the world no longer mattered to him a jot, only his own kind mattered enough that he would make their lives Hell-under-Earth. Or, so it would seem.

But Yulba had changed to a clockwork bird, number one million and one. Eyeless, still able to see, flapping over the melanic vistas of the demon country, blotting up the luminous twilight, cawing, clicking, letting fall droppings, yearning for the warmth of the Moon, yearning to be a Drin again, yearning for Azhrarn, and for Jaqir – who by that hour had already passed himself from the world, for demon time was not the time of mortals.

As for the *story*, that of Jaqir and Yulba and the Moon, it had become as it had and has become, or un-become. And who knows but that, in another little while, it will be forgotten, as most things are. Even the Moon is no longer *that* Moon, nor the Earth, nor the sky. The centuries fly, eternity is endless.

Moonblind

His mother kept the inn, and he was a child when he saw it first. The Hunt. Evading his chores, he had escaped into a high loft, from where he found it easy enough to climb out onto the roof. He lay along the thatch, looking down into the stony yard before the inn-house. Sunset had begun, the sky that night red from end to end. As the riders and dogs assembled, all redness fell and caught on them, as if they had been doused in a shower of freshest blood.

There were thirty men, thirty horses and sixty dogs.

The inn maids went round with the cups of drink, finest silver cups, somewhat dented, that the inn kept solely for those twelve nights. Even on the roof, the child could smell the strong wine, and the pungency of spice and herbs stirred in.

He noted the powerful horses and especially the dogs. These hounds were white and grey, long-haired, long-nosed, and bone-slim on long legs. All the men seemed loud and laughing, cracking jokes. Respected and revered, still they would boast of their participation in a Hunt. Already the child had heard how such men, wherever they went, whatever their birth or station in life, were treated like lords.

Next the red sky changed to a clear plum darkness, and the moon came up over the woods, round and white, with freckles on her surface. The Hunt saluted the moon, standing in their stirrups.

Then they slung the drained cups away, as if worthless, ringing on the stones and, turning their horses' heads, at a sudden gallop raced from the yard, among a streaming torrent of dogs.

It was as they left the light and shadow of the inn that the moonlight instead caught them. What had flashed and dripped scarlet at sunfall now blazed up like a bonfire of molten silver. On the roof, the boy was dazzled, eyes and brain. Ten years later, dazzled still, he presented himself to the Hunt Master in the Big House on the hill.

'You'd be happier and – and far more safe – staying on in your family's inn.'

'So I've heard, but here I am.'

'What of your poor mother? Don't you care how she'll fear for you? How will she manage if you're killed?'

'She'll manage. And I don't care a jot…'

Perhaps approving his impudence, the Hunt Master called his servant. He had the boy sent at once to undergo the proper tests. They were difficult and terrible, and he passed them all. By the time he was eighteen, Kevariz, the inn-woman's son, was himself a member of the Hunt.

Kevariz sat drinking at the inn.

He was twenty-nine years old, and it was the night before Full Moon, and Tyana expected him home. However, his mother had said she wished to see him. Now, if he came to see his mother, it was always a visit, an occasion. He had brought her a rose-silver luck charm to hang on the rafters.

She could brag that her son, who rode with the Hunt, had given it to the inn-house – but he doubted she would.

After the third tankard, he went up the cranky stair to her room above. Of course, he had been up here since his youth, but the room seemed every time more alien to him. Perhaps, even as a boy of nine or ten, it had been so – and all of the inn the same. He had thought himself made for another destiny.

'Mother. You're looking well.'

'Yes, you prefer me to be well. It lessens your guilt in leaving me.'

He put down the rose and the talisman beside it.

She nodded. 'Thank you,' she said, stiff and cold.

'You sent your boy for me.'

'I've had a Dream.'

Kevariz waited. His mother, when she reported this, meant only a single sort of dream; one which was prophetic. She had had them now and then, and her Dreams were always of something bad, and usually they came true. She had Dreamed, for example, of the wolf which killed Kevariz's father, on his journey back from the south.

Three days after she Dreamed it, men carried the body, what was left – not much – home to her.

Kevariz met her eyes steadily now. She was a grey-haired matron, well-off and proud. She had never liked his leaving her, let alone leaving her for a Hunt. On the days and nights he had come back from his training to help her at the inn, she treated him with scorn. Always she carped and chided, but never once had she said she did not *want* him to go, to please, *please* not abandon her and throw himself in the way of such danger. As a girl, she had elected to perform her Town Service in the silver mine, alongside the young men. Girls were never forced to do this, and few volunteered; they liked the softer work better, sorting the ore, or helping in the metal shops. But it showed her character.

He thought now, *she'll tell me she Dreamed I'm going to die tomorrow.*

What if she did? It could make no difference. No man could resign from a Hunt, once he had joined it. Any who deserted before his fiftieth year was thrown in the jail to rot. It was like that everywhere.

'Well, Mother,' he said.

'I Dreamed,' said Kevariz's mother, 'that you had a son. No, don't interrupt me. He wasn't what you'd care for. He was a wolf.'

'God's Silence, Mother!'

She had at last managed to shock him.

Not since she had beaten him first, when he was five years old, had she knocked him back like this.

'Sit down,' she said.

He sat, and she put one of the best pottery cups in his hand. It had brandy in it – she had kept it ready.

Kevariz drained the brandy.

She added nothing. It was her moment of triumph after all, twelve years waiting to pay him back, one year for every one of a year's Hunt Nights. It must feel as good as the strap had in her hand, when it rang on his shoulders.

'It was a true Dream, you'd say?'

'Yes.'

She stood by the mantlepiece, and he sat turning the pottery cup.

In the end he said, 'I suppose you think Tyana's betrayed me with some – with someone who has the strain.'

'She's your woman. What do you think?'

'Four years, we've taken care – we've no children. That suits me fine, and her too. So far as I know, she's never strayed from my heel.'

'Better be sure,' said his mother.

'All right.' He spoke shortly. He got up. 'Thanks for your

warning. I must be going, tomorrow is...'

'I know what tomorrow is, Kevar. Haven't I watched you ride off at every tomorrow of Full Moon, in your silver, and on your horse and with your dogs?'

He would not look at her; he could hear the mockery and rage in her voice clearly enough. He thought: *Is it that she didn't want to lose me, or that she wishes she could take my place?*

She was a hard woman, his mother.

Tyana was not like that, but wild and fey and loving, passionate and all for him. Or so he had thought.

When he climbed up the hill to his house, the lamp burned its yellow welcome in the window. Tyana was there, laying out the supper plates. Her hair was the colour of copper, a fiery veil as she bent above the candles or the fire.

She came at once to greet him, shoving the two great dogs away so she could kiss him first.

Tyana seemed just the same. Her scent of warm flesh, cinnamon and mint, her hungry mouth, unchanged and solely his.

As they ate the food, he said, 'Sergan's woman's in the family way again. And when Tyana agreed, he added, 'You're not missing that, perhaps?'

Tyana laughed. 'I? No. I want only you...'

'But a child, Yana...'

'I've no fondness for children.' She frowned, apparently uneasy. 'Is it you that wants me to have children? I will,' she said, 'if I must, to please you. But I can care for you better if it's just the two of us.'

After all, he saw the stubborn streak in her then. Of course, if he had insisted, by law she must obey and allow herself to conceive. She had taken up with a Huntsman and knew the rules. But, oh, he could tell, in that case he would have been made less comfortable. She would make sure of that.

But well, then, she was not presumably pregnant by some other, or she would have jumped at this excuse. Nor, he thought, would her reluctance let her get herself so.

'Why all this about children?' she asked.

Kevariz said, 'I thought, sometimes, those times I'm away with another Hunt – you might like the companionship.'

'No, because you leave the dogs with me then, and they're companions enough.'

'You're too attached to the dogs. Dogs get slaughtered every Full Moon, somewhere or other.'

Heartless despite her smile, Tyana said, 'Then the Master would give you another pair.'

We grow unfeeling, Kevariz thought later, as he lay beside Tyana, relaxed and sleeping after sexual love. *Heartless. Yes, I'm like that, too.* He was. He knew it. Though he *made* love with Tyana, he did not love her. Nor had he ever loved his mother. Neither did he love his comrades, nor, as some men did, his dogs or his horse, though he would groom them so carefully. *Do I like anything?*

Yes, he thought, *I like the Hunt, God help me. That's what I like and love.*

As for his mother's Dream – it could have been a lie – just her malice. She was getting old, nearly fifty herself. She was a woman.

He turned on his side and shut his eyes and for a moment was in the black-green forest, not riding but running, and there was fur on him, and he had four feet. Waking with a start, he lay an instant in suspended horror. Then it passed. They all dreamed things like that, once in a while. Had the Master not told him, told them all in the beginning, 'You'll become partly what you Hunt, and *they* are also partly like you. But remember, they're of the earth, and *you* are of the world. That's what keeps you separate.'

Kevariz the Huntsman was dressing for the Hunt, with the help of his woman, the excited dogs leaping about in the room below, barking, till he shouted for them to be quiet.

Tyana, very skilled after four years, laced him into the linen and leathers, helped push on his boots. She plaited his hair, added as she did so the silver ribbons that must mingle with the braids. She had scrubbed his back in the iron bath and shaved his jaw and cheeks with care. There must not be a nick on his face, nor any open cut anywhere on his body – if any were found, the wound must be cauterised with a hot metal rod and sealed by wax. She was adept at all of that, Tyana, but really, all the women on the hill were adept. They had had their training, too.

After the dressing and hair-braiding, Tyana opened the chest and undid the box. She performed this duty with ceremony, as Kevariz sat like a prince in his chair.

The box was of black-lacquered wood, inset with palest mother-of-pearl in a design of leaves and crossed knives. When she undid it, the low sun splashed up again from what lay there. The box was full of silver, and piece by piece, with the correct attention and reverence, Tyana brought the pieces out and laid them before him, and then, as he selected, she put them on his body.

Through the piercings in his ears and nostrils and chin went the silver studs and rings. Around his neck and wrists, and over the ankles of his hoots, were clasped the larger rings. Into the lacings of his garments silver chains were threaded and done up with silver locks. Silver buttons were attached to his coat, not by thread, but with silver claws. Onto his fingers slid ten silver coins set in silver. Then he stood up, and raised his arms, and around his waist was cinched the great belt of silver plates, each with its hammered crescent moon, but the buckle was shaped like the sun. Penultimate from the box, out from under a velvet cloth, the woman drew a pistol of white bone chased with silver, a silver-handled knife, and a long, incised, silver-hilted dagger.

'There,' she said. 'We're almost done.'

And finally, then, almost slyly, like a secret treat put by for a child, she drew from the bottom of the box the velvet bag and handed it to him. Kevariz himself loosed its drawstrings. He shook into his palm the cache of silver bullets.

'How beautiful you look,' Tyana said. Her eyes glowed, catching the glimmer of the silver. 'As if the moon had rained white fire on you.'

She always said similar things. She wanted sex then against the wall. This frequently occurred at that hour, and not only with them, but among other couples on the hill. He gave her what she wanted, it took little enough out of him, because at such times she was quick as any man.

Downstairs, the dogs were already dressed. He had seen to it as always, when earlier he groomed them. They, too, had their earrings and studs of silver, their collars. Their legs had thin silver rings, their claws were painted thick with silver, and silver wires were fastened in the long hair of their backs.

Out of the door they walked, he and they, along the hill, to the Big House.

The houses of Huntsmen clustered the hill, each with its grove, its little orchard, vineyard, kitchen-garden, which the servants and women tended. No one went without any good thing here. There was always plenty of food, and sufficient drink, women, fine clothing, even books if desired.

In the late afternoon light, dense and rich as amber honey, the trees were dark, and where the workers stood to watch, they clapped their hands and waved the men on.

All the Hunt was pouring up toward the Big House. Fifty men this season, and a hundred dogs. From the stables on the hilltop the horses, readied like the dogs that morning, neighed and stamped, calling and eager to be off.

As the Huntsmen greeted each other, at first sober, brief, and business-like, the grooms began to lead their horses out.

Kevariz saw his gelding appear, black as any night, and with a moon-white mane and tail – a classic horse he had bargained with the Master for, three years ago, after the original horse was eviscerated in the woods. The gelding also had silver through its ears, silver bells plaited in its mane, silver embroidery on the saddle-cloth, and flat studs fixed through the saddle. While over stirrups and the iron hooves, silver was newly-plated. This was common with all the horses.

He took the bridle from the groom. Among a crowd of men who did the same, he stroked the face of his horse, the long arch of neck, and the bells shook and made their faint sound. Up into the saddle Kevariz sprang, and the two tall dogs pranced around the horse, as all the dogs did – well-behaved now, used to the mounts, and to each other since they had kennelled together in their puppyhood, and run out together ever after. Only if sent to some other Hunt Meet must a man leave his own hounds behind. He must take loan of the wolfhounds of the Hunt that required him, to save the dogs quarrelling. Kevariz had never minded this, providing the loaned animals were healthy and well got-up.

Golden light played on silver. Kevariz recalled how he had seen it first, all that metal blazing in the moonshine. Dazzled, still dazzled. It had been easy, in a way, to be brave and single-minded, and to forego almost every other thing.

Just then the door of the Big House opened, and the Master came out in his blood-red brocaded coat and antique silver adornments passed, father to son, for sixteen generations.

The men cheered the Master. They always did. He bowed to them, as always too, and the servants and grooms clapped again.

'It's a fine night,' called the Master. 'A clear moon white as starch. We've heard, haven't we, there's one main pack this month, down by the river road. It's those we'll take. And any stragglers. Not too unworthy a job of work.'

The first cups went round. These were made of black bronze, and the wine had accordingly a bronze tang. Sergan said, joking, 'It'll taste better at the inn.'

Kevariz considered his mother a moment, when they were in the inn yard. He puzzled, did she truly spy on him, unseen, from a window?

Why had she told him that stupid fool's rigmarole?

Probably because it could haunt him forever, if he let it. For there were other women he had and could sleep with, and any one might announce she was to give him a son.

One day – one *night* – they would have wiped the strain, this strain of Hell, out. Scoured it off the face of the earth. So they always swore.

He put his mother and her Dream from his mind.

It was the earliest training, to be able to clear the brain on a Full Moon Night.

The sun sank into the land. The inn wine had been consumed. They saluted the rising moon. They flung away the silver cups, symbol of their own recklessness in the matter of their own lives, rode for the woods and the forest, flying now, the hounds, horses, and men. This was what Kevariz knew best; this fearful time, strangely, was when he felt the most secure.

The dogs started the first one down by the old mill-pond.

As they tore around the tarn, with its water-wheel standing obsolete now, in a moonlit verdigris of moss, across the clearing there loped something thin and white.

The hounds were belling, yowking. The men shouted excitedly. The moon-blaze of silver was all around, and through it, as if through an iridescent fog, Kevariz made out the shape of the wolf as it sped away, threading itself like an ivory needle back into the trees.

But the dogs were hot on its heels.

The Master yelled. They broke across the clearing and pelted down the ancient overgrown road beyond the ruined mill. Ten years since that mill had been in use. One night, the mill folk had died, all of them, murdered and eaten. There was barely enough left lying about for the town to identify. But this was what wolves did, a wolf-pack, and usually they were in packs. This individual, running in front of the hounds, though solitary, would be making for the familial lair.

Now the creature ahead, wanting more speed, dropped to its four feet – that was, what passed for feet. It bounded, ungainly, appalling, *swift*, leaping across obstacles along the road, the upthrust paving, the tussocks of weeds and bramble clumps.

Kevariz had seen every action it made before, and countless times. He kicked at his horse's sides, howling like the dogs. longing to catch up to their quarry and have it down.

But as usually happened, the dogs got there first, catching the wolf in the second it swerved and tried to head off again into the deeper forest, away now from where the river was and the lair.

It had made no sound until then, as the dogs sprang on it. When the biting fangs and silvered claws sank in, it began to emit the noises of its fury and agony – a horrible and filthy guttural screeching and growling.

The dogs swarmed over their captive. Huntsmen rode forward into the melee. It was strong, the wolf, as always. One dog was flung up and over, just like the silver cups in the yard – spinning, dented and silent – broken. One of Kollia's pair, Kevariz vaguely thought, his gelding stampeding forward, shaking its head. The bugle yapped, calling the dogs away. As they let go, sprawling down, the guns were out, and their voices barked in turn.

The bullets spat forward in stinging silver jets. Kevariz saw his own shot go home, deep into the shaggy face of the thing writhing now, bloody, wrecked, and refusing to die, there on the forest floor. Kevariz found himself out of the saddle. He ran in. Into his hand, almost before he expected it, came the great coarse ruff. He pulled the head upward and felt the claws of the beast scrape at him, sliding on leather, burnt by silver, gouging the flesh between.

'*Goodnight, shitspawn.*'

Kevariz plunged the long silver-hilted dagger in at the side of the neck, through fur and skin, flesh and skeleton. He heard the spine crack, felt it, saw the knife reappear on the neck's other side. The beast sagged. Its eyes, black as the darkness, each holding a miniature of the moon, stared into his. They looked blind, blind as his own.

The thing was dead.

Kevariz stood off. Hands clapped him on the hack, and a flask arrived. He swallowed brandy, as in his mother's room. Then they were all up in the saddles again, the living joyous dogs, bearded with blood, yipping for more, and the bugle summoning them on, for the rest.

Where the river opened up the forest, in places the banks were steep and full of holes and caves. Frequently this was where they chose, the wolf-packs, to lair. As the Hunt had been told, tonight it was the same.

Two males came bounding out, one nearly pure white and one much browner. They leapt at the horses, straight up, and Kevariz saw Zivender's mare fall shrieking, even as Ziv seized the monster's hair and stuck in his knife. Then they were lost in a kaleidoscope of limbs and weapons.

A female came out next, after the males were down. They had heard this pack comprised four or five members, which meant, when the dogs had also got the female down, and the Master himself had ridden over to dispatch her, that one more beast might still be inside the cave. Presently, as the shouts and shots died away, and the bubbling growling was silenced, they heard the final wolf, there inside the bank. It had begun howling, enraged, or frantic, but it did not come out.

The hounds were fierce, their blood was up, and the same for the men. The Master pointed. Sergan, and Ziv, who had struggled off his dying horse unharmed, but weeping with sorrow and anger, scrambled up the bank, their four dogs moving belly-down beside them, like snakes. They all vanished in at the maw of the cave.

Utter quiet was maintained outside. The Huntsmen there waited, guns positioned, their well-trained horses rock-still, so even the bells made no noise, the dogs crouched ready yet motionless.

The interior hubbub of battle was brief. The last wolf was one against six. Though these things had the strength of devils, seldom could even the larger packs of ten or more do much against the amalgamated might of a Hunt, protected by its silver – for which any town's youth were prepared to die in the mines – armed and organised like warriors for war.

After a few minutes the disturbance in the cave stopped, Zivender and Sergan's dogs instead bayed in triumph. They alone, having entered the lair, would be allowed the hearts and livers, the rest of the hounds must make do with a chop or two. The Master had done excellently, selecting Sergan for the honour, and Ziv, who had loved his horse as much as his woman, and would mourn her for months.

He was not the first to enter the cave. The Hunt Master had called to Kevariz and embraced him for his bold kill of the previous wolf. Possibly, when they all dined that night in the hall of the Big House, the Master would publicly title Kevariz "son". They were related that way, because Kevariz lived with Tyana, one of the Master's own daughters, but it was always "son" not "son-by-law" that the Master titled Kevariz when he had been particularly effective in a Hunt.

The brandy had gone round once more. Next, they would quarter the woods hereabouts, to be sure. But the reliable reports had only been of this one pack. As a rule, there was at least one wolf to be dealt with every month. No sooner had a Hunt burned out a nest, than more of the creatures slipped into the area, often inadvertently driven in from other spots, by other Hunts. Only twice, in all the years Kevariz had been a Huntsman, had they ridden all night without a single kill.

It was Zivender who asked Kevariz to go into the cave.

'I've lost my pocket-watch, damn my carelessness. No, it's not on poor Selina.' Selina was the dead mare. 'It must have dropped out of my coat in the lair. It's silver...'

'I know,' said Kevariz.

'My father gave it to me for my first Hunt. I'd go back in but I've got Selina to see to, can't just leave her lying.'

'I'll be glad to have a look for the watch. Do what you have to here.'

And so Kevariz climbed up to the cave.

The moon was going over by now, toward the west, and shone diagonally through the trees below, and across the inky water stretched a pointing finger of bleached fire.

So beautiful, the moon, that stirred up so much stinking dirt.

Kevariz had seen and entered other lairs. They were generally similar. Bones lay about, reeking and foul, though wolves, unless very old or sick, would empty their bladders and bowels elsewhere. There were always possessions in the lairs – sometimes a new Huntsman was unnerved to find a hairbrush or a doll. They had furniture too, many of them. Not the rough wooden stools and mattresses stuffed with dried grass that were normally found, but wonderful things that perhaps had come from great houses – a carved chest or decorated ebony chair. However fine, no man coveted them. The lair would he fired and burned out, and anything like that with it.

There was some furniture in this cave, but only of the crudely-made sort. The bed, though, had a raised wooden frame, and he discovered the dogs and men had killed the last wolf on it. It was another female, and initially he thought the copious bloodstains were only from the slaughter.

Ziv's silver watch was nowhere Kevariz could see, despite spending a while turning over the stuff in the lair, even picking about in the cold fireplace. In the end, Kevariz bent down to look under the bed-frame, for during the skirmish the watch could have rolled there.

Something had.

When he saw the glint of light, he took it for silver, and reached out and only snatched back his fingers in time. Under the bed, where the female must have thrust it when the Hunt approached, was a wolf-cub, not two days old. Kevariz stared in at it. It was too young yet, for much to happen with it on a Full Moon. To the unaccustomed eye, it looked only like a baby, rather thick-haired and downy, with wide, gleaming eyes. Even the dogs had overlooked it, its small scent hidden by the odour of the lair, the blood, and entrails.

'God's Silence.' Kevariz stood up. He had heard of, but never before had to contend with, such an eventuality. To butcher the full-grown ones, even if he had been told to do it at other times of a month, when they appeared nearly human, would have been seen to without a qualm, once he was sure. He had witnessed this once, a female wolf in her woman shape, hanged in the market by a silver rope, her feet weighted by iron. He cheered with everyone else when the rope pulled off her head. But this – this cub – this *child* – Kevariz stepped back, knelt down, peered again in under the bed-frame. It was crying now, the – the cub. So tiny and feeble, it made scarcely any sound, as he had sometimes found with sickly human infants when so young.

It was female.

'Devil's turd' Kevariz said to it. *'Werewolf,'* he said, giving it for once its full title. He hated it. He pushed his hatred in at it, like a blade. The baby only lay crying under the bed, under the mattress, and the corpse of its mother, whose heart, liver, and lights had already been removed and thrown to the hounds of Zivender and Sergan.

'God,' said Kevariz.

He stood up again, again stepped backward, and trod with a crunch on the face of Ziv's silver watch, lying unseen among the general mess.

Kevariz sat drinking at the Master's table.

It was the Hunt Dinner, and Tyana would not expect him home much before the third hour of morning. None of the women were present. The Dinners at Full Moon, especially after such a successful Hunt, were often rowdy.

The men recounted what they had done, over and over – the audience, which had already seen most of it, was not bored.

They told how Zivender and Sergan had gone into the cave, how Kevar had wrenched back the first wolf's head and sliced its spine. They told the courage of the dogs, the rewarding offal. They admired the claw-scorings on Kevariz's arm, which Tyana had already attended to.

'You see, son,' the Hunt Master said to Kevariz, putting an arm about his shoulder, 'when I was your age, I was the same. Riding through, getting a grip. That second when the knife *bites* – God and Hell, there's nothing like it. Not even sex.'

Kevariz nodded. 'It's like true love...' he said.

'Yes – you're right. *Love.* We *love* the brutes, don't we? We *love* them, and we kill them. Can't do the one without the other.'

They laughed. The fortified wines by then were passing round, purple in colour, heavy and fiery after the meats and sweets.

The welter of blood had not put any of them off the food.

When they staggered back to their houses on the hill, most of the Huntsmen would he busy with their women.

But *Better than sex...*

'Did you ever kill a cub?' Kevariz asked, as if curious. His face was happy, flushed with wine and good-will.

'It was my luck, just the once. They look like real babies, even on Full Moon. Mostly.'

'I heard of a man once...' Kevariz said. 'My mother told me about it at the inn – it made him ill to do that, though he was a terror with the grown ones, male or female, they could hardly hold him off from them.'

'Your mother? She was trying to put you off,' said the Master.

'Yes, I believe she was.' Kevariz nodded.

'If ever you come across a wolf-cub and you're squeamish, son, you call for me. I'll see you through...'

'I...' said Kevariz. His voice was weak suddenly, with recollection. But the Master never noticed, as he had not suspected the lie of Kevariz's mother's tale. Instead the Master was getting to his feet, calling out another toast for the night and the victory in one more battle.

Play-fighting, some of the Huntsmen crashed onto the table, and the remains of food, cutlery, and some wine spilled on the ground. The Master only laughed again. He valued his men. He was a good sort.

Tyana sat up from his body and gazed down at her by-law husband. She was surprised and disappointed

'I'm sorry,' he said. 'I drank too much at dinner at the Big House.'

'You drank too much – that's happened before on Hunt Nights. It makes no odds. You still want me.'

'I want you. But I'm unable.'

She sighed. He saw now she could be petulant, as well as stubborn. Her attractions, even her glory of hair, tonight grated on him like the stinging salves she had applied to the scratches the wolf had made as he killed it.

Soon she gave up on him. She lay down, sullen, and turned her back. 'You don't love me so well as you did.'

I never loved you, said the voice in his heart. He had only fancied her body and needed a woman to keep his house better than a servant, and the Master anyway had said to him, playfully, 'My Yana looks at you a lot.' The Master had thirteen daughters by various of his women, but no sons. He must get sons, therefore, through liaisons between his Huntsmen and his daughters. Was Tyana the loveliest daughter? Was Kevariz likely to be the one the Master chose to follow him in the Master's role? On other nights, when he called Kevariz "son", Kevariz had thought it might be so.

Kevariz said, 'I love you like the spring, Tyana. Now close your eyes and go to sleep.'

'How can I sleep without...?'

Kevariz felt himself heave out of the bed, landing on his feet on the night-frigid floor. 'Be quiet!' he bellowed at her.

Then he saw her looking up at him in fright, afraid of a blow that would spoil her looks. Kevariz shook himself. He sat down leadenly in the chair by the hearth.

'Listen, Yana, tonight I had to kill... I had to kill a cub.'

'A wolf-cub?'

'Yes. What else would I mean? God's Curse, it was hard for me. It looked just like a human baby. And – it cried so.'

Her face was all incomprehension. Well, she had said she had no feeling for children. But the face of any one of his comrades would be the same. *It* had not *been* a human baby. It was a *wolf's* child. Left to live, it would grow, swiftly as any actual beast, to adulthood – and then the murder of the real children would begin, and it would rejoice as it ate their meat.

These lands were rife with wolves. Indeed, it *was* a war. And although a child in an ordinary war might be spared, *not* a child that, less than two years on, would wield the powers and blood-lust of a full-grown, supernatural enemy.

'Oh, I know,' Kevariz said. 'Oh, Yana, I won't hurt you. Stop cowering and lie down. Go to sleep. I'll take a walk along the hill. Clear my head. The dawn's coming and the moon's down. It's safe enough.'

Did he realise, as he walked along the slope? Maybe he did. All the lights were out in the houses, save for the lamps left here and there in a porch. The windows of the Big House glistened only with the dim return of morning and the sky was hollow. The grass was wet with dew. Kevariz walked on, toward the woods, the forest.

He knew and had known. Of course, he had known. He had come out of the lair and coined at once his beginning lie. 'Ziv – look – I found it like this on the floor. You or Sergan must have trodden on it as you slaughtered that thing on the bed.'

And Zivender's long face, not just his beloved mare dead, but now his family keepsake smashed.

On another night, Kevariz would have told him the facts. That *he* had inadvertently trodden on the watch. He would have paid in the town for a repair, which anyway very likely would be done free for any Huntsman. But Kevariz lied, to practice.

Then, Kevariz had strolled off a way into the trees, mentioning he

195

needed to relieve himself. No one was suspicious, why should they be?

He thought it might have smothered, bundled there inside his coat, and the silver button-claws scorching it. It was so little, not one of the others had taken it for anything more than the pack of cloth he held in there, to a non-existent wound. Nor did it cry anymore, frozen by its contact with this otherness – Kevariz – which had dragged it from beneath the bed-frame, parcelled it into the cloth kept for staunching blood, clutched it between a coat and an inimically silvered body that, to the cub, must scratch, scald, and *smell* so very wrong, a human man whose odour was not of wolf, but of wolf-killing.

The dogs still did not nose it either. Even his two, when they came bouncing at him – but to them he smelled properly of butchery, and besides, he threw them the chops that were their lot. That was what interested them.

Down in among the trees, out of sight, he had found a bush of wild eucalypt, removed the baby and rolled the cloth in the bush. Then he put the baby back into the perfumed cloth and stowed it in one of fifty craters in the tree trunks, well off the ground, higher than his own head would he, when he rode a horse.

He thought he was giving it, the cub a chance. But later, after they had ridden through the woods and no one had discovered the child, or even wondered if anything was in a tree, Kevariz grasped the thorny idea that really he had only given it a slow, painful death – instead of a painful death that was fast.

Again and again that night, he cut himself on this idea, while thrusting it from his mind. For always it came back.

Now *he* was going back, back to the cratered tree, around the tumble of the river bank.

He knew what he would find and found it. Light by then was coming through the wood like rosy smoke. In the soft rays, as he lifted the cub from the tree, a human baby lay in his hands, watching him with clear and fully-focussed eyes that were like two blue moons.

Kevariz carried her down to the river and washed her gently in the water. By this he demonstrated to himself he knew also she was far more than human. No human child so young could have stood the water's dawn cold – but she did not mind. He too was now clean of the tang of blood. He fed her the milk he had stolen from his own cupboard in the house; the home the Master gave him that was no longer his. The wolf-child drank the milk. She was far more couth and coordinated than the human baby she seemed to be. She could already help hold the crock. Tomorrow, he must find a cow on the edge of the town, where they went out to pasture after Full Moon. But soon she could be weaned to easier stuff.

Kevariz tucked the baby in his arms, sitting under the tree, as sunlight bloomed in a giant flower of flame, and altered the forest from shadowed savagery to innocence.

It was as if he had been waiting for this hour.

Kevariz felt no compunction. As he had not when he left the inn, as he had not ever when he slew a wolf. He was pitiless, even in compassion, Kevariz.

The baby slept. Idly he rocked her, as he had seen women do.

For now — for a year and a half, at most two — she would be his child, the child he had never wanted, and now did. Then she would be grown, like all her kind, into a young woman of about seventeen years — Tyana's age, when he courted her. As in a pack it happened, they would thereafter be different with each other, the wolf-girl and Kevariz the Huntsman.

Except, he would never Hunt in that way again.

He would have to become one with her, live as she did, always potentially concealed, canny; if located then pursued. With Kevariz and his Huntsman's education to help her, she — and he — could perhaps survive a great while. But, if he considered sensibly, in fact they would not last long at all.

Already he had removed his silver, dropped it under the hill. The dogs, sleeping by the fire, had glanced up. He had nodded and gone out of the door.

He recalled now the Master's words, 'You'll become partly what you Hunt, as *they* are also partly like you.' They were of the earth, the Master said, but men were of the world — this was not honest. Kevariz did not believe it finally. Men too were of the earth, men too were wolves, or how else, in the case of *her* kind, could they ever be both at once?

Startling him, despite everything, the child spoke her first word to him at that moment. 'Da,' she said. 'Da...'

'Yes, baby, I'm your da.'

And in two years, he thought and knew, he would be her husband, by the oldest law there was. She was very fair, blonde and pale. Once a month, she would be one of the pure white ones.

Soon he got up, and walked them deeper into the forest, into those areas he had come across in the past, the wolf-places. For now, secure enough.

They would think, at the Big House, on the hill, he had lost his nerve and become a coward, as sometimes Huntsmen did, after which they ran away. They would search for him in the town, and in other towns – never in the woods. They understood Kevariz the Huntsman was too wise to hide there from jail, where the wolves might get him.

How many others, through the years, had done as he did?

It had been waiting for him, oh, yes. He who had never loved or liked, not mother or wife, not child. Not even friend, not even loyal horse and hound. And when he killed the wolves – *loving* it – it had been *fear* of love, not *love* at all that had made him brave and mad. Protesting too much, he had blinded himself, as at the start the silver ornaments had blinded him, in the moonlight. Now, he saw. He had seen the instant he had looked at her, beneath the bed.

Like his mother, however, Kevariz had discovered he possessed the prophetic streak. His Dream was a waking one, as he walked away into the wolf-heart of the forest, beyond the lairs of men.

He saw it all before him. The way she would grow, his adopted daughter. He saw the way, at each Full Moon, she changed, coated in fur, running now upright, now on taloned hands and feet, her back raised impossibly, her face all eyes and fangs. He saw it did not count anymore, the numbers of her kind he had killed, nor the countless numbers of his kind, killed by hers. He saw that she would never, even as a beast, harm a hair on his head. While he, to save her, would die.

He beheld them living in caves, the boles of dead trees, or running fleetly from a shouting pack of silver-clad men. He beheld them lovers, and their own first, and only, child – a boy, who, naturally, would inherit her blood, not his. His son that, as Kevariz's mother had foretold, would be a wolf. Somewhere too he watched them slain together, all three of them – but yet there was so much before that to come, so much of *life*, a living life Kevariz had never known. Surely it was worth the price.

The baby slept. This deep in the forest, even by day, the world grew darker and more profound. Since he had prophesied like his mother, and because of her foretelling of his fate, he decided he would call the child in his arms by his mother's name, Sosfiya.

ISRABEL

Israbel ran through the streets of Paris. The cobbles were slick with filth and wet. The city was made of thick grey rain. Israbel was sixteen – probably, who could be quite sure? Her mother was long dead, her father always unknown. Somewhere behind her waited a man with his belt drawn off, like a sword to smite her with. Israbel ran.

The narrow streets were mostly empty now, for night was coming. A fellow with a torch went by to light the lamps along the front of some tavern. Wet cats, thin as strings, shot across the alleys, or slunk over the roofs above.

When Israbel turned a corner into the *Place Du Coeur*, she did not know where she was, but in the deepening dusk one further cat came slinking out to cross her path. This cat was not like the others. It was very big, the size, she was afterwards to believe, of a horse. Though the light was gone, some peculiar sheen on the darkness showed her the faint dapplings along its back, its neck, which was longer than that of any ordinary feline, and the narrow ruff about its head. Its eyes were luminous and grey as the death of the light. It stopped.

She too, the running girl, had halted.

She thought, confusedly, *it's escaped from the great circus up at Montmartre.*

Israbel had heard of a circus, that is had many curiosities, including both people and beasts of weird appearance and characteristics.

She was not afraid of the cat. That is, not more afraid of it than of the darkness, the sadist she had escaped, the world, everything. And so, she did not, now, run away, only stood watching it, as it stood also watching *her*.

A hundred years later, when Israbel, still sixteen, rich, lovely, and, in her own way, dangerous, came occasionally to explain about the great cat, she would always add, 'Its pelt was so soft and warm, so smooth and plush, like the double velvets of Venice. Like my hair, you say? Well, perhaps very like that. But truly, its pelt was much better than my hair.'

'She is the woman I intend to be my wife.'

Plinta stared, a moment. He thought, *Your wife?* And then: *She looks like an insect. Oh, a beautiful insect – some sort of exquisite beetle, with gilded black wings.*

'Really?' he said.

'You don't approve.'

Plinta shivered – but unseen: inside his mind. 'Does it matter to you that I approve?'

'Well, no.'

By then, the woman – the *creature* – was approaching them, slipping between the candlelit marbles of the salon.

Dumière held out his hands. She paused, smiling, and took neither.

'Good evening, my love,' said Dumière. 'May I present my friend, Monsieur Plinta, the painter.'

She looked at Plinta.

Her eyes were like a flash of blackness seen through blue smoke.

Yes, she was beautiful. A perfect, sculpted face, large dark eyes – blue? – black? – whose lids were just barely touched with kohl, a long aquiline nose, (perhaps she was a Jewess), a wonderful mouth, not large – yet full, and capable of lengthening its shape – blushed either with rouge or uncommon good health.

She was not young. That is, she was about twenty-five or so, Plinta thought. Not that, physically, she seemed much older than sixteen. Yet her eyes knew things. Perhaps her clear and unlined eyes were even older – thirty, *forty – fifty?*

Plinta, the artist, now realised why he had thought of her pictorially and specifically as a beetle. Her black dress wrapped her closely, thrusting up a velvet glimpse of breasts, holding her corseted waist like two tight ebony hands ringed with gold. Her hair, too, which she wore partly loose, was quilled and rayed with gold – wings.

He thought, distinctly: *She is a vampire.*

'Madame,' he said, and bowed.

'Oh, but, Monsieur,' she said, 'I'm not married.'

'Not yet,' agreed Dumière. Now he reached out and took hold of her, like the tight hands of her dress on her waist. 'Come on, let's dance.'

As he led her away, she glanced back once, and directly into Plinta's eyes.

What was her name? Had Dumière not told him?

The next evening, as Plinta, who had just left his bed, lay on the sofa reading the morning's journals and drinking bitter coffee, his shambling servant Colas showed Israbel into the studio.

Plinta did not get up. Then he thought he had better, to be rude was too obvious. So he rose. But, when he did that, she laughed at him.

She said, 'I saw last night, Monsieur Plinta, you'd penetrated my disguise.'

Today she wore very dark blue-green, with a lemon plume in her hat. She was still like a beautiful beetle. Or maybe a lizard.

'Disguise? I didn't know you'd worn fancy-dress, madame.'

'Oh yes, of course. Always. But you saw right through to me, didn't you? As if I were – naked.'

Plinta felt at once an unmistakable and vivid surge of lust. Positioned high in his own brain, he looked down at the lust, tingling and flaring about in his body, and said, cautiously, 'I don't know what you mean, madame.'

'I'm not "madame". I have only one name. Israbel. Under that name I sometimes sing and act at the *Opéra*.'

'Very well,' he said. 'Please sit down.'

She too, he sensed, saw right through *him*. She knew what he felt, still felt. She knew, too, he was still in command of himself.

Israbel seated herself. She drew off the plumed hat, and her hair fell all around her, down to her waist. There were no longer golden quills and spangles in it, yet it glittered with strange gilding.

'I want you,' she said, 'to paint my portrait.'

'You honour me. Alas, I'm very busy.'

'No, you are not. You haven't had a commission, nor any paid work, for eighteen months. You mustn't forget, I know Dumière, who knows *you*.'

'Dumière doesn't know everything about me, I'm afraid.'

'No. You're a secretive man. But your painting is interesting. Wouldn't you like me to sit for you?'

'Frankly, Madame Israbel...'

'You wouldn't,' she finished for him.

The door opened. In blundered Colas with more wood for the

stove, for it was a chilly evening. Israbel watched Colas, then she turned her eyes back to Plinta. And, annoyed, he realised he had been hungry for their return to him, sulky in the split second of her looking away.

Colas banged the stove door shut again and lumbered out. Like two interrupted lovers, they resumed their murmured conversation.

'Dumière may have told you, monsieur, I'm well-off. I can pay you handsomely for your portrait of myself.'

'Why do you want such a portrait?'

She said, without hesitation, 'I'd like to look at it. I'd like to see myself in it.'

And, before he could quite stop himself, if he had even meant to stop himself, Plinta added, 'That being because a portrait is the only way you ever *could* see yourself. Am I correct, madame? You don't reflect in mirrors.'

Israbel smiled once more. It was difficult to take your gaze away from her mouth – unless you looked into her eyes; and then you could only look at those…

'I note you understand my predicament, monsieur,' she said, as if they had spoken of something dull.

Plinta decided not to reply.

Israbel got up, and as she did so, even clothed in her fashionable Parisian dress, something fell from her like a seventh veil. 'Others are fooled, of course,' she remarked. 'It's commonly thought no one can make out a vampire in a mirror. But naturally anyone can see us reflected there – save only we, ourselves.'

'Then you have kindred!' said Plinta, between wonder and alarm.

'Perhaps – but I've met none of them. No, no, I'm quite alone. I speak of them only in the historical and mythic sense. I belong, you understand, monsieur, to an ancient sisterhood, brotherhood, packed with persons. Except I've never met any of them…'

'Then how did you become what you are?'· Plinta asked, inevitably.

'If I tell you that, will you paint me? Will you give me my mirror, Monsieur Plinta?'

He turned his back, walked off to the window.

Standing by the frozen glass, he gazed down at the icy, hardly-lit streets running toward the River Seine; the bell-clanging local church; then, to the sky like black lead. But talking to her was a game he seemed unable to give up playing.

'Why do you want to see yourself, madame? Anyone else's face can tell you how beautiful you are.'

'Not yours,' she said.

Plinta lurched inside his skin. In utter silence, she had drawn physically close to him. Her narrow hand was on his shoulder. Almost as tall as he, she leaned to his ear. 'I'll tell you my story anyway,' she murmured. 'Perhaps.'

Plinta did not move. He wondered if she would sink her teeth, or some other blood-letting implement, into his neck. But he felt only her perfumed warmth, and then a coldness, and turning, he saw she was once more seated far off across the studio, her feet stretched out to the stove, drinking coffee like an ordinary human woman.

She did not appear at the *Opéra* very often. When she did, she always took some small cameo part, usually limited to a single appearance lasting maybe five minutes, during which she sang an aria by Handel, Rameau, or Voulé. Her voice was good, if not especially brilliant, but nevertheless, a great hush would grip the theatre while she voiced her lines and sang her music. She was always rapturously applauded, and flowers rained on the stage.

She was said to have slept with some of the richer or more notorious patrons – bankers, poets, that sort. None of them had ever seemed any the worse for it. That is, none of them mysteriously died or otherwise disappeared. None of them, perhaps, more to the point, metamorphosed in any way. They merely went on with their own earthbound lives, long after they parted from her.

Men did become infatuated, of course. One had drowned himself, Plinta thought. Plinta had never paid her name much attention, nor even seen her, until Dumière became in turn obsessed by her.

Dumière took Plinta to dinner at the *Café d'Orléans*. Here they ate oysters and various roasted meats and drank wine and liqueurs. Dumière spoke mostly – solely – of Israbel

Plinta, to his own consternation, listened with interest and completely failed to be bored. He had already agreed with Israbel to paint her. There had seemed to be nothing else he could do. He did not tell Dumière, however, as if this was a dirty secret. He sensed Dumière would call him out over it to a dawn duel in the *Bois*, and perhaps shoot him dead from jealousy.

Dumière was not really Plinta's friend. Dumière used him as a sort of social musical instrument, a piano perhaps, coming up to him and playing him with enthusiasm for a few hours now and then, even in public, in restaurants and salons, then forgetting Plinta again entirely for months – years – on end.

Plinta watched Dumière all through the dinner. Even over the crystallised fruits, brandy and cigars. Dumière seemed the same as ever: handsome, spoiled and charming.

Finally, when they were drunk enough, Plinta said to him, 'Have you had her yet?'

'*Had* her?'

'The kiss that is more than a kiss.'

'Why, Plinta, what do you think? Aren't I irresistible? Isn't *she*?'

'You have, then.'

'You prude! Do you want me to describe it?' Amused in victory, Dumière glowed above the glowing cigar. 'Well? I will if you like.'

Plinta thought he *would* like, that was, his *body* would have liked to hear every detail. Conversely, his clever, appraising mind was also highly curious. 'No, thank you.'

'I'll tell you this, Plinta, she isn't like any other woman I've ever known.'

'Doesn't the new lover always think that?'

'No, of course he doesn't. How absurd. We *pretend* we do, but we don't.'

'Then…' Cautious still, Plinta leaned back. 'Then how is she *different*? Is she perverse?'

'No such luck. Not that anything like that is necessary with her. Oh, her skin's soft and smooth, her hair's a marvel. She has a special scent she wears – like spice. Her body's lithe as a snake. It isn't any of that.'

'And *do* you mean to marry her?' asked Plinta, as Dumière fell silent, hypnotised by absorbing thoughts of Israbel.

'I might. I wouldn't mind it. Just to keep her to myself.'

'Do you think you could?'

'Yes. I'd put her in a cage. Like a panther. She only lets me visit her at night. She's nocturnal, like most panthers.'

'A cage…' Despite himself, Plinta was shocked, mostly at Dumière's suddenly active imagination.

'Oh, I mean a house, man, a big glorious house – but I'd have the only key. I'd keep her there. Do you know,' he added, 'the strangest thing is when she looks into a mirror. I bought her one, you see, a gorgeous thing from Italy, silvered glass, gilt cupids – she stood in front of it nearly half an hour. Staring at her reflection. She had such a puzzled look – a sad look – as if she were searching for something she couldn't find – I wonder what...?

Her soul, thought Plinta.

Worse than Dumière's invented cage-house, a door slammed in Plinta's heart then, trapping him inside with Israbel.

Israbel told Plinta at once she wanted to pose for him in the nude.

This, rather than excite, made cool sense to him. After all, if she wanted to see *herself* – which no mirror could now ever show her, she wanted to see her flesh *not* her *clothes* – she need only look into her wardrobe to behold those.

When she came out naked to the lamplight from behind the studio screen, he noted, unsurprised, her body was beautiful. But Plinta had seen the beautiful unclad bodies of women – and men – often in his trade.

What moved him was Israbel herself. Her gestures, expressions. Even the sound of her voice. For she would talk to him as he began his sketches.

Her voice was pleasant, restful. It was elusive too. Neither young nor old, barely even feminine. A slightly tarnished silver voice to vie with the gold glints in her eyes and hair.

He found her easy to capture on paper, and presently on canvas. Even her colours were simple – cream and black, with highlights of turquoise, navy, and warmer tones, like shining metals. But her red mouth burned for him.

What would it be like – not to kiss – but to be *bitten* by the teeth of that burning mouth?

Plinta recalled that awareness he had had before – of the casting of a seventh veil, less the provocative act of a dancing Salomé, it had been as if Israbel *cast a skin*.

She had not yet, despite her pledge, told him the tale of how she became what he knew she was, a vampire, who lived on the blood of others. But for that matter, he did not know when or how she took blood. She had never approached him in any way, either in seduction or attack. Naturally, she would want the portrait completed to her satisfaction first. However, one day he would finish.

He actually considered, twice, following her when she left the studio, to see her method of predation. Yet he never did.

What would he do if she suddenly turned her attentions on him? Would he allow her his blood? Would he be able to prevent her?

He was not afraid of Israbel. He was not in love with her. But obsessed he *was*. Intellectually and artistically at least as much as physically and in his emotions.

A winter dusk brought her early, while a thick sunfall bubbled behind the church like sweet apricot preserves.

The painting was almost done, and he permitted her, when she asked, to see it. She had never asked before.

She stood a long while staring at it, just as Dumière – whom, now, Plinta had not seen for two months – had described with the costly cupid mirror. For one awful second, Plinta thought perhaps she could not see herself in the painted picture, *either* – it was a very exact likeness.

Then she said, 'Oh thank God. There I am again. Oh, yes. Thank God.'

'Do you know, can you guess,' she whispered presently, when he had sat her down, wrapped her furs about her, given her cognac, 'what it's like – never *again to see your own self*? Oh, there are whole peoples, I know, who never have mirrors and so never look into them – but even so – they may see a reflection in some surface. And here in this city – a polished table top – window – a pool. Think of me, I was so young. Gazing instead at my hands – my feet – my *shadow* – because my shadow I still have – trying to remember myself from that. I pulled my hair across my eyes, too, and looked at my hair. But myself – my face, my eyes, my mouth – forever gone. All of *you* could see them, *all of you* – all, save I myself. And they were *mine*.'

'The penalty for everything else you've gained,' he said. Was this harsh? No, only a fact.

'True,' she said. 'Nevertheless, I have outwitted the penalty, or I *shall* do so. With the help of Plinta the Painter. Do you know, Plinta, the oddest thing – I'd only seen myself four or five times in any case, before I lost the ability to view my own reflection. In my – shall I even say *home?* – in the slum where I was born, there were few mirrors. Despite that, as I've said – once in a windowpane, and once a table polished with my hand – and once in a pool of rainwater in a gutter, and once in the side of a bottle – but once a man gave me a piece of looking-glass. I looked, and truly saw myself, and he said, *Now you do as I say, or I'll cut that face you see across with my razor.* I did what he said. He still took off his belt to beat me. I hadn't pleased him, you understand. That was when I ran. This, Plinta, was about a hundred, a hundred and seven years ago. It was in the era just before the Revolution. Paris was raw and smarting, not yet seething – I didn't notice. The city was like a model made of wet newspaper. Unreal. And I must only escape. So, I escaped, as you see.'

He said, 'You became what you are now.'

Then she told him.

The great cat in the *Place Du Coeur* had approached her so suddenly and swiftly, seeming to move as if on wheels, that Israbel had had no time to think, or to decide after all once more to run away. Next second, its body touched hers.

The body of the cat was warm, she said, as a hearth, or a summer stone, and its pelt was smooth, velvet-soft, yet prickling with electric life. The instant they were in contact, a vast soothing, in fact a feeling of *content* flood Israbel. 'It was like the first time I ever tasted good brandy.'

The Place du Coeur was now, she said, long felled, its yards and hovels squashed and built over. Alleys attenuated from, it however, then and still, creeping towards the *Ile de la Cité*.

Israbel remembered only this, walking very fast with the great leopard, whose neck was long and who was as tall as a horse, both it and she unseen and incredibly un-noted, through shadows and night. Here and there, bleary lights shone in the rain. Sometimes loud displays of inebriation, rage, or merriment flowed around the edges of their progress. For everything like that seemed divided by their passage, like a river, which they swam together, she and the cat, effortlessly. They came eventually out into the open spaces before the Cathedral.

Notre Dame, Our Lady of Paris, was that night herself lit to gold and smoky red. In her windows, dark blue fires and rubies. Far above her, demonic gargoyles craned, peering over and down at the city, their wings locked until midnight should strike in some other dimension, and let them loose.

But the leopard drew Israbel away down a sort of slope, and into a cavern under the street. She could not say exactly *how* it drew her.

It was as if she had become invisibly connected to its skin, the vibrant *spirit* of its short dense fur, which led her along like a benevolent leash.

'What did I think or feel? I was only happy. I felt quite safe, going down into the dark. If instead it had somehow drawn me up to the very heights of the Cathedral, I couldn't have been afraid.'

In the cavern – no, she had sometimes, in later years, looked for this spot by *Notre Dame*, never found it, nor any entrance to it – was the leopard's lair. The stone floor was dry and thick with straw and rushes and scraps of material. The air was warm yet clean, faintly tinged with the incense of *Notre Dame*, freshened by little cracks and other apertures. She smelled the river, too, wholesome as the rest.

She lay down against the cat, which held her between its great muscled forelegs, the paws resting around her, without a hint of talons. It breathed into her face. And its breath was healthy and clean, and smelled only a little salty.

'Some of those I tell this story ask if the cat then ravished me, as lions can be trained to do with human women. Yet no such thing happened at all. Oh, it wasn't like that. It was as if I lay again, a child, in the arms of my mother or a father who loved me tenderly. I never felt so secure, nor have I ever after. So I slept, my head on one of the huge arms, against the breast of dappled fur, to the rhythmic hymn of its breathing.'

Israbel paused. This hiatus went on and on.

Plinta said finally, 'And then?'

She sighed. 'I woke up. It was twilight. I felt well and strong, as if I'd eaten a nourishing meal and drunk a little wine. And as if I'd bathed in hot, scented water – that was how I now smelled. I wasn't under the city anymore. I was on a back street, against a wall, out of sight, where it must have taken me when it was done. I might have dreamed everything, but for knowing I was glad it wasn't daytime, and for the sense of wellbeing, of *vitality* – neither of which have ever left me since. Even so, I started to cry. I ran about, trying to find the way back down to my beloved friend – for yes, the great cat had become my only friend and all the family I had. Of course, I detected no way and not a single clue. I never saw my leopard again. Presently, instead, my own – no *human* kind – discovered me. And so I learned my powers over them, what I could do and gain. What I had become.'

'A vampire.'

'An immortal thing. Naturally limited to the night, but otherwise able to exist as she wishes. And fed – *cherished* – by mortal blood.'

Plinta roused himself. He felt cold and sleepy, inert and depressed, all the opposites of what she described her own feelings to be.

'But how had – this cat – taken *your* blood – how had it refashioned you?'

'Do you really wish to know?'

'Yes…'

Israbel lowered her eyes of black turquoise. 'The pelt,' she said simply, in a sad, low voice. 'The beautiful fur of it – every fibre leached every atom of my blood away and filled me in return with the ichor of the vampire race.'

'It's *fur!*'

Plinta surged up. He strode up and down the studio, rubbing circulation back into his numbed hands and arms, stopping only to shovel more wood into the stove. The room seemed hot – yet he was freezing.

When he happened to glance at the clock, he was astounded: two hours had passed since Israbel had first arrived. The moment he looked at her now, she too got up. She had not taken off any but her outer garments, the furs. It seemed she did not, tonight, mean to pose for her portrait. Certainly, she did not, for she said then, 'Monsieur, your picture of me is all I could ever hope for. You've given me a very special gift. Now I shall pay you.'

'It isn't finished!' Plinta exclaimed. He himself heard the panic in his tone. It was not only the unfinished painting that troubled him. It seemed their commerce, hers and his, was at an end.

But Israbel only nodded gravely.

'Not quite finished, I agree. But that's as it should be – as it *must* be, don't you think? For neither am I, monsieur, *finished*. Nor, perhaps can I ever be. The picture has reached the very stage I myself am at. Like me, it must remain there, or how can I see myself in it?'

Plinta stood still. He stared at Israbel, memorising her, her grace, elegance, and otherness.

'And *so*,' she said gently, 'let me settle my account with you.'

'I don't know,' he said, 'what this picture can be worth.'

'Everything.'

'Do I ask everything of you, then?'

209

'You know that I'm rich.'

'Don't pay me,' he said, 'in money.'

'Then how?'

As she questioned him like that, Plinta saw in her a total fatal innocence. It had nothing to do with naïveté or foolishness. *I must never lose her.* Aloud he said, 'Show me.'

'Ah.'

'Show me how – *pelt* – can take blood – *how you feed yourself.*'

The crudeness of the words he had used, and his desire to find out, both appalled him. He was humiliated by himself, and trembling, but even so would not deny what he had said.

She answered, 'If you wish. But – I'm hungry, Plinta, Monsieur Plinta the Painter. If it's to be you…'

'*Me.* Who *else?*'

'Then, I shan't hold back. You must become as I am. Do you want such a thing?'

Plinta thought about it. But he had been thinking of it constantly, behind a screen of debate, arguing with himself that in fact, it was not possible. But it was.

'Madame Israbel, I have so much to learn of my trade. That alone would need immortality. I'd like the time. I don't subscribe to the idea that, being always myself, I must become less. I think one must be able to *evolve* – even in the same continuing body. Yes, I'd give up the daylight. But I too am already partly nocturnal. I sleep through a day, rise at sunset. But more than that – I want to *know*…'

Israbel turned her head. This was as if she listened, obediently, to some angel at her right shoulder, who now told her what she must do. It seemed she knew the angel of old. Its advice was always sound.

Before, he had seen a seventh veil fall from her.

Now Israbel touched the bodice of her dress, and the yellow silk parted and dropped, like a veil, and all else with it. As before, she stood in front of him naked. Her hair, loose and gleaming, framed her face, neck, and upper body.

Plinta felt a stab of sexual appetite so intense it hurt him. Then he grasped it was not sexual at all.

She came to him as her kind did, as the great cat had come to her – sudden and swift, gliding as if over burnished ice.

And as she came, her hair, her *hair,* lifted up on her head in two wide, black-flaming wings, glittering with tines and prisms of diamond, topaz, and gold, and as it fastened on him, and her flesh met his own clothed body, he felt the touch of her, hair, skin, her eyes, her lips. Oh, not like mother or father. This was like the meeting of mortal man with God.

Plinta seemed to lie that night high up on the roofs of the Cathedral, among the army of gargoyles which, as a white moon rose, flew back and forth, scratching their claws on the parapets, their eyes full of misty smoulderings.

Here, Israbel took his blood, not biting, but through her skin and her hair, the soft persuasive caresses ebbing and swelling like a symphony.

He understood that, in the future, he too must take sustenance in this way. But *her* hair, so long and thick, had become two wings, like those of some giant Egyptian hawk. She too, he saw, as he lay quiet between the delicious bouts of her feeding, flew off the roof, into the sky and stars. Sometimes she even gripped the gargoyles, held them, while both they and she soared across the moon, her hair coiling them, their tails wrapped around her. Did she take blood also from their carved stone, replacing it with immortal vampiric essences? Of course, how else were they able to fly?

Near dawn she closed his eyes with her lips, a kind of kiss.

'Sleep now. Be at peace. Asleep, the sun can't harm you. Tomorrow night you will be changed.'

'Then tomorrow, where shall I meet you?' he said. But Plinta discovered he could not, now she had shut them, open his eyes, and she did not reply, and had drawn away. A colossal slumberousness stole over him. He sank into it, not minding.

In the dream then, a sleep, which itself held a dream. In this second trance, he saw Israbel after all, her face framed now by the velvet and silk curtains of a stage. Wings flew out from her skull. Her eyes were highly reflective – like a pair of looking-glasses. Otherwise, her face had no features at all. It was a *faceless* face, a perfect, blind face, of fabric stretched taut on bone.

Colas found him the next evening. Plinta lay stiff and marble cold, and looking bloodless as marble, there on the studio rug, splashed by the dregs of a sunset.

Colas gave a yowl. Howling and yelping like a wolf, he rolled Plinta about the floor and, when neighbours rushed up the stairs, wailed that Plinta had died, was dead, and now Colas would be slung out on the street – Colas' only actual concern.

'No, you dolt. Look, he's waking up. *Dead? Plinta?* Only drunk…'

Plinta woke. He stretched, and Colas who genuinely had seen him minutes before dead as the deadest corpse, backed away gibbering.

But Plinta himself felt wonderful, like a prince who is in love and has, besides, dined on a banquet. He threw a boot at Colas, and Colas, at last reassured his patron was the same as ever, tramped off to fetch the coffee.

Already the marvellous dream – of the Cathedral, the gargoyles, the vampire, and her attentions – was fading. Of the dream-within-the-dream did anything remain? Maybe not. But Plinta soon noticed Israbel had taken her portrait away with her. Why not, when she had bought it, and at an excellent price? Next time he saw it, the picture, he would be again with her.

One last splinter of dream-memory did linger, however. He had asked her where he should meet her, Israbel his sister, *now*, in blood. But he had been stupid to ask, for Plinta had not needed to. Tonight, as much of Paris knew, Israbel was due to act and sing her glimmering five minutes at the *Opéra*.

Plinta threw his mirror into the cupboard before he left the studio. Now a vampire, he could never again see himself reflected and had duly proved as much with one or two contemptuous glares at the glass.

Would she be glad, at last, of his company? They were brethren, and she had admitted she had discovered no kindred, just as never again had she located the supernatural cat.

Two moods possessed Plinta as he walked the glacial streets of Paris, moving toward the golden ornament of the theatre. One was an elation not unmixed with eager fear. The other was a deep melancholy, a sort of shadow. The first state he comprehended. The second puzzled him. Was he in mourning then for his purely *human* life, now ended? What did that matter? Nothing, not at all. But no, it was not that.

He stood in the light-spiked dark and thought: *Perhaps immortality is only formed, for us, from those countless days we may never now experience. A life of nights, doubled.*

All things are paid for. Even Israbel had paid for the painting he had made of her.

Plinta took a box at the theatre, a rare extravagance. He soon glimpsed Dumière across the auditorium in a box of his own, with other friends. Dumière saluted Plinta, pleased to see him at a distance. But how jealous Dumière would be, if only he knew. Had he offered Israbel marriage? Israbel and Plinta *were* married, in more than religion or legality.

One flesh...

Where shall I feed? Plinta thought, as the curtain rose on some spectacular unimportance. *She will show me. She will be my teacher.* Then he sat back, watching the acts of the play through half-closed eyes, and all about the theatre rustled and murmured, whistled and called, alienly alive. He imagined it was like being in the zoological gardens. He had never felt a part of them, the human race, and now was not.

To great clapping and calls, Israbel came out in the fifth act, as the program stipulated, to perform her part and sing her aria, which that night was by Rameau.

Plinta sat forward. His eyes widened. His heart, or some more profound mechanism, slammed high into his chest, then leapt away, down into a chasm. Tears rolled, helpless to save themselves, from his eyes.

If he had been able, in those minutes, like the Biblical Samson, he would have risen, grabbed vast pillars of the *Opéra* temple, and brought it crashing down.

Samson had lost all. Plinta too, had lost.

Now he could never know, he who must learn *everything* – whether or not he had loved her. Instead he would be, like the rest of his kind, bereft, and quite unique.

On the stage Israbel sang, and the audience hung in wild suspense until the last note, then bellowed its applause and flung its flowers. And across the theatre, Dumière sprang up and raced, fever-flushed from his box, to seek her in the dressing rooms.

But Plinta stayed where he was, still as when Colas had found him and thought him, rightly, dead. Only the mobile tears ran on from Plinta's eyes.

For she had warned him, had she not? Even his mirror, in its own cruelly amusing way, had done so. Certainly, his inner dream of facelessness. No vampire could see itself in reflection – only human things could see it there. But that was not *only* in mirrors. No vampire could see *any* vampire – themselves or another – either in a mirror, or anywhere in the whole crystal globe of the heartless, lonely, reflective world.

On the stage, Israbel was taking her bow. Plinta alone did not applaud. To him she was now entirely inaudible and invisible, just as he was now entirely inaudible and invisible to Israbel, and to all their kind.

Stalking the Leopard

From a Future-Urban Myth by John Kaiine

Avly leaned her slim white arms on the balustrade, her ruby bracelets dripping along the stone. She was young, beautiful, and rich, and lived in one of the most picturesque cities of northern climes, Dophan, beneath the great, man-made rainbow known as The Arch.

Still lit up after dark, its seven burning colours glowed across the dusk sky. More subtly, its rays painted the parks, tree-hung boulevards, and mansions below, including Avly's balcony, her pale skin, and fashionably-short black hair.

How bored she was, this elegant young woman.

Nothing engaged her interest. Avly had known only attractive and glamorously stimulating things all her twenty years. By now, even the rainbow itself, at which tourists would stand gaping, both on the ground and in the jewelled flying vehicles, had become, for her, samey.

One of these vehicles, however, now dipped toward the balcony. She saw, with slight affront, it was the private car of her most recent ex-lover. They had parted amiably, and at Avly's wish – perhaps for that very reason she did not want to ride with him to this evening's party.

'Avly! Glimmering creature. Do get in, we're late.'

Avly got into the car and sank back on the cushioned seat. A glass of champagnist alighted in her hand. She sipped and glanced sidelong at her handsome ex, who wore a silk cloak.

Whatever had she seen in him? But oh, what had she seen, ever, in *any* of her several lovers?

The driverless car whirled them through the sky, under The Arch, deftly and automatically avoiding other similar traffic, most of it intent on pleasure.

They landed on the roof of a brightly-lamped mansion. Massive trees grew from stems of water set into concrete. Polished diamonds winked in tiles. Fortunately, another woman came at once and claimed Avly's cast-off. Now Avly stood again, bored and lethargic, at one more balustrade, staring across into the shining apartments over the way, where similar parties raged. Was there anything interesting *there?* No. Everything might as well be a mirror. Including this roof-garden.

'Oh look! Look at that – down in the Violet Quarter!'

The quarters of the city were named for the colours of The Arch, but Violet, like Indigo and Orange, was one of the poorer, shabbier areas.

Party-goers poured in a tide across the garden, and Avly went indifferently after them, not expecting to see very much. However, from the north side of the roof, she and everyone else soon stared exclaiming at a distant but colossal column of smoke and fire.

'Several of the old houses on Velvet Street must be burning.'

'Let's go and see.'

Accidents and disasters were rare in Dophan. The last vehicular crash had happened before Avly was born, the last fire when she was ten – and she had been interested then. But now this ghoulishness irritated her, and she wanted to decline the offer of the two nearest guests, who were already guiding her into the flow of persons hurrying back towards the vehicle-park.

'Avly, come *on*. What a spectacle it must be – you can't *miss* it – and the horror – perhaps there are several dead!'

Ennui, distaste even, strangely decided Avly on non-resistance. She allowed them to pull her into the car, and moments later they were zooming north across the city. From many buildings around, countless others did the same.

What would she feel? Alarm, sympathy, fear... Would she feel *anything?* People, as a rule, no longer seemed quite real to Avly – that is, when she thought of them in any depth.

The fire, though, was impressive. It towered into, and presently dominated, the sky. Black and purple smoke, sequined by embers and sparks, plumed two blocks of flaming masonry. Even as the car settled on an adjacent landing-pad, one of the houses collapsed with a roar, and a mixed swarm of darks and lights shot upward.

Sightseers piled out of their transports, carrying Avly with them, helpless and contemptuous. Shouting and laughing, the crowd struggled to approach as close as possible to the safety barriers already erected in the street. No firefighters or medical vehicles seemed in evidence. Only a street marshal stood by with some twenty of his men. They were there simply to maintain order.

Another house collapsed.

'They don't bother with them now, you know,' someone said. 'These poorer streets can't afford any insurance.'

Avly found herself pressed to the high, transparent, fire-resistant barrier. No smoke stung her eyes or ash stained her frock. Like everyone else, she gazed fixedly into the heart of the fire.

Was it only beautiful? Or only terrible?

Had anyone survived?

Startling her, at that very moment Avly saw a tall figure emerge from the crimson hell.

She was astounded. He was dressed darkly, and his long, fashionable cloak flared away from him like a single black wing. His hair was also long and black. From this distance, through the slight distortion of the barrier and the unfelt ripples of heat, she could not make out his features, save for a dark bar of brows, eyes…

He strode from the conflagration – *untouched*. How was that credible? All around him, the cascading flames – sparks swirling through his hair, the wild wing of the cloak brushing against a crumbling mass of brickwork and fire. Was he wearing some extreme protective clothing? He did not look like either a firefighter or a medic. Down the charred tumble of the steps he walked, with unlikely ease, into the street.

Without a backward glance, he strode away.

'That man,' said Avly.

The woman beside her remarked, 'Yes, I thought I saw somebody too – a survivor, perhaps. I couldn't be sure. Where is he now?'

Avly stared. She could no longer see the man who had walked out of the fire. He must have entered the crowd, been lost there among the many other young, tall men with long hair and cloaks.

The woman said to Avly, 'An optical illusion, actually, I now think. Have you ever seen a fire before? Illusions can happen. I wasn't sure, myself, if I really saw anyone.'

Avly was sure that she herself had.

Just then, the last buildings gave way together. A golden bombshell of curdled fire hit the sky, then the black dust started drifting, even finally across the tops of the barriers. Careful of its garments, the crowd began to disperse.

During the night Avly had a recurring dream. It was of the man who had stridden out of the fire. In the dream she had detached herself from the crowd and now walked after him, taking some care not to be seen, and so keeping to the shadows beyond the streetlamps. Always he stalked some eleven or twelve meters ahead of her. Following, pursuing him with stealth and tenacity, Avly experienced a continual frisson of – excitement.

Never, since earliest childhood, had she felt such a thing. She had, probably, forgotten until now, what excitement *did* feel like. Besides, there was another element, beyond anything childish. It was, she realised on waking, both romantic and sexual.

What was happening? Really, she did not mind what it was. It had been – quite amazing. Was it still? Yes. She tried, accordingly, to return into sleep in order to undergo the pursuit, and the emotion it entailed. But now sleep eluded her.

She spent all day, as usual, in the most unimportant, superficial activities. Lying down at midnight, which was very early for her, she waited, tingling at the chance of dreams. But that night, she dreamed of nothing. Nothing at all.

Avly was in a store that was hung with crystals, strolling about with two acquaintances. A fountain played unwetly over all. Avly was *not* bored.

The moment she had left her apartment, she had begun to look out for him, the man from the fire. It was ridiculous; really made her inwardly laugh – something too that recently had seldom occurred. How could she ever hope to locate one man, unnamed, unknown, amid the teeming sprawl of Dophan? All she could assume was that he was fully rich, even though he had stepped from the fire in rundown Velvet Street. His clothes, his hair, his *demeanour* had conveyed complete assurance and security – therefore wealth. Avly had not lived among them for twenty years without coming to recognise her own clan. Although, if anything, the stranger was more princely than any man of Avly's class she had met, more arrogant.

A doll of the store, in the form of a tawny lion-beast, trotted over and presented the tray of perfumes, wines, and stimulants resting on its back.

Each woman plucked something up. The air filled with scent and bubbles.

But Avly's eyes slid to the edges of all the rooms, trying to find the man. After the three women had been right through the ten storeys of the store, and she had looked everywhere in it – 'But, Avly, whatever are you *looking* for?' – unanswered – she was eager to go back outside. Once there, she quickly sloughed her companions and began to patrol the boulevards alone. It was mid-afternoon, the sunlight brilliant and The Arch rainbowing down the most succulent mixed tones of colour on pavements and burnished trees. Avly looked everywhere but pavements, trees, and sky.

Nevertheless, she did not see the man at all. Not even anyone who resembled him. It had been, perhaps, foolish to suppose that he would simply arrive in her vicinity. No, she must take the initiative and mount a proper search.

What did she have to go on? Frankly, only one thing. Which was that, since he was rich, he must live either in the Yellow, Green, or Blue Quarters to the west of the city. Maybe he *had* been sightseeing in Violet on the night of the fire.

If only she knew something else about him, or better still, possessed something personal of his – for those who could pay, a DNA register was available. But she lacked either kind of clue.

A minute's intense disappointment flooded Avly. This in turn interested her, however. Was she – was she "In Love"? But she had been in love with many men, a few women too. It had never felt like this – this desperate electric *hunger* – this excitement and anxiety.

Avly summoned one of the individual public air-cars. As it swooped towards her, a silvery shiver ran up her spine. She swiftly got into the car and ordered it to fly her to the Green Quarter.

Between the glamorous greenstone mansions, Avly wended her way and never saw her quarry. Here and there, in be-glittered bars and stores, she paused to make conversation with groups of her peers. Into each brief chat she inserted leading questions. She had heard, she said, from one of her friends, that an eccentric man from this quarter liked to play the tourist in the rundown areas of the city. But everyone she spoke to looked at her in bewilderment. They had heard of nobody like that. What, anyway, would be the point of visiting such slums?

'Oh, during the fire in Violet,' supplied Avly vaguely. 'My friend thought she saw him there.'

'But,' they replied, slightly thrown, 'almost all of us *were*. After all, that *fire* was something worth seeing. Did you know,' they added, 'there were nineteen dead?'

As evening fell, Avly caught another individual public flyer. She rode south again, over into Yellow.

She was growing tired, not exactly physically, but in a slow internal way. She was thinking now she would never find him, and so she believed she *must*. For yes, she *was* in love. And love gave her the *right* to find him. Even so, hers was a difficult task, almost like those set lovers in ancient legends and stories...

The car alighted by one of the great parks of Yellow. Avly walked along dusk avenues between lemon-trees, across lawns bordered by giant primroses and saffrons.

A scatter of other pedestrians passed her. Now she asked no one anything. None of them was him.

Leaving the park at a wide gateway, Avly took a road lined by mansions of cream stucco. Already the delicate streetlamps were burning up on their stems, and windows warmed. All this seemed abruptly sad to Avly. Her eyes filled with tears, and deep, deep within herself she felt a fiery joy at her new-minted depression.

Then – *then* – she saw him.

She froze to marble, there beneath a lamp-standard, its illumination full upon her.

He was on the same side of the paved sidewalk, approaching her, the long cloak swinging as he strode. She saw his face properly because, one after another, the street lamps described it. It was a patrician, pale, terrible face – terrible in its flawless ordinariness. Was he handsome? Ugly? Avly could not be sure. His eyebrows were black, the eyes too seemed black. His hair and clothes were black also – as she recalled from the last time. He was gloved.

While he approached swiftly nearer and nearer, Avly shrank away as if from too fierce a glare of light. But he – he glanced once at her, just as he reached her. Glanced once, and then away, striding on along the street.

Avly shrivelled from the seemingly amused contempt of this one brief look and revelled peculiarly in the comfortless thrill. There had, besides, been more to his glance, she thought. For such disdain seemed to come from foreknowledge. As if he *knew* her and so could discount her entirely. And of course he did not and could not know her. Thus it was for her to change his mind. It seemed to her, weirdly stranded, moth-like, under the lamp, that his very dismissal had been an *invitation*. So, it said, make me aware of you, make me take an interest in you. Show me something I have never seen in any other, for I too am bored here.

Avly drew in a breath. She crept silently back from the lamps and in among the trees of the street. Once concealed in their shadows, she followed the man.

Unlike her dreams, however, there was no need to go far. In less than three more minutes, he turned and mounted a long flight of steps. Above, a door opened for him, and he passed into the house.

Shattered by her success, Avly leant back against a tree. This then, most probably, was where he lived, his apartment.

She gazed up the length of the building. Amid the carvings and cornices, all the windows beamed with light. Which were his? The house was too high for her to be sure if the faint occasional traces of movement she saw cross the windows were, any of them, his.

After a space of time, she went up the steps herself and keyed the panel by the door for the names of those who resided there. Having mechanically glimpsed her status in the city, the panel gave them up to her. But of course, of all the twenty-seven people living, in couples, trios, or singly in the mansion, only ten of them male, none had a name she knew or could know to be his.

Impatient, curbing urgency, Avly withdrew to the watch-post of her tree.

The night was young as she herself, so inevitably in party prone Dophan, he would next come out again – either that or he would be sponsoring some festivity of his own in the house. Might she, if enough persons attended this, add herself independently to the guest-list?

At the idea her head spun. Laughter welled in her mind and throat. *I am happy!* How bizarre.

But, too, how wonderful the street, the lamps, the stars far above beyond the rainbow. *His* street, lamps, stars. That she had located him so quickly was certainly destiny.

An hour went by. Avly took off her high-heeled shoes and stood barefoot. Then she sat down under the tree, as sluts and waifs did in the rough quarters of Dophan. Avly did not care.

Another hour. Avly started awake – she had not meant to doze – had she *missed* him? No, impossible. Some invisible galvanic thread, which joined them, would have tugged at her if he had reappeared. What then had woken her so suddenly?

Avly jumped to her feet and put on her shoes. She stood by the tree watching, in a kind of indifferent dismay, as a medical vehicle, siren mooing, dropped from the sky to the sidewalk.

Savage white radiance exploded from its interior as two medics and a medical doll shaped like a trolley with ramps leaped out and plunged up the steps of the very house where he lived. Only then did Avly grow rigid with fright. Had something happened to *him*?

Above, far up the façade of the mansion, one window filled with chaotic activity. In the vehicle itself machines chattered, and Avly heard a flat mechanical voice: 'Seven people, you say? All the same? Poisoning? How rare. Yes, from the roof will be best.'

Then the vehicle lifted up and sailed to the landing-pad on the house-top, presumably to ferry casualties via the roof elevator.

Avly's heart pounded. She decided she must herself run into the building.

Before she could stir a muscle, the front door reopened. And it was the man who came out.

He moved down the steps exactly as she had seen him do at the site of the fire. He was calm and self-contained. Gaining the pavement, he looked neither left nor right but turned south along the boulevard.

Avly found she could not, after all, quite make herself follow him. She stared after his tall, spare figure, the swagger, the gloved hands. Realisation had reached her. He did not live in this house at all. As the medical vehicle, siren loud and warning beacons flashing, rose from the roof with its – dying? – cargo, Avly put her hands and forehead against the trunk of the tree. She understood at last. The fire, and now – poison. Her lover was an assassin.

How many drooping days went by, Avly knew precisely. She marked them on a calendar. There were seven. Perhaps, in some remote manner, she was observing an unconscious vigil for the seven poisoned dead from the Yellow Quarter.

She had read about them, too, in the journals, for to die in this way was, as the voice of the vehicle had remarked, *rare*. It seemed the cause had been contained in some vintage alcohol they had drunk. Investigations were in progress.

Did Avly consider reporting to the city authorities what she suspected, or rather, was sure of? That this was no vintner's blunder, or domestic accident, just as the fire had not been, and that *he* was responsible for all the deaths? Momentarily she did. Then she saw she could not betray him. She was, for one thing, certain he would then reason exactly who had witnessed him and find her before officers of the law apprehended him. On the other hand, the notion of such a nightmare event brought her only one more perversely violent thrill. Common sense, meanwhile, instructed Avly that such a dangerous man's retributive anger should be avoided at all costs.

She could not stop thinking of him. Or dreaming of him.

Every night of the seven days, she pursued him through a surreal Dophan which, in sleep, had become deserted and vegetal and jet-black, with narrow shimmering defiles, where he sprang forward, cat-like, and she slunk after, trembling with nerves and desire. She never caught up to him in the dreams. He never turned and looked at her. Yet at those times she knew he was aware of her, and that she had a right never to give up. However, something else then occurred.

Information came to Avly, in a dream, of the assassin's forthcoming whereabouts. This was on the seventh night, and the message – for such it must be – was entirely clear. Slinking after her lethal prey through the jungle of the dream-city, Avly beheld a tall tower that loomed out of the darkness. It had a glacial azure globe on its roof, and Avly knew it in a dream-second as the Communications Building in Blue. Across the sky above it were littered two sparkling numerals: 9 and 35.

When she woke on the eighth morning, Avly deduced that this had been relayed directly to her, by means of telepathy. Evidently, he would be in the vicinity of the tower tonight – tonight, of course, since he was a nocturnal being. The hour was nine o'clock.

The other number – thirty-five – almost paralysed her with a sense of shock and dread that sank through her bones like syrupy spice. The *other* number, presumably, related to the tally of victims he expected to kill, by or near the tower.

Avly did not entertain a moment's doubt about this psychic signal from his brain to hers. But she did suspect he might not be aware that he had contacted her. Her acute interest in him had tuned her in, perhaps, to the frequency of his mind, which must after all blaze like a torch with its skills and crimes. Fate had taken a hand and sent her these facts, for her use.

All day she lay about the apartment, not answering calls, not doing anything save brood and rehearse her now almost mystic role.

I believe I am quite mad, she finally told herself.

This seemed to liberate her entirely. She got up and went to make herself exceedingly beautiful for the coming night's adventure.

As Avly, dripping with rubies and scarlet, moved on foot through the city, experiencing all things in a sort of new wonder, Dophan blossomed to neon night.

At last, in the Green Quarter, she caught an individual public flyer. It bore her north, into Blue. An oddly magical ride.

Even the stars had a light navy colour this evening, outside the iridescence of The Arch.

On foot once more, music floated to her from bars, with the crystalline chink, like breaking thermometers, of goblets and bottles knocked together. Avly's sober blood itself seemed aerated with the spangles of champagnist or vodsinthe.

The crowds parted, smiling benignly, to let her through. She seemed to be the heroine of the drama, they obliging bit-players.

How many would die? Thirty-five. A momentous figure. This would be a catastrophe. Was he paid to do this work, or was it only an act... of love?

A vibration from some time-piece flittered out the essence of a quarter to nine, one minute after Avly had positioned herself in a wide plaza beneath the tower of the Communications Building. She stood looking up the tower's tiered storeys. The windows were long and narrow, and it was sculpted from deep blue concrete, the globe from white sapphire.

Someone paused beside her. Avly knew it was not the one she had come here for, but still she half-turned, made nosy at this ultimate juncture by her fellow humans.

A blond young man stood close by, talking into a jewelled cell phone the size and shape of a beetle, and set in a ring.

'Naturally I know the tale. I read a screening of it only yesterday.'

Avly's attention left him. Would he be one of those who would die?

'Yes, and she made this gesture that frightened him. So he ran to his employer,' droned on the young man, annoyingly, 'and asked permission to escape to Bokhara.'

What a pretty name, Avly inconsequently thought: *Bokhara*. Her knowledge of geography was limited.

'But when the employer confronted her, she just denied everything. What? Oh, yes, I forgot. And that's how it ends.'

Avly's eyes opened wide, gleaming like the edges of sharp knives. Across the square, she had seen him.

Seen *him*.

He was like a piece fallen out of the dark. His hair, his cloak and clothes. She watched him as intently as if she were a surveillance machine. And so she saw him cross the plaza, and as he passed, his arm, the cloak, brushed over someone, only as if, courteously, he ushered this other out of his way – but the man tottered, choking, and all at once crashed down.

Avly caught her breath. He must be a genius at his art. Only that brushing of the arm and cloak, only that. Yet too, she was confused. She had anticipated a major disaster being caused, to account for the deaths of as many as thirty-five people. A bomb, perhaps. But no one else even collapsed, and the plaza was merely full of sightseers pressing forward to watch the fascinating spectacle of someone else dying on the paving.

The assassin though had moved northward, away. Already his form dwindled in distance. Avly hurried from the square. Despite her gilded shoes, she ran. She did not mean to lose him now.

He walked, and so therefore did she. It became like her dreams too, when they left the Blue Quarter after some twenty minutes and moved diagonally on into Violet. Here there were fewer and dimmer lights. The shells of unoccupied buildings stood like cliffs, open only on caves of blackness. Most of the streetlamps, even where they remained standing, were unlit. As for the rainbow Arch, this part of it seemed to have gone out, or to be obscured from below. It was only a colourless high ghostly bridge, arcing above, that, miles off, grew luminescent again astride other places. Weeds rioted from cracked pavement and walls, into enormous forests. So all her dreams, then, had been prescient. Did he not know she paced behind him? They had walked by then, he some eleven or twelve meters ahead, for over an hour. He never looked about at her, she never looked away from him. And if any lived in the surrounding houses, yards, and streets, tonight they had hidden. Unless it was only that, now, Avly had eyes for no other but one.

They had reached a landing-station for public flyers. In the slums of Violet, Indigo, and Orange, these vehicles were never individualised, but served as many as a hundred people at a time. The landing-station was crowded, so much so that, even if Avly had until now been blind to everyone else, she could not choose but see them here.

The poor had serious faces, or so she thought. Serious and hard, or, if any mirth broke out among them, it seemed raw and barbarous, and definitely too loud. Their garments had no attractiveness, in her opinion. She felt faintly sorry for them.

If he had come here to kill some of these persons, probably he did them a favour, as he had previously with the fire. The sole puzzle was why any of them required killing. They had no power, no influence or money, and died quickly enough anyway.

But everything he did intrigued her and appeared intellectually viable, if obscure. Any scruple about his work she had evaporated in the ecstasy of seeing him where she had believed she would, of following him along the lonely, jungled streets of Violet. She cared only for him. Tonight, they must meet, must talk. Perhaps do more than talk.

He and she. Destiny combined them. Avly knew this as absolutely as she knew her own exquisite image in a mirror. He might play at cat-and-mouse with her, but in the end, why should he not succumb? She had everything he must want.

Out of the black sky – even stars did not show above these quarters – the dull-lighted, heavy-hulled flyer approached.

It landed gracelessly on the pad, and the crowd milled forward, thrusting itself into the interior, in and in, without any caution. Surely it was overloaded, and more than a hundred men and women were now inside the car?

All this while of waiting at the station, Avly had kept sight of him, although he roved through the crowd. This time he caused no disturbance, nor had anyone expired. She assumed his current murder plot involved the flyer and he would carry it out when everyone was assembled. Compunction warned her not to stand too close. She was about to retreat a little, when *he too* stepped into the vehicle.

Avly knew one split second of reluctance. Then she burst

226

forward and drew herself after him, and all the rest, into the hot and jumbled body of the car.

There was nowhere left by now, naturally, to sit. But he also was standing, against the rail provided for patrons who had no seat.

Some ten or so people had already wedged themselves between him and Avly.

The muddy lights of the flyer dulled further, as it lifted, not very smoothly, back into the sky.

It was apparently bound for the Indigo Quarter, and then for Orange, or so the illuminated strip across the roof promised. But then, it did not matter where they went, it only mattered where *he* might go.

What was he doing on this cumbersome thing? He seemed to have no concern about anyone aboard and stood like most of the rest who must do so, his face a blank.

None of the flying cars, even these out in the slums, had drivers; they were operated by their own intricate mechanical intestines. This one lumbered through the air, and Avly frowned as slight turbulence seemed to hit the vehicle. None of the other passengers, needless to say, paid any attention, used to such inferior transport.

Was he simply travelling, as the others were, to another area of Dophan? Yet he was rich. Why would he need to employ an unaesthetic public car – not to mention the sort of resentful squintings some had cast at Avly, boarding in her finery? No one seemed to react to him, however. Maybe he often came this way. Besides, now she studied him, although he was not dressed in the un-fashions of the poor, nor did he wear the gemmed attire of the wealthy classes. Perhaps this was the most clever form of disguise.

His face drew her eyes again and again. She found it difficult to gaze at him for very long. Her vision blurred, her heart raced, waves of heat and cold chased up and down her body. Seldom – never – had she been so exhilarated or so *terrified*. She had begun to speak a mantra to him in her mind, enticing him, persuading him, *making love* to him. If nothing came of this partial meeting, Avly felt she would not be able to bear it. She would fall into some despairing abyss. His darkness lit the gloomy car for her like a smoky sun.

They landed – bumpily – five times in the purlieus of Indigo, and much of the crowd streamed away. They were like ants, Avly thought, watching them mill down the ramps from the landing-stations, off into the dreary channels of their quarter.

But eventually, after the fifth stop, only some thirty or so people remained on the flyer. Thirty-five? The fatal number? What now would he do?

Before Avly could collect herself, he had left the rail, and as the flyer once more dragged itself skywards, he sat down on one of the long, otherwise empty seats.

From there he looked back, directly at her.

Avly felt her physical body drop through itself onto the floor, while heart and soul rushed upward.

His face was no longer blank. His eyes, very obviously, saw her. He nodded. As if this were their arrangement, and they had both come here deliberately to meet.

Avly, in a half trance, also left the rail. His gaze stayed on her as, shaken about and clinging to handholds, she made her precarious way to the seat. She sat down beside him.

'Where are you going?' she asked him, when he did not say a word.

Still he looked at her, taking in everything about her, she believed, noting her appearance, her jewels, how she had dressed and scented herself to appeal to him.

Then he said quietly, for her ears alone, 'Where do you think?'

His voice too was dark. It was musical and rhythmic.

It made her reckless. Breathlessly she said, 'With me?'

'Ah.' The pause hung like a scorching wire in the air between them. He added, softly, 'Or is it that you are coming with me?'

Rather than being forced now by her emotions to turn away from him, Avly could not take her eyes from his. They were black, his eyes, a silvered black, deep to depthlessness, yet inaccessible. She longed to fall into them and drown, but as yet they would not let her.

The flyer gave a lurch and began again to descend. Below, only half seen on the rim of sight, lightless Orange swelled to meet it.

'This is the last southbound stop,' he said.

The car barged home on its landing-pad. Avly expected him to rise, as the other passengers were doing. He ignored them and the opened doors. Presently the car was empty but for he and she, and the doors closed.

'But,' she said, 'don't you have to follow them?'

'Why should I?' His wonderful voice hypnotised her, as his eyes had done.

'But they – they were the thirty-five, surely, the ones you intend to destroy…'

She did not care she had revealed her knowledge. And he – he laughed.

His laugh. She stared, enraptured and transfixed. It was like the most astounding symphony, distilled to a single cadence. The laughter ended. He said, quite gently, 'You have applied the idea of thirty-five wrongly. Thirty-five is the number of the *last* one to die in Dophan, tonight. You see, thirty-four are already dead.'

Something cool and static was in Avly's mind and changed everything in her, excitement, hope, lust – bone, sinew, blood – to a fluid silence.

She looked away from him as if it had always been easy.

The flyer, returning now to its shed in Indigo, was rising once again, more steadily than before. It chugged over the unlit buildings, and far beyond and behind Avly noticed, indifferently, the bright towers and mansions of the better quarters, bangled with their lamps.

'And I,' she whispered, 'am to be the thirty-fifth person. I'm the last one who will die tonight.' Then she gazed back at him. He too seemed further off, but curiously, also near. She knew him, after all. Perhaps she had done so from the first. Doubtless anyone would.

Nevertheless, she asked, 'Who are you?'

'Death,' he responded.

The next moment the failing flyer, its systems most unusually, but not quite impossibly, breaking down, plummeted from the sky to smash a vast crater in the wilderness of weeds and ruins at the edge of the Orange Quarter.

No one resided immediately in the neighbourhood, either to be fatally struck by the car, or to witness the solitary passenger who left the wreckage and strode away without a backward glance. He was a tall man with long dark hair, and a cloak as black as the grave.

The Ancient Myth

A servant ran to his master, a merchant, in great fear, saying that he had met Death in the marketplace, and she had made a threatening gesture at him. The servant begged the merchant to let him fly at once to Bokhara, many miles away. The merchant agreed, and the servant speedily rode off. Later that same day the merchant himself happened to see Death in the city. He drew her aside and asked why she had frightened his servant with a gesture of threat. 'No, he mistook me,' said Death. 'The gesture I made was in fact one of surprise at seeing him here – for tonight I have an appointment with him, in Bokhara.'

The Thousand Nights and a Night

En Forêt Noire

At school, in the 1920's, my mother was taught (among many terrific things, all of which – including a library of faultless literature and maths – she retained till the end of her life) a little song from France. She recalled all the words, and the melody. And I, happy magpie that I am, stored references to the song in my 1981 werewolf novel 'Lycanthia'. 'En Forêt Noire je vais les soirs', part of the song began... 'Into the dark forest I go in the evenings'. Years after, John Kaiine suggested a scenario to do with a very dark forest. The plot was compelling, and quickly established itself with cast, actions and denouement. The title, of course, had only been waiting.

While the carriage was trundling towards the small city of Arlin, through the dusty summer fields – that was when Louis Corbière first saw it. The forest.

'What's there?' It was not Louis, but the fat lawyer travelling with his thin wife, who inquired.

Only one person, the wrinkled little clerk, knew.

'The Forest of Arlinacque. An ancient wood, said to have existed since the era of Charlemagne.'

'Impossible!' exclaimed the lawyer, who, despite his question, believed he knew everything.

And the clerk said no more.

Later, at dinner in the inn on the Arlin Road, Louis mentioned the forest to the innkeeper.

'That place. Oh, monsieur. It's too close for my comfort.'

'Close? But it lies – what? – ten miles away from your inn here.'

'Too close. I said.'

'Why?'

'A bad spot, monsieur. Rotten. Dark in more than darkness.'

Louis pondered, as he ate the roast meat and drank the wine. The Forest of Arlinacque had indeed looked very dark. Even in the blistering scorch of the late afternoon sun, it was entirely black in form, impenetrable. Huge pines, monumental yews, and other conifers, tangled together, were reaching high up into the thick, hot air. It had taken the coach, travelling quite fast, half an hour or more to pass the trees. But though Louis had striven to squint between them, he had seen very little. The aisles of the forest were like caves full of shadows. Beyond, the fields resumed, and beyond them, the hills, and finally the shape of the mountains was scratched out thinly on the sky.

Reverie ceased. The inn was generally rather noisy, seeming packed with soldiers, and shouting drinkers.

As Louis was retiring for the night, a stooped and very elderly and eccentrically old-fashioned man approached him on the inn stair.

'I heard you ask about the forest, monsieur. Perhaps you would care to glance in this book, which carries the legends of many areas, including that of Arlinacque.'

'You're too kind.'

The old man smiled and said, 'I'm merely old, monsieur, and have been so for a long time. The only real pleasures left to me are to be either very kind, or very cruel.'

Louis was young, not yet twenty-two, and old age was like another country to him. He felt sorry for its inhabitants. After all, life was dangerous and uncertain; he might never have to enter the country of the old.

Upstairs, he lit extra candles, and sat propped high in bed, reading the book the old man had given him.

It was, like the donor, an antique, published, it seemed, around the time of Louis XIII. As the Bourbon namesake turned the pages, ordinary Louis Corbière found fascinating anecdotes of ghosts, undines, dragons in hidden valleys, beautiful women imprisoned beneath ruined castles, and so on. Eventually he located a reference to Arlinacque. By then the candles were burning low, and he was tired. The ornamented print fluttered against his eyes, and before he had read more than five or six lines, he fell asleep.

Even so, the idea of the forest stayed with him, and followed him down into unconsciousness.

Louis dreamed he ran between dark trees, in darkness. Somewhere high above, a moon shone, flashing through pine-needles and branches like a silver sword. Ahead lay no safety – and behind was terror. Race as he might, he could not outrun the awful unknown horror which pursued him. His only hope would be to find a way out of the forest. And he had no chance of that, he thought, none at all.

He woke near dawn, sweating, his feet and fists stinging, because he had clenched them so hard.

Presently he laughed at himself. He was a grown man, on the way to visit his betrothed, for the first time in her family home. She was a pretty girl, who liked him. How foolish to succumb to childish fears.

In the morning, he bore the book, the passage on the forest unread, down into the main room of the inn. The elderly guest who had loaned it was nowhere to be seen – apparently not yet risen from his bed. Louis therefore left the book in the guardianship of the innkeeper, whose puzzlement might be a cover for intended theft. But Louis could do nothing else. The coach was due to leave in ten more minutes.

Dinner the next night was a quite different affair. Célie's parents, the de Lejays, had welcomed Louis, just as they had in Paris, bemoaned as usual his lack of a servant to travel with and take care of him, and presented him, laughing, to their blushing daughter. The afternoon progressed happily enough, through a rose-hung garden, to a pleasant enough evening, during which endless visitors arrived to greet Louis, culminating in a lavish supper. The table was swagged in lace, jewelled by candles and the best china and crystal, elegant, if often chipped. Sixteen people sat down to dine. Unfortunately, one of them was Célie's brother, Marcellin.

Marcellin had never cared for Louis, or the betrothal, and made this plain in various "playful" ways – as if only joking with Louis, rather than trying to catch him out or demean him. Louis' father had formed his wealth in trade, and so ably that Louis himself had not been required to enter the business, and instead had pretentions to study. The de Lejays meanwhile kept up minor aristocratic habits but had fallen on hard – that was moneyless – times. Hence the match, with which everybody, saving Marcellin, seemed well-pleased.

'And how do you find the country, hereabouts?' asked Marcellin sneeringly of Louis, across the festive candles.

'Countrified,' said Louis, smiling.

Célie's father laughed, and so did Célie, but Marcellin continued, 'Come, come, Monsieur Louis. Surely you made out some difference between our region and the tame rambles around Paris? Or can you really not tell a hawk from a handsaw?'

Louis said, 'Even Hamlet could do that, apparently, when the wind was blowing the right way.'

'Oh, bravo. I'd forgotten you were a scholar. You must be,' Marcellin added, 'to go bouncing about in a public carriage without your servant.'

Madame de Lejay raised her hands in alarm.

Louis said, mildly, 'I prefer to travel that way. And on journeys, servants get underfoot, I find.'

'Then you should train them otherwise, monsieur. My Jeannot is never under my feet. He knows too well what I'd do to him if he got in my way.'

Louis mentally considered Marcellin's Jeannot a moment, a villainous, leering fellow, with a scar across his forehead which, supposedly, Marcellin had given him years before.

Louis decided to change the subject. 'I did see one thing that interested me greatly, as we drove here. A huge black forest of pine trees that someone told me is called Arlinacque.'

Madame de Lejay gasped and crossed herself. A number of others at the table looked nervous.

'I beg your pardon,' said Louis. 'But – is it truly such a terrible place?'

'One never knows,' said Monsieur de Lejay. He added sombrely, 'A great many people have vanished there.'

'Oh, worse than that!' cried a blonde lady across the table, who was a cousin of Madame's. 'Men walk into that forest – and never come out of it. They are never seen again – nor any who go there to search for them.'

'There is the story of a soldier,' said Monsieur de Lejay, now even more heavily. 'This happened only a few years back. He was seeking employment, having been wounded in the Prussian War, and was on foot, having given his horse for his debts. So he took an unfamiliar track to Arlin, and happened across the edges of the forest. An old woman was out on a field nearby, hurrying to get home in the dusk. But she ran over to him and clutched his arm. "Don't go into the wood," she said to the soldier. "Why's that, Granny?" he asked her. She said that none who went in there ever came out again. Things were there, inside. Dreadful things, that sucked away blood and bone, and left only ashes blowing on the ground.'

Louis glanced about him. What theatre! No one seemed to breathe. Even Marcellin looked uneasy, his eyes fixed on his father. Yet Louis himself, amused though he attempted to be, felt abruptly a sinking at his heart. He told himself it was nothing, and that he was too sophisticated to be made afraid by this provincial telling of horror-tales.

Monsieur de Lejay, however, went inexorably on. 'The soldier told the old woman, as others reported later, that he would heed her warning, but obviously he did that only to restore her calm. He had no intention of tramping all the way round the forest in order to avoid going into it, looking for the Arlin Road. He was already footsore, and perhaps thought very likely he would meet gypsies in the wood, or charcoal-burners, who might keep him company, and share some wine with him, through the night. So, soon after, he set off into the trees.'

Monsieur paused.

'And then?' demanded one of the other relatives, a young lady with curls, who maybe had never heard this story before.

'And then – nothing, I fear. He went into the wood and, like the rest, never emerged from it. Although some persons from a nearby village, who were out on the pastures above, heard, during the night, hideous screams coming from among the pines. Such things had been heard before. They did not dare go to look. Then, in the days following, six of the soldier's companions from the war, discovering their comrade had vanished, went also to the Forest of Arlinacque – and one of these men returned.'

Louis said, 'But, monsieur, forgive me, I thought you said no one ever did.'

'Ah, my dear friend. This young soldier had not gone into the forest, only to the very edge of it, from where he watched his brothers walk away through the trees. It seems he, too, had a wound, a sword-cut to the leg, and had sat down to rest, meaning after a minute to catch them up. But instead, as he told it, a fearful coldness and lethargy swept over him, almost a stupor, so he thought he would faint. And then it came to him how no sound was in the forest, not the rustle of an animal passing through, not the rattle of a bird's wings, nor any song or call. A silence was there, and a darkness was there – and his companions were in the midst of it – but in that very moment, as he forced himself to his feet to pursue them – he heard them shrieking, and so ghastly were the

235

noises – this, to a man who had recently served in battle – that he fell down in a swoon. Later, he dragged himself to the nearest town. He spoke to the priest and the notary. His account is on record, and anyone may see it.'

So absolute now was the silence also in the dining-room that when a wick popped suddenly in one of the candles, two or three of the ladies cried out.

'But,' Louis said, 'what things are they reckoned to be, in the forest?'

Madame de Lejay spoke leadenly, her eyes cast down as if afraid even to talk of it, 'Vampires.'

'Oh, Louis – where do the souls go, when their bodies are the victims of vampires?'

Louis frowned at Célie, in the moonlit garden of the de Lejay house. He could smell roses, *vigne-de-miel*... and Célie's perfume. He wished they could discuss other matters.

Nor would he say what he had read, here and there, in his studies – that any victim of a vampire became himself a vampire, too. Why, anyway, must this be the case? Surely it must depend. Who could know?

'All good souls,' he said sternly, 'go to God, whatever the manner of their death. I believe that, Célie. And so must you.'

His sternness seemed to console her. She liked to be guided; he had observed that on the three previous occasions they had been together. But this was the first time they had been allowed to be alone. He looked at her, her sweet face, and saw how her eyes admired him, and thought that, as well as liking her, he might fall in love with her, too. How splendid that would be.

'Célie, we must trust in God.'

'And – in each other?'

To kiss her was a delight. He experienced vast joy, simply because things were turning out so beautifully.

But raising his head, the perfect moment was spoiled. For over there, against the vine-grown wall, Marcellin stood, smoking his pipe, unseen till then, but seeing, watching the lovers with the flat, gelid eyes of a snake.

Louis stayed in the de Lejay house four days and spent a lot of that time with Célie. He began to desire her greatly, and was also appreciative of her talents, especially when she played the family harpsichord. The parents were affable. Everyone appeared glad. Even Marcellin, Louis was thankful to find, seemed to have become grudgingly resigned to the marriage of his sister to a tradesman's son.

On the fifth morning, the whole household was up early to bid Louis farewell. He was to catch the public coach to Paris, which left the market square at seven o'clock. To his surprise, after a tender parting from Célie, Marcellin fell into step with Louis. 'I'll see you safe on the coach, my dear brother-to-be. And look, here's Jeannot to carry your bags.'

Louis felt an immediate misgiving. Though the general good will might have made his perceptions cloudy, he now suspected a plot. However, to resist might well give offence to the beaming parents of his betrothed. So he accepted Marcellin's offer urbanely.

In the square, a few persons waited for the coach, and soon it clattered into sight. The brown church was striking a quarter to seven from its clock, as Jeannot, his grinning face like that of an ill-treated, ill-natured dog, threw Louis' bags – rather carelessly – to their place. Then Marcellin spoke. 'Do you know, I think I'll travel a short way with you Louis.'

'That's not necessary, thank you.'

'No, no. I can do with an excursion. As far as Guistanne maybe. That's about an hour off, is it not? Then I'll hire a horse and jog back. Jeannot,' he added, in a jolly tone that was patently false, 'what do you say?'

Jeannot only grinned.

Louis said, 'But there'll be no room on the coach.'

'There, there. We can squeeze in. See how few other passengers there are. You get in, Louis, and Jeannot, you also. I'll just have a word with the driver. I never met one of his sort would pass up the chance of some francs for a drink.'

Very reluctantly, and still punching his brains to find a way to deny these unwanted companions, Louis got into the coach. Jeannot hopped in at once behind him and thumped down on the seat at his side. Presently Marcellin joined them, all smiles and charm, flirting with the two wives in the coach, speaking very respectfully to the cleric in the corner. At Louis, he showed his long white teeth in disturbing satisfaction.

Louis could only smile too and put up with it all. At Guistanne they would get out, presumably. Yet he feared they would not. Oh, then, let them go all the way to Paris, if they must. There, he could make firm excuses to slough them. Even if, as he sensed would be necessary, he would then have to "loan" Marcellin the money for lodging, both in Paris, and on the way there, not to mention the fare for the coach back to Arlin.

They reached the inn at midday. Here everyone got off and dined, Marcellin too, for needless to say neither he nor Jeannot had removed themselves at Guistanne.

Over the meal, Marcellin's conversation was unctuous and gloating. Louis conceived a strong urge somehow to elude him, and his servant, while at the inn. Louis had a crazy notion of hiding somewhere, until the coach had left with them. But then, of course, he doubted they would leave, without him. He told himself fiercely however not to be a fool. He must put up with them. For what could these two wretches do to him, after all?

He had, in the haze of blooming love and general success, forgotten the Forest of Arlinacque.

It was about ten miles, the forest, from the inn, as Louis had previously pointed out to the innkeeper.

The coach bounded off from the inn-yard at about two in the afternoon, but then, after some seven or eight miles, it mysteriously slowed, then stopped altogether.

Consternation had the passengers craning from the windows, Marcellin with them.

The driver had got down and came round to the door. 'All will be well, mesdames, messieurs. Just a tiny adjustment is needed. We'll be off again in twenty minutes.'

'Twenty! Oh,' said Marcellin to Louis, 'let's stretch our legs, shall we?'

The carriage was unbearably hot, parked where it had come to rest, out on the road between the fields, under a brazen, pallid sky.

Nevertheless, Louis did not want to leave the carriage. He said he would remain.

But, 'What nonsense! Doesn't know what's good for him, my brother Louis...' and somehow, in a couple of swift manoeuvres, Jeannot and Marcellin had ungently lifted Louis off his seat and out of the vehicle.

Once they were down on the road, Louis thrust them away. 'What in God's name are you at?'

'Why, I'm concerned for you, my dear. What else?'

At that very second, the driver's mate went running round the carriage. He slammed the door shut and leapt up on the driver's box. The driver was, it appeared, already there. Next, the long lizard-tongue flick of a whip set the horses racing away down the road, the coach rumbling behind them, only a startled face or two peering back through the windows at the three men left on the road.

'My bags…!' exclaimed Louis.

'Damn your bags. But that coachman's a good judge – he can tell who has the class, and who has not. He did just as I told him. Meanwhile, you and I, we've other business.'

Truly horrified now, Louis turned to see Marcellin had produced a smart, silver-chased duelling pistol. He aimed it at Louis' head, while Jeannot stood gobbling and spitting like a rabid dog.

'What do you want, Marcellin? Are you planning to murder me?'

'Maybe not. But since you're to wed my sister, I'd like to find out if you're worth anything, you common little lout. Worth anything, that is, apart from your dirty money. What do you say? Shall we take a walk?'

They walked, of course, along the road for about two miles, by which time they had reached the outskirts of the forest.

It was black as pitch, exactly as Louis remembered it. Some crows, which were flapping over a cornfield nearby, seemed always, even in their widest circlings, to avoid the outposts of the trees.

Marcellin halted, and so therefore did Louis, while Jeannot prowled up and down behind them.

Louis had considered trying to break away. But he had not convinced himself Marcellin, who now seemed both stupid and insane, might not take a shot at him if he did so. Such guns were notoriously unreliable – and, even not meaning to wound Louis fatally, Marcellin might still accidentally do it. Besides, there was nowhere here to escape to. The carriage, in the charge of the bribed driver, was far off. And though he had heard of villages and towns nearby, Louis did not know their location. As for the inn, it was some eight miles back along the road.

'Well, now,' said Marcellin. 'There it is, this vampire-haunted wood. What do you say, Louis? Shall we take a stroll in it?'

Louis, naturally, had been aware this was Marcellin's plan – been aware of it, if in some vague unrecalled way, since luncheon.

He felt, Louis, a deep, ominous reluctance to enter the forest. But he knew that if he refused, this fiend, and the fiend's degenerate servant, would drag him in among the pines, or, perhaps more likely, the two of them would give Louis a violent beating, and leave him lying on the track.

So Louis shrugged. 'If we must.'

'Oh, yes. We must. Not scared, are you, dear brother?'

Louis said nothing. And Jeannot laughed in his own unmusical neigh.

They walked on up the road.

After maybe five minutes, a path appeared through the fields, which led towards the forest. It was an overgrown path, evidently infrequently used. They took it. All around, the dry yellow stalks of ripened grain stood like watching sentinels at a death-march. Then the shadow of the pines came spilling down, cool, cold, smelling of a strange hollowness, less verdant than empty.

The silence was all at once immediate, and implacable. It was a silence like a loud noise. Louis thought, in order to be heard above it, he must shout. But he said nothing, and when Marcellin spoke again, his voice sounded only dulled – yet it had taken on a very different tone.

'I remember old tales about this forest,' said Marcellin. 'Yes. A place of the Devil. Look, do you see between the trees? All the slight undergrowth there is stays entirely undisturbed. No one comes here. No one dares... They say no animal or bird will ever enter it. If ever one strays in here, it too vanishes and is never found.'

He is trying to frighten me, Louis concluded. But when he glanced at Marcellin, his enemy's face was pale, and Marcellin's eyes darted uncertainly about the dim, barely-to-be-seen avenues between the pine-trunks. They were on the very brink, staring in. Yet even now it seemed to be too late. They were already trapped in some web of sticky darkness and horror, and could not move away, only forward.

Even Jeannot looked wary at last, though he said not one word.

'Perhaps...' said Marcellin. He hesitated.

Louis waited, hoping Marcellin would relent, and they might still get free of the trees.

But no. Marcellin frowned suddenly, and said in a harsh, low growl, 'Come on then, brother Louis. Onward!' And he waved the pistol.

They stepped in among the trees, and Jeannot plodded after them.

Then all the shadows dropped together. It was like the curtain of night. Louis paused, to allow his eyes to adjust. Marcellin and Jeannot did the same, the latter cursing. But the blackness was uncanny. Even the densest forest, in early afternoon, should not change to midnight... And though Louis had waited, still he could hardly see. Less shadow, then, more a fog – a miasma – sheathed the area.

Childishly, he turned and looked back, and saw daylight framed brightly, in slender ovals, between the nearest trees.

Out there, less than six metres away, lay sunburnt fields and open pasture. And yet – though the glow of day stayed visible – it did not, even faintly, reflect into the forest. Incredibly, not one single shaft of daylight pierced the gloom.

Above, boughs heavy with needles and black as ink, crossed and wove against each other. Tiny flecks of sky were to be glimpsed, but they were opaque, and remote. On the forest's floor not a fragment, not a splinter of light had fallen.

'A – strange spot,' said Marcellin. Did his voice tremble? Was he acting?

'Yes, it is,' said Louis.

'I think,' said Marcellin, 'it would be easy to be lost here.'

'No doubt.'

'But we are brave, bold fellows. And you, Louis, bravest of all, so you shall be our leader.' Louis regarded Marcellin who now smiled again with utmost malice. 'Courage, my valiant leader. Lead on!'

It was obvious enough what was in Marcellin's mind. Louis was to be made, still at gun-point, to move away ahead of the other two. No doubt, they would soon sidle off and leave the forest, for here, despite all misgivings, the way back to the fields was yet in view, and so it must – surely – be possible to get out there. But Louis would be forced to go deeper in, and thus might lose himself, being only a tradesman's son, an upstart, an idiot.

Yet, too, Louis had noted that Marcellin at least partly believed in the legend of the forest.

How he must hate me! In his heart he really wishes me to be slaughtered here, and so never return.

However, if by going on, he might in the end avoid Marcellin and the servant, Louis was prepared to obey.

Accordingly, he strode briskly forward, along one of the smoky avenues, not once now looking back.

He tried to measure his progress in time as well as in distance. He counted minutes in his head, one minute, then two, stalking along the corridor between the trees.

But the forest began, even so soon, to confuse him. Though he could hardly see them, the trunks of the pines, crenulated and barbarous, soared up like pillars in some macabre church. Yew trees like black bears crouched across adjacent vistas, other coniferous trees, also dark and thick-furred, struggled up between, sometimes swaying a little at some unseen unfelt current of air. The undergrowth was sparse. Here and there, a skeletal bush, a dead bramble. No birds called. And everything always the same, as if – as if in passing each column or blot of tree, Louis walked in an unnoticed circle, and so passed each one again, and then again, round and round – even though the avenue was itself in fact, unnaturally, as straight as a road.

After three minutes, Louis stopped, and pretended to ease the cuff of his right boot. He had heard no more from his vile companions. They seemed to have disappeared into the substance of the pines. He supposed – and prayed – they had now retreated.

So then, presently, he did turn, and looked back the way he had come.

All evidence of external light was gone. The smothered cracks of day which had showed between the first trees, were no longer to be seen. Only the avenue could be made out, and not very clearly, stretching along its straight pillared line. And no one was there. The evil Marcellin and the disgusting Jeannot, unable to decide between viciousness and unease, had apparently made off.

Well, it was no great thing, was it? Louis had not deviated from the path. He need only retrace his steps along the aisle, and he would come, after three or four minutes, to the forest's edge, where daylight had formerly showed – and still must. He might then linger a little, to be sure his tormentors had really gone. And after that, emerge, and go up the road again to the inn, which should not take him more than two hours. Notions that Marcellin might be lying in wait for him along the route, Louis dismissed. He was beginning to think after all he had been unwise to give in to a bully. For all Marcellin was his future wife's brother, Louis decided if any further threat was tried, he would throw off his coat and make a fight of it, pistol or no.

He was about halfway back along the avenue, and had not yet identified any glimpse of daylight through the trees ahead, when a curious sound came out of the thunderous silence of the forest.

It was a sort of prolonged whining note. At first, he took it for some mechanical noise – of a bellows, or cartwheel, away across the fields. Then it seemed it must be the cry of a small animal in a snare. It went on and on, sometimes becoming louder, falling off, beginning once more.

Louis halted. The noise was unpleasant. It set his teeth on edge. He wished it would stop, for now it seemed very loud indeed...

Next moment the whining shattered into a pistol shot – and then a duet of screams. They were the most appalling thing he had ever heard, frankly indescribable, combining a kind of guttural choking with high, irresistible shrills of enormous pain and fear.

Sweat burst out all over Louis' body. His guts churned, and he thought he would vomit. He wished only to run away, to bury himself deep in the ground and so hear the dreadful outcry no longer.

But then, the ice-cold thought sliced through his panic. That is cunning Marcellin, and Jeannot too. They are copying the stories, reproducing the awful shrieks of the tales.

They wanted to scare Louis out of his wits and had almost done so. He shook himself. Let them howl, then, if they must. He would be patient.

The noises ended abruptly. Probably they had hurt their throats.

Louis gave them fifteen more minutes, counted out in his head, before completing his return journey along the avenue to the edge of the wood.

There was no light. It had been crushed. And what he had taken for the first trees, though he walked forward into them with the determination of the desperate, did not, now, open onto the fields. Nor were they the first trees.

Had he taken a wrong turning? It was not possible. He had not left the avenue. Unless... Had the sameness of the pines and yews deceived him? Had he somehow gone astray?

He must have done. It was the only answer.

Except for one other answer he would not consider. Which was that the trees themselves had somehow altered, shifting to close an open path.

I will not give in to superstition, even though I feel it. I will not be beaten by old stories and old trees, nor even by that devil Marcellin.

Soon after this, moving cautiously forward in the direction he continued to judge to be the way back to the road, Louis found Marcellin, and Jeannot.

It was actually quite remarkable that he did so, and had he been even a few minutes, indeed a few seconds, later, certainly he would not have done. For there was not much left of them.

Louis stood rooted to the ground – as maybe the trees were not – glaring at what lay across the track: two long heaps of rusty, greyish dust, shining a little, and so able to be seen. At the end of each of these mounds lay a pair of skeletal feet, unshod, all bone. At the other end, a face rested eyelessly, like a mask, upon a blob of darkness – all that persisted of either head or skull.

But even as Louis bent over them, his own eyes starting from his own head, as if red-hot nails drove them out, the bone feet and the masks of papery skin dissolved to ash, and in an unheard eddy of wind, blew off and away among the trees.

Between the columns of the pines, Louis ran. He dived and sprang and galloped. When he must rest, panting, he crouched low against the barren earth of the forest, among its arched, craggy roots. As soon as he was able, again he leapt forward, and on – like a hunted deer.

Yet, as even Louis understood, he was clever, no fool. And he knew all this running was of no use whatsoever.

A bleak thirst assailed him. He chewed his tongue to release moisture, not wanting even to take up a bit of the bark, or the tiny pebbles, which were occasionally lying about under the trees, to suck on. He did not weep. And only once he prayed to God. But, being no fool, he sensed even God was shut out of this forest. It was a department of Hell.

Although there had been absolutely no proper light at any time, in the end, the unseen illumination ebbed quite away. And then the forest was as black as if he were inside a locked chest, hung closely with thick black draperies. Outside this filthy place, worldly night must have arrived. Louis felt despair. For he guessed he would never see night, nor day, again.

Despite all that, so far, he had evaded the things – the demons or vampires, whatever they were – of the forest. But he was aware too, that perhaps, just as Marcellin had, they were playing with him. Teasing.

After the true ebony black of night soaked through the trees, Louis ceased to run. He only walked, creeping along, sometimes biting on his hand, as he had done in childhood, when afraid of the big dogs of his father's country house.

But he tried not to think of his father, or his mother, both of whom he loved, nor Célie, whom he had begun to love. He tried to beat his mind into finding a solution to all this.

He would, of course, never discover a path from the forest. That much was obvious. While whatever lurked here, toying with him, was only waiting for some self-chosen, special moment to emerge, and do to him – oh God – what had been done to Marcellin and Jeannot – and to all the rest.

Finally, exhaustion covered Louis like the night. He sat down, having no choice, his back against a tree. He was so weary and repulsed by everything that had happened to him, that he was almost ready to confront death. Not quite.

Sitting, he felt something inside his coat grate against his side. He put his hand on it and drew it out. Forgotten in bewilderment – flint and tinder – the means to make light – and fire.

Louis sat there, holding these ingredients of civilisation in his hand. He did not think in words, but in pictures. The pictures were simple, of a dry summer forest – set alight and burning.

It was then, in the instant of revelation, that the touch came on his shoulder. First on his shoulder, then encircling all his body, his torso, legs, arms – his face. A soft touch, or sequence of touches, almost loving, almost amorous. He did not even flinch. He struck, with one rapid motion, the flint – and a spray of flame split the dark.

Louis saw, by the light from his tinder-box, great arms embracing him, long hands of longer fingers, stiff and glittering hair, mouths like those of gigantic living statues...

No eyes. They had none. Had no need of them.

It was – the trees – the trees themselves. Nothing lived in the forest. It was the forest which lived. They grouped around him, rank on rank, circle on circle, rootless, pressing in, spreading down their needled boughs, uncoiling their trunks like serpents. Wooden claws caressed him, hair of pine-needles scratched eagerly at his face. Faceless heads, lacking eyes, opened their mouths and breathed in his essence with adoring greed.

The forest. The forest was the vampire.

From the throat of Louis issued one long, wailing cry. But in that instant, he cast the fire away from the tinder, and like a star he saw it plunge, there among the jumble of the half-seen serpents, their thirsty needles and searching spikes.

As a new scarlet light began to bloom, like the sun fallen upwards from below, though the floor of the forest, Louis prised himself from that unthinkable union. And as the mouths lapped and snapped after him, he flung himself once more away.

Over boulevards lined by clutching, snatching things, that grasped at him and lost him, lost him, torn, milked like a goat from the pastures, bled, he ripped his way, tossing the flowers of fire again and again among them, until the talons of their loveless hungry love withdrew.

He saw their empire wither in the flame. He saw them consumed. Yet too, he felt himself dissolving. He ran screaming on legs made only of dust.

Even so, by the vivid light of the conflagration, Louis hurtled on, the roar of a huge forest fire all about him, amid the limbs of demons disintegrating. A rain of sparks descended.

He tumbled out suddenly – out, sobbing and praying – and out – out – on to the hard stones of – a road. A road. While at his back, towers blazed red, and ruby fields dazzled, and purple smoke streamed into the sky, and drowned, in its rivers, the moon.

Louis lay face-down on the road, crying. Sparks went on showering over him. They scorched his hands and the back of his neck but did not hurt. Nor were his clothes burnt, nor torn; he was amazed to see it, even through his tears and hysteria.

He thought the local villagers would soon come hurrying now, if only to try to save their crops from the wild arson of the nearest fields. But no one came. No one. They were too frightened.

The fire – the forest – was a crimson cloud that bellowed up into the sky. Where there had been silence was a symphony of rage and agony.

Louis got up in a while. He trudged away from it, along the road, his head hanging, stupefied and near to collapse. Nothing seemed real to him. Not even what he had done.

It was almost midnight when he reached the inn, or so he thought. He had journeyed slowly, and the walk had seemed to take him years. Lights still shone, however, in the inn's main room, and in several other chambers above. Louis was dully surprised none of the people here looked out to see what the other light was, blaring ten miles back along the road, where the forest went on burning.

Louis himself cast one last look in that direction. The lower sky was flushed, the stars there inflamed. Then he pushed open the inn door.

The main room contained a large drunken party of some kind. Men raised their glasses and bawled out patriotic songs. In the shadowy corners of the room, beyond the candlelight, a few other patrons were quietly sitting. Louis saw the group of soldiers he had observed on the first evening he stayed there, and then the old gentleman in his strange antique clothes, who had offered him the book of legends. This ancient man perched by the low summer fire, reading, but now he lifted his eyes and met Louis' glance. The soldiers too, Louis was aware, had turned his way. Yet the drunks at their festivity had interest it seemed in none but themselves and each other.

Now the innkeeper and two of his assistants hurried in, bearing jugs of hot brandy, fruit and sweets.

Louis attempted in vain to catch their eye. He sighed. He would have to wait.

It was then that the old man got up and hobbled towards him.

'So, you have come back, monsieur.'

'It seems I have,' answered Louis.

'I believed you would. Despite this, I tried to warn you. Yet, the very fact that I was able to do so, to speak to you at all, indicated, alas, that already, probably, your fate was sealed.'

'I beg your pardon?' Louis saw the innkeeper approaching and hailed him again. To his dismay, but somehow not to his astonishment, the innkeeper paid Louis no attention, simply walking straight by him and out of the door. Lamely, Louis gazed at the old man in the old-fashioned coat. 'The forest burns,' Louis said. 'Has no one seen the purple light in the sky?'

'I have, monsieur. They have.' The old man gestured graciously towards the soldiers in the corner, who in turn bowed to him. 'But it has burned before, the Forest of Arlinacque. Or rather, we have thought it has. For the forest, alone of all things, can never die. Nor can it ever be left hungry.'

Total stillness flowed from the night and settled within Louis like a sort of poison.

'What are you telling me?'

'I am telling you that this is now your home. As I once did, as our friends the soldiers once did, also, and as others have done, who now exist inside this inn, you entered the forest, and the forest took you. But that is over. There is no more to fear. Those persons that the trees kill, when they are wicked, they go elsewhere, and those who are saints, they too, if to another destination. But we who are only ordinary men, we come back to this inn. And the inn is full of us, dear monsieur. Look about you and see.'

Louis looked. He saw. They were everywhere, at the edges of the room, on the stairs, moving between the shadows and the candles. Old and young, wealthy and poor, male and female. They were nodding to him, smiling not unkindly, sorry for him, for the shock he experienced, now, which they too, long ago, had also felt. While in the centre of the room, brilliantly lit, the boisterous, fleshly, mortal drinkers saluted each other, and saw no one else at all.

In a misery that seemed, even this early, quite familiar, Louis watched, in his mind's eye, Célie slipping away from him, his parents, his youth, his future, the world itself.

'I did not, then,' he whispered, 'escape. I thought I had.'

'You did not escape. None ever do.'

'Oh God, what has become of me?'

The old man replied, in the most gentle of voices, 'It is nothing so very unusual, dear monsieur. You are only dead.'

THE SNAKE

A Story of the Flat Earth

The snake lay under a low, flowering tree, at the side of the forest path. The snake seemed like a small spill of amber that the sun had firmed and coined with scales.

A woman passed, on broad bare feet. The snake watched from eyes like darts but did not change its position. Later a scholar wandered by, gazing at this and that. He paused some while to inhale the perfume of the flowers, leaning into the lower branches of the tree, but his mind was so fixed on the minutiae of esoteric things, he never glimpsed the snake. The snake however saw the scholar, and watched him, yet did not stir, made no move either to strike at him or retreat. Eventually, the scholar wandered off into the forest, thinking of stars and gods and other lives he had lived.

An hour later, a young man came riding along the path on the back of a jet-black horse. It was adorned with golden bells and had a garland round its neck, and the rider was elegantly dressed in satin and silk, with boots of fine blond leather. He was handsome also, and seemed happy, looking up into the sky as if he saw in it all sorts of kind and generous creatures, each of which smiled lovingly back at him.

The snake suddenly flicked its amber tail.

Though small, the snake by its action caused the lower and most flowery branches of the tree to begin shaking. *Swish-swish* they went – and the rider glanced down at them.

'The favourite flower!' he exclaimed. And dismounting gracefully at once, he reached into the tree to snap off the largest bloom. In less than a second the snake uncoiled all its length and rose upright on its tail. Its shining head shot forward. A single hiss escaped its jaws and its poisonous fangs stabbed deep into the young man's palm.

As gleaming death spilled from his fingers he stood transfixed. He stared at his hand, then upward at the sky that, moments before, had been so crowded with sweetness, yet now seemed filled with fire and doom. For him it was. He stiffened, choked. Tears poured from his eyes. Rigid as a stone statue he crashed to the ground, where two or three inadvertent stony ripples ran over his body, after which he was motionless, and dead as yesterday.

The horse, frightened, galloped off along the path. The snake too had vanished.

Perhaps three hundred heartbeats after, a noise of music and laughter began to be audible, and then a large company of riders, all richly-clad and mounted on horses strung with bells, came dancingly into view.

Instantly an awful cry went up. The cavalcade was halted.

Living men bent over the dead man on the path.

'Look, see there, the marks on his palm. Already he is turning black with venom.'

'And the flower beside him,' said one, 'he went to the tree and plucked it for her, since this one is her favourite. But he disturbed a snake…'

'The gods,' said another 'can never be trusted.'

Zerezel waited among her maidens, on the terrace before her father's palace, all morning, and through the flame of noon, the thick gilt of afternoon. At first, they joked: had the handsome prince met another he preferred on the very road to his wedding? And they were amused, for they, and she, knew he loved only Zerezel, while even the patterns of the stars had confirmed this. Then more serious things were said – the great forest was full of tigers and lynx, robbers, ghosts – but certainly the young prince was brave and intelligent enough to defeat or elude all such dangers. Besides, he had ridden that way before, and now as always travelled with a vast company of men and servants. Perhaps he might have ridden a little ahead, impatient to reach his lover, but only by three hundred heartbeats, or four hundred heartbeats – no more.

When the gilded afternoon turned to jasper and swung low into the western sky, the old prince, Zerezel's father, sent some of his soldiers out along the road.

Then the maidens began to weep. It was Zerezel who calmed them. She moved among them gently, with her long hair that was the colour of the western sky, her slender wrists ringed by pearl. 'All will be well.' But there began to be a shadow on her beautiful face. For now it was the time for shadows. They rose up their full length and stood on their tails among the carved and painted trees of columns, they spread like poisonous stains over the patterned floors. And then the shadows burst out of the forest, shouting and calling, and making too a sound like that sound a heart makes, when it falls down through some inner chamber of the body, and into a place of blackness under the earth, which men say does not exist, and which does *not*, yet which any who have ever suffered know, and have visited often.

'He is dead, Princess. He is dead.'

'*Is* he dead?' she asked. 'Why then, so is the world.'

And so for her the world died. And she went in and lay down, and the edges of her bridal robes, and her marigold hair, poured like tears along the floor, and the darkness could come up from the hell under the earth, and veil it all in black.

'*She will die too.*'

This was what they said.

It was known by then also that her betrothed had plucked a flower for her, her favourite flower that did not anymore grow in his own land. And that was how he met the snake and death. She lay in her apartment, on a floor, and drank nothing and nibbled at the air. She heard no one speak to her. She said not a word. Only the medicinal spells of sages kept her in her body, and this barely. A month passed from the calendar.

Another month began to pass.

'Send,' her father said, 'to the four corners of the earth, send to the tops of mountains and the cellars of the seas, to deserts of sand or wind or snow. Tell any there anything I can give them I will render, to one that can save my daughter.'

The messengers rode out. They scattered like thrown grains of rice along the world.

They had a great many adventures on their various journeys, each of which, probably, would crowd a whole book. But there was one among them, Keshom by name, who travelled northward and then farther north, beyond the limit of any then-drawn map.

Gradually, the land turned cold, and white. Keshom assumed this was from that fabled element known as "snow", which clothed the heights of the tallest mountains – apparently. Yet here, the land was not so tall. It went up and down, and the *white*, which was like marble, or purified cream, was combed all over it. Here and there too Keshom seemed to see some word or other, even now and then – if only when he was very tired – whole sentences decoratively written on it... most strange.

After a while, however, the terrain did rise consistently. So Keshom, of course, rode upward with it.

All at once he came over a kind of ridge – and there before him stretched what he took at first to be some giant's smashed mirror of corrupt and misted glass. From its centre lifted a curious tower, very black, but with veins of a glistening red.

Presently he realised, as if reason only now returned to him, that the area of broken glass ahead was a lake, seemingly frozen.

Meanwhile a red light had burgeoned at the apex of the tower.

Exactly then there occurred a snowfall.

Keshom sat his horse, and he and it observed how this snow dropped everywhere. The messenger put out his hand and caught one flake and peered at it in dismay. For there *was* a word on it, and so it seemed to him, written clearly, and he read it. *Thus*, it said. But then snowflake and word melted together. Keshom was glad.

He did not advance until the snowfall ended. But when it did, he picked toward the tower.

'Does some mage live there?'

Prudently, rather than cross the ice, Keshom rode around the lake, and after perhaps three-tenths of an hour, he reached a causeway of high snowy stone, which led out to the tower. Nothing marked this but for a great skull at its beginning, which Keshom took to be that of a tiger or leopard. It was black.

From the vantage of the causeway he could see a single window that burned with a cool grey light, and matched the heavy sky now settling to evening.

Keshom went along the causeway and arrived at the base of the tower.

Above in the grey window nothing had been, or was to be seen, and there was no indication of a door whereon to knock, let alone to enter by.

But Keshom raised his well-trained voice.

'My prince sends me, as one of his messengers, to all four corners of the earth, to mountaintops and sea cellars, to deserts of sand, wind, and snow. I am to tell you, he will give anything he can render to one that can save his daughter.'

'What is this daughter's name?' said another male voice.

It seemed to speak directly in Keshom's ear and was both quiet and overwhelming at the same time.

Keshom shook his head to clear it of the sound. He thought, *This one has power.*

He answered, 'Zerezel.'

At this a huge panel slid back in the tower-side. Beyond, Keshom saw a dimness, lit only by the failing light of evening. Yet through the dim appeared a flight of cranky steps.

'Enter,' said the other voice, more softly and even more distinctly now.

Keshom hesitated. 'Great sir,' said he, 'may I ask *your* name?'

'*Thus,*' said the voice.

And on the stair a line of grey tapers lit, to indicate, needlessly, the way.

In the far country where Zerezel lay suspended between life and death, albeit with one of her narrow feet already well across death's threshold, a full year had been sloughed from the calendar. The old prince had aged not one but a hundred years. His complexion and his hair were white as any supernatural snow. And if a word were written on *him* it was *Despair*, plain for all to see. He paced about night and day. Only once at each dawn and once at each moonrise would he step into his daughter's chamber, where, by now, they had laid her on a couch. She herself was beyond all human contact. Her slenderness had grown thin, and in her bright hair too some strands of white had appeared. Her eyes were shut. She did not speak, and only a physician's glass could show she breathed. She had no awareness of the world that had died for her, nor of any person in it. She had lost everything but one thing, and that was her beauty, which still clothed her like her wedding finery, impervious. Only magic kept her alive, and this was *all* it could do. And often now, gazing at her actually lifeless deathlessness, her father would chide himself, and believe he should order the safeguards removed, that she could fully die and have peace. For perhaps in the waste of the deadlands she might find her beloved again. But the old prince had never been certain any afterlife existed, despite the teachings of the priests. For if it did, and was worth anything, why had the gods themselves preferred to be immortal?

And perhaps one can be found who will save her...

But few of the messengers had returned, and those that had brought no help. In every country they had encountered not a single man or woman of power who had reckoned themselves able to assist.

'We can part oceans and topple stars,' they would say, 'but Lord Death we may not bargain with. And since only her lover, restored to life, would bring your princess from her deadly state, save her we cannot. Nor none can. Such a love as hers, broken, slays those who otherwise would not die. For such a love is greater than death. Go home, then. We offer nothing but to pull down another star.'

There was an evening when it was to be a night of no moon. On such a night the old prince spared himself a visit to Zerezel's chamber. As he sat alone, a servant came to him and told him the messenger Keshom waited nearby.

Soon Keshom knelt before the prince.

'Sir, I bring news.'

The old man stared at him with a heart that quailed. Keshom looked stern and troubled. But then he spoke:

'In the farthest north, among the dry white snows, I chanced on a magician of extraordinary power. For name he takes only the word *Thus*. But he has said to me he alone can rid your daughter, exquisite Zerezel, of her killing sorrow. And I was convinced.' Keshom's face, during these sentences, had altered. He seemed merely earnest now, and perhaps his former look had been due to exhaustion.

The old prince rose to his feet. He summoned his court to hear what Keshom had said, and what else he had to say. Keshom continued: having left his horse at the base of the tower, he climbed the stair in the half-light for several minutes, until he emerged directly into a vast stone space, lit with a sort of dusk, above which, in the ceiling, burned a non-illuminating red glow like that of a setting sun.

No other was to be seen, though on all sides were cabinets stacked with scrolls of vellum, and large books bound in ebony and horn, or else in what seemed to be black or white human skin. The whole area was round and had no corners. But at the walls, equidistant from each other, were four stone beasts. One was like a griffin, and one an alligator, one a man with the head of a dog, and one a fox with the face of a child. Each of these creatures had in its forehead a jewel. The eagle brow of the griffin had a jaundiced topaz, and that of the alligator a sable pearl; the dog-headed man bore a dull purplish spinel, but the child-faced fox wore a gem Keshom had neither seen before nor heard of – it was the colour of decay. From the jaws of each beast there curled out vapour. But this was odourless and faint, neither increasing nor ceasing.

Keshom had paused, rather terrified, yet in command of himself, for he had been well-trained in his duties.

At length the disembodied and inimical voice he had heard outside spoke to him again from the air.

'Shall I appear?'

'That would be welcome,' said Keshom.

'Do you suppose so?' the voice asked ominously.

Abruptly a cloud-like fog filled the space. It did not issue from the mouths of the four beasts, but simply straight down from the redness above.

It swirled then cleared, and when it had done so a tawny leopard crouched there, in the chamber's centre. It snarled at Keshom too, showing off its fangs and blood-red mouth. But Keshom did nothing. He waited.

Then the pelt of the leopard wrinkled and poured off, and it stood upright and became a tall and slender man, whose golden hair flowed from his head over his wide shoulders. He was clothed in velvet. His face, as Keshom currently told the old prince, was of a wonderful handsomeness. Never, said Keshom, had he seen any man, nor even a woman, aside from Zerezel, whose beauty was as noble, or as instantaneously persuasive.

'Now, besides knowing the name I use, you behold my true human likeness,' said the paragon to Keshom.

Keshom bowed low. 'Sir,' he said, 'the sun has set on the world. I must ask if you are one of the Demonkind, even if you are their lord, Azhrarn himself?'

('Indeed, murmured several of the prince's court when they heard this, 'and was he as beautiful as that?')

But the man, the magician, had only smiled a little at Keshom's inquiry. 'Unlike that of any demon, my hair is yellow,' said he, playfully quite underestimating the glamour of his hair. 'Besides, note that I wear golden rings, as no demon could, or would deign to do. No, I am not one of Azhrarn's fine troupe, though others now and then have made the same error as yourself.'

Keshom once more bowed low.

The magician resumed. 'I know of your master's daughter, Princess Zerezel. She is said to be the fairest maiden now living. What therefore ails her that she must be saved from it?'

Keshom punctually related the tragic events. He added that she lay now close to death, while her father, and all the land, mourned.

'And can none of your own scholars offer rescue?'

'None. Nor any other I have met with, despite great ability. For they say love is stronger than death and such a love it is that slays her.'

A change passed over the face of he who named himself solely *Thus*. While across the room, the stone beast that resembled a child-faced fox blinked both its eyes – even Keshom gasped – and the mortifying jewel in its forehead gleamed for an instant coldly green.

'I have heard this said before,' murmured the magician, 'this of love and death. Very well, return to your prince. Tell him I alone can save Zerezel. But my price shall be high.'

'He would give you his own life, great magus, I assure you, in payment.'

'And so I should,' agreed the old prince now. 'Oh, can it be possible her saviour is at hand? But,' he added, 'where is he? Surely he has travelled with you?'

'No sir. He said he would remain in his northern tower until your answer.'

'Alas! The way is so long, never now will he reach us in time – for despite any magic woven about her, I can no longer blind myself – she sinks and fades like guttering candleshine.'

Outside, a wind blew along the terraces of the palace, and the forest trees bowed down as it went by. A vague smoke for a moment seemed to hide the stars.

'Fear nothing,' said a voice at the old prince's ear. 'I am already with you.'

And there he was, the magician, tall and fabulous as Keshom had described him, or more so perhaps, much more.

The Prince spoke to him without faltering, also well-trained in his duties. 'Lord Magus, you are welcome as summer. But how am I to call you?'

'As your slave did, *Thus*. For that is my name.'

It had not, however, always been his name.

Some twenty odd years before that moonless night, the magnificent and puissant magus, Thus, was only a spindly youth, drab of skin and shaven-headed, who drove camels for an unkind master, and went by the name of Drahn – which meant, in those regions, *Hardship*.

Drahn had been sold to camel work, at the age of six, by his mother, who demonstrably had not wanted him. If anything, she had been more unkind even than his owner, who through the ten years of their acquaintance simply half-starved him, and whipped him if he transgressed – only punching and kicking him groundlessly during bouts of drunken wrath. The camels also were harsh with Drahn, being themselves ill-treated. They too kicked him, and stinkingly spat at him. One morning, the most violent of them, a huge red animal, kicked Drahn so cruelly he lost his senses. And when he woke again, the caravan had moved on, either not noticing they had mislaid Drahn, or reckoning him worth less than other rubbish shed along the route.

Where Drahn had dropped was in the middle of a desert – this one not of snow but *salt*.

Here, for two or three blazing days, and the cold nights between, he staggered or crawled about, croaking with thirst and fear.

Finally, he tumbled down a slope and fetched up by a horrible little pond of black, salty liquid. Nevertheless, partially crazed, Drahn attempted to drink it. The result was ungood.

After this episode he abandoned himself to death.

He was accordingly amazed to be woken by a tall, ancient man, who held a flask of clean water to Drahn's lips, and firstly prevented him from drinking too much, which after the dearth, would have killed him more certainly than his thirst.

One salt-preserved tree grew by the pond. It had a whitish trunk and even leaves, these like strips of fossilised gum.

Here then the ancient man sat sheltering, and Drahn beside him, while the blade of the sun sliced its slow agony from east to west.

Drahn had little social chat.

Neither had the ancient one. *He* spoke only facts.

'I am glad to have met with you, Drahn,' he said, 'since Lord Fate decrees I must perish here of old age, and all my mighty magecraft cannot prevent it.'

'Pah! What magecraft, you old goat?' politely inquired Drahn, who of course had learnt his manners from sadists and camels.

'Why lad, such as this…'

At which the filthy pond-puddle changed to a pool of crystal water, and the salted-down tree to a towering palm, pineapple-trunked with fronds like malachite.

'Ahhh!' screamed Drahn.

'Yes, yes. But to continue, I have been caught unawares by my own demise – which I confess I had not bothered to predict, which prediction is in any case an inexact science, just as King Death himself does not always know when he must rise up and strike us down. Unawares, I say, I despaired of finding any to whom I might pass on such quantities of power as I contain. (For you must understand, I possess also the knack of gifting my brilliance to anyone, at my death.) However, despair be gone! Here *you* are! And yes, poor boy, you are such a ghastly specimen, ugly, brainless, and vile, that I shall be able to fill you to the brim with greatness, glory, strength, and genius, not to mention vast physical beauty, and magery beyond all dreams. *You* will far excel even myself. For I was cultured, a clever and educated man at the hour these attributes came to me, and handsome too. Which left less room for improvement. With *you*, the tide of power will work in unimpeded transfer. The dreary vacant vessel which is yourself will be flooded, and so enlarge. After all, it is always better to gather water in an empty jar. Or write on a blank page.'

(Drahn snorted and gobbled in confusion.)

Taking no notice, the sage finalised: 'Now brace yourself for the torrent of benefits. Also for extreme amounts of time in which to exercise and enjoy them. For though this cannot make you either invulnerable or immortal, and one day you, as I, must die, (and should be careful meanwhile of accidents), with reasonable care longevity is yours. I myself have lived hundreds of years. But death encroaches. I feel his hand upon me – therefore, receive all – *Thus*.'

Then the sage stretched out his own hand, and as one finger of it touched Drahn, a blow far more conclusive than that of a camel's hoof threw him into oblivion.

Waking, the gods knew how, much later, he found himself in a luxurious oasis of palms, dates, and orange trees, where wholesome fountains sparkled, and deer and hyenas drank together in harmony at the lustrous pool. The sage had vanished. Only some bones, picked pristine, lay along the pool's rim.

And Drahn? Drahn was gone.

The *he* that had woken was not the *he* that he had been.

In the water, he saw the new *he* that he now was.

And presently, without effort, translocating himself from the oasis to some other spot miles off, he laughed aloud and renamed himself: for the last word he had heard when in mundane human form.

The old prince and his court conducted the Magician Thus solemnly up the winding ways of the palace, to the life-death chamber of Princess Zerezel.

All were afraid – but the magician.

They flung open the doors – an act of fear.

Beyond the extended teardrops of windows, the moonless night hung black as a curtain, torn and fanged with stars.

In the glimmer of a solitary lamp, a single couch. And on the couch lay Zerezel. Hair of sunset and winter frost. Skin of silk and silence. Beauty of the world, *despising* the world. Alive. Dead. In her wedding garments of baffled, thwarted love.

Not a word, let alone a phrase, was spoken by any of them.

Not even Thus spoke in his mage's voice.

Keshom though, who had come up to the chamber with the rest, glanced at the magician warily. And saw that in the magus's face the skull stood out like a knife.

Then he alone moved forward, the magician Thus, and standing by her bed, he looked directly down at her. If never before had he seen her, surely even like this, he must love her now. If ever before he *had* seen Zerezel, he must have loved her then.

He was, it was a fact, much handsomer than the man she had adored and meant to wed. Thus truly did possess the perfect gorgeousness credited to demons.

And when he bent toward her, and his mane of hair, in the lamp's low gleam like a rush of volcanic rain, furled round her, who could not believe that these moments had been preordained. As, in a way, they had.

The sage's tower, when Drahn-now-Thus had first came to it, rose from a lake of glassy water, amid a plain of blowing grass. It was, the tower, of marble, and veined with luminous rainbow colours.

Imbued with the learning, wisdom, sorcerous genius, and memory of the sage, Drahn-Thus recognised the tower instantly, and entered it.

A white stair went up to the sage's library, which was sunny both day and night. The walls were lined with scrolls and books, cased or bound in covers of precious materials, none of which seemed earthly in origin. Above in the ceiling beamed a constant sunlight. Equidistant from each other, four marble beasts guarded the chamber. They were a feathered lion, a graceful lizard, a smooth-coated dog, and a little child with butterfly wings. On the forehead of each shone a gem. The lion had a sky-blue topaz, the lizard a silvery pearl, the dog a crimson spinel. But the child's jewel was clear and flashing as water. It was a diamond.

Knowing how, Thus made his home in the tower.

From the tower, also knowing how, he came to rule all the land about.

In his brain was the memory of the mage-sage. The sage had been benign, gentle, and trusted. Wherever therefore that Thus took himself, he was greeted with gladness, and at once recognised as the sage's heir.

For one bred to abject slavery and misuse, lessoned only in cruelty, to one unattractive, mindless, and foul, such happenings were a tonic.

Years passed, on bare broad feet. Decades wandered by, scholastically gazing at this and that.

From the mouths of the four beings in the tower faint smokes began to issue. They could tell Thus of so many matters, and he questioned them very often, determined to learn, to understand and grasp. He had indeed been empty, was greedy now.

The sage had known, seeing Drahn in the desert of salt, that to give him too much water too swiftly in his great thirst would physically ruin and destroy him. Yet this careful sage had also deluged Drahn with psychic power, not even thinking twice.

He did not set a hand on her, the woman who lay before him.

All saw this, the throng in the lamplit chamber.

Yet, despite the brazen rainfall of his hair, it was obvious to them that he bent toward Zerezel like a stooping hawk. Most realised next, with a sudden start, he had placed his lips upon hers.

He kissed her.

He kissed her, and from the night all about a composite sigh, a breeze, a breath, winged up.

For *kindness* kisses. Honour kisses. *Love* kisses.

He did not linger then, but raised his head, and stood above the lovely spill of her body.

Soundlessness followed the sigh, and stasis, and in the solitary lamp the flame faltered as if it must go out – before leaping high, filling the whole chamber with light.

Where had she been to, Zerezel? Oh, she did not think or know or care. Somewhere, nowhere. Where the beaten soul will drag itself, wishing too it should die.

Yet there, after millennia, something brushed against her, as a leaf may glance across a sleeping hand.

It was more than that. Weightless, formless, yet it had to it a peerless bitter-sweetness, and an *edge* like honed steel. It had the sort of *voice* which called more loudly than any trumpet note, more subtly than any murmur uttered either side of life.

She lifted her face from the ashes of nothingness. Sightless and deaf, she waited to see and hear again this *thing*. At a loss. And when the summons did not come again, still she turned and broke the surface of the ash entire, and she flew out like a bird toward the sun – outward, upward, into the living world.

In the chamber with the lamp, it was as if a glass screen shattered.

She had seemed dead, the prince's daughter. Now in one movement she rose straight up from the couch, kneeled there on it, and death fell from her like a veil.

Her eyes were wide and full of a vital searching.

She spoke hoarsely, for her voice had been dumb some while.

She spoke only to one.

'How?' she asked. 'How? How have *you* done this?'

Then the magician flaunted himself before her. It was his vanity, and few could miss it. (Did she?) But after all, why should he not be vain, when he had worked such a miracle?

How *had* he done it? Through his great power, evidently, his force of charisma.

But 'I have done it,' he told Zerezel, 'through love.'

'Then,' she whispered, '*I love you.*'

After which she fell back on the couch, too weak to offer anything other. Which hardly mattered, she had offered all. And her eyes anyway stayed open and burned on the magician. It was noted, by some regretfully and by others in approval, that never had she gazed with such hypnotised fascination at her former bridegroom, even though his death had nearly slain her.

The palace rang with celebration. Flags of scarlet and saffron dripped from ledges. Firecrackers were being made ready to fill the sky with arcs and orbs and showers of rose-red stars. Keshom entered the princess's apartment.

How changed everything was. The floors and walls dazzled with polishing and sunshine. Most burnished of all, the young woman who stood before him. She had given orders, and the couch was taken away on which she had lain so long. It was an emblem of sadness and ill-omen and had been burned.

Now Zerezel's eyes burned. The fire in them was very bright, all her sorrow seemingly consumed there.

She spoke at once. 'Tell me of him.'

Of course, Keshom had no doubt of whom she wished to hear. Yet it was quite curious, for in another day and evening that same man and she were to be married. This was the price Thus had demanded of her father – Zerezel herself. The old prince had been glad to pay it. As for the girl, she had already consented, for had she not whispered before them all: *I love you?*

'Lady,' said Keshom, 'what would you know? I was with him only that one hour inside his room of magic.'

'Tell me of that, then,' said Zerezel.

So Keshom described again what he had seen, and what had been said and done.

She listened attentively, occasionally nodding. And as he spoke, Keshom saw how she was strong and well, a bloom of health on her from the magician's healing kiss, even the white that had come in her hair disguised and coloured over. One would not know, to look at her now, she had suffered any loss.

When Keshom concluded his account, she said, 'And after? What did you learn *then*, when you had left him?'

Keshom frowned.

'That is,' she said, 'when you travelled back from the tower. You will have passed through the lands best known to the Lord Thus. Surely they talked of him there?'

Keshom frowned worse. It was true enough; the magician *was* talked of, if one should ask about him, as Keshom had during his return journey.

'They praised his erudition, lady, and his looks. They told of wonders he had performed, incredible feats of marvel. Although...'

'Although?'

'They were afraid of him too.' Keshom lowered his eyes, for now her *eyes* blazed only with great anger. Certainly, she must think he slighted her second suitor. Quickly Keshom added, 'Such power as his may terrify. As I have said, even to me he showed himself as a leopard. He is able to assume such forms, and it would be impossible not to be afraid of it. Besides, I have heard the stone creatures in his tower tell and show him everything he desires. He is like a god on earth. One may adore and admire and *also* fear such prowess.'

'Yet, though long-lived, he is not an immortal, nor invulnerable,' said Zerezel, rather doubtfully. 'So I have heard. Can this be so?'

She dreads she will lose him like her last lover, thought Keshom. And he said, 'So too I heard – that he is vulnerable and mortal both. Yet, we concede, so mighty in power, he is well-equipped to defend himself.' After which Keshom bit his tongue, for he wished the magician might not be so armed in his own defence, that he *might* be lost to Zerezel, and to the palace, and to the whole earth.

For Keshom *had* asked for stories in those lands of the Magus Thus, and first he was given only the most fulsome praise of him. Royal messenger as he was, Keshom had known this at once for the subterfuge of pure terror. And gradually he weaned some of them to mutter the truth, or scraps of it. And these tiny scraps were like huge blots of filth soon smeared all over the image of the magician. Thus was to the people round about his tower a beast, not only in his shape-shifting, but in his inhuman cruelties and viciousness, his greed and evil-doing. They had another name for him, too. Here and there Keshom had seen, or been shown it, scratched into some wall or fence as a warning, and the magician had not, lion as he was there, bothered to smite the scratches away. *Drahk*, that was the harsh name the people of those regions gave him. *Drahk*.

Keshom himself had known but too well he could not cross such a mortal demon. (Demonkind might have been nicer to deal with. They had their own oblique codes and would sometimes make bargains.)

The monster however would merely kill him, and worse, vent his displeasure on those who spoke ill of him. And therefore Keshom had come home and delivered the magician's message, and all the rest followed.

Much alarmed, only one item *perplexed* Keshom at this point. That a being of such enormous and unfastidious power should trouble to save Zerezel, let alone require to wed her.

The princess meanwhile nodded. Her eyes were dark. Was she then content with what he had said? Approaching Keshom, she gave him a silver ring with a white gem in it. 'You are a good man, Keshom.'

He thanked her and went away, and raged at himself that he had not confessed the horror to her. But it would have been no use. Thus – or *Drahk* – had each of them in his thrall. And she, poor maiden, *loved* him.

The wedding day arrived.

Dawn till sunfall they rejoiced.

Birds were loosed in multi-coloured drifts; incenses spiralled upward; night closed and was undone with fireworks.

After the banquet, with garlands and singing, Zerezel went up to her bridal bower. Never had any woman looked so lovely, or so glad. Presently her husband, the magician, followed her. Never had any man looked so god-like, or so sure.

Priests blessed the bed, the rafters, the doorway, and all nine windows of the room. Wine and perfume were spilled. A guard of attendance waited in the antechamber as custom decreed: three maidens chosen for their virtues, and three gentlemen chosen likewise for theirs. It seemed Zerezel had asked that Keshom be one of these. It was a bestowal of much favour, for which he was envied. He would, needless to say, rather have been placed in a dungeon for the night.

Outside, beyond the festive gardens, the forest hushed and rustled, asking itself perhaps what went on now in that huge lighted house, where, for a year, only lament and silence had visited. And perhaps too certain trees asked each other, or the sky above to which they prayed with the upraised wooden fingers of their branches: *has she forgotten him so soon? Has she forgotten her beloved one? He that died against our feet from the bite of a little golden snake?* But to that, neither the trees nor the sky gave answer.

Drahk who was Thus, Thus who was Drahk. Years he ruled that land, the kind, pompous sage had governed, and that had expected something similar from Drahk. But Drahk had been Drahn and Drahn had been scum. And for every particle of mystic brilliance that entered his brain, still Drahn too lurked in there, skulking like a venomous insect in the corner of a golden palace filled by lights, or, as a poisonous snake might do, of course.

People and lands were soiled and spoiled. The landscape was altered to a desert, and then came the scourges of winds, and then the snow dropped dry and adamant, white, like salt. The lake too froze and broke and froze. The ethereal rainbow marble of the tower went black and seemed to run with blood, the blood of those savaged by Drahk who was still Drahn and taught by camel-kicks and the fists of dead-souled human *things*.

The sage, dying, for all his genius forgot his common sense. He knew not to give a man perishing of thirst too much water. He did not consider that this might apply also to the giving of flawless knowledge and magecraft to one dehydrated of all goodness, thought, and heart. Oh, that power...

In it had gushed.

Another receiving it would have died. Alas, Drahn-Drahk lived on. And on and on, for though not invulnerable, as Keshom remarked, Drahk's cunning and defences, once marshalled, were never overcome.

So he ruled his ruined lands. And when he grew bored with his sin, he asked questions of the wise stone beasts, the feathered lion and giant lizard, the dog, the child with butterfly wings. And the topics he asked to hear of and see, converted those arcane creatures to a predatory griffin, an alligator, a man with a dog's head – and the child lost its beautiful wings.

But then there came a night when Drahk considered he had seen and learned and done all that could interest him. And boredom gnawed. So then he said to all four beasts: 'I am the best of men. I am master of the earth. I therefore disdain to conquer and rule more of it than these few miles, for it is all the same. Instead I will have something else. For any woman I have seen that I have wanted – I took. They were all dross. Yet maybe there is one who is not dross. A virgin, and the most glorious. Find and show me that one. The fairest woman on earth, as I am easily the most handsome among men.'

Vanity, always that, with him. He had had nothing, now had, could have, it all. Boasted and wanted to partner his grandeur. A moon to his sun, a satellite to his world.

The beasts obliged. That was their fate.

The griffin revealed a wondrous woman in the east, but she was too old for Drahk. The alligator revealed a more wondrous and younger woman in the west, but she was a harlot. The dog-man revealed one younger and more wondrous still, but she was newly deceased, and had lain three days in her tomb. Drahk cursed his servants. Then he said to the wingless child, 'Now, you. And be sure *you* do not fail me.'

And the child revealed Zerezel, in the far south, and she was young and virgin and the most beautiful woman living on earth. But she loved another man and was due to wed him.

Drahk said, 'If *I* go to her, she will instantly forget the fool. She will want only me.'

But the child answered softly, 'No, lord magician. For true love is blind. True love can only love. Such love is a sword, stronger even than death – therefore beware of it!'

At these words Drahk, entirely at last frustrated, felt the sword of true love pierce *him*, through the heart he had never properly had, either as Drahn or Drahk. And so he cursed the stone child too, whose wings had already been ripped away.

From his curses the jewels of all four creatures were muddied. But the child's turned a dreadful shade. Yet as the child was also robbed of its form, becoming a fox with only a child's face left to it, it *laughed*, though this seemed just the barking of the fox.

And here now is the puzzle of the magician.

Evil and ignorant he was. Fantastically enlightened and made a genius as well. And in that way his spirit was at war with nature within him. Though *he* wished only to exercise his vileness, the power that had become his mind yearned for sanity and goodness and pulled and struggled and rent at him. Because of this he had hoped to find some way to outwit his better side, to blind it in one eye – which was that of the intellect and soul.

And unfortunately, the manner was to hand. Arch-mage that he had become, could he not shape-shift?

Like one donning another coat, Drahk had put on him the form of a leopard, and went out to kill and rape and raven. Or he wore another mantle for it, that of the bear, or of the unicorn, or the shape of a tiger or the wolverine. So he indulged his pleasures, so he outwitted himself

And this method did not, even in his new ecstasy of love, desert him.

The clean power always refused to allow him the act of murder, but once no longer human he was without conscience. And he was used, by then, to splitting himself in twain. It was surprisingly very easy.

He had obsessively studied Zerezel some while. He knew, amongst other things, her favourite flowers.

Drahk blighted all of them in her lover's country, and instead grew a tree of them beside a forest path, along which her betrothed would travel, a little ahead of his retinue, as Drahk had seen he always did.

Drahk then contemplated and selected the most fitting alternate form to put on. He assumed it. And lay under the tree of flowers and waited patiently.

When the bridegroom entered the bed-chamber, his bride stood before him. She was clothed as if in silken mist and her hair was like a waterfall.

Her eyes rested on him with the most profound hunger.

How could she help but love him? And he loved her.

He knew this.

Love stronger than death.

He had used up so much carnal passion in unspeakable scenarios, that now he paused a minute, gazing at her, wanting to delve in himself for some wholesome dream of lust, of longing, and certain he did so.

Zerezel seemed faultlessly to suit herself to his mood. Only after some time did she address him.

'My beloved lord,' she said, 'you brought me from the outskirts of death's kingdom. And you are the mightiest mage known upon earth. How can it be you – *you* – a god among mankind, have chosen *me*?'

'Ah,' he said. A fakery of dismissal.

'Beloved,' she said, 'I do not deserve you.'

Something struck a spark then in his vain, divided mind.

Tanith Lee

With a hint of – was it *petulance*? – he said, 'Nor I you, it seems. Since you loved and would have wed another.'

'He is *nothing*,' said the woman immediately. And her eyes revealed without doubt that only Drahk (Thus) filled her thoughts.

'You did not reckon him nothing once,' said Drahk. 'Nor myself anything at all.'

'How might I? I had never looked on you. Nor had you beheld me either.'

'Suppose,' said Drahk quietly, 'I were to tell you that, even before that man's untimely end, I *had* seen, and *had* desired you?'

Was she stunned by this? It seemed so. 'My lord – I must ask you why then you hesitated? For if you had come to me then, and I had seen *you*, could I have wanted any other?' (And beyond the windows the forest rustled and hushed, lifting its praying wooden arms to the sky.)

Drahk mused. 'Could you not? But if you had loved me better, what then of your betrothed? The contract was too firm to break.'

She grew deadly pale and answered, 'I should have despised him, having looked on you. I would have begged that someone kill him and rid me of him instantly.'

'One did kill him and rid you of him.'

'A snake, they say. How I wish I might see that snake! I would have them make a temple to its glory.'

Drahk preened himself. 'Oh, I could show it to you.'

'What, can you summon it?'

'In a way. I could take on its form.'

She laughed then. It was a melody, her laughter, played only for one man. 'I know, lord, you are a shape-changer. But, beloved love, lord of earth and forever, a leopard is your form, or a lion – some kingly beast – or an eagle, a dragon – never a snake. How could you become such?'

Drahk smiled. Was his smile playful too, or very dangerous? 'Do you doubt it?' he inquired. 'Are you unable to picture it?'

She lowered her beautiful and fiery eyes.

It was midnight.

A moon had risen late.

The amber debris of the firecrackers still clouded the forest, and the moon itself smouldered like a ruby, even when it reached the apex of the sky.

It was then that Keshom heard a voice call to him, and only to him, from Zerezel's inner chamber.

The other five attendants had fallen asleep. Only he, burdened with his misery, had not.

Nor could he tell, disoriented as he had become, quite whose voice it was that called, whether that of male or female, or even if it were that of some ghost which wailed from the forest.

He rapped on the door, and his hand was cold.

'Enter,' said the voice, '*Thus.*'

The magician had not, even as the sage had not, been able to predict all things. That Zerezel would almost die, for example, had not entered his calculations. But that her father must thereafter send for help was nearly traditional. And by some kind of influence too, Drahk had then made sure one messenger at least should find him.

A single question however remained outstanding.

The fox child in the tower had warned Drahk that Zerezel could not love him, could love only her first lover – even dead. And since these stone creatures were all-knowing, even vain, self-blinded Drahk believed it, and accordingly *slew* her first lover. Why then and how had Drahk's own kiss *restored* Zerezel to life, let alone to utter instant love of *him* – a love that even denied the former lover, forgot or wanted him slain? She, who had been so faithful. Love stronger than death…

Now the answer to that lingering question lay before Keshom. Though he did not quite see it yet.

He saw only the room, the marriage bed – untouched, unused – and Zerezel the maiden, who stood there wrapped in a silken shawl, the ends of which pooled over and around her feet. The lamps were out, but red moonlight filled the room from three of nine windows. No other was present. The Magician Thus, or Drahk, was not to be seen.

'I wish to thank you, Keshom,' said Zerezel, in a mild, low tone, 'for bringing him to me. For delivering him up to me. This man who, in the form of a little yellow snake, slew my only beloved with his venom.'

'Lady!' cried Keshom, galvanised, 'I failed you, rather, for I told you nothing of my suspicion of him. Let alone that he had killed your prince – for I swear that *this* I never guessed.'

'You need tell me nothing. You had only, as you did, to confirm the mage was facile in the craft of shape-shift, and vulnerable too. Capable of dying.' (Outside the forest made no sound, listening with all its million million leaves. And the moon, like Keshom, stared with an amazed wild face.)

'I had learned who was the murderer – yes, even in the oblivious nothing where I wandered. And also how the murder had been done. I knew from the moment I felt the touch of his lips. For on his lips I tasted the skin of my one true love, and mingled with the unique fragrance of his flesh – the taint of some dire poison. It seems my lover's body was the last human element the magician had touched with his mouth, before that mouth kissed mine. Oh,' she said, and from her eyes the moon-hot tears fell out like blood, 'at once I woke and flung back to regain the world and view the assassin. I gazed at him with burning loathing, and with deep hunger for his death – which others, and even he, mistook for *love*. And when he came to me tonight, I wooed and coaxed him to put on the shape he used to work his crime. Boastfully he did so. And when he coiled there on the floor, slender and little and scaled and venomous, I went to him with cries of praise and delight, and see...' She let drop the shawl and it slid away. '...*how I rewarded him.*'

And there on the floor in the strange light, spine-snapped and crushed in one second under her heel, lay a golden snake, dead as yesterday, unmade as tomorrow.

OUR LADY OF SCARLET

During a visit by the plague, it was thought the colour red was a means of warding off sickness. The colours of plague, after all – like those of death – were quite otherwise. Red meanwhile symbolised the shade of untainted blood. For this reason, then, red draperies poured from windows or clad beds of the rich. Red flowers were grown, red wine was the popular beverage. While those also cunning or wealthy enough to afford expensive dyes and ornaments, put on coats and gowns of crimson, and trinkets of ruby, or ruby-tinted glass.

Andelm, however, believed in none of this.

He was in his twentieth year, well-favoured and talented, and the student of a secretive society both alchemical and scholastic. Andelm accordingly foresaw for himself a shining future, which even plague could not interrupt, let alone dismantle. He had placed his faith in different powers. They had nothing to do either with red, or with God.

In the dawn-early street, therefore, as he took himself to his studies, or in the summer twilight as he returned, he did not flinch from the dreadful carts, which trundled up and down the thoroughfares. Actually, he looked them over with a certain merciless interest. Pulled by one or a pair of pale, gaunt nags or desolate donkeys, each had its driver and sometimes a secondary man.

These fellows were usually coarse and pitiless themselves. Either they had been condemned by utter poverty, or drawn unlucky lots, to take on this work. They feater moment by moment almost certain infection from the carts' mortal contents. Or else they had already had the plague and survived it, which would tend to leave them scarred, and some strange way psychically poisoned, both by the disease and their recovery from it.

Now and then, student and self-certain as he was, Andelm persuaded the live men on the carts to let him look more closely at the dead ones. On the mobile wooden table, corpses lay thick as a catch of herring. They were bound for the plague pits outside the city walls. Here they were flung in and coverleted by quicklime – or else burned on a communal fire. (By now the city was massed with such smokes, and too the smokes or burning tinctures and herbs said, like red, to protect.) Many of the cadavers were naked. Even those who had been dressed, especially the *well*-dressed, had had most or all of their clothing stolen by any, as for example the cart drivers and their mates, who no longer had cause or margin to fear contagion.

So Andelm was able easily to inspect many aspects of plague death. Its black swellings and their reeking leakages; the wrongly-coloured greenish or black blood that here and there issued; the composure or reverse of the dead. He beheld in this way disturbing sights. Such as a beautiful young woman, cool and pale as alabaster, laid in the cart in a poor little shift no one had wanted to steal. All unsightliness was either hidden or absent. Perhaps she had in fact died of some other malady, even been murdered. Another time Andelm had marvelled at the assorted contortions of death agony. And once at two children, sat in the cart bolt upright, with blank eyes wide, their hands locked each in the other's in a heart-searing final clutch; now, due to morbidity, inseparable.

It must be said Andelm's own heart was not wrung, though no scene ever left him unmoved. His purpose in this wicked world of sins and ailments was, he believed, to *learn* and so to grow powerful in knowledge. Only then might he assist Mankind. Rather than weep or faint or curse at the horrors of the plague, he sought to be tutored by them. When once or twice the strings of his heart gave off a human twang of shock or grief, he mastered them with the thought that one day he might alleviate or prevent such happenings.

And then he would pass calmly on to his lessons and work at the academy, and return after to his further reading and his work in his modest lodging, above *The Sun's Head Inn*.

That night Andelm returned there very late.

He had been forced to wait, if not without curiosity, as a procession of priests went along with lit candles, singing a Mass for the soul of some aristocratic person just then claimed by plague. The casket lay closed, on a bed of dripping silks, (none of these red), and was drawn by two black horses. Many mourners accompanied the hearse, they carrying long black or white feathers.

The rumour was the mighty man had also been a writer of note. Andelm had never heard of him nor, did he much care. The student had scarce time for books that were not educational, none for poetry or plays.

At last reaching the inn, Andelm went through the yard into the common-room, which formerly, since the disease began to stalk, was almost or totally vacant. Tonight, though, a change had come about. Despair itself produces symptoms, this being one of them. For reckoning themselves lost, a crowd of people had gathered to mingle in the normal way, eating much and drinking vastly, and now acting too in the most lascivious manner, man with woman, woman with woman, and man with man.

Andelm did not linger long. He was neither offended nor aroused by the view of some pairs of naked breasts, not the flash of active buttocks in a shadow beyond. He had already glimpsed such things in other places, and himself took no interest either in sex. He had no spare moments for it.

Despite this non-diversion, on his gaining the upper floor, something *did* give Andelm pause.

A large neglected room along the narrow corridor, some fifty paces from his own, had been opened wide. In the past, various lumber was stored there, and occasionally a drunk had got in and made a nest, filling the area briefly with stink.

Now the room was altered. It had apparently another purpose.

Andelm, concealed by the darker corridor from the room's currently well-lit space, stood a few seconds to watch what went on.

Then he moved away, and undoing his own door went inside.

Even there, however, with the wood of the door muscularly shut and bolted against the rest of the inn's noise, Andelm was soon aware that sounds from the neighbouring room yet penetrated his sanctuary in a way the general row did not.

He found himself disturbed.

He at first considered this might have had to do solely with the fact that what went on in the upper room, unlike the carnality in the common-room, bore a similarity to certain rites, practiced at intervals by the alchemic secretive society of which he was a member. Both they, and those in the room, had a semblance of the religious. Both were formal, possibly archaic in origin, immeasurably intense – and fully Godless. On the other hand, Andelm, seating himself to dissect the matter, did not think mere appearances had much bearing on this reaction. No, rather it was the sense of *power* that might ritually be conjured among the students of his society. The same perception that an equal, if quite *unlike*, power was rising there, in the upper room, only fifty odd paces from him. And their door stood wide, so any might witness it.

Some while Andelm wrestled with his thought. He ignored the sparse and well-known furnishing of his chamber, the half loaf and dish of now-cold broth put ready for him with his pot of ale. He ignored his two books and the sheaf of papers lying ready, with pen and ink.

Presently, he admitted to himself he must go back and take a second glance at the other room. Maybe he had been mistaken. Maybe the hot, smoke-stifled streets, the later hour, had made him fanciful. And maybe something even more significant than he believed went on along the corridor.

Within the room... any rubbish was cleared away, the old broken chairs conceivably chopped for winter fuel. The bedframe had been taken apart and stored elsewhere. All other former items had also vanished. Nor did any human stench loiter. The room had been scrubbed and some aromatic burned there, as on the streets outside.

Candles threw a dense, ruddy glare from the iron wall spikes, and in their own vulpine light the melting wax on them ran like thin, reddish blood.

Some twenty or twenty-five people of both genders were in the room. They crushed together in a snake-like, circling formation, their hands fixedly clasped, (reminding Andelm, in sudden uneasy memory, of the two dead children in the cart). Each head was turned, in several cases almost wry-necked, so every one of them might gaze of what dominated the room's farthest end. There, where the old bed had been, with mice busy in the mattress, now rose a stand of some sort, concealed beneath a blood-red drapery. And on the stand...

In height, the carven figure, that of a female, was not much more than two feet, far less than half the height of a man. Nor was it of any fineness, but rough in outline and feature. And yet, in candle-red it glowed and had great presence.

Andelm could see at once it had been made to mimic, if not replicate, figures of the Virgin Mary. Unlike the Virgin, though, the woman it represented was shown wearing a plain yet revealing gown, that clearly described the shapes of breasts and thighs beneath. The carved robe had been stained a ripe red, and the figure's unveiled head was garlanded with hair painted the shade of the rusty Eastern spice known as ginger. The face, too, while having no subtlety of line or expression, possessed much vitality. The red lips curved in a hungry smile; the dark eyes, rather than convey the deadness of the statue, glittered hard as jet stones. She seemed amused, this immodest red Virgin. She seemed more than – yet essentially *kin* to – *human.*

Going back, Andelm had been incautious. Probably, despite their averted heads, they had noted him go by before, even expected his return, been *waiting.*

From the group he immediately heard call the strong loud voice of Stollia, the inn-wife. 'Come in and join us, Master Andelm. Any may attend. Don't stand aside on ceremony. There's no disrespect we offer you. All are one at this.'

Andelm had the urge to fly. He was unused to such feelings, brave as he was with his self-assurance and selfless self-absorption.

But he forced himself rather to reply with a question.

'What is it then, mistress, that you do?'

'What does it look like? We worship Our Lady here.'

'Is she your Lady?' asked Andelm, as coolly and sensibly as he could. 'Surely our only Lady is the Mother of our Lord, Virgin Marya, who steps between us and God's wrath.' He himself credited none of this, of course. He had been educated much beyond it from his seventeenth year. But he knew the ways of the unlessoned world and was always careful to pay lip-service to any other unavoidable dues to the majesty of the Church.

But Stollia said straight out, 'God forsakes us, and Christ forsakes us, and the Virgin Marya has gone deaf to our pleas. Otherwise wouldn't the plague death have been blown away?'

('True, it is true,' muttered other voices in the heated, perfumed, reddened room.)

'So we have found another saviour. Here she is, for Tibar the carpenter fashioned her to help us. She *hears* us. *She* will listen. She is the Red Virgin. She knows the proper colour of our blood and will take care of us. Step in and pray to her, master. It'll lift your spirits better than ale.'

But Andelm had stepped back until his spine touched the wall of the passage, through his coat and his skin.

Where he had never feared privately to mock the Virgin Marya, or even God, with his disbelief, Andelm knew now a deep and feral terror of this scarlet icon. He would rather, it seemed to him, spit on the feet of Christ upon the church crucifix, and before the priests too, than give a single word to *this* one.

'I thank you, but I must get to my studies,' he said, still in a polite, cool tone. 'May you be happy in your new faith.'

And turning abruptly, while they made a slight, sullen scornful noise behind him, he hurried back to his chamber, again closed and bolted the door, and now also propped there a heavy chair with both the heavy books on it. About an hour after this, he additionally sprinkled salt across the inner threshold.

Throughout that night, he sensed a Presence at the inn, inside its confines. He sensed the movement of this being, below in the ultimately unenthusiastic tumble of the common-room, from which, post-midnight, only a few groans and lamentations issued, coincidentally in the passage outside the upper rooms.

It had been born, he knew, in the *adjacent* room.

It was, he knew, the essential volatile element of the creature he saw on Stollia's improvised altar. The Red Virgin.

Rising before dawn as always, but now leaden and nervous from lack of sufficient sleep, Andelm detected how the horrible travesty slipped back, if only a short distance, from the outside of his door. It was flirtatious, it seemed, with one who instinctively disliked yet also was afraid of it.

To admit fear was novel for Andelm. To be afraid was quite alien to him. A further lesson, this one appeared more unpleasant than even the most upsetting of those ordeals he had willingly endured in order to enter the secret order. The fear was worse, too, he supposed, than any ordinary fear of death. That hunter in black, whose scythe swept so often across the streets outside, Andelm had acknowledged but never so far shrunk from, certain no harm would come to him, no price be exacted, for his youthful days were to be long, and his destiny fixed.

His intention was to go straight to the academy, and there seek advice from the Grand Master. However, arriving at the academy doors he found them boarded up, and daubed with the plague sign.

Presently, he learned from a fellow student in a nearby tavern that the Master had been taken sick in the evening and died before sunrise. His flock had scattered. Most of them feared they too were marked by disease, as did this fellow, who now sat drinking and weeping. 'What use, then, all our learning and cunning, Andelm?' he wretchedly asked.

Andelm would have chided him, but saw with his apothecary's eye the sweat of fever already on the man's face, and that his armpit seemed sore.

The city was clogged everywhere by now with the ceremonies and accessories of the plague. Drunkenness and sexual events were on display in doorways and alleys, and even the street itself, only part concealed by smokes. Though carts still passed inexorably along their never-ending journeys to and from the outer burial-and-burning grounds, other traffic had come to a standstill, and in many places undisguised robbery and other violence occurred. Everywhere were scrawled the plague signs, and everywhere the smoke, and the red cloths hanging down like arrested tongues. The dirty, killing air was full of vague moaning and sudden slicing shrieks.

Andelm returned to *The Sun's Head*. He found there a yet more strident daylight recreation of the previous night's orgy. A young woman and man came to Andelm at once. They began to paw him, spilling their red wine over his coat. 'There! An anointing – we worship the Red Virgin! She'll keep us safe. Come, let us anoint you another way... No? Don't you carry a rod in your breeches, then?'

But Andelm thrust them off and ran upstairs to his chamber. Emerging from it that morning, and feeling the Presence had withdrawn, he had seen the door to the other room was ordinarily shut. But curious smears were all over the passageway. They were like those an enormous snail might have created, if it had slid back and forth – and its slime was scarlet. That had alarmed him, but he had had his plan to take refuge at the academy.

Now Andelm had no other sanctuary save this one. With some unspeakable something passing below and closely up and down beyond his door.

It was true, his dread had increased. His horror of the rough-carved figure, or rather its *essence*. He was certain it could and would protect none of them. Wrongly conceived and conjured, it was in itself both malign and acquisitive. It had been grown out of general terror of the plague, and so had become, in some unreasonable yet appropriate way, a component of and assistant *to* the plague. (Added perhaps also to his fear besides, was Andelm's no doubt unconscious abhorrence of women, that was, their carnal possibility.)

By now the red slime had dried and turned dark as old blood in the corridor. Andelm sprang past and over it and into his room.

Here he locked and bolted the door, then flung off all his clothes and his shoes and sprinkled both them and himself with a measure of the precious salt. Taking other occult ointments from his cupboard, unguents he knew well from his training, he set about protecting his room as best he could. The chamber had become his castle besieged.

All that remained to him of food was the half loaf he had not tasted, some cold broth and ale from the previous night's supper, besides a stale slab of cheese in a box he kept to tempt mice away from his books. He had a stoop of water too; three days old it was, but better than none.

Many persons had done similar things to that which he now did, but their efforts had been all to avoid plague. His care still was not that. It was solely to avoid – *her*. *She*, the Red Virgin who had made her lair at this inn.

It was Stollia's fault, he had decided. Stollia – Woman, authoress of the Downfall of Man. For, without crediting religion, its analogies and ciphers he had taken to heart. If not made from a rib, if not ever having eaten of a deceptive apple and – worse – *shared* it, yet Andelm knew Woman was more bestial, the less to be trusted, and the fount of a power ungovernable and uneducable: fatal.

And Stollia, (Woman), had given orders for the carving and painting of the Red Virgin. Stollia was the priestess. Stollia had always lorded over her weak husband, therefore over the inn. Now her creation, birthed from the womb of Stollia's frightened animal mind, lorded over *all* – even the plague itself. For *she*, Our Lady of Scarlet, was an anathema. To a lucid man, no devil, but the demon-enemy of logic, swept out, burning bright, into the hell of life.

It was virtually an axiom then, the rest being so, that Andelm would be of prime fascination to *her*. *Him* she would mean to hunt down.

She was there in the night, after the midnight chimes had struck from the single clock that still sounded then.

He heard her pass across the door, over and over, soft as the paw of a colossal cat, all its claws ensheathed – yet ready.

Under the door a faint rosiness bloomed, faded.

She tried him only once that night, and only for an hour. But he did not sleep again until daylight came.

The first day of his siege he began more earnest work for his own protection, taking out implements and charts from his second box in the cupboard.

Diligently, he sacrificed a candle, puddling it down before making up its altered shape from the warm wax.

He undid one of the books, leaving one in place on the barricading chair, since drunk revellers had also come to beat on his door during the day. But the door anyway was enhanced by now through the High Art Andelm had learned. Nothing human at least could breach it.

She was active only at night. Of course, she was the hot dark of unreason, the red-blackness of shadowy ignorance and fear. And the second night he knew she would return.

Return she did.

Now in the silk stroking of the paw along the wood he heard the first delicate scraping of her claws. Her red light came and went, deep as crimson, pallid as a girl's watered lip-paste. He smelled her too. She did not have a mortal odour, not even female, maybe to his surprise. No, she smelled of fresh meat and wine and roses. She smelled of ginger and incense and a hot, hot iron; a *scorch*.

Most of the night she bothered him with her second visitation.

During it he wished he might have prayed. But he did not believe in God, or gods. He spoke chants only of alchemic teachings.

Near dawn she left off, and he sank asleep.

How long, he asked confusedly in his dreams, how long could he withstand her? But waking again, again he set to work, paring and finishing the wax and getting it as it must be. Then replacing one book and taking up the other, he opened that too, breathing in its profound and fearsome lesson, its instructions written in a code ancient as the pyramids, of the Aegyptians.

Beyond the window, in the outer world, endless unpleasant and maddening sounds arose, but the smokes were now so dense that even morning was full twilight. In this murk, only the occasional running torch might be seen. Finally, during the second day, a group of such torches marched to the inn, and he heard the rumble of a corpse-cart coming near and stopping at the yard gate. Voices murmured, then wailed. Soon enough the cart went off again, and after this there was screaming and pleading. Then came the heavy blows as the doors of *The Sun's Head* were hammered shut and boarded. The sound of the plague sign scribbled there was too mild for him to pick out. When the torch-party too had gone, the outcry sank inside the inn.

Andelm wondered which of the Red Virgin's worshippers had succumbed after all to the disease, saddling all the rest with imprisonment here until they should die also. He pondered if any might survive. He considered if some would come to assault his door once again, now militantly, or if they had in this new extremity forgotten him. Certainly, nobody came, and by the hour of sunset, when the smouldering city outside turned iron black as a coffin's interior, (an example of which Andelm had once seen), all discernible human sounds had ended in the building.

He had by then one finger's breadth of water and one swallow of ale, a dish of bread turning colour as if itself sick, some cheese, no broth. But he could not leave the room.

She came at ten, when the church clock, for the first, did not chime.

Andelm was standing on the floor inside his circle of salt and silver, chart to hand.

The paw smote the wood and its claws *raked*. The timbers shook. The lock gave a shiver.

Andelm roared arcane words and dashed lightning from one hand. It caught the tiny wax figure on the ground.

'Rise up, Kephyon, warrior and knight! Defend this fortress!'

And the wax figure, by those means invested with a surrogate life-force, *waxed* in size and ascended to the height of the door lintel.

Though made of a yellowish substance, now most like eldritch ivory, it had the form of a tall and mighty man, clad in armour, helmed, and armed with sword and pikestaff – these resembling metallic, yellow amber.

Without another moment lost, the *investrum* passed straight through the closed door, which reformed behind it. From the corridor came immediate savage and uncanny notes of battle. The clang and slither of weapons, the oddest rhythmic guttural, a sort of snarling, so low and almost inaudible that no doubt only the psychic ear could note it. Sometimes the door was thrust against, inadvertently or in a fury. Under it, a repulsive tangle of saffron and scarlet lights locked and relocked in combat.

Time seemed altered. The night, as if afraid, fled over and away from the city and the inn. Hours chimed – not on the silenced clock – but on the skin of Andelm's mind.

In the last minutes before dawn, the duality of colours under the door was changed. They melded to a hideous orange, and in that instant a long broad tear broke through the spellbound wood. Via this generous crack, Andelm must watch then as his *autometary vestrum* Kephyon burst into a hundred pieces.

Andelm uttered a loud cry.

In that moment, a flare of red gleamed over the inside of the door, as if a spray of blood had splashed it. But the blood seemed to be a mouth, which laughed at him. The he saw that the redness was the bloody reflection of the sun, lifting sombrely from the smoke for a few seconds. Already the hour was midday. *She* had left him. And his guardian warrior, Kephyon, modelled and summoned without fault, and according to antique lore, was vanquished entirely. Not even a trace of him remained, as Andelm could clearly see through the break in the door.

Next day he did not mean to sleep.

He opened once more the second book.

From this, Andelm made his own chart, as in the past. He was assured that, in the fashioning and calling of Kephyon he had made no error. The unclean other power had simply proved too strong. What he must call on now therefore demanded from him not only meticulous labour, but an epitome of personal strength.

He used in its manufacture nothing so concrete as wax, but only ink from his ink-horn, (fluidity), and the flame of a struck tinder, (heat).

While the prior night had fled so fast, the day containing this venture seemed to expand. And he was bemusedly reminded of some episode in The Bible, to do with the staying of time by the extraordinary jurisdiction of the Biblical God, in whom Andelm himself had no faith.

Eventually, exhaustion overcame Andelm. But he supposed by then he had completed his endeavours. So he indulged in two hours of sleep, his own discipline awaking him. He ate the last of his bread and cheese rind, and drank the last gulp of ale and water.

Below and all about him in *The Sun's Head*, he heard no noise at all, beyond the odd croaking of a beam as day cooked to noon, or when a mouse, indifferent to plague, scurried busily through the walls. Andelm thought that all other persons there must now be deceased, or so approximate to death they were dumb, at least indecipherable. An awful pity did stir in him then, despite everything. He felt he might have mourned and wept for them at this ultimate juncture. But he had no space to give to it. He wiped his eyes on his bare arm, as a boy would have. And maybe he had *done* when a boy, turned so quickly from youthful things to momentous studies, which at that date were harsh, and all beyond him.

But, hardly perceptible in the black fog of smoke, the sun was going down.

Andelm roused, and made the circle of force upon the floor, closing himself within. Then summoned with his Voice and his own blood, and the thin whistling of a slender reed pipe, his only other saviour: The Angel of Duskfall, Uzt.

The angel arrived in a rushing, like a great storm of winds and rain. It entered the chamber from out of the invisible air, which was seen briefly to rip wide as a torn sail. In colour the entity was a deep violet-blue.

Andelm stood and confronted the angel. It had less the face of a man than of a lion, and was maned with blue flames that writhed and crackled. Where the *vestrum* Kephyon had been tall as the upper limit of the door, the head of the Angel Uzt reached nearly to the ceiling. Behind its robed and towering form, which like the mane, also sinuously writhed as fire would, four wings stirred and shimmered, the feathers of them like those of a blue phoenix. It seemed angry and already prepared for war. A glittering sword was gripped in each many-fingered hand. Its eyes, smoothly blue-blank as stones, also shot off sword-edge sparks.

'Greeting, Uzt,' said Andelm, for the angel must be acknowledged.

'I am primed,' Uzt answered, in a voice of tempest. 'Why, and for what?'

'She approaches.'

This was sure enough. *She* even now smeared her forecasting scarlet taint through the door's unmended crack. (Andelm had known to attempt repairing the door would be redundant. Once she had breached the way on the third night, she would be quite able to penetrate his chamber on her return, mend or spell it as he might.)

So she did, and instantly.

Even as the Angel of Dusk raised both swords, the bloody deluge of the Red Virgin gushed into the room, smashing the rest of the door's timbers as it came.

The chamber reeled as opposing forces clashed.

Galvanics and thunder-bolts sizzled and exploded. Splinters showered out from the wood of beams and furnishings, plasters from the walls. The floor itself appeared to be erupting, as if the earth quaked; indeed, panes of the very world seemed to have shattered and now to cascade through space. The surges of atmosphere stung like vipers. Meanwhile the brightest and blindest flashes of light alternated with abysmal blinks of pure blackness. Between could be glimpsed insane wrestlings of crimson and scarlet with the beating of indigo blades and wings.

The uproar was so vast, Andelm believed he must go deaf. He fell to his knees inside the circle, aware that only its power would protect him from the battle. (But even as he knelt there, he beheld how little sections of the circle were flaking off, dissolving like bread touched with acid.)

The terminating moment came. Blue and red burned up as one, immovable even among the black and white lashes of vision. And Andelm saw how both colours wooed, then wed each other. They fused, inseparable, changing abruptly to the extravagant purple of ancient Tyre, for which Caesars had contended. *Something,* now colourless and screeching, detached itself, and was loosed upward like an arrow – was gone. After this, all colour died, and dimness began. After *this*, a silence.

Not deaf or blinded despite the onslaught, Andelm stared through the clearing stasis of the room. And saw what stood there now, the victor, less than thirteen paces from him. It was she. Of course. Uzt she had routed, at least the configuration of him. The angel was gone, and piece by piece instead her corrupting light spilled throughout the chamber.

All was glowing. All was red. She had won.

Although grown in size, she looked to him, as no doubt she must, exactly like the statue old Tibar had rough-carved – unfinished and grotesque, ugly and omniscient. Her eyes spangled and her mouth grinned, and over her lascivious robe her raw spice hair trickled like serpents.

He had, Andelm, no further defence, nor any strength left to attempt it, nor any time to activate it, even had vigour and skill allowed.

For she was here. She was, though motionless, nine paces from him, seven paces, and now four – the number of the nights he had held out against her.

She did not speak. She *breathed* on him. Her breath hurt and shamed him. It said: *Now worship me for you may have no other god.*

He understood, had always done so, that she meant to be his death. And it was to happen, and to be now, though he had never thought to die in such a way, nor so young, his true power unlearned and work undone. But there was no help. No rescue. She would put her carapace against his human one, and like all others he would be destroyed. By the flesh, the grossness and futility of life – and thus by the plague, fever, agony, and extinction.

Andelm shuddered. Humiliated and in despair, he bowed his head.

Sun, stand thou still... and thou, Moon... And the sun stood still, and the moon stayed... So the sun stood still in the midst of heaven, and hasted not to go down about a whole day.

It was Yezua who had done this, Yezua praying only to his God.

How curious the idea should come to Andelm now, even some of the words from The Bible, which outlined the event. Evidently, Yezua's God, then, had stopped time, letting it continue only for Yezua's army and the army of those he fought – inside some kind of impervious bubble.

But what had this to do with Andelm?

And what had that other thing to do with him either, that peculiar shadow, which was growing there upon the floor. *She* did not cast it for she had none, and *he* did not cast it, certainly, for it was of something standing upright behind him.

Andelm could not move to look about and see. He had become a block of stone, but stone not blind or deaf. He saw that the shadow was not dark, indeed had no colour in it of any sort. And yet it was very definitely there on the floor, stretching out and out, as if the shape had been cut from *time itself,* and this shape, robed and hooded and slender and huge, held in its right hand, even supposing it possessed a hand to hold anything, a wide and curving sickle, like the crescent, maybe, of a moon that stood still, or a quartered, still-standing sun.

He had no notion, Andelm the student of alchemic mysteries, what this creature was. And he could not even raise his eyes from its shadow to see what *she* would do – or could she not see it, as he himself could not actually *turn* to do?

But the being which cast the timeless shadow spoke.

It had a voice, needless to relate, that was not to be heard. And every syllable sounded loud as trumpets, soft as a sigh, vivid as molten glass.

'Now is not his hour.'

This was what the voice said.

'He is to live into his eighty-ninth year, the third month of it, the fifth day of that month, the twentieth hour of that day, and only then to die, replete with long life and famous among men. Not until then can any form of dying have sovereignty over him, and then only *I* shall have it, for then, then only, may I claim him. But soon or late, all yield to me. Even gods, even God perhaps at Eternity's ending. Even *I*, myself, last of all lasts, must yield, to me.'

Andelm's head, without his volition, snapped up and he beheld the face of the Red Virgin, transfixed in a mindless terror of its own. But over Andelm's head, so close he felt the hissing flight of it, the great scythe passed with its sharpest sickle edge. It clove the body of the demon in half, and she fell in two portions – that vanished in foul-smelling nothingness before ever they reached the ground.

The shadow had already disappeared.

Nothing was there then but for the damaged room, the silent inn, the city outside where rain was falling, flattening the smokes, and a single bell rang in a far-off church. And the young student, well-favoured and pale, who got up from the floor and looked about him once only, knowing now he would survive and prosper,

Tanith Lee

through all calamity and against all odds....

But also knowing the Year, the Month, the Day, the *Hour* of his death.

Author's Notes:

There really was a belief (at least in Shakespearian England) that wearing red etc. could protect from the bubonic plague. (The setting of this story, however, is somewhere on the European mainland.)

The Biblical reference and quote are from the Old Testament Book of Joshua (Yezua in the story), Ch. 10, V:12-15.sa

About the Author

Tanith Lee (1947-2015) was born in London. Because her parents were professional dancers (ballroom, Latin American) and had to live where the work was, she attended a number of truly terrible schools, and didn't learn to read – she was also dyslectic – until almost age 8. And then only because her father taught her. This opened the world of books to her, and by 9 she was writing. After much better education at a grammar school, she went on to work in a library. This was followed by various other jobs – shop assistant, waitress, clerk – plus a year at art college when she was 25-26. In 1974, her career as a writer was launched, when DAW Books of America, under the leadership of Donald A. Wollheim, bought and published *The Birthgrave*, and thereafter 26 of her novels and collections.

Tanith was presented with a Lifetime Achievement Award in 2013, at World Fantasycon in Brighton. During her lifetime, she also received the World Horror Convention Grand Master Award, as well as the August Derleth Award and the World Fantasy Award for short fiction (twice).

In 1992, she married the writer-artist-photographer John Kaiine, her partner since 1987. They lived on the Sussex Weald, near the sea, in a house full of books and plants, and never without feline companions. She died at home in May 2015, after a long illness, continuing to work until a couple of weeks before her death.

Throughout her life, Tanith wrote around 100 books, and over 300 short stories. 4 of her radio plays were broadcast by the BBC; she also wrote 2 episodes (*Sarcophagus* and *Sand*) for the TV series *Blake's 7*. Her stories were read regularly on Radio 4 Extra. She was an inspiration to a generation of writers and her work was enormously influential within genre fiction – as it continues to be. She wrote in many styles, within and across many genres, including Horror, SF and Fantasy, Historical, Detective, Contemporary-Psychological, Children and Young Adult. Her preoccupation, though, was always people.

Publishing History of the Stories

Taken from *Daughter of the Night, An Annotated Tanith Lee Bibliography*,
compiled and maintained by Allison Rich
http://www.daughterofthenight.com/

The Story Told by Smoke (From the Journals of St. Strange)
Realms of Fantasy. Vol 1 No 3, February 1995

Doll Skulls (a Paradis novelette)
Realms of Fantasy. Vol 2 No 3, February 1996
*Hunting the Shadows: The Selected Stories of Tanith Lee vol 2, Wildside Press
2009, pbk 2012*

Death Loves Me
Realms of Fantasy. Vol 2 No 6, August 1996
*Tempting the Gods: The Selected stories of Tanith Lee, vol 1, Wildside Press, 2009,
pbk 2012*

Old Flame (From the Journals of St. Strange)
Realms of Fantasy. Vol 3 No 3, February 1997

The Lady-Of-Shalott House
Realms of Fantasy. Vol 4 No 1, October 1997
*Tempting the Gods: The Selected Stories of Tanith Lee Vol 1, Wildside Press,
2009, pbk 2012 USA*
Ghosteria 1: The Stories, Immanion Press, 2014, UK

I Bring You Forever
Realms of Fantasy. Vol 4 No 5. June 1998
*Myriad Lands 2: Beyond the Edge, edited by David R Stokes, Guardbridge Books,
2016 UK*

The Woman in Scarlet
Realms of Fantasy. Vol 6 No 4, April 2000
*Lord of Swords: Thirteen Stories of Heroic Fantasy, Pitch-Black Books, 2004,
edited by Daniel E Blackinton*
*Hunting the Shadows: The selected stories of Tanith Lee vol 2, Wildside Press 2009,
pbk 2012*
*The Mammoth Book of Warriors and Wizardry, edited by Sean Wallace, Robinson,
2014 (UK) and Running Press, 2014 (USA)*

The Children of His Old Age
Realms of Fantasy. Vol 7 No 1, October 2000

The Man Who Stole the Moon (A Story of the Flat Earth)
Realms of Fantasy. Vol 7 No 3, February 2001
Year's Best Fantasy Stories 2, edited by David G Hartwell & Kathryn Cramer,
Eos 2002, USA
The Mammoth Book of Angels and Demons, edited by Paula Guarn, Running
Press, 2013, USA

Moonblind
Realms of Fantasy. Vol 9 No 4, April 2003
Year's Best Fantasy Stories 4, edited by David G Hartwell & Kathryn Cramer,
Eos 2004, USA

Israbel
Realms of Fantasy. Vol 10, No 4, April 2004 (Note: this issue was misnumbered
as Vol 10, No 3, April 2004)
The Mammoth Book of Best New Horror 16, edited by Stephen Jones, Constable
Robinson, 2005, UK
The Mammoth Book of Best New Horror 16, edited by Stephen Jones, Carroll &
Graf, 2005, USA.
Blood 20: Tales of Vampire Horror, Telos Publishing, 2015, UK

Stalking the Leopard
Realms of Fantasy. Vol 10 No 5 June 2004 (Note: this issue was misnumbered as
Vol 10, No 4, June 2004)
Space is Just a Starry Night, Aqueduct Press, 2013 USA

En Forêt Noire
Realms of Fantasy. Vol 12 No 2, December 2005
Cold Grey Stones, NewCon Press, 2012 UK, limited edition hardback
Colder Greyer Stones, NewCon Press, paperback edition of Cold Grey Stones,
including a bonus story.

The Snake (A Story of the Flat Earth)
Realms of Fantasy. Vol 14 No 5, June 2008

Our Lady of Scarlet
Realms of Fantasy. Vol 15, No 5, August 2009

BOOKS BY TANITH LEE

Series

The Birthgrave Trilogy (The Birthgrave; Vazkor, son of Vazkor
[published as Shadowfire in the UK], Quest for the White Witch)
The Blood Opera Sequence (Dark Dance; Personal Darkness; Darkness, I)
The Flat Earth Opus (Night's Master; Death's Master; Delusion's
Master; Delirium's Mistress; Night's Sorceries)
The Lionwolf Trilogy (Cast a Bright Shadow; Here in Cold Hell;
No Flame But Mine)
The Paradys Quartet (The Book of the Damned; The Book of the Beast;
The Book of the Dead; The Book of the Mad)
The Venus Quartet (Faces Under Water; Saint Fire; A Bed of Earth;
Venus Preserved)
The Vis Trilogy (The Storm Lord; Anackire; The White Serpent)
The FOUR-Bee Series (Don't Bite the Sun; Drinking Sapphire Wine)
The S.I.L.V.E.R. Series (Silver Metal Lover; Metallic Love)

Novels and Novellas

34
The Blood of Roses
Companions on the Road
Days of Grass
Death of the Day
Electric Forest
Elephantasm
Eva Fairdeath
The Gods Are Thirsty
Kill the Dead
Heart-Beast
A Heroine of the World
Louisa the Poisoner
Lycanthia
Madame Two Swords
Mortal Suns
Reigning Cats and Dogs
Sabella
Sung in Shadow
Vivia
Volkhavaar

When the Lights Go Out
White as Snow
The Winter Players

Young Adult and Children's Fiction

Animal Castle (picture book)
The Castle of Dark
The Claidi Journals (Law of the Wolf Tower; Wolf Star Rise,
Queen of the Wolves, Wolf Wing)
The Dragon Hoard
East of Midnight
The Piratica Novels (Piratica 1; Piratica 2; Piratica 3)
Prince on a White Horse
Princess Hynchatti and Other Surprises
Shon the Taken
The Unicorn Trilogy (Black Unicorn; Gold Unicorn; Red Unicorn)
The Voyage of the Bassett: Islands in the Sky

Story Collections

Blood 20
Cold Grey Stones
Colder Greyer Stones
Cyrion
Dancing in the Fire
Disturbed by Her Song
Dreams of Dark and Light
Fatal Women
Forests of the Night
The Gorgon
Hunting the Shadows
Nightshades
Phantasya
Red as Blood – Tales from the Sisters Grimmer
Redder Than Blood
Sounds and Furies
Tamastara, or the Indian Nights
Space is Just a Starry Night
Tempting the Gods
Unsilent Night
Women as Demons

Tanith Lee Titles Published by Immanion Press

The Colouring Book Series

Cruel Pink
Greyglass
To Indigo
Ivoria
Killing Violets
L'Amber
Turquoiselle

The Blood Opera Sequence

Dark Dance
Personal Darkness
Darkness, I *(forthcoming 2018)*

Novels and Novellas

34
Ghosteria Volume 2: The Novel: Zircons May Be Mistaken
Madame Two Swords

Collections

Animate Objects
A Different City
Ghosteria Volume 1: The Stories
Legenda Maris
The Weird Tales of Tanith Lee
Venus Burning: Realms: Collected Short Stories from 'Realms of Fantasy'

Of Interest to Tanith Lee Enthusiasts…

Night's Nieces

This anthology is a tribute to Tanith Lee, comprising short stories written shortly after her death by some of her writer friends to whom Tanith was a profound influence and inspiration: Storm Constantine, Cecilia Dart-Thornton, Vera Nazarian, Sarah Singleton, Kari Sperring, Sam Stone, Freda Warrington and Liz Williams. With an introduction by Tanith's husband, the artist John Kaiine. Illustrated throughout by the contributors and with photographs from Tanith Lee's personal collection.

IMMANION PRESS

Purveyors of Speculative Fiction

Songs to Earth and Sky edited by Storm Constantine

Six writers explore the eight seasonal festivals of the year, dreaming up new beliefs and customs, new myths, new dehara – the gods of Wraeththu. As different communities develop among Wraeththu, the androgynous race who have inherited a ravaged earth, so fresh legends spring up – or else ghosts from the inception of their kind come back to haunt them. From the silent, snow-heavy forests of Megalithican mountains, through the lush summer fields of Alba Sulh, into the hot, shimmering continent of Olathe, this book explores the Wheel of the Year, bringing its powerful spirits and landscapes to vivid life. The Deharan system of magic explored in these stories reinvents the Pagan Wheel of the Year with an androgynous focus and will be fascinating both to fans of the Mythos and those who are new to it. Nine brand new tales, including a novella, a novelette and a short story from Storm herself, and stories from *Wendy Darling, Nerine Dorman, Suzanne Gabriel, Fiona Lane* and *E. S. Wynn.* ISBN 978-1-907737-84-8 £11.99 $15.50 pbk

Madame Two Swords by Tanith Lee

An unnamed narrator, in the French city of Troy, finds an old book of the writings of the revolutionary, Lucien de Ceppays, who lived and died in the city two centuries before. She feels a strange bond to the life and thoughts of this long-dead man – what is the mysterious truth behind her obsession? Perhaps she did not find the book at all – perhaps it found her. Some years later, impoverished after the death of her mother, the narrator – in a state of desperation – find herself inexorably guided to meet the peculiar and unnerving Madame Two Swords, an old woman with a history, and her own enduring bonds to Lucien – as well as the book. For the narrator, reality seems to unravel, as she begins to penetrate just how intimately she is connected with Madame Two Swords and Lucien. Previously only available as a limited-edition hardback in 1988, the long-awaited new edition of this vintage-Tanith novella includes illustrations by Jarod Mills. ISBN 978-1-907737-81-7 £11.99, $15.50 pbk

Salty Kiss Island by Rhys Hughes

What is a fantastical love story? It isn't quite the same as an ordinary love story. The events that take place are stranger, more extreme, full of the passion of originality, invention and magic, as well as an intensification of emotional love. The stories in *Salty Kiss Island* are set in this world and others, spanning the spectrum of possible and impossible experiences, the uncharted territories of yearning, the depths and shoals of the heart, mind and soul. A love of language runs through them, parallel to the love that motivates their characters to feats of preposterous heroism, luminous lunacy and grandiose gesture. They include tales of minstrels and their catastrophic serenades, dreamers sinking into sequences of ever-deeper dreams, goddesses and mermaids, sailors and devils, messages in bottles that can think and speak but never be read, shadows with an independent life and voyagers of distant galaxies who are already at their destinations before they arrive.
ISBN: 978-1-907737-77-0, £11.99, $15.50 pbk

The Lightbearer by Alan Richardson

Michael Horsett parachutes into Occupied France before the D-Day Invasion. He is dropped in the wrong place, miles from the action, badly injured, and totally alone. He falls prey to two Thelemist women who have awaited the Hawk God's coming, attracts a group of First World War veterans who rally to what they imagine is his cause, is hunted by a troop of German Field Police who are desperate to find him, and has a climactic encounter with a mutilated priest who believes that Lucifer Incarnate has arrived…*The Lightbearer* is a unique gnostic thriller, dealing with the themes of Light and Darkness, Good and Evil, Matter and Spirit.
"The Lightbearer is another shining example of Alan Richardson's talent as a story-teller. He uses his wide esoteric knowledge to produce a story that thrills, chills and startles the reader as it radiates pure magical energy. An unusual and gripping war story with more facets than a star sapphire." – Mélusine Draco, author of "Aubry's

http://www.immanion-press.com
info@immanion-press.com

NEWCON PRESS

http://newconpress.co.uk/

The very best in fantasy, science fiction, and horror

Best of British Science Fiction 2017, edited by Donna Scott

Editor Donna Scott has selected the very best short fiction by British authors published during 2017. Featuring 22 tales, from established names and rising stars: Robert Bagnall, Chris Barnham, Eric Brown, Sarah Byrne, Anne Charnock, Ian Creasey, Matt Dovey, Jaine Fenn, Katie Gray, Tyler Keevil, Ken MacLeod, Tim Major, Laura Mauro, Karen McCreedy, Jeff Noon, N. J. Ramsden, Adam Roberts, Philip A. Suggars, E.J. Swift, Natalia Theodoridou, Lavie Tidhar, Aliya Whiteley Available as a numbered limited-edition hardback, each copy signed by the editor, and an A5 paperback. ISBN pbk: 978-1-910935-73-6 £12.99 pbk, £24.99 hbk

For Love of Distant Shores: Tales of the Apt by Adrian Tchaikovsky

In a narrative reminiscent of Phileas Fogg meets Professor Challenger, *For Love of Distant Shores* features the exploits of scientist-cum-adventurer Doctor Ludweg Phinagler, as recorded by his (semi-)faithful assistant, Fosse. Maverick academic Phinagler is able to charm almost everyone he meets... except for his fellow academics at Collegium. He mounts expeditions to the far-flung corners of the world during which he confronts ancient mysteries and deadly dangers. Includes 4 separate adventures.

Tales of the Apt provides a companion to the best-selling *Shadows of the Apt* decalogy. Available as an A5 paperback and a signed hardback edition, limited to 100 numbered copies ISBN pbk: 978-1-910935-71-2 £12.99 pbk, £24.99 hbk

TANITH LEE FROM NEWCON PRESS

Cover Art by John Kaiine

Colder Greyer Stones

A unique collection of twelve stories from Britain's foremost Mistress of the Fantastic; all are previously uncollected, two have never appeared in print before and six stories are wholly original to this collection, including the bonus novelette, exclusive to this edition, 'The Frost Watcher'. The first edition of this collection, *Cold Grey Stones*, was released in November 2013 to commemorate the author being honoured at that year's World Fantasy Convention with a 'Lifetime Achievement Award'. ISBN: 978-1907069604, pbk: £9.99

Tanith By Choice

Tanith Lee is one of the finest writers ever to grace the field of speculative fiction and has left one heck of a legacy. I would never dream of attempting to compile a 'Best of' collection, so instead I've let others do so for me. This book features many of her finest stories, as chosen by those who knew her. – *Ian Whates, editor.*

With contributions from *Storm Constantine, Craig Gidney, Mavis Haut, Stephen Jones, John Kaiine* (Tanith's widower), *Vera Nazarian, Sarah Singleton, Kari Sperring, Sam Stone, Cecilia Dart-Thornton, Freda Warrington* and *Ian Whates*, each story is accompanied by a note from the person responsible for selecting it explaining why this tale means so much to them. Available as a paperback and a numbered limited-edition hardback. ISBN: 978-1-910935-57-6 hbk, 978-1-910935-58-3 pbk

http://newconpress.co.uk/

www.ingramcontent.com/pod-product-compliance
Lightning Source LLC
Chambersburg PA
CBHW021218260626
47172CB00002B/482